Rickshaw Boy

Rickshaw Boy

A Novel

LAO SHE

Translated by HOWARD GOLDBLATT

HARPER**PERENNIAL** MODERN**CHINESE**CLASSICS

NEW YORK • LONDON • TORONTO • SYDNEY • NEW DELHI • AUCKLAND

HARPER**PERENNIAL** ● MODERNCHINESE**CLASSICS**

HarperCollins books may be purchased for educational, business, or sales promotional use. For information please write: Special Markets Department, HarperCollins Publishers, 10 East 53rd Street, New York, NY 10022.

FIRST EDITION

Title page image © Kuznetsov Alexey and is used under license from Shutterstock.com

Library of Congress Cataloging-in-Publication Data is available upon request.

ISBN 978-0-06-143692-5

11 12 13 14   OV/RRD   10 9 8 7 6 5 4 3 2

INTRODUCTION

Lao She (Shu Qingchun, 1899–1966) remains one of the most widely read Chinese novelists of the first half of the twentieth century, and probably its most beloved. Born into an impoverished Manchu family—his father, a lowly palace guard for the Qing emperor, was killed during the 1900 Boxer Rebellion—he was particularly sensitive to his link to the hated Manchu Dynasty, which ruled China from the mid-seventeenth century until it was overthrown in 1911. The view of one of his biographers is difficult to dispute: "The poverty of his childhood and the fact that these were also the years when the dynasty was collapsing and the Manchus were becoming a target of increasingly bitter attacks left a deep shadow on Lao She's impressionable mind and later kept him from personal participation in political activities. But his alienation strengthened his sense of patriotism and made his need to identify with China even more acute."[*]

After graduating from Beiping Normal School, Lao She spent half a dozen years as a schoolteacher, primary school principal,

---

[*]Ranbir Vohra, *Lao She and the Chinese Revolution* (Cambridge: East Asian Research Center, 1974), 2.

and school administrator. Then, in 1924, after joining a Christian society and studying English, he accompanied a British missionary, Clemont Egerton, to London, where he taught Chinese at the University of London's School of Oriental Studies. Among his lesser-discussed activities there was the acknowledged assistance to Egerton in his translation of the "indecent" classical novel *The Golden Lotus*, in which the racy parts were rendered in Latin. During his time away from the classroom, Lao She read voraciously. He has written of his fascination with British novels, in particular the work of Charles Dickens, whose devotion to the urban downtrodden and use of ironic humor Lao She found particularly affecting; they would inform much of his own work, particularly the early novels and stories.

Lao She's literary career began during his five-year stay in England, where he wrote three novels: *The Philosophy of Lao Zhang* (1926), a mostly comical look at middle-class Beiping residents and modeled, in the author's own words, after *Nicholas Nickleby* and *The Pickwick Papers*; *Zhao Ziyue* (1927), a generally unsympathetic exposé of the activities of a group of college students; and *The Two Mas* (1929), the tale of a Chinese father and son living, and loving, in London. All three were serialized in China's most prestigious literary magazine of the day, *Short Story Magazine*, before Lao She returned to China, in 1929, after a six-month stop in Singapore, where he taught Chinese in a middle school; there he wrote most of a short novel, *The Birthday of Little Po* (1931), the only one of his novels that focuses entirely on a child, a Cantonese boy living in Singapore.

Upon Lao She's return to China, he landed a teaching job at a Shandong university, where he continued to write and publish. His first novel written there, *Lake Daming* (1931), was set to be published in 1932, but the author's only manuscript was lost when a Japanese bomb destroyed the publishing house. Later in 1931 a dystopian satire set on Mars entitled *Cat Country* (1932) appeared, followed closely by *Divorce* (1933),[*] a tale of domestic strife. Taken together, the two novels give witness to Lao She's increasing dejection over deteriorating social and political conditions in China and the rise of nationalistic, even revolutionary, tendencies throughout the country in the wake of the Japanese occupation of Northeast China (Manchuria) in 1931, with the establishment of the puppet state of Manchukuo, followed by a Japanese attack on Shanghai the same year.

While *Cat Country* and *Divorce* broaden the author's critique of the weakness of the Chinese character, castigating it as a malaise that affects the whole nation, not just pockets of middle-class urbanites, Lao She continued to see the salvation of Chinese society in the Confucian ideal of individual moral integrity, the vaunted *junzi*, a man of virtue. This begins to change with the slight novel *The Biography of Niu Tianci* (1936),[†] in which the author entertains doubts that "individual heroism could be of any use in a generally corrupt society."[‡] Lao She's political ambivalence had begun to give way to more active political engagement. The bankruptcy of individualism in the face of a corrupting and dehumanizing social system is both the political and moral message of his next novel, *Rickshaw Boy*, which was first serialized in a magazine edited by Lin Yutang, *Cosmic Wind* (1936–1937), and published as a book in 1939; it has been republished many times in China, Taiwan,

---

*An English translation entitled *The Quest for Love of Lao Lee* was published in 1948.

†An English translation entitled *Heavensent* was published in 1986.

‡C. T. Hsia, *A History of Modern Chinese Fiction*, 3rd ed. (Bloomington: Indiana University Press, 1999), 180.

Hong Kong, Singapore, and in Chinese communities in the West.

Not only had Lao She matured as a writer when he wrote *Rickshaw Boy*, but he also had finally been able to quit teaching, a job he admitted he did not like, and devote all his time and energies to his craft. The polished structure, language, and descriptions of this complex novel made for a fitting debut as a full-time writer. After producing a series of novels that dealt with middle-class urbanites, minor officials, college students, and the like, in *Rickshaw Boy*, Lao She chose an illiterate, countrified common laborer as the vehicle for his ongoing social critique. Though a case can be made for viewing the novel as an "allegory of Republican China" in which "the Chinese people were bullied by imperialist powers, misled by the false promise of capitalist modernization, and betrayed by corrupt government, miscarried revolution, and their own disunity,"[*] at its core it "portrays the physical and moral decline of an individual in an unjust society"[†] and, for the first time, hints at a way out: a move away from individualism and toward collective action. Lao She himself wrote of the novel in 1954, "I expressed my sympathy for the laboring people and my admiration of their sterling qualities, but I gave them no future, no way out. They lived miserably and died wronged."[‡] For a twenty-first-century reader who knows how things have turned out in China, the novel can be read as commentary on the sorts of struggles the

---

[*]Thomas Moran, "The Reluctant Nihilism of Lao She's *Camel Xiangzi*," in Joshua Mostow, ed., *The Columbia Companion to Modern East Asian Literature* (New York: Columbia University Press, 2003), 453.

[†]Bonnie S. M. McDougall and Kam Louie, *The Literature of China in the Twentieth Century* (New York: Columbia University Press, 1997), 118.

[‡]Lao She, "Afterword," *Camel Xiangzi*, tr. Shi Xiaojing (Bloomington: Indiana University Press, 1981), 230.

underprivileged of the world face daily and the powers that keep them that way. It is also a stark but edifying picture of the early-twentieth-century city in which Lao She was born and died.

During the war years (1937–1945), Lao She spent most of his time in the interior, where he devoted his energies and lent his patriotic zeal to the publication of anti-Japanese magazines and to the chairmanship of the All-China Association of Resistance Writers and Artists. There he began a novel set in one of Beijing's traditional quadrangular compounds, *Four Generations Under One Roof*, which he would not finish until several years later. He did start and finish a novel—*Cremation*—which he considered to be an utter failure, owing primarily to a lack of understanding of life in areas under Japanese occupation: "If a work like *Cremation* had been written before the war," he wrote, "I would have thrown it into the wastepaper basket. But now I do not have that type of courage."[*] For a variety of reasons, not least of which were the demands upon writers to serve the war effort, Lao She's major achievements during this period were in patriotic plays, most of which were forgotten after the war. It is important to keep in mind that during these troubled times, when the Japanese invasion was further complicated by the irreconcilable strife between Communist and Nationalist forces, and the continued presence of warlords, particularly in the north, Lao She was the only cultural figure who commanded enough respect by all sides to serve in a leadership role of patriotic literary and art associations.

The war with Japan ended in 1945, only to morph immediately into four years of civil war between the forces of Chiang Kai-shek and Mao Zedong. Lao She was absent from China

---

[*]Vohra, *Lao She and the Chinese Revolution*, 129.

during most of those years. Owing largely to the surprising popularity of an English translation of *Rickshaw Boy*—it was a Book-of-the-Month Club selection—Lao She was invited by the U.S. Department of State to visit America in early 1946; though the initial invitation was for a year, he did not return home until the establishment of the People's Republic, reportedly at the request of Zhou Enlai. Soon after he arrived in the U.S., at a gathering in his honor, he made a point of informing his American audience, which knew little about Chinese literature, other than a bit of classical poetry and the translations of Arthur Waley and others of premodern novels, that new literary trends had taken hold back home. "The younger school of Chinese to which [I belong]," a *New York Times* story on May 19, 1946, quoted Lao She, "is only about thirty years old and it is distinguished from the older by its break with the classical vernacular and by its subject matter, which has less to do with flowers than with social themes."

While in the United States, Lao She wrote a novel he called *Drum Singers*; it was published in an English translation (1989) long before the Chinese version appeared. He also completed his long novel dealing with the lives of several generations of families living in a traditional Beijing compound, *Four Generations Under One Roof*, and worked with an old China hand, Ida Pruitt, on an abridged translation into English she called *The Yellow Storm* (1951); the Chinese original appeared in three volumes, published in 1946, 1948, and 1951.

A celebrated cultural figure in the People's Republic for the first seventeen years of its existence, Lao She held a variety of important or symbolic offices after his return in 1949, and while he appears never to have been completely comfortable with the system or ideology under which he lived and worked, he wrote prolifically, devoting his creative talents almost exclusively to the production of dramas, some of which continue to be read and performed. *Teahouse* (1958), which treats the Chinese revolution in three periods, from the late Qing reform movement through the early postwar era, was made into a successful film, starring Ying Ruochen. It remains Lao She's most impressive work from the period and is also the first of his creations to feature Manchu characters, one of whom declares, "I am a Manchu, and the Manchus are also Chinese."* Thus spake Lao She!

Lao She's final novel, *Beneath the Red Banner*, was begun in the early 1960s but never finished; the partial manuscript, which was not published until 1979,† following the lead of *Teahouse*, features a number of Manchu characters.

In 1966, shortly after Mao launched his Cultural Revolution, Lao She was interviewed by a foreign couple who subsequently published the exchange. His remarks regarding himself and his generation of writers are telling: "I can understand why Mao Zedong wishes to destroy the old bourgeois concepts of life, but I cannot write of this struggle because I am not a Marxist, and, therefore, I cannot feel and think as a Peking student in May 1966 who sees the situation in a Marxist way. . . . We old ones can't apologize for what we are. We can only explain why we are and wave the young ones on their way to the future."‡ Not long after that, Lao She was visited at the offices of the Chinese Writers Association by Red Guards, who dragged him outside, where they interrogated, humiliated, and probably beat him. He was

---

*Vohra, *Lao She and the Chinese Revolution*, 163.

†An English translation was published in 1987.

‡Vohra, 164.

ordered to return the next day, but, according to reports, when he saw his "courtyard strewn with all his possessions, his house looted, his painting and sculpture wrecked, and his manuscripts, the work of a lifetime, in shreds . . . he did not enter his house but instead turned and walked to [a nearby lake], and there he drowned himself."

Lao She has been unevenly translated into English. Some of his novels, particularly the early ones, remain untranslated, while others, and many of his excellent short stories, have been translated more than once, in China and in the West. *Luotuo Xiangzi* (sometimes translated as *Camel Xiangzi*), his signature novel, besides remaining popular in Chinese communities throughout the world, is available in translation in many countries. While it has previously appeared in three English translations, it has not fared particularly well. In 1945, Reynal & Hitchcock of New York published a translation entitled *Rickshaw Boy* (the author's name is given as Lau Shaw), by a translator using the pseudonym Evan King, reputedly a prisoner of the Japanese in Northern China when the work was done. Beautifully illustrated by Cyrus LeRoy Baldridge, it was a bestseller, thanks in part to the popularity of the Book-of-the-Month Club. Unfortunately, King's translation reflects little of the style or intent of the original. Larding his rendering with grand flourishes that are found nowhere in the Chinese, the translator took it upon himself to rewrite portions of the novel, delete others, and move sections around in ways that, quite frankly, make little sense. Then, in one of the most egregious betrayals of an author's autonomy of purpose, Evan King changed the ending, completely distorting the author's intent.

After a shelf life of more than three decades, King's translation was superseded by one that takes none of those liberties. Nor, unhappily, does it do justice to the artistry of the original or appeal as a representative of good English writing, however laudable the impetus to end King's reign may have been. Frequent misreadings and non-idiomatic English, plus an outdated spelling system for Chinese, seriously mar the work. Published by the University of Hawai'i Press in 1979, Jean James's *Rickshaw* is a valiant if ultimately unsatisfactory attempt to bring the novel faithfully across to a new generation of readers, for which the editorial staff at the press must share responsibility.

In an afterword to a revised Chinese edition of the novel in 1954, Lao She wrote: "The Chinese edition of this book has already been reprinted several times. In this present edition, I have taken out some of the coarser language and some unnecessary descriptions." Whether this was an altogether voluntary undertaking remains a mystery, although there is evidence that it was not, and whether the result is a better novel is a matter of taste. One must not, however, be fooled by the understated confession into believing that the changes were, in fact, minimal. Several passages considered by some to be delicate or unsuitable in a Communist milieu have been excised, disrupting the logic of the narrative where they occur. And as for coarse language, it's still there; but the author had to say something, I suppose.

In 1981, China's Foreign Languages Press and Indiana University jointly published a translation of the novel under the title *Camel Xiangzi*, which includes a preface by Lao She's widow, artist Hu Jieqing, and a translation of the author's essay "How I Came to Write the Novel 'Camel Xiangzi,'" from a delightful little book of Lao She's essays on his writing, *An Old Ox and a Beat-up Cart* (1935). The translator, Shi Xiaojing, has based her readable, if uneven, rendering on the 1954 revised edition—minus, shockingly, the last chapter and a half! Echoes of Evan King. In 2005, the translation, with the ending restored, was republished in a bilingual edition in Hong Kong, with an extended introduction by the literary scholar Kwok-kan Tam. For obvious reasons, anyone interested in this translation should choose this edition.*

Having enjoyed, if not necessarily accepted, the counsel of my earlier translators, I have undertaken this project, a goal I set for myself two decades ago, in hopes of making available a complete, faithful, and readable English version of one of China's modern classics. In doing so, I have worked from a facsimile of the original (1939) Renjian shuwu edition, but have consulted the 1941 Wenhua shenghua chubanshe edition, in which minor errors in the earlier edition have been corrected.

For a novel that is more than seventy years old, anachronisms are unavoidable. For the most part, I have opted for contemporary relevance over period prose; since this is a translation, the illusion of absolute authenticity is already compromised, so I see no reason to be quaint. There are two major exceptions. First, the title. The Chinese title, *Luotuo Xiangzi*, is the protagonist's name, the literal meaning of which is "fortunate son," preceded by the word for camel (*luotuo*). Xiangzi is, of course, a young man, not a boy, and while only a few of the characters associated with rickshaws are, in fact, boys, at the time of writing, pullers were known among foreigners as rickshaw "boys" (waiters, servants, and other menial laborers all suffered the indignity of being called boys, irrespective of their age). However distasteful it seems now, "rickshaw boy" fits the period and the tone, and so

---

*Hong Kong, the Chinese University Press, 2005.

I follow Evan King in his choice of English title. As for the city in which most of the narrative takes place, China's current capital has had a number of names over the years. In the Republican era (1912–1945) it was officially called Beiping ("northern peace"); it reverted back to the earlier Beijing with the establishment of the People's Republic in 1949. Lao She used Beiping; so have I, along with two of my predecessors.

If I have failed in my goal of giving Lao She's masterpiece the translated version it deserves, it is not because I had no help along the way. The editors at HarperCollins, my agent, Sandra Dijkstra, and my wife, Sylvia Lin, supplied encouragement and assistance whenever I needed it. Finally, a tip of the hat to a couple of killer Chinese Web sites that made sense of the many elusive and highly colorful Beijing-isms no longer in common use.

—Howard Goldblatt

Rickshaw Boy

CHAPTER ONE

I'd like you to meet a fellow named Xiangzi, not Camel, be-cause, you see, Camel is only a nickname. After I've told you about Xiangzi, we'll deal with his relationship with camels, and be done with it.

The city of Beiping has several classes of rickshaw men: first are those who are young, energetic, and fleet-footed; they rent handsome rickshaws, put in a whole day, and are free to come and go as they please. They stake out a spot at a rickshaw stand or by a manor gate and wait for people who are looking for speed. If luck is with them, they can land a fare right off, earning as much as a silver dollar or two. But if luck passes them by, and they don't make enough to pay for that day's rental, well, so what? This group of running brothers has two ambitions: one is to land a job as a private hire; the other is to buy one's own rick-shaw, to own one outright. Then it makes no difference if they get paid by the month or pick up odd fares, since the rickshaws are theirs.

The second class includes men who are slightly older and who, for health reasons, cannot run as fast, or whose family situation will not allow them to go all day without a fare. For the most part, their rickshaws are in good shape, if not particularly

new. Since they manage to keep up appearances, they can still
demand a respectable fee for their services. Some of these brothers work a full day, others only half a day. The half-day workers
generally choose the night shift, even in the summers and winters, since they have the energy to handle it. Working at night
requires special care and skill, so there's more money to be made.

Men over forty or younger than twenty have little chance of
falling into either of these classes. They rent beat-up rickshaws
and don't dare work at night, which means they must set out
early in the morning and work till three or four in the afternoon
in hopes of earning enough to pay for that day's rent and food.
Given the poor condition of their rickshaws, speed is out of the
question, so they wind up earning less for running more. Most
of their fares come from hauling melons, fruit, and produce to
market; the pay is low, but at least they can run at their own
pace.

Some of the under-twenty men start out at the age of eleven
or twelve, and few become top runners after the age of twenty,
as they'll have suffered too many injuries to maintain decent
health. They can pull a rickshaw all their lives and still not make
the grade. Those over forty will have been at it for at least a de-
cade, which takes its toll; settling for mediocrity, they gradually
become resigned to the knowledge that one day they will collapse and die in the street. Their style of running, their shrewd
bargaining abilities, and the deft use of shortcuts or circuitous
routes help them relive the glories of their past, which is why
they turn up their noses at younger men. But past glory has no
effect on their current dismal prospects. And so they sigh as they
wipe the sweat from their brows. But the suffering of these veterans pales in comparison with another group of pullers, men
who never imagined they would one day have to scrape out a

living by pulling a rickshaw. Not until the line between life and death has blurred for them do they finally pick up the shafts of a rickshaw. Laid-off policemen and school janitors, peddlers who have squandered their capital, and out-of-work laborers who have nothing more to sell and no prospects for work grit their teeth, swallow their tears, and set out on this road to oblivion. Having mortgaged their youth, they are reduced to spilling the blood and sweat derived from coarse corn cakes on the city streets. They have little strength, scant experience, and no friends; even their laboring brothers avoid them. They pull rundown rickshaws whose tires go flat several times a day, and must beg forgiveness from passengers who, if they're lucky, will give them fifteen cents for a ride.

Yet another class of rickshaw men owes its distinction to the peculiarities of environment and intelligence. Those native to Xiyuan and Haidian naturally ply their trade in the Western Hills or around the universities at Yanjing and Tsinghua; those from Anding Gate stick to the Qinghe and Beiyuan districts; while those outside of Yongding Gate work in the area of Nanyuan. Interested only in long hauls, these men disdain the short, penny-ante business. But even they are no match for their long-distance brethren in the Legacy Quarter, who take passengers from the diplomatic sector all the way to the Jade Fountain, the Summer Palace, and the Western Hills. Stamina is only one reason why most pullers will not compete for this business, for this group of men can deal with their foreign passengers in their own languages: when a British or French soldier says he wants to go to the Summer Palace or the Yonghe Monastery or the Eight Alleys red-light district, they understand. And they will not pass this skill on to their rivals. Their style of running is also unique: at a pace that is neither particularly fast nor too slow, they run

with their heads down, not deigning to look left or right as they
keep to the sides of the roads, aloof and self-assured. Since they
serve foreigners, they do not wear the numbered jackets required
of other rickshaw men. Instead, they dress in long-sleeved white
shirts, black or white loose-fitting trousers tied at the ankles
with thin bands, and black cloth-soled "double-faced" shoes—
clean, neat, smart-looking. One sight of this attire keeps other
pullers from competing for fares or trying to race them. They
might as well be engaged in a trade all their own.

Now with this overview of the rickshaw trade, let's see where
Xiangzi fits in, in order to place—or at least attempt to place—
him as precisely as a cog in a machine. Before he gained the
nickname Camel, he was a relatively independent rickshaw man.
That is to say, he belonged to the young, vigorous set and owned
his own rickshaw. He was master of his own fate—an altogether
high-class rickshaw man.

That was no small accomplishment. Only after a year, then
two years, and then as many as three or four years—shedding
one drop, two drops, unknown thousands of drops of sweat—
did he manage to buy a rickshaw. By gritting his teeth through
wind and rain and scrimping on food and tea, he finally put
enough aside to buy it, a tangible reward for his struggles and his
suffering, like a medal for valor. In the days when he was pulling
a rental rickshaw, he ran from morning to night, from east to
west and from north to south, spinning like a top, and never his
own man. But his eyes did not falter and his heart would not
waver, as he thought of the rickshaw waiting for him, one that
would guarantee his freedom and independence, one that
counted as his arms and legs. Owning a rickshaw meant never

having to suffer mistreatment or do the bidding of people who rented them out. Relying on his strength and his own rickshaw, all he needed to do to make a living was to stay alert.

Hard work never bothered Xiangzi, nor was he affected by any of the excusable yet reprehensible bad habits so common among other rickshaw men. A combination of intelligence and diligence ensured that his dream would come true. If he'd been born into a better family or received a decent education, he'd never have been reduced to joining the rubber tire crowd; no matter what trade he'd taken up, he'd have made the most of his opportunities. Unfortunately, he had no choice, so, all right, he'd prove himself in the trade he was saddled with. Had he been consigned to hell, he'd have been one of the good demons. Born and raised in the countryside, he had come to the city at the age of eighteen, after losing his parents and the few acres of land they had worked. He brought with him a country boy's powerful physique and honesty. At first he survived by working at a variety of backbreaking jobs, and it had not taken him long to discover that pulling a rickshaw was an easier way to make a living. At the other jobs his wages were fixed; pulling a rickshaw offered more variety and opportunities, and you never knew when and where you might do better than you thought. Naturally, he realized that chance alone was not enough, that a good-looking, fast-moving man and rickshaw were essential. People knew a high-quality product when they saw it. After thinking it over, he concluded that he had most of what it takes: strength and youth. What he lacked was experience. You don't start out at the top, with the best equipment. But that was not going to hold Xiangzi back. With his youth and strength, he figured it would take no more than a couple of weeks to be running with the best of them. Then he'd rent a new rickshaw, and if all went well, he'd soon be on the payroll of a private party. Finally, after a couple of years, three or four at most, he'd buy a rickshaw, one that outshone everyone else's. As he flexed his muscles, he was confident that it was only a matter of time before he reached his goal. It was not wishful thinking.

Xiangzi's stature and muscles outstripped his years. He was tall and robust not long after his twentieth birthday, and even though his body had not reached maturity, he was no longer a boy—he was an adult, in face and figure, who retained a look of innocence and a mischievous nature. After watching the top runners in action, he decided to tighten his belt as far as it would go to show off his hard chest muscles and powerful, straight back. He looked down at his shoulders, broad and impressive. After fixing his belt, he'd put on a pair of baggy white trousers and tie them at the ankles with a band made of chicken intestines, to call attention to his large feet. Yes, he was going to be the finest rickshaw man in town. The thought nearly made him laugh out loud.

All in all, he had run-of-the-mill features; the look on his face is what set him apart. He had a smallish head, big, round eyes, a fleshy nose, and short, bushy eyebrows. His shaved head glistened. There was no excess flab in his cheeks, and his neck was nearly the same thickness as his head. His face was ruddy, always, highlighted by a large red scar that ran from his cheekbone to his right ear—he'd been bitten by a donkey while napping under a tree as a youngster. He paid little attention to his appearance yet was as fond of his face as he was of his body, both hard and solid. He counted his face as one of his limbs, and its strength was all that mattered. Even after coming to the city, he could do handstands and hold them for a long time, making him feel that he was like a tree that stood strong and straight.

He really was like a tree: solid, silent, and full of life. He had his plans and his aspirations, but he kept them to himself. Among the brethren, injustices and hardships were constant topics of conversation. At rickshaw stands, in teahouses, and in tenement compounds, the men discussed, described, and argued about their lot, until these things became public property, like popular songs passing from mouth to mouth and place to place. As a country boy, Xiangzi lacked the conversational skills of men from the city. If eloquence was a natural gift, he'd never received it, and he had no desire to imitate the sharp-tongued men around him. He knew what he was about and took no pleasure in talking with them; that gave him more time to think, as if his eyes were focused only on his own heart. Once he made up his mind, he followed the road his instincts told him to travel. If that led nowhere, he'd lapse into silence for a day or two, clenching his teeth as if biting down on his heart.

He made up his mind to pull a rickshaw, and that is what he did. He rented a beat-up rickshaw to try out his legs. The first day he earned next to nothing. The next day was better. But then he had to take a couple of days off, for his ankles had swelled to the size of gourds, putting his legs out of commission. He put up with the pain, no matter how bad it got, knowing that it was inevitable, a necessary passage on the way to where he was going. Without passing this test, he would never be able to go out and run as he wanted.

As soon as his legs were healthy, he went out again. He was a happy man, knowing that there was nothing more to be afraid of. He knew the city well and was never bothered if he took the long way round, since he had a reservoir of strength. How to run never presented much of a problem, either, thanks to his experience of pushing, pulling, carrying, and lifting heavy objects. Besides, he'd worked it out that as long as he remained within his limits he'd be safe. As for negotiating a fare, his tongue was slow, and he was too easily rattled to compete with the wily old rickshaw men. Recognizing this shortcoming, he avoided rickshaw stands, waiting instead in places where his was the only rickshaw. In those out-of-the-way places he could take his time when negotiating a fare. Sometimes he didn't even bother. "Climb aboard," he'd say, "and give me what you think it's worth." People seemed eager to deal with an honest man who had such a likable, innocent face, convinced that a simple young man like that would not overcharge them. Even those who had misgivings would suspect only that he was too new to the city to know his way around and so did not know how much to charge. "Do you know the place?" they'd ask. He'd play dumb and grin, leaving them scratching their heads.

It took only two or three weeks for Xiangzi to get his legs into shape, and he knew he looked good when he ran. Running style was proof of a rickshaw man's ability and qualifications. Those who ran with their feet splayed like a pair of palm-leaf fans had obviously just come in from the countryside, while those who ran with their heads down and shuffled along at a walking speed that only looked like a run were in their fifties or older. Old-timers who lacked physical strength had their own way of running: with their chests drawn in, they strained forward and lifted their legs high in the air, jerking their heads forward with each step, appearing to run but never moving faster than a brisk walk. They relied upon style to retain their self-respect. Needless to say, none of this appealed to Xiangzi. With his long legs, he took great strides, his hips hardly moving, and made little sound as he ran, each step like a spring, keeping the rickshaw level and his rider safe and comfortable. When told to stop, no matter how fast he was going, he planted his feet and pulled up smartly. His strength infused every part of the rickshaw as he bent his back slightly and gripped the shafts loosely. He was lively, nimble, and precise, fast without looking rushed, never flirting with danger. All this was rare even among men who pulled for private parties.

Xiangzi traded in his beat-up rickshaw for a new one, and on that day he learned that rickshaws with soft springs, solid brass fittings, large rain hoods with flaps, two lamps, and thin-necked horns cost more than a hundred yuan. For a little less, he could buy one that had so-so paint and fittings. That was all he needed to scrape together. If he put aside ten cents every day, in a thousand days he'd have a hundred yuan. A thousand days! He tried to calculate just how long that was but failed. Yet that did not faze him. A thousand days, even ten thousand days—it wouldn't matter. He was going to buy his own rickshaw. With that in mind, he decided to hire out to a private party and went looking for an employer with an active social life, someone who often attended dinner parties, at least ten a month, which would translate to two or three yuan in tips. That, on top of the one yuan he could save from his monthly pay, would add up to four or five yuan a month, or fifty to sixty a year, bringing him even closer to his goal. He did not smoke, he did not drink, and he did not gamble. With no bad habits and no family burdens, there was nothing to keep him from his goal as long as he persevered. He made a vow to himself: in a year and a half, he— Xiangzi—would own a rickshaw. And it had to be brand-new, not refurbished.

He found an employer. But his hopes were not favored by reality. He persevered—that was the easy part—but a year and a half later his vow remained unfulfilled. He had his private hires and was prudent and cautious. What a shame that the affairs of the world are not always simple, for that did not keep his employers from sacking him. Sometimes he lasted two or three months, sometimes only eight or ten days, after which he was out looking for steady work again. Meanwhile, he took as many fares as he could while he looked for another monthly hire, which was like riding one horse while looking for another. He simply could not remain idle. That led to mistakes, as he threw himself into his work, not only to make enough to fill his belly but to continue saving up to buy a rickshaw. And yet, hard work alone was not enough. His mind wandered as he ran, with thoughts crowding into his head, and the more he thought, the more fearful he grew, and the more indignant. At this rate, when would he ever have enough to buy a rickshaw? Why was this happening? Was he not trying hard enough? Such confusing thoughts led him to throw caution to the wind. He'd run over sharp pieces of metal on the road, causing a blowout, and that would be it for the day. But there were worse mishaps: he sometimes ran down a pedestrian or two, and once even lost a hubcap by failing to squeeze through a narrow opening. None of that would have happened if he'd had a steady job, and his disappointment at not having one made him clumsy and careless. Naturally, he had to pay for damages to the rented rickshaws, which increased his anxieties, like throwing oil on a fire. One way to avoid a serious accident was to spend all day in bed, but when he opened his eyes in the morning, he chastised himself over the loss of a day's wages. To complicate matters, the more he agonized over his situation, the worse he treated himself, stinting on regular meals. He considered himself made of strong stuff, but that did not keep him from getting sick. Too tightfisted to spend money on medicine when he fell ill, he tried to tough it out, which only made things worse, until he not only had to spend even more on medicine but had to take several days off to recuperate. To these troubles he responded by gritting his teeth and working even harder, which still had no effect on the speed with which he saved up money.

Eventually, he scraped together a hundred yuan, but it had taken three long years.

He could wait no longer. Originally he had planned to buy a fully outfitted, brand-new rickshaw satisfactory in every respect. Now it was a matter of whatever a hundred yuan could buy. No more waiting. What if he ran into more trouble and had to spend some of that money? As luck would have it, a custom-made rickshaw that the customer could not afford to pick up became available; it came very close to meeting Xiangzi's expectations. The original price had been over a hundred, but since the customer had forfeited his down payment, the shop was willing to lower the price a bit. Red in the face, his hands trembling uncontrollably, Xiangzi laid down ninety-six yuan. "I want this one!" Wanting to hold out for a round number, the shop owner talked and talked as he took the rickshaw outside and brought it back in, set the rain hood and put it back, and tooted the horn, every action accompanied by the finest sales pitch he knew. Finally, he kicked the steel spokes and said, "Hear that? Like a bell. Go ahead, take it out. You can use this till you pull it to pieces, and if a single one of these spokes buckles, bring it back and fling it in my face! A hundred yuan, my final offer."

Xiangzi counted his money one more time.

"I want this one. I'll give you ninety-six yuan!"

The shop owner knew this was no ordinary customer. He looked down at the money, then looked up at Xiangzi. He sighed.

"Might as well make a friend. It's yours. Six-month warranty. If you ruin the frame, that's on you. Anything else goes wrong, I'll repair it for free. Here it is in writing. Take it!"

Xiangzi's hands trembled more than ever as he tucked the warranty away and pulled the rickshaw out, nearly in tears. He took it to a remote spot to look it over, his very own rickshaw. He could see his face in the lacquer finish, and was willing to overlook even those things that strayed a bit from his ideal. Why? Because it was his. He could, he thought, take a little time off while he examined his rickshaw, so he sat on the newly padded footrest and gazed at the shiny brass horn. It occurred to him that he was twenty-two years old. Since his parents had died when he was very young, he had forgotten the day of his birth and had not celebrated a birthday since coming to the city. All right, he said to himself, I bought a new rickshaw today, so this will count as a birthday, mine and the rickshaw's. Easy to remember, and since the rickshaw had come about as a result of his blood and sweat, there was nothing to stop him from considering man and rickshaw as one.

Now, how to celebrate this double birthday? He had an idea: his first ride had to be a well-dressed man, not a woman. Ideally, he'd take him to Front Gate or, second best, Dongan Market. There he'd treat himself to a meal at the best stall around, including some quick-fried lamb in pocket bread. After he'd eaten, he'd look around for a good fare or two, but if nothing suited his fancy, he'd knock off for the day—his birthday!

Life improved for Xiangzi now that he had his own rickshaw, whether it was a steady job or individual fares, since he no longer had to worry about the rental fee. Every cent he took in was his. At peace with himself, he was friendly with his passengers, and that meant even more business. After six months of pulling his own rickshaw, his wish list grew. At this rate, in two years—no more—he'd be able to buy a second rickshaw, then a third . . . he could open his own rickshaw shed!

But wishes seldom come true, and Xiangzi's were no exception.

CHAPTER TWO

Xiangzi's happiness buoyed him; with a new rickshaw, he ran faster than ever. He took great pains to be careful—it was, after all, his own rickshaw—but each time he stole a look at it he felt he'd dishonor it by not running hard.

Since coming to the city, he had grown more than an inch, and instinct told him that he would keep growing. As his physique hardened, his skin seemed to fit him better, and a few scraggly hairs appeared on his upper lip. And yet he wanted to be taller still. Whenever he had to duck to walk through a door or gate, his heart swelled with pride, though he never said so. He was, he felt, an adult who was still a bit of a child, and how fascinating that was.

A big man pulling a handsome rickshaw, his very own, with flexible shafts that made the bar come alive in his hands. The carriage glistened, the mat was white and clean, and the horn made a crisp, loud sound. Why *wouldn't* he want to run fast? That was how he honored himself and his rickshaw. It had nothing to do with vanity; it was a sense of duty. Not running fast, not flying down the street, kept him from giving free rein to his strength and showing off the rickshaw's grace. It was a wonderful rickshaw that within six months seemed to develop a consciousness and emotions of its own. When he twisted his body or stepped down hard or straightened his back, it responded immediately, giving him the help he needed. There was no misunderstanding, no awkwardness between them. When they were on a level stretch of deserted road, he could take the bar in one hand, and the tires would chase him along, making a sound like whistling wind and pushing him to a fast, steady pace. When he reached a destination, he'd wring puddles of sweat out of his shirt and pants, as if they had just been taken out of a laundry basin. Exhausted? Sure. But happy and proud. It was the sort of exhaustion you get from riding a galloping horse.

There is a difference between boldness and recklessness, and Xiangzi was never reckless; he ran with confidence. Not running fast would be unfair to his passengers. But going so fast that he damaged his rickshaw would be unfair to himself. The rickshaw was the center of his life, and he knew how to take care of it. Combining caution with daring enhanced his confidence, convincing him that he and his rickshaw were made of hard stuff indeed.

As a result, not only did he run fearlessly, but he also gave no thought to the hours he kept. To him, making a living by pulling a rickshaw was proof of moral integrity, and there was no one to stop him when he felt like taking his rickshaw out. He paid little attention to rumors floating around town: soldiers have appeared at Xiyuan; more fighting at Changxindian; forced conscription outside Xizhi Gate; the closing of the city gate at Qihua. He took note of none of it. Naturally, shops along the streets were boarded up, and armed police and security forces flooded the streets; but he stayed clear of such places, taking his rickshaw out of service, like everyone else. While he refused to believe the rumors, caution was his watchword, especially since the rickshaw was his. But he was, after all, a country boy who, unlike the city folk, did not hear the wind and mistake it for rain. Besides, he had faith in his body, and even if the rumors proved to be true, he would know how to stay out of harm's way. He was not someone to be pushed around—not a strapping, broad-shouldered young man like him.

War and rumors arrived like clockwork every year during planting season. Wheat tassels and bayonets were symbols of hope and of despair for northerners. Xiangzi's rickshaw was six months old when farmers began hoping for spring rains to nourish their crops. The rain did not always come when they wanted it, but war arrived whether they wanted it or not. Rumors, real events. Xiangzi seemed to forget that he had once been a peasant himself. How badly war destroyed farmland was not his problem, and he had no time to worry if the rains came or not. Only his rickshaw mattered. It was the source of everything he ate; it was a fertile field that dutifully followed him everywhere, a living piece of land, a precious possession. Then the price of grain rose, owing to a shortage of rain and a surplus of war. That was something Xiangzi did know. But like the city folk, he could only complain, not do anything about it. The cost of grain has gone up? So be it. After all, no one knows how to make it go back down. That attitude had him focused solely on himself; all thoughts of calamity migrated to the back of his head.

When city folk do not know how to deal with something, they create rumors—sometimes they are total fabrications and sometimes they are based on a kernel of truth—as a means of showing that they are neither stupid nor feckless. They are like fish that rise lazily to the surface to release useless bubbles just to please themselves. Of all the rumors, those concerning war are the most interesting. All the others start and end as rumor, on the order of ghost stories in which all the talk in the world can never make a ghost appear. But where war is concerned, since accurate news is unavailable, rumors are prophetic, like setting up a pole to see its shadow. In the case of minor details, rumors fall wide of the mark; but with war, eighty or ninety percent of the rumors are based on fact. "There's going to be fighting!" That cry invariably comes true. Who is fighting whom, and how, depends on who you are talking to. Xiangzi was not unaware of that, but common laborers—which include rickshaw men—while not looking forward to wartime, do not necessarily suffer because of it. When war breaks out, the first to panic are the rich, who think only of fleeing at the first sign of trouble; wealth is their ticket out of town. Obviously, with feet weighted down by riches, they cannot just pick up and leave on their own, so they must hire a phalanx of people to get them on the road: people to carry their luggage and vehicles to transport families—male and female, young and old. At such times, men who sell their muscle find that their arms and legs are suddenly worth a great deal.

"Front Gate, East Train Station!"

"Where?"

"East—Train—Station."

"Oh, give me one yuan forty and we'll call it even! No haggling, war is raging everywhere!"

That was how things stood when Xiangzi took his rickshaw out of the city. Rumors had flown for at least ten days, and the price of everything rose; yet the fighting was far away from Beiping. He went out each day as usual, not taking time off despite the rumors. One day, after hauling a passenger to West City, he noticed something unusual. He made a few turns around the area but saw no one at the western intersection of Huguo Monastery Road and New Street hailing rickshaws to familiar destinations:

"Xiyuan?"

"Tsinghua University?"

He heard that no vehicles dared leave the city, for they were being seized outside at Xizhi Gate—wagons, large and small, donkey carts, and rickshaws, no exceptions. Deciding to stop for a cup of tea, he headed south to take a break. The rickshaw stand was unusually quiet, a sign that danger lurked. Xiangzi was no coward, but neither was he one to walk blindly into harm's way. As he pondered the situation, a pair of rickshaws pulled up. The passengers appeared to be students. One of the rickshaw pullers shouted, "Anyone for Tsinghua University? Tsinghua!"

None of the men at the rickshaw stand replied. Some smirked; others sat on their rickshaws smoking pipes without looking up.

"Are you all mutes?" the man shouted. "Tsinghua!"

"Give me two yuan and I'll go!" replied a short youngster with a shaved head, half in jest.

"Come on over. Who else?" Both rickshaws pulled up and stopped.

The young fellow froze, not knowing what to do now, since no one else made a move. Xiangzi did not have to be told that going outside the city gate was risky, but two yuan to Tsinghua University—a trip that usually cost no more than twenty or thirty cents—why wasn't anyone interested? Like the others, he did not want to go, but the shaved-head youngster appeared to be willing. As long as he wasn't the only one, why not do it?

"You there, big guy, what do you say?"

"Big guy." Xiangzi had to laugh. It was, he knew, a compliment, and he took it to heart. The least he could do was help out the shaved-head young man, who had plenty of spunk for someone so short, not to mention the two yuan he'd be earning; that was not something he saw every day. Dangerous? What were the odds? Besides, over the past couple of days he'd heard that the Temple of Heaven was a massing spot for soldiers, but he'd been there and had seen neither hide nor hair of a soldier. With these thoughts running through his mind, he pulled his rickshaw up.

When the group reached Xizhi Gate, there were few people around, which Xiangzi took as a bad sign. His young companion did not like what he saw, either.

"Let's keep an eye peeled, pal," he said with a little laugh. "It might be trouble, it might not be. But we've come this far." Xiangzi had a premonition that something bad was about to happen, but after all these years on the street, his word meant something. He could not start acting like an old woman now.

After passing through the gate, they did not see another vehicle anywhere, and Xiangzi lowered his head to keep from looking around. His heart felt like it was bumping up against his ribs. Once they were on Gaoliang Bridge, he sneaked a look. Not a soldier anywhere, and that made him feel a little better. Two yuan, after all, was two yuan, not a sum for the faint of heart. Though he was not given to idle chatter, it was so deathly still he felt a need to say something to his companion. "Let's take a dirt path. This road . . ."

"Just what I was thinking," the youngster said. "We might have a chance if we stay off the road."

But before they made it to the dirt path, Xiangzi, his shaved-headed companion, and their passengers fell into the hands of a dozen soldiers.

Although it was the time of year to burn incense at the temple on Mount Miaofeng, a thin shirt was no protection against the cold. Xiangzi was wearing only a thin gray tunic and a pair of blue cotton army trousers, both reeking of sweat and little more than rags—they'd been like that before he put them on. All he could think of were the white jacket and indigo-dyed lined pants he was wearing when they took them off him—they were so clean and so smart. There were nicer clothes than that in the world, but he knew how hard it had been for someone like him to be dressed that way. The sweat-stink of what he was wearing now reminded him of all he'd struggled for and made what he had accomplished seem nobler. The more he thought about his past, the deeper his hatred for the soldiers. They had taken his clothes, his shoes, his rickshaw, even the sash he used as a belt, in return for bruises and welts all over his body and blisters on his feet. The clothes didn't count for much, nor did his injuries, since they'd heal soon enough. But the rickshaw he'd bought with his blood and sweat, it was gone! The last he'd seen of it was when they took it to their barracks. In the past, he'd had no trouble putting his suffering and difficulties out of his mind, but not his rickshaw!

Xiangzi was not afraid of hard work or suffering, but he knew what it would take to get a second rickshaw—years. All he'd achieved had come to nothing. He'd have to start over again. The tears came. He didn't just hate those soldiers—he hated the whole world. What right do they have to do this to me? "What right?" He was shouting.

But this shout—though it made him feel a little better—reminded him of the dangers he faced. Only one thing counted now: escape.

Where was he? He couldn't be sure. He'd been on the march with the soldiers for days, the sweat running from his head down to the bottoms of his feet. Always on the move, carrying or pulling or pushing things for the soldiers. When they stopped, he had to fetch water, light fires, and feed the livestock. All day long his only thought was how to force the strength he'd need into his hands and feet; his mind was a blank. At night, the minute his head hit the ground, he slept like the dead, and never waking up again did not seem like such a bad thing after all.

At first, he vaguely recalled, the soldiers were in retreat toward Mount Miaofeng, but when they reached the back side of the mountains, he focused on climbing, knowing that one slip could send him into the stream below, where birds of prey would eventually pick his bones clean. He put all other thoughts out of his mind. They wove their way over and around mountains for days on end, until one day the footpaths virtually disappeared. With the sun at his back, Xiangzi saw a distant plain, and when the call went out for the porters to return for the evening meal, soldiers came back to camp with camels.

Camels! Xiangzi's heart skipped a beat, and suddenly he could think again, like a lost man spotting a familiar sign; a plan formed in his head. Camels are no good in the mountains, so they'd obviously reached the plain. He knew that people raised camels in the western suburbs of the capital: places like Balizhuang, Huang Village, Northern Xin'an, Moshi Pass, Wulitun, and Sanjiadian. Was it possible that all that travel had brought them right back to Moshi Pass? He wondered what kind of strategy these soldiers—who were good for little more than marching and plundering—

had. What he did know was, if they really were at Moshi Pass, they had given up on the mountains and were looking for an escape route. Moshi Pass was an ideal spot; heading northeast would take them to the Western Hills; heading south they'd reach Changxindian or Fengtai; heading west out of the pass was the best option. While plotting for the soldiers, he was actually figuring how he was going to escape; the time had arrived. If the soldiers turned back to the mountains, even if he managed to get away, he might starve. It was now or never. He was confident that if he ran, he could make it back to Haidian. It wouldn't be easy—he'd have to pass through many towns and villages, but all places he'd been before. He shut his eyes and tried to picture the route: Moshi Pass is here—I hope to heaven I'm right! Head northeast, past Gold Peak Mountain and Prince Li's Grave, to Badachu; turn east at Sipingtai to Xingzi Pass and Nanxinzhuang. He'd need to hug the foothills for cover as he headed north from Nanxinzhuang, through Wei Family Village and Nanhetan; keep heading north to Red Hill and Prince Jie's Palace, all the way to Jingyi Gardens. From there he could find Haidian with his eyes closed. His heart nearly leaped out of his chest. Over the past several days, all his blood seemed to flow into his limbs; now, suddenly, it rushed back to his heart, which burned hot, while his arms and legs went cold. Feverish hope made him tremble from head to toe.

Late at night Xiangzi was still awake. Hope buoyed his spirits; fear made him jittery. He tried to sleep but couldn't, and lay on his bed of straw feeling as if his arms and legs had left his body. He was surrounded by an eerie silence, the stars above the only witnesses to his pounding heart. The silence was broken by the sorrowful brays of a camel. The camels were very near. It was a good sound, like the crow of a rooster before dawn, simultaneously forlorn and comforting.

He heard cannon fire, distant but unmistakable. He didn't dare move, but then he heard an uproar in the camp. He held his breath. This was his chance. He knew that the soldiers had to retreat and that they'd head back into the mountains. His time with them had taught him that they fought like bees trapped inside a room, flying blindly into walls. The soldiers would react to the sound of cannon fire by running away, so he had to be ready to make his move. Slowly he began to crawl along the ground, holding his breath as best he could as he searched for the camels. He knew they wouldn't be any help, but, like him, they were prisoners, and that ought to elicit a bit of mutual sympathy. Pandemonium reigned in camp. He found the camels kneeling on the ground and looking like a cluster of hillocks in the dark, the only sound their raspy breathing, as if peace reigned all around. That lifted his courage. He crouched down beside one of the camels, like a porter hiding behind a sandbag, where he was struck by an idea: the cannon fire was coming from the south, and even if they weren't shooting at anything, they were warning everyone that there was no passage. What that meant was that the soldiers had to retreat into the mountains, and they'd not be taking the camels. So the animals' fate was tied up with his. If the soldiers were not willing to abandon the animals, he had no chance. But if they forgot the camels, he could escape. By putting his ear to the ground, he could tell if anyone was coming his way. His heart was racing.

He had no idea how long he waited there, but no one came for the camels. Time to take a chance. He sat up and peered between the two humps. Nothing to see but darkness. He ran. Whatever happened, good or bad, it was time to flee.

CHAPTER THREE

Xiangzi had run twenty or thirty steps when he stopped. He couldn't leave those camels. All he had in the world now was his life, and he'd have happily picked up a length of rope if he could have found one. Even something that worthless would have brought him a sense of well-being; in other words, with that in his hand, he'd at least have something. Escaping was essential, but what good was a man's life stripped bare of everything else? He had to take the animals with him, though he had no idea if they might come in handy; but they were, after all, something, and something quite big.

He began pulling the camels to their feet. Clueless as to how to handle them, he wasn't frightened; he'd come from the countryside, where he'd spent a good deal of time around domestic animals. Slowly, very slowly, they stood up. He had no time to worry whether or not they were tied together, and as soon as he realized he could get one camel to follow him, he started walking—one or all of them, it didn't matter.

He regretted the impulse as soon as he started out. Being accustomed to carrying heavy loads, camels walk slowly. And they aren't just slow—they are cautious, fearful of slipping. Any water puddle or patch of mud can result in a sprain or a cracked knee.

The value of a camel rests only in its legs. A damaged leg can put it out of commission. Meanwhile, Xiangzi was fleeing for his life.

Years of pulling a rickshaw had honed Xiangzi's sense of direction. But that did little to calm his confused state of mind. Finding the camels had at first made them the focus of his thoughts. But once he had them on their feet, he realized he didn't know for sure where he was. It was so dark and he was so anxious that, even if he knew how to travel by the stars, he wouldn't put his trust in them, since they—it seemed to him— were more anxious than he. They seemed to bump into each other in the dark sky, and he forced himself to stop looking up. Head down, he kept walking, slowly, his anxiety growing. He began to ponder his situation: since I'm walking with camels, I need to get away from the mountain paths and find a road. It's a straight line from Moshi Pass—if that's where I am—to Yellow Village. That means a real road and no detours. The words "no detours" carried considerable weight to a man who made his living pulling a rickshaw. But the road offered no possibility of concealment. What if he encountered another gang of soldiers? And even if he didn't, did he look like someone who tended camels, given the tattered army clothes, his dirty face, and his long, unruly hair? No, not in a million years! What he looked like was a deserter. A deserter! It wouldn't be so bad if soldiers caught him, but if villagers spotted him, he could look forward to being buried alive! That thought made him tremble. The sound of the camels walking behind him gave him a scare. His only chance of getting away was to abandon the camels, since they were holding him back. Maybe so, but he held on to the rope that was fixed to the lead camel's nose. Let's go, keep walking. We'll wind up somewhere and deal with whatever's waiting for us there. If I make it out alive, I've got camels to show for it. If I don't, those are the breaks.

He slipped out of his army clothes, tore off the tunic collar, and plucked off the last two conspicuous brass buttons and flung them into the darkness. They fell without a sound. Then he draped the collarless, buttonless shirt over his shoulders and tied the sleeves together in front of his chest, as if he were carrying a bundle on his back. That made him look less like a soldier on the run. Finally, he rolled the pant cuffs up just under his knees. He knew he still didn't look much like a camel herder, but at least people wouldn't spot him right off as a deserter. His dirty face and sweat-soaked body probably gave him the appearance of a coal miner. Ideas did not come to Xiangzi quickly, but when they came, they were well formed and immediately put into practice. The night was so dark that no one could have seen him, and there wasn't a pressing need for him to act right away; but he couldn't wait, since he did not know what time it was. For all he knew, daybreak wasn't far off. He was avoiding mountain paths, so once the sun came out, he'd have no place to hide. If he traveled during the day, he'd have to convince people that he was a coal miner. That's what he thought, so that's what he did, and it made him feel better, as if the danger had passed and he'd soon be back in Beiping. He had to make his way into the city, and soon; with no money and no food, time was his worst enemy. Another idea came to him: he'd save energy, which would help stave off hunger, if he rode one of the camels. But he wasn't sure he could manage. The ride would be steady enough, but he'd first have to find a way to get the camel to kneel. Nothing was more important than time, and that would be more trouble than it was worth. Besides, if he was up there, he couldn't see the ground in front; if the camel stumbled, it would take him with it. No, just keep walking.

He had a sense that he was on a highway but could not be sure exactly where he was or in which direction he was walking. The late night, the exhaustion of many days, and the risks of running away made him uneasy in mind and body. After walking awhile, his steps steady and slow, his body began to demand sleep. As a chill penetrated the darkness, uncertainties multiplied. He kept looking down at the ground, which seemed to his eye to undulate, though every even step belied that vision; extreme caution and the tricks his mind was playing on him disturbed him to the point of visible agitation. Might as well stop looking down, he thought, and concentrate on what's ahead. He shuffled forward, feet dragging on the ground. He couldn't see a thing, as if all the darkness in the world were waiting there for him. Each step in the darkness took him into more of the same; the camels followed without making a sound.

As he grew accustomed to the dark, his mind seemed to stop functioning and he could no longer keep his eyes open. Was he still walking, or had he stopped? All he sensed was a wavelike motion in his head, like black ocean swells; the darkness attached itself to his mind, unsettled, flustered, confused. Suddenly he was jolted awake, as if something had occurred to him, maybe a sound, he couldn't be sure. He opened his eyes, and he knew at once that he was still walking—the momentary thought was gone. Nothing was happening anywhere around him. His heart lurched for a second before he calmed down. Keep your eyes open, he told himself, and no wild thoughts. Getting into the city as quickly as possible is all that matters. But his mind would not cooperate. His eyelids kept drooping, and he knew he had to think of something quick to stay awake. If he could lie down, he could sleep for three days. Think, he said, think. His head was reeling, his body was uncomfortably wet, his scalp itched, his feet were sore, and his mouth was dry and bitter-tasting. The best he could come up with was self-pity, but even that seemed impossible, since his head was empty; he no sooner had thoughts about himself than he forgot them, like a dying candle that won't light. Enveloped by darkness, he felt as if he were floating inside a black cloud. Though he was aware of his existence and that he was walking forward, there was no evidence of where he was headed. He was like a man tossed about on the open sea, no longer able to believe in himself. Never in his life had he felt so bewildered, so downhearted, so very alone. Never one to place much importance on friends, he feared nothing, no matter what it was, so long as he was out in the light of day, with the sun shining down on him. Even now he felt no fear, but the inability to make necessary decisions was more than he could bear. If the camels had been as intransigent as, say, mules, he might well have focused his attention on them. But they were so obedient they began to get on his nerves, and as his mind wandered, he was not even sure they were still behind him, and that gave him a scare. He was ready to believe that the hulking beasts had somehow gone off in a different direction in the darkness without his knowing it, like a melting ice block pulled behind him.

At some point along the way he sat down. If he were to die yet retain memory after death, he would be unable to recall how he'd come to be sitting on the ground, or why. He sat there for five minutes—or maybe it was an hour, he didn't know. Neither did he know if he'd sat down and fallen asleep or if he'd fallen asleep and then sat down. Probably the latter, since by then he was so exhausted he could have slept standing up.

He woke up abruptly, not the normal return to wakefulness but with a start, as if transported to another world. It was still pitch-dark. He heard a rooster crow, clear as a bell, almost as if something had pierced his brain. He was wide awake. The camels, what about the camels? That was his first and only thought. The rope was still in his hand; the camels were there beside him. What a relief! He did not feel like getting up. He was sore all over, too sore to stand. But he didn't dare go back to sleep. He had to think, think hard, come up with something. And it was at this moment that he recalled his rickshaw. "What right?" he shouted.

It was an empty shout that served no purpose. He stood up and felt one of the camels. How many were there? He didn't know. He went from one to the next—three, he counted. Not too many, too few. He concentrated on them. Unsure of what to do with three camels, he had a vague thought that his future was tied to them.

"Why not sell them and use the money to buy a new rickshaw?" He nearly jumped in the air. But he didn't, probably because he was embarrassed that he hadn't thought of something so natural, so easy to accomplish, before this. In the end, happiness won out over shame. He knew what he was going to do. Hadn't he heard a rooster crow only a few minutes before? Well, even when they do that at two in the morning, daybreak cannot be far off. And where there were roosters, there had to be a village. Maybe Northern Xin'an. The people there raised camels, so he mustn't waste any time. If he reached the village before sunup, he could dispose of his camels, go immediately into the city, and buy a rickshaw. With war raging all around, they must be selling them cheap. That thought crowded out all others. Selling his camels would be easy.

Xiangzi's spirits rose. His soreness was gone. If he could have exchanged his camels for a hundred acres of farmland or a string of pearls, he would not have been nearly as happy. Standing up straight, he got his camels up off the ground and started walking. He had no idea what a camel sold for these days, but he'd heard that in the past, before trains came to town, a camel was worth three dabao, or fifty ounces of silver. They're strong and they eat less than mules. Three dabao was probably out of the question, but he had hopes of getting eighty or a hundred yuan, enough to buy a rickshaw.

The sky was turning light, starting up ahead of him, which meant he was heading east. Even if he was on the wrong road, he'd still be heading east. The mountains were to the west, the city to the east. He knew that much. The darkness was retreating all around, and though no colors were visible, the fields and distant trees were coming into view in the haze. The stars were vanishing, as the sky filled with a layer of gray that resembled clouds but could have been mist—still fairly dark, but rising higher and higher. Finally he mustered the courage to look up. The smell of grass grew stronger and he heard bird songs. Now that he could distinguish shapes, his ears, his eyes, his mouth, and his nose were back in working order. He looked down and saw that he could make out parts of his body, a reminder of the sorry shape he was in. At least he had proof that he was alive. Like waking from a bad dream, he was struck by the thought of how joyful it was to be alive. After briefly examining himself, he turned to look at his camels. They were as sorry-looking as he, and as wonderful. They were molting, pinkish-gray skin showing through in clumps, the sloughed-off hide hanging from parts of their bodies; pulling it off would have required little effort. They looked like big, lumbering beggars. The long necks were the most wretched-looking: long, hairless, curved, ungraceful, stretched out in front like frustrated dragons. But

Xiangzi did not find them disgusting, no matter how disreputable they might appear. They were, after all, living creatures. He was, he felt, the luckiest man alive, for the heavens had sent him three treasures that he could swap for a rickshaw. Things like that did not happen every day. He laughed out loud.

Red streaks appeared in the gray sky, casting shadows over the ground and the distant trees; little by little the reds and grays merged, turning some of the sky a washed-out purple and some of it bright red, but mostly the purplish gray of grapes. A few moments later, gold borders framed the red, creating rays of sunlight that were all the colors of the rainbow. Then, as if a switch had been thrown, things came into view. The morning colors turned dark red, in vivid contrast to the blue sky. The red began breaking up, releasing golden sunbeams—layers of color intersecting with the sun's rays. Gorgeous spiderlike webs formed in the southeastern corner of the sky, as fields, trees, and wild grass turned from dark green to the color of jade. The trunks of ancient trees were dyed a golden red, sunlight glistened off the wings of passing birds, and everything seemed to be smiling. Xiangzi felt like shouting at the layers of red and gold, for he did not recall seeing the sun even once after being seized by the soldiers; he had spent the days grumbling and cursing inwardly, head hung low. He'd had no thoughts of the sun and the moon; the sky had disappeared from his life. Now he was walking freely, feeling more hopeful with each step. The sun painted the dew on grass and leaves with a coat of gold and had not only brightened his hair and brows but had warmed his heart as well. All his troubles, all the dangers and suffering, were forgotten. His shabby appearance did not matter, for he had not been cast out from the sun's light and heat. He was once again living in a bright, warm world, and was so happy he could shout.

He looked down at his threadbare clothes, then at the molting camels behind him, and he laughed. How uncanny, he was
thinking, that four such sorry individuals had actually managed
to get away safely and walk into the sun. It made no difference
who was right and who was wrong, as far as he was concerned,
since it was all written in the heavens. With a sense of relief, he
walked with slow assurance; with the heavens as his protector,
he had nothing to fear. Where were his feet taking him? Men
and women were out working in the fields, but he did not care
to ask them. Just keep walking. Even the possibility that he'd be
unable to sell his camels right away did not concern him. He'd
worry about that after he reached Beiping, a city he desperately
wanted to see again. No mother and father were waiting for him
in a place where nothing belonged to him. But it was his home,
all of it, and he'd know what to do when he arrived. He saw a
village off in the distance, a fairly large one, with a row of tall,
green willows standing guard, bending low over the squat rooftops from which kitchen smoke curled upward. He heard the
barking of dogs—music to his ears. He headed for the village,
not expecting any sort of windfall but to show that he feared
nothing. The villagers posed no threat, since everyone was
bathed in the glorious, peaceful rays of the sun. He'd like a drink
of water, if that was possible. But if not, so be it. A little water
meant nothing to someone who had come out of the mountains
alive.

Barking dogs announced his approach; he ignored them. But
the eyes of the village women and children made him uncomfortable. He must have looked like a very strange camel herder.
Why else would they be gawking at him that way? He was
deeply embarrassed. To the soldiers he'd been less than human,
and to the people here in the village he was a freak. He didn't

know what to do. Size and strength had always been a source of self-esteem and pride for him, but recently he had become a victim of injustice and privation through no fault of his own. As he looked over the roof of one of the houses, he saw the sun, with its promise, but now it didn't seem so lovely.

Worried that the camels could slip and fall in the foul-smelling puddles of toxic water mixed with pig and horse urine on a street that ran through the village, Xiangzi felt like resting. He spotted a relatively lavish house to the north of the street with a tiled building behind it. The gate and gatehouse were missing; only a slat door remained. Xiangzi knew what that was: a tiled building—a rich man; a slat door and no gate—a camel dealer! All right, this was the place to take a rest and see if there might be a chance to say good-bye to his camels.

"*Seh! Seh! Seh!*" Xiangzi commanded the camels to kneel. It was the only camel command he knew, and he proudly put it to use. Now the villagers would see that he knew what he was doing. The camels knelt and he coolly went over and sat beneath a young willow. People were watching him, and he was watching them. That, he knew, was the only way to lessen their suspicions.

He had been sitting there awhile when an old man came out. Wearing a blue jacket, open in front, he had a face that glowed, and one look told Xiangzi that this was one of the village's wealthy men. He made a quick decision.

"Have you got some water, old-timer? I could use a glass."

"Ah!" The old man rubbed caked mud from his chest and gave Xiangzi a long look. Then he eyed the three camels. "I've got water. Where are you from?"

"Out west." Xiangzi couldn't give a name because he wasn't sure.

"Aren't there soldiers out that way?" The old man was staring at Xiangzi's army pants.

"They grabbed me. I just got away."

"I see. No problem getting the camels through the western pass?"

"The soldiers went into the mountains. The roads are safe."

"Uh-huh." The old man nodded slowly. "Wait here, I'll get you some water."

Xiangzi followed him into the yard, where he spotted four camels.

"Why don't I leave these three with you, sir? You can put together a camel train."

"Hah! A train? Thirty years ago I owned three trains. Things have changed. Who can afford to feed camels these days?"

The old man stopped to stare at his four camels. "I was thinking about getting all the neighborhood camels together and letting them go out beyond the pass to graze," he said after a moment. "But I didn't dare, since there's fighting in the east and in the west. I hate keeping them penned up here. Just look at all the flies. It'll be even hotter soon, and that will bring the mosquitoes. I can't stand watching these fine animals suffer, I tell you!"

"So why don't I leave my three with you? That way you can take a train out to graze? Animals need to be on the move, and if you keep them here all summer, the flies and mosquitoes will eat them alive!" Xiangzi was nearly pleading.

"Who has the money to buy them? These are bad times to raise camels."

"I'll leave them with you and you can give me what you think is fair. That way I can say good-bye to them and go into the city to make a living."

The old man sized Xiangzi up. He didn't seem like a bandit or

anything. Then he turned to look at the three camels out beyond the gate. Apparently, he liked what he saw, though he
knew no good could come of buying them. But a book lover can
be counted on to buy a book, and a horse fancier cannot pass up
a stud for sale. A trader who's owned three camel trains is no
different. Besides, Xiangzi had said he'd sell them cheaply, and
whenever a connoisseur sees a bargain, he tends to forget
whether or not he should be buying the thing in the first place.

"If I were a rich man, young fellow, I'd be happy to take them
off your hands." It was an honest statement.

"You can have them for whatever you think is fair," Xiangzi
said with such sincerity the old man seemed slightly embarrassed.

"I mean it, young fellow, if this were thirty years ago, they'd
be worth three dabao. But times have changed, there's fighting
everywhere, and I . . . maybe you'd better try your luck somewhere else."

"Just give me what you can!" Xiangzi did not know what else
to say. He knew the old man was telling the truth, and he had
no interest in running around the country trying to sell his camels. What if no one wanted them? That would mean even more
trouble.

"Look, I'm embarrassed to say it, but I could manage twenty
or thirty yuan, and even that's not easy for me. I tell you, these
times, I've got no choice."

Xiangzi's heart fell. Twenty or thirty yuan? That wasn't nearly
enough to buy a rickshaw. But he couldn't let this business slow
him down, and what were the chances he'd meet up with another trader like this? "Just give me what you can, sir."

"What do you do for a living, young fellow? Obviously, you're
not in the camel business."

Xiangzi told him.

"So, you risked your life to save these animals!" The old man's sympathy was conspicuous. He was also relieved, assured that the animals were not stolen. Actually, they probably had been at some point, but the soldiers presented a second layer of ownership. During wartime, normal practices fly out the window.

"How about this, young man—I'll give you thirty-five yuan. I'd be a liar if I said I wasn't getting them cheap, but I'd also be a liar if I said I could give you even one yuan more. I'm over sixty. I don't know what else I can say."

Xiangzi, who had always been tightfisted, did not know what to do. But after his days with those soldiers, to suddenly hear the old man speak to him with obvious sincerity and sympathy, he knew he mustn't haggle. Not to mention the fact that thirty-five yuan in his hand meant more than ten thousand in his dreams, even though it wasn't much to risk your life for. Three living, breathing camels could not possibly be worth only thirty-five yuan! But what choice did he have?

"They're yours, old-timer. Just one request. Give me a jacket and something to eat."

"Deal!"

Xiangzi drank his fill of cold water, accepted the thirty-five bright one-yuan coins and two big cornmeal cakes, and headed off to the city in a tattered white jacket that barely covered his chest.

CHAPTER FOUR

Xiangzi was laid up for three days in a little inn in Haidian, chilled one minute and feverish the next. He was in a fog, his mind a blank; purple blisters had erupted on his gums. All he wanted was water; he had no appetite. Three days without food had dissipated the heat in his body, leaving him as weak as a piece of soft candy. Sometime during those three days he must have dreamed about his three camels and muttered aloud, for when he was conscious again he had gained a nickname: Camel Xiangzi.

Xiangzi had been his name, his only name, the day he entered the city. Now that Camel had been tacked onto it, no one cared what his family name might have been. He himself didn't care whether he had a family name or not. But he was bothered by the fact that not only had he traded three living animals for that little bit of money, but he now had a not altogether welcomed nickname.

Once he struggled to his feet, Xiangzi felt like going outside to look around. His legs, unfortunately, were not up to the challenge. He barely made it to the door before they came out from under him and he landed on the floor, where he sat in a daze for a long time, his forehead beaded in a clammy sweat. He put up with this the best he could until he managed to open his eyes. His stomach rumbled. Now he was hungry. Moving slowly, he got to his feet and went outside to find a wonton peddler. He ordered a bowl of wontons, which he ate sitting on the ground. The first slurp of soup nearly sickened him, but he held it in his mouth until he could force it down. He had no desire for more, but when the second mouthful slipped down into his stomach a moment later, he belched, proving he was going to make it.

Now that he had some food in his stomach, he took stock of himself. He was thin as a rail and his pants were unimaginably filthy. He did not feel like moving, but he had to get back to the clean, neat person he'd been before. He refused to enter the city looking like death warmed over. But cleaning up meant spending money: a shave and new clothes, including shoes and socks, would not be free. He should not have to spend any of his thirty-five yuan, already much less than what a new rickshaw would cost, but he felt sorry for himself. Despite the fact that he'd only been held by the soldiers for a short time, all that had happened seemed like a bad dream, one that had aged him, as if he'd grown years older in a matter of days. Those big hands and feet were his, no doubt about that, but they seemed like objects he'd found somewhere—he could not have felt worse. He tried not to think about the grievances he'd suffered and the dangers he'd faced in recent days, but the memories persisted; it was like knowing the sky is dark on an overcast day without looking up. He was too fond of his body to make it suffer more than it already had. Though he knew that he was still very weak, he stood up. He did not want to wait any longer than was necessary to pull himself together. All he needed to be strong again, he felt, was to have his head shaved and put on some new clothes.

To get to that point, all it cost was two-twenty: one yuan for a coarse pair of pants and a jacket, eighty cents for a pair of black cloth shoes, fifteen cents for some coarse cotton socks, plus twenty-five cents for a straw hat. He got two boxes of matches for his cast-off clothes.

Clutching his matches, he headed off toward Xizhi Gate, but he hadn't gotten far when his body began to fail him again. He gritted his teeth. No riding for him. How could someone from the countryside consider a couple of miles too far to walk, especially a man who has pulled a rickshaw? More to the point, it would have been laughable for someone as strong as Xiangzi to be felled by a minor illness. If he pitched to the ground and could not get back up, he'd crawl into the city if necessary. Xiangzi would not give up. His survival depended on his making it into the city today. The one thing he believed in was his body, and no sickness was going to keep him down.

He staggered along and had barely left Haidian when he began to see stars, and had to lean against a willow tree to steady himself and wait for the world to stop spinning. Not for a minute, however, did he sit down. Slowly the world stopped spinning, and Xiangzi's heart returned from some distant spot to the middle of his chest. After wiping the sweat from his forehead, he started walking again. Now that his head was freshly shaved and he had on new clothes and shoes, he was feeling better about himself. So his legs had to do their bit—keep walking! He didn't stop again until he had reached Guanxiang, where he saw bustling crowds of people and horses, where his ears were bombarded with a cacophony of noises and his nose was struck by a dry stench. As he stepped on the spongy dirt road, he felt like getting down on his hands and knees to kiss the ground, the stinking, lovable ground that supplied him with a living. Having no parents, no brothers or sisters, no family at all, Xiangzi

had but one friend: this ancient city. It had given him everything, and he'd rather starve here than thrive in the countryside.
There were sights to be seen here and sounds to be heard; all
around him there was light and there was noise. If he worked
hard, there was money to be made, lots of it, more food than he
could ever eat, and more clothing than he could wear in a lifetime. A beggar in the city might dine on meaty broths, while in
the countryside maize cakes were the best a person could hope
for. When he reached the western bank of the Gaoliang Bridge,
Xiangzi sat down and shed hot tears.

To the west, the setting sun decorated the crooked tips of
aged riverbank willows with flecks of gold. The river was short
on water but long on algae, giving it the look of a long, greasy
sash, narrow and dark green, and emitting a dank, slightly fishy
odor. Beards had already appeared on the squat, dried-out wheat
stalks north of the riverbank; a layer of dust covered the leaves.
Lotus plants floating on ponds south of the river were under-
sized and anemic; tiny bubbles broke the surface amid the plants
from time to time. On the bridge east of where Xiangzi sat, lines
of pedestrian and vehicle traffic were unbroken and, under the
afternoon sun, seemingly rushed. As dusk neared, a feeling of
unease appeared to affect the travelers. For Xiangzi's senses, this
all conspired to spark delight and adoration. Only this strip of
water counted as a river, and only those trees, stalks of wheat,
lotus leaves, and the bridge were worthy of the name, because
they were all part of Beiping.

He sat there, happily idle, filling his eyes with familiar, affectionate sights; if he never moved from that spot, he'd die a happy
man. After sitting a while longer, he got up and went to the
bridgehead, where he ordered a bowl of briny bean curd, with
vinegar, soy sauce, pepper oil, and chives; when heated, it

smelled so good it took his breath away. His hand shook when he accepted the bowl, with bright green chives floating on top. He took a bite, and the bean curd burned its way down. He put down the bowl and added two spoonfuls of pepper oil to the mixture. By the time he'd finished, his pant sash was wet with sweat. His eyes were half closed as he handed back the bowl. "Another," he said.

Now, as he stood up, Xiangzi felt human again. The sun hung at the far western edge of the sky, turning the water in the river a soft red. Feeling like shouting for joy, he rubbed the smooth scar on his face, then felt the coins in his bag before gazing up at the sun resting atop the bridge. He forced the recent illness out of his mind, along with everything else; his aspirations restored, he was now ready to enter the city proper.

All manner of vehicles and people crowded through the city gate, and though no one dared to rush, they all wanted to get through as quickly as possible. Sounds—cracking whips, shouts, curses, horns, bells, laughter—merged and were amplified by the gate's acoustics, with, it seemed, everyone creating noise at the same time, one loud buzz. Moving ahead by stepping where he could and elbowing his way through the crowd, he squeezed into the city like a fish riding the waves. The first thing he saw was New Street, broad and straight. His eyes lit up, like the glinting of the sun on rooftops south of where he stood. He nodded his appreciation.

Since his bedding was waiting for him at Harmony Shed on Xi'an Gate Road, that was where he was headed. With no family to worry about, he'd bunked there even when he wasn't renting one of their rickshaws. The boss of Harmony Shed, Fourth Master Liu, was nearly seventy but did not live up to the honest notion of a man his age. As a young man, he'd been a guard at

an army depot, had run gambling dens, had dealt in slave traffic, and had profited from usury. He possessed all the attributes
and talents required in these callings: strength, shrewdness,
tricks, connections, and reputation. He'd been involved in gang
fights and had kidnapped young women from good families
before the fall of the last dynasty. For that, he had been tortured;
without begging for mercy, and by standing firm at his trials, he
had earned a reputation. His release from prison coincided
with the establishment of the new republic and a rapid increase
in the authority of the militia. Fourth Master Liu could see that
the heroes of an earlier age now belonged to the past, and even
if the legendary Li Da and Wu Song were to reappear, their
skills would find no outlet. So he opened a rickshaw rental
shed. Thanks to his experiences in low places, he knew how to
deal with poor people, when to tighten the ropes and when to
loosen them. In short, he was a master of manipulation, and
none of the rickshaw men dared stand up to him. Glaring at
them one moment and laughing with them the next, he had
them so cowed they felt they had one foot in heaven and one in
hell; he always prevailed. Eventually, he owned more than sixty
rickshaws, all in good to excellent shape—no run-down rickshaws for him—for which he charged a higher rent than his
competitors. But he gave his men an extra day's pay at each of
the three major holidays, and Harmony Shed supplied quarters
for bachelor pullers, no charge, except for the vehicle rent. Men
who did not pay up or who argued with Liu had their bedding
confiscated and were thrown out like discarded canteens. But if
one of them had an urgent matter to attend to or was laid low
with an illness, all he had to do was tell Fourth Master. Without
the slightest equivocation, he was ready with a helping hand,

and nothing would stop him, not a fire and not a flood. That is how one earns a reputation.

Fourth Master Liu was like a tiger. Despite his age, he had a straight back and thought nothing of walking two or three miles. He had big, round eyes, a large nose, a square jaw, and a pair of protruding teeth that gave him the look of a tiger when he opened his mouth. He was as tall as Xiangzi and, like the younger man, had a shaved head that fairly shone and no beard. He liked to think of himself as a tiger, but he had produced no male cub. He had an unwed daughter of thirty-seven or eight, and anyone who knew Fourth Master Liu knew his daughter, Huniu—Tiger Girl. She, too, looked like a tiger, which scared off all the men, but she was a great help to her father; she just couldn't find a man willing to marry her. In fact, she might as well have been a man, the way she cursed and carried on, and that was only the beginning. With Fourth Master Liu taking charge of the rickshaws and Huniu taking care of business, Harmony Shed ran like a well-oiled machine. It enjoyed the status of authority among rickshaw sheds, and talk of how Liu and his daughter ran their business was often on the lips of rickshaw men and their bosses, the way scholars quote the classics.

Before he'd put away enough to buy his first rickshaw, Xiangzi had rented from Harmony Shed and had handed his earnings to Fourth Master Liu for safekeeping. When he finally had enough, he took the money from Liu and bought his new rickshaw.

"What do you think of my rickshaw, Fourth Master?" Xiangzi asked.

The old man looked it over and nodded. "Not bad."

"I'd like to keep staying here, at least until I get a monthly hire. I can move out then." There was pride in Xiangzi's voice.

"Fine." Again Fourth Master Liu nodded.

Eventually, Xiangzi did find a monthly hire, and he moved out. He was told that any time he went back to picking up rides, he was welcome at Harmony Shed.

Bedding down in Harmony Shed without renting one of Fourth Master Liu's rickshaws was, in the eyes of other rickshaw men, a rare occurrence, so some guessed that he must be related to the old man. But even more of them assumed that the old man had his eye on Xiangzi as a possible groom for Huniu and a replacement son for him. While this assumption was clearly informed by a measure of envy, if one day it turned out to be true, then when Fourth Master Liu died, Harmony Shed would pass on to Xiangzi. For the moment, however, this was just idle gossip and not something anyone dared to bring up in Xiangzi's presence. What they didn't know was that Fourth Master had other reasons for treating Xiangzi differently. He saw him as being capable of sticking to the old ways in new surroundings. If he were to join the army, he wouldn't start acting stupid just so he could bully people when he put on the feared uniform. He kept busy when he was in the yard, and once he stopped sweating, he looked for something to do: cleaning rickshaws, pumping up the tires, airing out the rain hoods, oiling the moving parts . . . no one had to ask him to do these things, he did them on his own and was happy to do so; it was his favorite form of entertainment. Twenty or so men bunked in Harmony Shed, and when they brought their rickshaws in, they either sat around shooting the breeze or slept. All but Xiangzi, the only one who was never idle. At first, the others thought he was sucking up to Fourth Master Liu. But it took only a few days for them to realize that that was the furthest thing from his mind. He was sincere, he was artless, and he had nothing to say to anyone. Old Man Liu never uttered a word of praise or ever gave him a special look. But he had things worked out in his head. He was well aware that Xiangzi was a good worker, which is why he was willing to let him stay there even when he wasn't renting one of Liu's rickshaws. With Xiangzi around, the yard and gate were always swept clean, to give but one example. And Huniu was fond of this foolish big fellow. Xiangzi always stopped to listen to what she had to say, and he never quarreled with her. The other men, plagued by suffering, often talked back to her. She was not afraid of these men, and she usually ignored them, saving whatever she wanted to say for Xiangzi. So when he found a monthly hire, Fourth Master and his daughter felt as if they'd lost a friend. Then the next time he returned, even when Fourth Master was yelling at one of the men, he didn't seem so angry—almost kindly.

Xiangzi walked into Harmony Shed clutching his two boxes of matches. Night had not yet fallen, and Fourth Master and his daughter were having dinner. Huniu put down her chopsticks the minute she saw him.

"Xiangzi!" she shouted. "Did you get taken off by a wolf? Or maybe you went gold prospecting in Africa!"

"Hmm" was all Xiangzi said.

Fourth Master ran his eyes over Xiangzi but said nothing. Still wearing his new straw hat, Xiangzi sat down across from them. "Join us if you haven't eaten," Huniu said, as if welcoming a close friend.

Xiangzi did not budge, but a warm, hard-to-describe feeling flooded over him. Harmony Shed had always been home to him. He'd have a series of monthly hires, and then he'd be out

on the street again for a while. And all that time he had a place
to stay, right here in Harmony Shed, and someone to talk to.
After barely escaping with his life, he was back among friends,
people who invited him to join them at the table, and he'd have
been forgiven for thinking that this was all a cruel trick. But, no,
he was nearly in tears.

"I had two bowls of bean curd a while ago," he said politely.

"Where have you been?" Fourth Master Liu asked, his eyes
still fixed on Xiangzi. "Where's your rickshaw?"

"Rickshaw?" Xiangzi spat in anguish.

"Come eat first," Huniu said as she pulled him up to the
table, like an affectionate elder sister. "We won't poison you, and
two bowls of bean curd hardly make a meal."

Instead of picking up a bowl, Xiangzi took out his money.
"Fourth Master," he said, "would you hold this for me? Thirty
yuan." He returned the small change to his pocket.

"Where'd you get it?" Fourth Master's eyebrows formed the
question.

Xiangzi related his experience with the soldiers as he ate.

"You young fool," Fourth Master said, shaking his head. "If
you'd brought those camels into town and sold them to a slaugh-
terhouse, you could have gotten ten or fifteen a head. In the
winter, when they're done molting, they'd have brought in sixty
yuan!"

Xiangzi already had qualms, and this news only made him
feel worse. But on second thought, selling three living, breathing creatures to face the knife didn't seem right. He and the
camels had escaped together, and they all deserved to live. He
said nothing, his heart at peace.

While Huniu was clearing the table, Fourth Master looked
up, as if mulling something over. He smiled, revealing those two

fangs, which were getting harder with age. "What a simpleton you are. You say you fell ill at Haidian. Then why didn't you take the Yellow Village road straight back here?"

"I went the long way around the Western Hills to avoid running into trouble. If the villagers thought I was a deserter, they'd have come after me."

Fourth Master smiled and rolled his eyes. He'd been afraid that Xiangzi was lying about where he'd gotten the thirty yuan, and he wouldn't have been able to hold it for him if it had been stolen. As a young man, if it was illegal, he'd done it. Now he declared he was on the straight and narrow, and that required caution, something he had gotten good at. There had only been that one hole in Xiangzi's tale of woe, but his explanation made it possible for the old man to breathe easy.

"What do you plan to do with this?" he asked, pointing to the money.

"You tell me."

"Want to buy another rickshaw?" Once again, the fangs appeared, which seemed to mean "You plan to use your own rickshaw but live here for free, is that it?"

"There isn't enough. I'm only interested in buying a new one." Xiangzi was too occupied with his own thoughts to notice Fourth Master Liu's fangs.

"Want a loan? Ten percent interest. For others I charge twenty percent."

Xiangzi shook his head.

"Better to pay me ten percent than borrow from a loan shark."

"I say no to both," Xiangzi said, almost spellbound. "I'll save up, little by little, until I've got enough to pay cash."

The old man looked at Xiangzi as if he were a written character he'd never seen before. No matter how unpleasant things might be, he could not get angry. After a moment, he picked up the money. "Thirty? You're sure that's all?"

"That's all!" Xiangzi stood up. "Time to turn in. Here's a box of matches." He laid a box on the table, stood there vacantly for a moment, and then added, "Don't tell anyone about the camels."

CHAPTER FIVE

As promised, Old Man Liu told no one of Xiangzi's experiences, but the camel story quickly spread from Haidian into the city. In the past, people had found little fault with Xiangzi, except that he was stubbornly antisocial and a bit difficult to deal with. But "Camel Xiangzi" was a different matter. Though he continued to work quietly and stayed clear of people, they began to see him in a different light. Some said he'd found a gold watch, others that he'd come into possession of three hundred yuan, and one person, who considered himself to be the only one in the know, nodded confidently and said that Xiangzi had brought thirty camels back from the Western Hills. The stories differed, but the conclusions did not: through shady dealings Xiangzi had struck it rich, and anyone who came in to easy money, whether he was on good terms with people or not, was worthy of respect. Selling one's muscle is a hard way to make a living, so who could be blamed for dreaming of ill-gotten riches, no matter how long the odds? No wonder such people were seen as favored by fate. And so, sullen and standoffish Xiangzi was transformed into a man of distinction who had every right to be taciturn and was worthy of being fawned over.

"Come on, Xiangzi, tell us how you got rich!" It was a refrain he heard every day. He remained tight-lipped. If they pressed him, the scar on his face turned red and he said, "Rich? Then where the hell is my rickshaw!"

And that was the truth. Where was his rickshaw? That got them thinking. But commiserating with people is never as easy as congratulating them. And so they forgot all about Xiangzi's rickshaw, focusing instead on his good fortune. For a few days, that is, until they saw him pulling a rickshaw again instead of taking up a new trade or buying a house or some land, and their attitude cooled off. Now, when someone mentioned Camel Xiangzi, no one bothered to ask why he was called camel, of all animals. They just accepted it.

Xiangzi, on the other hand, could not forget what had happened to him. He was burning to buy a new rickshaw, but the greater his impatience, the more he thought about his first rickshaw. He pushed himself, working hard with no complaint, but not even that erased the memory of what had happened, thoughts that nearly suffocated him. He couldn't help wondering what good it did to try so hard. The world didn't treat you any fairer just because you tried hard. Not a world in which his rickshaw had been taken from him! Even if he managed to get another one right away, who was to say the same thing wouldn't happen again? It was a nightmare that destroyed his faith in the future. He often watched enviously as the other men drank and smoked and visited whorehouses. If trying hard was a waste of time, why not enjoy life for a change? They had it right. Though he wasn't quite ready to go to a whorehouse, he could at least have a drink or two and relax. Alcohol and tobacco suddenly held a strong attraction; neither cost much, and both brought a bit of comfort, an incentive to struggle on and help a man forget past suffering.

And yet he could not bring himself to try either one. Every cent he saved brought him that much closer to his goal of buying a new rickshaw. Not buying one was unthinkable, even if it was taken from him the day after he got it. It was his ideal, his aspiration, almost his religion. He had no reason to live if he could not pull his own rickshaw. He did not aspire to become an official, or get rich, or start up a business. His talent was in pulling a rickshaw, and his unwavering hope was to buy one of his own; not to do so would have been a disgrace. Day and night, this was the thought that occupied him and the reason he counted his money so carefully. The day he forgot this would be the day he forgot himself, and he'd then be little more than a beast that knew how to pull a rickshaw, lacking all traces of humanity. Even the finest rickshaw, if it was a rental, he pulled half-heartedly, as unnaturally as if he were carrying a rock on his back. He didn't slack off just because it was a rental; he always cleaned it up after bringing it in for the day, and took pains to keep from damaging it. But he did this to be prudent, not because he enjoyed it. Yes, taking care of his own rickshaw brought the same satisfaction as counting his own money. He still neither smoked nor drank, and would not even treat himself to a cup of good tea. In teahouses, reputable rickshaw men like him, after burning up the streets awhile, would spend ten cents for a bag of tea and two lumps of sugar to revitalize themselves and cool off. When Xiangzi ran until sweat dripped from his ears and his chest felt the strain, that's what he'd have liked to do, not out of habit or to put on airs but because it was what he needed. Yet after a moment's thought, he'd settle for a one-cent bag of tea dross. There were times when he felt like cursing for being so hard on himself, but what was a rickshaw man set on putting a bit of money aside each month to do? No, he'd endure whatever

it took to buy a rickshaw. After that, who could say? Owning a
rickshaw made everything worthwhile.

He was miserly with his money and tenacious about making
more of it. He took monthly hires when he could and spent all
day picking up fares on the street the rest of the time, going out
early and returning late, and only then if he'd earned his daily
quota, regardless of the hour or the state of his legs. Some days
he stayed out well into the night. Until then, he'd refused to steal
other pullers' fares, especially the old, the frail, and disabled
veterans. Given his strength and superior rickshaw, they would
not have stood a chance in a fight for business now. He was no
longer so scrupulous. Money, every single coin, was all that mattered, not how much the effort cost him or who he had to fight
for it. He was single-minded in reaching his goal, like a ravenous
wild animal. As soon as someone was in the seat behind him,
Xiangzi ran; he never felt better than when he was running, firm
in his belief that stopping was an impediment to his goal of buying his own rickshaw. But his reputation suffered. On many occasions, when he stole a fare, a volley of curses would follow
him. He never responded, merely lowered his head and ran as
fast as he could. "If I didn't need to buy a rickshaw," he said to
himself, "I'd never shame myself like that." It was an unspoken
apology. At rickshaw stands or in teahouses, when he noticed
the disapproving glares, he wanted to explain himself. But since
they all gave him the cold shoulder, compounded by the fact
that he never drank or gambled or played chess or simply passed
the time with them, he forced the words back down and kept
them inside. Embarrassment gradually turned to resentment
and suppressed rage. When they glared at him, he glared back.
When he thought about how they had looked up to him after
his escape from the mountains, their change in attitude rankled.

Alone with his pot of tea in a teahouse or counting his earnings at a rickshaw stand, he swallowed his anger. Not one to look for a fight, he would not back down from one, either. That was also true for most of the other men, but they thought twice before mixing it up with Xiangzi, since they were no match for him, one-on-one, and ganging up would be a disgrace. Forcing himself to keep his anger in check—the only way he knew how to deal with the situation—he would endure it the best he could until he had his own rickshaw. Once he was free of the need to come up with a day's rental, he could be generous and stop offending other pullers by stealing their fares. That was the way to look at it, he thought to himself as he eyed the other men, as if to say, "Wait and see."

But back to Xiangzi. He ought not to have pushed himself so hard. He'd barely returned to the city when he began pulling a rickshaw again, before giving his body a chance to fully recover. Never one to bow down to adversity, he tired easily. Even then, he refused to rest, convinced that the way to overcome soreness and sluggishness was to run more and sweat more. Knowing the pitfalls of starving himself, he nonetheless refused to eat good, nutritious food. He could see he was thinner than before, but he was still bigger and taller than the other men and was reassured that his muscles were still hard. He believed he could put up with more hardships than they, and it never occurred to him that his size and the hard work he forced upon himself required more nourishment. Huniu often said to him, "If you keep this up, don't blame others when you start spitting up blood!"

He knew she meant well, but because things were going badly and he was not taking care of his body, he was irritable. With a scowl, he grumbled, "If I don't keep at it, when will I be able to buy my rickshaw?"

Anyone else who scowled at Huniu like that would never hear the end of it—but not Xiangzi, on whom she doted and whom she treated with unwavering courtesy. She merely curled her lip and said:

"Buying a rickshaw takes time, even for someone who thinks he's made of steel. What you need is a good rest." She saw he wasn't listening. "All right," she said, "do it your way, but don't blame me if you drop dead along the way."

Fourth Master Liu wasn't pleased with Xiangzi, either; going out early and returning late after driving himself to the point of exhaustion was bad for the rickshaw. Rental agreements were good for the entire day, with no restrictions on when rickshaws were taken out or brought back in. But if every puller worked as hard as Xiangzi, the rickshaws would be worn out six months before their time. Even the sturdiest vehicle could not stand such punishing treatment. And that was not all the old man lost. Neglecting everything but hauling fares meant that Xiangzi had no time to clean rickshaws and help out with other chores. No wonder Liu was unhappy. But he kept it to himself, since all-day rentals were the rule in the trade, and doing odd jobs in the yard was an act of friendship, not an obligation. It would have been unseemly for a man of Liu's reputation to complain to Xiangzi, so all he could do was cast disapproving looks out of the corner of his eye and keep his lips clamped shut. At times he felt like throwing Xiangzi out, but he didn't dare, because of his daughter. While he did not see Xiangzi as a prospective son-in-law, he avoided anything that might upset Huniu, who seemed to have her eye on the impetuous young man. He had only one daughter, a woman with no marriage prospects, and chasing away her friend would have been unwise. There was no denying that she was a big help in the yard, and he selfishly was in no hurry for her to get married; maybe his guilty feelings made him a little afraid of her. All his life, he had feared neither heaven nor earth, only to arrive at old age afraid of his own daughter! He was able to rationalize the embarrassment by attributing his fear of her as proof that he was not totally heartless, and that on his deathbed he would not have to suffer retribution for his misdeeds. Acknowledging a fear of his daughter justified not driving Xiangzi away. That was not to say he would brook any nonsense from her in regard to marrying the man. Absolutely not. He could see that this had crossed her mind, but Xiangzi had so far not taken advantage of that to improve his situation.

All Liu had to do was be watchful—no sense upsetting his daughter.

Xiangzi was oblivious to Fourth Master's watchful eye, for he had no time to worry about such things. If he decided to leave Harmony Shed, it would not be personal; a monthly hire was the only thing that could lure him away. He'd grown tired of picking up passengers on the street, partly because the other men hated him for stealing their fares and partly because his income varied so widely from day to day—more today, less to-morrow—making it impossible to predict when he'd have enough to buy his rickshaw. For him, a steady income was the best, even if he could make a little more picking up stray fares. That way he'd know exactly how much he could put away each month, which brought hope and peace of mind. He was a man who liked things neat and tidy.

Xiangzi found his monthly hire, but it turned out no better than picking up stray fares. Mr. Yang was from Shanghai, his wife was from Tianjin, and his concubine was from Suzhou. One man, two wives, a brood of children, and a host of local dialects. Xiangzi's head was spinning his first day on the job. The man's wife called him out bright and early to go to market. After that, he had to deliver the young masters and mistresses to their respective schools: kindergarten, primary, and middle. Different schools, different ages, and different appearances, but each one as unpleasant as the next, especially when riding in the rickshaw; even the best-behaved among them seemed to have two hands more than a monkey. After depositing the children in their schools, Xiangzi had to take Mr. Yang to his government office, and then return home to pick up the concubine to take her to Dongan Market or to visit friends. After that, it was time to pick up the children and bring them home for lunch. Then back to school. That done, it was time for Xiangzi to eat, but the man's wife called out in her Tianjin accent for him to fetch water. The family's drinking water was delivered from outside; water for washing clothes was part of the rickshaw man's duties. Though this chore was not spelled out in the contract, Xiangzi let it pass to stay on good terms with his employer. Without complaint, he filled up the water vat. That done, he picked up his rice bowl, only to be sent by the concubine to buy something. The two women did not get along, but where family business was concerned, they shared a philosophy: point one, servants must never stand around idle; point two, servants are to eat their meals out of sight. Not knowing this, Xiangzi thought only that his first day was an unusually busy one for the family, so he kept quiet. He even went out and bought some baked flatbread on his own. Despite his obsession with money, keeping the job was worth the outlay.

As soon as he returned from the shopping trip, the wife told him to sweep the compound. Mr. Yang, his wife, and his concubine always dressed nicely when they went out, but their house, inside and out, was like a garbage dump. Just looking at the

ground outside nearly made Xiangzi sick to his stomach, so he
threw himself into the task with such enthusiasm that he forgot
that a rickshaw man ought not to be given such jobs. Once the
compound was neat and clean, the concubine told him to sweep
out their rooms while he was at it. Still no complaints from
Xiangzi. What got to him, on the other hand, was how two
women who took such care of their appearance could live in
rooms too filthy to step foot in. But he went ahead and swept
them clean, just in time to have a grubby little one-year-old
thrust into his arms by the concubine. He was helpless. He was
not one to mind the hard work, but this was the first child he'd
ever held, and he clutched the young master with both hands. If
he relaxed his hold, he might drop him, but if he held him too
tight, he could crush him. He broke out in a cold sweat and was
determined to hand the little treasure over to Nanny Zhang—a
woman from northern Jiangsu with unbound feet. He found
her, only to be greeted with a barrage of curses. Servants seldom
stayed on in the Yang home more than four or five days. To Mr.
Yang and his wives, they were little more than personal slaves,
and if they hadn't worked them half to death, they felt they
hadn't gotten enough value out of the pittance they paid. Nanny
Zhang, on the other hand, had been with them five or six years;
she owed her longevity to her abusive mouth. Whether it was
the master or one of his wives, no annoyance went unnoted. No
one had been able to withstand Mr. Yang's withering Shanghai
curses, his wife's imperious Tianjin scolding, or his concubine's
Suzhou rebukes, until, that is, the arrival of Nanny Zhang, who
quickly earned their grudging respect. Appreciating her worth,
like a martial hero encountering a stalwart adversary, they kept
her on as the family enforcer.

Xiangzi had grown up in a northern village and could not

tolerate cursing in public. But, believing that no decent man raises a hand against a woman, he dared not strike Nanny Zhang, nor was he about to argue with her. He was reduced to glowering, and that silenced Nanny Zhang, who had likely spotted danger in his look. The silence was broken by the wife, who ordered Xiangzi to pick up the children from school. He thrust the grubby child into the hands of the concubine, who took it as an insult and gave him hell. The wife hadn't liked the idea of Xiangzi's holding the concubine's baby in the first place, and when she heard Xiangzi being bombarded by curses, she joined the fray in her oily voice. Attacking whom? Xiangzi, of course. Everyone's target of choice. Quickly picking up the shafts of his rickshaw, he made his escape, even his anger apparently forgotten. He had never before witnessed anything like this, and it made his head swim.

One after the other, he brought the children back to a compound that was noisier than a marketplace, with three women cursing and a bunch of kids bawling. It was as bad as the unruly scene outside a Dashala cinema when the show let out. Fortunately for Xiangzi, he still had to pick up Mr. Yang at the office, so off he went. The clamor of the street was easier to take than the pandemonium back at the house.

Xiangzi's chance for a breather did not come until midnight. He was worn out. Everyone in the family was in bed, but his ears rang with the sounds of bickering, as if three separate gramophones were playing in his head at the same time, keeping him on edge. He forced himself to think about nothing but sleep. But the minute he entered his room, his heart sank and all thoughts of sleep vanished. It was a tiny gatehouse room with doors on two sides, divided down the center by a wooden barrier; one side of the room was Nanny Zhang's, the other his.

There was no lamp, but a small two-foot window on the road-side wall under a street lamp provided a bit of light. The room, dank and musty, had a thick layer of dust on the floor and was furnished on his side with a cot against the wall and nothing more. Feeling the wooden slats with his hand, he knew that with his head at one end, his feet would be pressed up against the wall, but if he stretched out his legs, he would be in a half-seated position. He could not sleep curled up, so after looking at the situation from all angles, he moved the bed out at a slant, which would let him get through the night lying flat, with his feet hanging over the edge.

After retrieving his bedding from the doorway, he spread it out on the cot and lay down. But how was he supposed to sleep with his legs dangling in midair? He closed his eyes anyway and said to himself, *Get some sleep. You have to be up early in the morning. After all you've put up with, you can't let this stop you. The food is terrible and the work exhausting, but maybe they have mahjong parties or invite guests for dinner or go out at night. What are you here for, anyway, Xiangzi? For the wages. Do whatever it takes to put aside the money you need.* Comforted by that thought, he breathed in the air of the room and found it didn't smell as bad as he'd thought. As he was nodding off, he was dimly aware that bedbugs were biting him, but he was too sleepy to worry about that.

Two days into the new job Xiangzi was totally disheartened. Then, on the fourth day, some women showed up, and Nanny Zhang set up the mahjong table. Xiangzi's heart felt like a frozen lake over which a spring breeze blew. When the ladies of the house played mahjong, they turned their children over to the servants, and since Nanny Zhang was kept busy supplying the women with cigarettes and tea and hot towels, the little monkeys were Xiangzi's responsibility. He hated the little brats, but when he stole inside, he saw that Mrs. Yang was the banker and that she seemed to take the duty seriously. Maybe, he thought, even though she's a shrew, she might understand that this is a chance to give the servants a little extra. He showed unusual patience with the children, expecting a tip when the game was over. Treating them like little lords and ladies was the way to go.

When the game was over, Mrs. Yang told Xiangzi to take her guests home, and since two of them were in a hurry to leave, she had him call for a second rickshaw. When it arrived, she made a big show of looking for money to pay her guest's fare. The woman politely declined, drawing a disapproving shout from Mrs. Yang:

"You can't be serious, my dear! I won't let you come to my place without at least paying your way home. Come, my dear, up you go!" Finally, she managed to come up with ten cents.

Xiangzi saw that her hand shook as she handed over the paltry sum.

When he returned from taking the guest home, Xiangzi helped Nanny Zhang tidy up after the game. Then he glanced at Mrs. Yang, who told Nanny Zhang to get her a glass of water. As soon as Nanny Zhang was out of the room, she took out a ten-cent bill. "Take this and stop looking at me like that!"

Xiangzi went purple in the face. He straightened up, as if he wanted to touch the ceiling with his head, took the bill, and flung it in her fat face.

"Give me my four days' wages!"

"How dare you!" she said. The look in his face stopped her from saying more. She handed him his four days' wages. Xiangzi picked up his bedding and stormed out the gate, followed by a barrage of curses from the yard.

CHAPTER SIX

An early autumn night, with breezes rustling leaves that cast their shadows on the ground by the light of stars. Xiangzi looked up at the Milky Way and sighed. Under such a bracing sky, he should not feel as if he were suffocating. He had too broad a chest for that; he did nonetheless. He felt like sitting down and crying his heart out. A man with his physique, his ability to endure so much, and his determination should not be treated like a pig or a dog and ought to be able to hold down a job. For this, he did not blame the Yang family alone. A vague sense of despair was taking hold, a feeling that he would never amount to much. His steps slowed as he walked along, bedding under his arm, as if he were no longer the Xiangzi who could easily run a mile or more without stopping.

The nearly deserted main street and bright street lamps made him feel even worse. Where should he go now? Where? Harmony Shed, of course. But that saddened him. People in business or those who sell their labor aren't as concerned about having no customers as they are about losing the ones they have, as when someone walks into a restaurant or barbershop, takes one look, and walks back out. Xiangzi knew that finding and losing jobs happened all the time—you're not wanted here, so you go some place where you are. But he had meekly done what was asked of him, at a considerable loss of face, in pursuit of his goal to buy a rickshaw, and as a result had worked a total of three and a half days, no different from those men who willfully went from job to job. That's what really bothered him. He wasn't sure he had the heart to return to Harmony Shed, where they were sure to laugh at him: "Well, would you look at this! Camel Xiangzi packs it in after only three and a half days!"

But if not Harmony Shed, where? Not wanting to worry about that, he headed for Xi'an Gate. The Harmony Shed façade was made up of three shop fronts. The middle one, the accounting office, was off-limits to the rickshaw men except for settling accounts or conducting business. They were forbidden from using it to enter the yard because the eastern and western rooms were the bedrooms of the owner and his daughter. The rickshaw entrance, next to the western room, was a double gate painted green, over which a bright, uncovered electric light hung from a thick wire, illuminating a metal plaque beneath it with the words "Harmony Shed" in gold script. This was the gate the pullers used, with or without their rickshaws. The green gate and gold lettering shone in the bright glare of the electric light, with handsome rickshaws going in and out, some black, others yellow, all highly polished and outfitted with clean white cushions that gave the men a sense of personal pride, a feeling that they were the aristocrats of their profession. Once inside, you entered a large courtyard with an ancient acacia tree in the center. The rickshaws were kept in buildings to the east and west that opened to the courtyard. A building south of the courtyard and several small rooms behind a tiny courtyard were the men's sleeping quarters.

It must have been after eleven when Xiangzi spotted the light above the door at Harmony Shed. The accounting office and eastern room were dark, but a light shone in the western room, which meant that Huniu was still up. He planned to sneak in quietly so she wouldn't see him. He did not want her to be the first to witness his defeat, since she held him in such high regard. But he'd barely pulled his rickshaw up under her window when she walked out through the rickshaw entrance.

"Oh, Xiangzi, what—" She stopped when she saw the dejected look on his face and the bedding in the rickshaw.

It was what he had dreaded; as humiliation filled his heart, he stood there like a fool, speechless, as he gazed stupidly at Huniu. There was something different about her that night. Whether it was the effects of the light or because she'd powdered her face, her skin was paler than usual, largely masking the ferocious expression she normally wore. Her lips were painted, lending her a seductive appearance. Xiangzi did not know what to make of this bewildering change. He'd never actually thought of her as a woman, and the sight of her reddened lips embarrassed him. She was wearing a light green satin jacket over a pair of wide unlined black crepe trousers. The overhead light lent her green jacket a soft and slightly doleful luster, and since it was a bit too short, it revealed a strip of her white waistband, highlighting the quiet elegance of the green. A light breeze rustled her wide black trousers slightly, almost as if sinister essences were trying to escape the bright light and become one with the dark night. Xiangzi lowered his head, not daring to keep staring, though the image of a glimmering green jacket stayed with him. As far as he knew, Huniu never dressed like that. The family was rich enough for her to dress in silks and satins, but daily contact with coarse rickshaw men dictated that she wear ordinary cotton clothing, with an occasional but muted touch of color. Xiangzi was seeing something new and exciting, yet familiar, and that mystified him.

He had arrived feeling terrible, only to encounter this strange apparition under a bright light, and he did not know what to do. Aware that it was not his place to move, he was hoping that she would either turn and go back inside or tell him what to do. The tension was more than he could take, like nothing he'd ever known. It was unbearable.

"Hey!" She moved closer. "Don't just stand there," she said, keeping her voice low. "Put your rickshaw away and come right back. I want to talk to you about something. I'll be inside."

Accustomed to helping out with things when she asked him to, this time he detected a difference and he needed time to think. But standing there thinking made him look as though he was frozen to the spot; not knowing what else to do, he took his rickshaw inside. The southern rooms were dark, so the men were either in bed or hadn't quit for the day. After parking his rickshaw, he headed back to her door, where suddenly his heart began to race.

"Come in," she said, sticking her head out the door, looking somewhere between lighthearted and impatient. "I want to talk to you about something."

He walked in slowly.

A pair of not quite ripe white pears lay on a table. Next to them were a decanter of liquor and three white porcelain cups. Finally, there was a large platter with half a stewed chicken, pieces of smoked liver, and some tripe.

"See what we have." She pointed to a chair and waited for him to sit down before continuing: "I'm treating myself tonight for all my hard work, and you can join me." She poured him a cup from the decanter. The peppery smell of the liquor mixed with that of smoked and stewed meats produced a pungent, heavy aroma. "Drink up," she said, "and try some of this chicken. I've already started, so you needn't wait. I tossed some divination tallies a while ago, and they said you'd be back. What do you think of that?"

"I don't drink," Xiangzi said, as he gazed spellbound at the cup of liquor.

"Then get the hell out of here! Don't you know when someone's being nice to you, you dumb camel? It won't kill you! Even I can drink four ounces of the stuff! You don't believe me? Watch." She picked up a cup and nearly emptied it. Closing her eyes, she breathed heavily and held the cup out to Xiangzi. "Finish it. If you don't, I'll grab you by the ear and pour it down your throat."

Xiangzi was incapable of expressing the resentment he felt. He wanted to react to the humiliation by glaring at her but had to admit that she had always treated him well and dealt openly with him. He did not want to offend her. Now was probably the time to tell her what he'd been through. Never garrulous, on this day a torrent of words was bursting to get out. He thought that Huniu might actually be showing tenderness, not mocking him, so he took the cup from her and drained it. A stinging sensation slid slowly, precisely, and potently down his throat. He stretched out his neck, threw out his chest, and belched twice, uncomfortably.

Huniu laughed. After he had forced down the liquor, the sound of that laugh made him turn to look at the eastern room.

"He's not there." She stopped laughing, though a smile remained. "The old man is off celebrating my aunt's birthday and won't be back for three or four days. She lives in Nanyuan." She refilled Xiangzi's cup.

There was something funny about all this, but he didn't feel like leaving, not with her face right there in front of him. Her clothes were so clean and silky and her lips so red that he felt stimulated in a way that was new to him. She was still ugly but seemed more full of life than usual, as if she'd become a different person; or maybe it was still her but with something added. He didn't have the nerve to try to figure out just what this new something was and, at least for the moment, was unwilling to accept it; on the other hand, he was not prepared to reject it, either. His face reddened. He took another drink, as if to boost his courage, and forgot all about telling her his troubles. Red in the face, he could not turn away, but the longer he looked, the greater his sense of turmoil, as that bewildering something about her was becoming more apparent, and a heated force emanating from her gradually turned her into an abstraction. Be careful, he warned himself, but he was beginning to feel emboldened. He drained three more cups and abandoned his normal caution. Gazing at her through a bit of a fog, for some reason he felt incredibly happy—and daring. He was on the verge of grabbing hold of a brand-new experience and happiness. Most of the time she frightened him, but now there didn't seem to be anything daunting about her. He, on the other hand, was the imposing one, the stronger of the two. He felt as if he could pick her up like a kitten.

The light went out in the room. The night was black as pitch. A star or two twinkled in the Milky Way or burned through the darkness, dragging red or white tails behind them, breezy or durable, falling earthward or racing across the sky, like dazzling explosions. They quivered and shook, investing the sky with heated upheavals, lighting it up. Sometimes stars flew through the sky alone or in pairs, sometimes in greater numbers at the same time, causing the silent autumn sky to shudder and bring chaos to all the other stars. From time to time a single giant star tore through a corner of the sky, its long tail emitting enormous sparks—reds turning gradually to yellow. With one last push, it lit up that corner of the sky, as if piercing layers of darkness to get to and frolic with milky white rays of light. When the light died out, the darkness sputtered a time or two before coming together again, as the stars quietly, lazily, returned to their places and smiled at the autumn breezes. Fireflies hovered just above the ground, searching for their mates and cavorting like the stars.

Xiangzi got up early the next morning and went out with his rickshaw. His head ached; his throat was sore. He had a hangover but didn't let that bother him. As he sat at the entrance to a small lane, with the early morning breezes cooling his head, he knew the discomfort would fade before long. But the problem preying on his mind depressed and confused him, and he didn't know what to do about that. The night's events brought doubts, shame, and sadness, not to mention the prospect of danger.

He did not understand Huniu. That she was not a virgin was something he had discovered only a few hours earlier. He had always respected her and had never heard any talk of promiscuity about her. Though free and easy in her dealings with people, no one talked about her behind her back; the worst anyone might say was that she was fierce as a tiger. So how had last night happened?

Foolish as it seemed, Xiangzi began to have suspicions. She knew he'd landed a monthly hire, so how could she have been waiting for him like that? If she hadn't cared who came by . . . Xiangzi lowered his head. As a young man from the countryside, he had plans for his future, though he hadn't yet given any thought to marriage. If he had his own rickshaw and life were a little easier, he could, if he wanted, go back to his village and marry a robust young woman who was no stranger to hard work, one who could wash clothes and do housework. Young men of his age nearly all slipped off to a whorehouse from time to time, even if they had someone to keep an eye on them. Not Xiangzi. To begin with, as someone who prided himself on his abilities, he was not about to throw money away on women. Second, he had seen foolish young men—some no more than eighteen—whose money had bought them nothing but grief; he watched as they pressed their heads against a toilet wall, unable to urinate. Finally, he would not be able to face his future wife if he didn't behave himself now. Since he would marry only a virgin, a spotless girl, he could ask nothing less of himself. But now, now . . . he thought about Huniu, who was fine for a friend, but as a woman, she was ugly, old, fierce, and shameless! Not even soldiers who had stolen his rickshaw and nearly killed him in the process were as hateful and disgusting as she. She had destroyed the innocence and decency he'd brought from the countryside. He was now a womanizer!

Even worse, what if Fourth Master Liu found out? Did he know that his daughter was used goods? If not, then all the blame would be Xiangzi's, wouldn't it? But if he knew and had no control over her, then what kind of people were they? And what kind of person would he be for mixing with the likes of them? He wouldn't marry her even if they were both willing, not even if the old man owned six hundred or six thousand rickshaws. He had to get away from Harmony Shed, sever relations with them, and do it now. He could buy a rickshaw and find a wife without relying on anyone else; that's how things were done. With this thought, he raised his head with renewed confidence in his manhood. There was nothing to fear, nothing to worry about. He'd get what he wanted; all he had to do was work hard.

But after losing two fares, his anxieties returned. He tried not to think about what had happened, but his mind would not cooperate. This was different from anything in his experience, and even if it was a problem he could solve, he couldn't brush it aside. His body felt unclean, and something black that had entered his heart could not be washed away. Despite his hatred of her, his disgust, she had her claws in him, and the more he tried to stop thinking about her, the more often she leaped out of his mind, naked, offering him both her ugliness and her beauty. It was like buying a pile of junk and finding amid the rusting metals a few irresistible baubles. He had never been that intimate with anyone before, and though it was a seduction that had occurred without warning, it was not the sort of relationship he could forget. He might try to push it to the back of his mind, but it would spin its web there and take hold. This was more than just a new experience—it also disturbed him in ways he could not describe. Feeling lost, he could not deal with her, with himself, with the present, or with the future; like an insect caught in a spiderweb, to struggle was futile.

In his disoriented state, Xiangzi pulled a couple of fares, but even as he ran he could not stop thinking about this business, and not in a clear, methodical fashion. Rather, random bits and pieces surfaced in his head—a particular meaning or feeling or emotion, vague and yet close and very personal. He had a strong urge to drink himself into oblivion, all alone. Maybe that would make him happy and lessen his torment. But he didn't dare start something that would be his undoing. He thought again about buying a rickshaw but could not stay focused, for something always interfered with his thoughts. It wormed its way into his head even before he could picture the rickshaw and blocked his thoughts like a dark cloud blotting out the sun. When night fell, and it was time to knock off for the day, he felt even worse. He had to return to Harmony Shed but was afraid to. What would he do if he ran into her? He wandered the streets pulling an empty rickshaw, nearing the yard but not entering it, like a truant child afraid to go home.

Strangely, the more he wanted to avoid an encounter, the more he actually looked forward to seeing her, and the darker the sky grew, the more intense was this desire. An audacious if confused obsession had a firm grip on his heart, even though he knew it was wrong. As a boy, he'd once stirred up a hornets' nest with a pole, a yearning to see what would happen driving out his fear, as if a demonic power were behind him, goading him on. In his uncertain mood, he now felt that a force greater than himself was rolling him into a ball and throwing it into a roaring fire. He was powerless to keep himself from moving ahead.

He made another turn around Xi'an Gate. This time he would not delay but would go looking for her. She no longer had an identity; she was just a woman. He felt hot all over and had barely reached the gate when a middle-aged man walked into the light of the overhead lamp. He thought he recognized the man but couldn't be sure. Instinctively, he said, "Rickshaw?"

The man stopped in his tracks. "Xiangzi, is that you?"

"Yes," Xiangzi replied with a smile. "Mr. Cao?"

Mr. Cao smiled and nodded. "Xiangzi, if you're not working for anyone, how about coming to my place? The man I have now is too lazy even to wipe down the rickshaw, though he does run like a racehorse. What do you say?"

"How could I refuse, sir?" Xiangzi seemed to have forgotten even how to smile. He wiped his face with a towel. "When should I start?"

"Let's see," Mr. Cao said, as he thought a moment. "How about the day after tomorrow?"

"Yes, sir." Xiangzi also paused to think for a moment. "Can I take you home now, sir?"

"No need. After I returned from that visit to Shanghai, we moved. I live on Beichang Street now and come out at night for walks. I'll see you in two days." Mr. Cao gave Xiangzi his new address, and then added, "We'll use my rickshaw."

Xiangzi was so happy he could fly. All the troubles of the past few days vanished, like paving stones washed clean by the rain. He had worked for Mr. Cao in the past, and though they had been together only a short time, they had gotten along well. Mr. Cao was a kind man with a small family—a wife and a young son.

Xiangzi ran his rickshaw back to Harmony Shed, where the light in Huniu's room still shone. He froze on the spot and stood there awhile before deciding to go in and tell her he'd found another monthly hire. After turning over the rental money he owed for the two days, he'd ask for his savings, and that would put an end to their relationship; she'd understand without his saying so.

First he parked his rickshaw, then walked back and, screwing up his courage, called out, "Miss Liu."

"Come in!"

He pushed open the door. She was sprawled on the bed in her

everyday clothes and barefoot. She didn't move. "So," she said, "back for some more of the good stuff?"

Xiangzi blushed, turning as red as a dyed egg. He was tongue-tied for a moment before he said slowly, "I've got another job—I start the day after tomorrow. He has his own rickshaw."

"You really don't know what's good for you, do you?" She sat up and, with an exasperated smile, pointed at him. "There's food and clothing for you here, but you can't be happy unless you're sweating like a pig, is that it? The old man has no control over me, and I don't plan to spend the rest of my days as a spinster. Even if he turns bullheaded, I've got enough put aside for you and me to own two or three rickshaws, which would bring in at least one yuan a day. Isn't that better than running your legs off day in and day out? What's so bad about me? I may be older than you, but not by much, and I can pamper you."

"But I want to pull a rickshaw!" It was the only argument Xiangzi had.

"You're a real bonehead!" she said. "Sit down. I won't bite." She smiled, showing her fang-like canines. Xiangzi sat down, obviously jittery. "Where's my money?"

"The old man has it. Don't worry, it's safe. But don't ask him for it now. You know his temper. Ask for it when you've got enough to buy a rickshaw. If you try it now, you'll be lucky to hold on to your soul! He's been good to you, and you won't lose it. If there's anything missing, I'll double it. You've got the head of a peasant, so be careful I don't bite it off!"

There was nothing Xiangzi could say, so he fumbled in his trousers to dig out the two days' rental fee and laid it on the table. "That's for two days." Then he added as an afterthought, "I'm turning in my rickshaw. I'll take tomorrow off." Taking time off was the last thing he wanted, but that made it a clean break. He'd turn in his rickshaw and not spend another night at Harmony Shed.

Huniu came over, picked up the money, and stuffed it back into his pocket. "You're a lucky guy, getting me and a rickshaw for two days free of charge. Just don't be ungrateful." She turned and locked the door from inside.

CHAPTER SEVEN

Xiangzi moved into the Cao home.

He felt guilty about Huniu, but it was her seduction that had caused the trouble. Besides, he had no designs on her money and did not feel that a clean break was in any way unfair. The one thing that did bother him was that Fourth Master Liu was holding his money. The old man might wonder what was going on if he asked for it now, but steering clear of them could set Huniu off, and if she revealed what had happened, he might never see his money again. And by trusting his savings to the old man, he was sure to run into her whenever he went to Harmony Shed—that would be awkward. Unable to concoct a way out, he grew increasingly uneasy.

Ideally, he could ask Mr. Cao for advice, but that would mean telling him what had happened with Huniu. Filled with remorse, he began to understand that the relationship could not be severed so easily. It was a stain that could not be washed away. Through no fault of his own, he had lost his rickshaw, and through no fault of his own, he now found himself in a quandary. He might as well admit it—his life was effectively over. However badly he wanted to outshine others, he was doomed to fail. After looking at the situation from every angle, only one thing became clear: in the end, he would have to put his pride aside and marry Huniu, but not because he wanted to. Could he have been swayed by talk of those few rickshaws? "A cuckold eats leftovers," as the saying goes. That was an unbearable thought, but it might come to that. He would just have to keep doing what he did best and see what happened. Keeping busy was good; waiting around was bad. Gone was his self-confidence. His size, strength, and heart all counted for little. His life was now in the hands of someone else, and a nasty piece of work that someone was.

By rights he should have been happy, since the Cao family was the best he had ever worked for. The pay was no better than at other places and was enhanced only by modest bonuses at the three annual festivals. But Mr. and Mrs. Cao were good-hearted people who treated everyone with kindness and dignity. Xiangzi was eager, desperate even, to earn a bit more, but having a decent place to live and enough to eat counted for quite a lot. The Cao home was always clean and tidy, including the servants' quarters; the food was appetizing and wholesome; and they never fed the help on leftovers. With a clean, spacious room of his own and the leisure to enjoy three meals a day, not to mention the humane treatment, Xiangzi—even Xiangzi—knew that there was more to life than the single-minded pursuit of money. An added benefit was that good food and lodging, when combined with a relaxed work schedule, made it possible to get back into shape. If he had been obliged to buy his own food, he would not have eaten nearly as well; now, with regular meals and no need to grovel for them, he'd have been a fool not to eat his fill. Food, after all, cost money, and he knew what that meant. Finding work that provided good food, a clean room, and the chance to be a presentable human being was nothing to scoff at.

Even though the Caos did not play mahjong and seldom invited guests over, which reduced the chance for a nice tip here and there, he performed odd jobs for them, which earned him a little extra. If, for instance, Mrs. Cao asked him to pick up some medicine for one of the children, she would add ten cents and tell him to hire a rickshaw for the ride, knowing full well that he could outrun the best of them. It wasn't much, but the gesture, an expression of understanding, meant a lot to him. Xiangzi had worked for several employers, nine out of ten of whom would be late paying wages to show that they would rather not pay at all, since, in their view, servants were little more than dogs or cats, if that. The Caos were different, and he was happy in their home. He gladly swept out the courtyard and watered the flowers without being asked. And they always rewarded him with a kind word. They even hunted up old, used objects for him to exchange for matches, though he would keep them for himself because they were still usable. This was the place for him, thanks to them.

In Xiangzi's eyes, Fourth Master Liu was like Tyrant Huang of the Yellow Turbans, in that he placed great importance on his image, despite his tyrannical ways, and played by the rules; for that reason he could not be considered all bad. Only two great historical figures existed for Xiangzi—Tyrant Huang and the Sage Confucius. All he knew about the Sage was that he had mastered many books and was a man of reason. Xiangzi had worked for both civilian and military employers; none of the military employers had been the equal of Fourth Master Liu, while among the civilian employers, which included university lecturers and officials with good jobs in the official yamen, all well-educated individuals, none was a man of reason. And for those who came close, their wives and daughters made life difficult for him. Only Mr. Cao was well read and reasonable, while his wife won Xiangzi over by her proper behavior. So Mr. Cao had to be a sage, and whenever Xiangzi tried to imagine what the great man had been like, Mr. Cao was the model, whether Confucius liked it or not.

Truth be told, Mr. Cao was not particularly wise, just a man of modest abilities who did a bit of teaching and engaged in other work of that nature. He called himself a socialist, as well as an aesthete, having been influenced by the socialist William Morris. While he had no profound views on politics or art, he had the ability to put his modest beliefs into practice in the trivial aspects of daily life. Seeming to realize that he lacked the talent to shake up the world, he contented himself with organizing his work and family around his ideals. While this did society no good to speak of, at least his deeds matched his words, which kept him from becoming a hypocrite. As a result, he paid close attention to small matters, as if to say that so long as his little family was happy and well run, society could do as it pleased. Sometimes this brought him shame, at other times gratification, for it seemed clear to him that his family was an oasis in a desert, one whose significance was to supply food and water to those who wandered in, and nothing more.

Xiangzi had stumbled into this tiny oasis after days of wandering in the desert, which he saw as nothing short of a miracle. He had never met anyone quite like Mr. Cao before and, for that reason, viewed him as a true sage. Maybe he was being naïve, or maybe there were simply too few such people in society. With Mr. Cao sitting in his rickshaw, dressed with understated elegance and full of life, Xiangzi took great joy in his work, proud of how he looked and how he ran, as if he were the only person in the world worthy of serving Mr. Cao. Their

home, where everything was always neat and peaceful, filled him
with a sense of well-being. Back in his village, he often saw old
men sitting outdoors on a winter day or beneath an autumn
moon, quietly smoking their bamboo pipes, and though he was
too young to imitate them, he took pleasure in trying to figure
out what made the activity so special. Now, though he lived in
the city, Mr. Cao's quiet lifestyle reminded him of life in the village and made him feel like smoking a pipe to experience that
something special.

Unfortunately, the woman and his modest savings preyed on
his mind. His heart was like a green leaf entwined in silk threads
by a caterpillar preparing its cocoon. He was so caught up in
these thoughts that he often gave wrong answers to people, including Mr. Cao, to his chagrin. The Cao family went to bed
early, leaving Xiangzi with time on his hands after nine o'clock,
time he spent in his room or outside mulling over his problems.
He even considered getting married in order to dash Huniu's
hopes. But how could he raise a family on what a rickshaw man
earned? He knew how tough life was for rickshaw men who
lived in crowded tenement compounds and whose wives had to
take in mending while their children scrounged for lumps of
coal and were forced to eat watermelon rinds they found on
garbage heaps in the summer and charity gruel in the winter.
That was not for Xiangzi. Besides, if he took a wife, he could say
good-bye to the meager savings Fourth Master Liu was holding
for him. Huniu would never let him off that easily. No, he
couldn't give up the money, not after risking his life for it.

He had bought his rickshaw the previous autumn, and now,
a little more than a year later, he had nothing but a measly
thirty-odd yuan that he could not get his hands on, plus a complicated entanglement. Depressing thoughts.

The weather began to cool off ten days or so after the Mid-Autumn Festival, and he would soon need warmer clothes. That meant money, of course. Since he could not spend and save at the same time, how could he ever hope to own another rickshaw?

One night, when taking Mr. Cao back from East City later than usual, Xiangzi took pains to stay on the street fronting Tiananmen Square. Wide and flat, the street was nearly deserted; accompanied by a slight breeze and soft lamplight, he ran with strength and ease, clearing his mind of the dejection he'd suffered for days. The sound of his footfalls and the shafts of the rickshaw helped him forget all his problems. He opened his shirt to let the breeze cool his chest. That was so invigorating he felt that he could just keep running, as far and as fast as his legs would take him, and die with no regrets. He was nearly flying down the street, overtaking one rickshaw after another. As he passed Tiananmen, his feet were like springs; they barely touched the ground before springing back up again. Behind him, the wheels were turning so fast they seemed to lift off the ground, the spokes a blur. Man and vehicle were swept along by strong gusts of wind. Fanned by the cool air, Mr. Cao dozed off; otherwise, he would have told Xiangzi to slow down. But Xiangzi was sure that a good sweat would help him sleep soundly that night, undisturbed by his thoughts.

They were approaching Beichang Street. The north side lay in the shadows of acacia trees by the red walls. Xiangzi was about to slow down when he stumbled on something. The wheels of his rickshaw hit the bump as he flew headlong to the ground, snapping one of the shafts in the process. "What the . . ." Mr. Cao was thrown from the rickshaw before he could finish. Without a word, Xiangzi scrambled to his feet. Nimbly sitting up where he fell, this time Mr. Cao got the words out: "What happened?"

A pile of paving stones had been unloaded in the middle of the street without a red warning light.

"Are you hurt?" Xiangzi asked.

"No. I can walk home," Mr. Cao said, having regained his composure. "Bring the rickshaw along." He groped among the stones to see if he'd dropped anything.

Xiangzi felt the broken shaft. "It's not a bad break," he said. "Please, get back on. I can still pull you." He dragged the rickshaw away from the paving stones. "Please, sir, get back on."

Though he'd rather not have, the pleading tone in Xiangzi's voice convinced Mr. Cao that it was the right thing to do.

When they reached the street lamp at the Beichang Street intersection, Mr. Cao saw that his right hand was bleeding. "Xiangzi, stop!"

Xiangzi turned to look. His face was bloody.

Mr. Cao was nearly speechless. "Hurry, hurry and . . ."

Xiangzi didn't know what to make of that, except to start running again. Which he did, not stopping till they were back home.

The first thing Xiangzi saw after bringing the rickshaw to a stop was Mr. Cao's injured hand. He ran into the yard to tell the mistress.

"Don't worry about me," Mr. Cao said, as he followed him into the yard. "See to yourself first."

As Xiangzi looked himself over, the aches and pains surfaced. Both knees and his right elbow were badly skinned. What he thought was sweat on his face turned out to be blood. Unable to act, or even think, he sat down on the stone steps and gazed blankly at the black-lacquered rickshaw with its broken shaft.

Two white splintered pieces of wood spoiled its look, like a paper figurine with stalks of millet where the legs are supposed to be. He gaped at the white ends.

"Xiangzi!" Gao Ma, the Caos' maidservant, called out. "Where are you?"

He sat without moving, his eyes glued to the splintered ends, as if they had pierced his heart.

"What are you up to, hiding from me like that? You've given me a real scare. The master wants you." Gao Ma was in the habit of interjecting her feelings into whatever she was talking about, which led to confusion yet was quite touching. A widow in her early thirties, she was neat and clean, direct and honest, hard-working and conscientious. Previous households had found her boastful, opinionated, often sneaky, and a bit mysterious. But the Caos liked their servants to be clean, straight-talking people, and were not bothered by minor eccentricities, which is why she'd been with them for two or three years; where they went, she went. "The master wants you," she repeated. But when Xiangzi stood up, she saw his bloody face. "Oh, my, you'll be the death of me! What happened to you? Get that taken care of right away, before you get a case of lockjaw! Get a move on! The master has medicine that'll take care of it!"

Xiangzi walked into the study, Gao Ma behind him, grumbling the whole way. Mrs. Cao was wrapping her husband's hand when she saw Xiangzi. She uttered a cry of alarm.

"He's taken a nasty fall, mistress," Gao Ma said, as if Mrs. Cao could not see for herself. After busying herself filling a basin with cool water, she chattered on: "I knew something like this would happen sooner or later, the way he runs, like a man with a death wish. And I was right. What are you waiting for? Wash that face so we can put some medicine on it. I'm telling you!"

Xiangzi stood motionless, gripping his right elbow. With blood all over his face, he felt out of place in such a clean, refined study. And he wasn't alone; the others, even Gao Ma, uncharacteristically silent, could sense that something was not right.

"Sir." Xiangzi broke the silence, head bowed, his voice barely audible but surprisingly strong. "You'd better find someone else. You can hold back this month's wages to fix the broken shaft and the cracked lantern on the left side. Nothing else was broken."

"We'll talk about that after you wash up and put on some medicine," Mr. Cao said as he watched his wife wrap his injured hand.

"Now wash up!" Gao Ma said, having regained her voice. "The master has said nothing, so don't get ahead of yourself."

He still didn't move. "I don't need to wash up. I'll be fine in a minute. A monthly hire who injures his employer and damages his rickshaw no longer has the face to . . ." Words failed him, but he was obviously on the verge of tears. Giving up his job and forfeiting his wages nearly amounted to suicide in Xiangzi's eyes. But at a time like this, duty and face were more important than life, because the person he'd injured was Mr. Cao, not just anybody. If he'd thrown Mrs. Yang, for instance, so what! It would have served her right. He could have dealt with her like a street fighter; since she had never treated him like a man, there was no need to be considerate. Money was everything; face meant nothing, let alone rules of behavior. But Mr. Cao was not like that, and Xiangzi needed to sacrifice money to preserve his self-respect. If there was anyone or anything to hate, it was his fate, and he had just about decided that after leaving the Cao home he'd give up life as a rickshaw man. Since his life was worth practically nothing, he could throw it away if he wanted. But he couldn't be so cavalier when it came to other people. What if he actually killed someone? That thought had never occurred to him in the past, but the accident with Mr. Cao changed that. All right, then, he'd forget the money and take up a new line of work, one that didn't put other people at risk. And yet, since pulling a rickshaw had always been his ideal trade, giving it up meant abandoning hope. He would just muddle his way through life from now on and forget his dream of being a model rickshaw man. But what a waste of such a carefully developed physique! Back when he was picking up passengers on the street, he was sometimes cursed for stealing fares from other men, a shameless act he justified by his desire to better himself and buy his own rickshaw; he had no trouble absolving himself. But now he had a monthly hire and what happened? He had an accident. If word got around that Xiangzi had bungled a monthly hire by throwing his employer and banging up his rickshaw, he'd be laughed out of the ranks. He had no choice. He must quit before Mr. Cao fired him.

"Xiangzi," said Mr. Cao, whose hand was neatly bandaged. "Go wash up. I don't want to hear any more talk about quitting. It wasn't your fault. They should have put a red lantern by the rock pile. Don't give it another thought. Go wash up and get some medicine on that."

"That's right, sir," Gao Ma injected her opinion. "Xiangzi's just upset. Sure, you threw your employer, and he hurt his hand, but Mr. Cao says it wasn't your fault, so enough of that talk. Just look at you, a big, strapping young man who's all worked up, like a child. You tell him, madam, to stop worrying." Gao Ma sounded like a phonograph record, going round and round and bringing everyone into it, with no beginning and no end.

"Go wash up," Mrs. Cao said. "I hate the sight of blood."

Xiangzi stood there not knowing what to do until he heard

Mrs. Cao complaining, and he immediately knew what he had to do to put her mind at ease. He picked up the basin, carried it over to the doorway, and cleaned the blood from his face. Gao Ma walked up with a bottle of medicine.

"Don't forget your elbow and knees," she said as she daubed medicine on his injured face.

"Never mind those." Xiangzi shook his head.

After Mr. and Mrs. Cao went to bed, Gao Ma followed Xiangzi to his room, where she stood in the doorway and laid down the medicine bottle. "Put some of this on. Don't let what happened out there upset you. Back when my husband was alive, I was always quitting jobs. The way he refused to better himself while I was slaving away infuriated me. I was young and headstrong then, and ready to quit if I heard a cross word. I was hired help, not a slave. 'You may be filthy rich,' I'd say, 'but even a clay figurine is made from earth. Nobody can wait on you, old lady!' But I'm better now. My husband's death solved a lot of my problems, and my temper softened. I've been here almost three years, I think—yes, I started on the ninth day of the ninth month. They don't give many tips, but they treat us like human beings. We earn our living by the sweat of our brow, and nice words can only go so far. But taking the long view makes sense. If you leave one job every two or three days, you're out of work half the year, and that's no good. You're better off sticking with a good-natured employer, and even if there aren't many tips, you can usually put something aside over the long haul. The master didn't say anything about what happened today, so why beat yourself up? Forget it. I'm not saying I'm old and wise, but you're a young hothead, and you can't fill your belly with a quick temper. For a decent, hardworking youngster like you, settling down here is a lot better than flying from place to place. It's not them I'm thinking about, it's you, especially since you and I get along so well." She paused to catch her breath. "Well, then, I'll see you tomorrow. Now forget this stubborn nonsense. I say what I mean and I mean what I say."

Xiangzi's right elbow hurt so badly he couldn't sleep. So he added up the pros and cons of what Gao Ma said and concluded that she was right. Only money is to be trusted. He'd keep saving up to buy his rickshaw, and threatening to quit was no way to fill his belly. That comforting thought brought him a bit of peaceful sleep.

CHAPTER EIGHT

Mr. Cao had the rickshaw repaired and deducted nothing from Xiangzi's wages. Mrs. Cao gave him two Thrice Yellow Precious Wax cure-alls, but he did not take them. No more talk about quitting. The incident caused Xiangzi much embarrassment over the next few days, but in the end Gao Ma's advice won out. Several more days passed and things returned to normal; gradually he forgot the accident and experienced a rebirth of hope. When he was alone in his room, his eyes sparkled as he calculated ways to save up to buy his rickshaw, muttering as he did so, as if bothered by anxieties. His calculations were rough, but he kept at it—six sixes are thirty-six—with figures that did not square with what he already had, but just saying the numbers boosted his confidence, as if he were really keeping an account.

He admired Gao Ma, who was wiser and more competent than most men. She was a straight-talker, and he was reluctant to pass the time of day with her. But if they met in the yard or one of the doorways, he eagerly listened to what she had to say, for that would give him something to think about for the rest of the day. He invariably pleased her with his silly grin as a sign of admiration. Even if she was busy with something, she'd stop and speak to him.

But where money was concerned, he dared not follow her advice. It wasn't that her ideas were wrong; they were just too risky. He liked listening to her, since that calmed him, and there was much he could learn from her. But he stuck to his old ways with money—he would not easily let go of it.

Gao Ma did have a way with money. Since becoming a widow, she'd lent out whatever was left over at the end of the month to fellow servants, local policemen, and peddlers, one or two yuan at a time, at thirty percent or higher interest. These people were often so desperate for as little as one yuan that their eyes would glaze over and they'd pay as much as one hundred percent interest to get their hands on it. It was the only way they'd ever see a bit of extra money, and they would take it, even knowing it could easily bleed them dry. It offered them some breathing room for today, and let tomorrow take care of itself. That was the best that life could offer such people. When her husband was alive, Gao Ma knew what the toxic side of money was like. He'd come to her, roaring drunk, and demand some from her; if she didn't have it to give, he'd cause a drunken scene in front of the house, forcing her to borrow the money, whatever the rate of interest. She took this experience to heart, lending out money not as a form of retaliation but as something perfectly reasonable, even timely and charitable. Some people need money; others willingly lend it to them. Like Zhou Yu pretending to hit Huang Gai—one ungrudgingly gives; the other cheerfully takes.

Since she had no qualms about what she was doing, she needed to ensure that she wasn't throwing her money away. That required a keen eye, finesse, prudence, and a ruthless hand, all perfectly aboveboard. She was as conscientious as a bank manager, since extreme care was essential. The amount could be great, it could be small, but the doctrine did not vary, because they lived in a capitalist society. It was like pouring money into a big sieve with tiny holes: as the money sifts down, little by little, less gets through. At the same time, the doctrine also sifts down through the sieve, but there is always as much at the top as there is at the bottom, because a doctrine, unlike money, is nonphysical and shapeless; it can slip through no matter how small the holes. Everyone said that Gao Ma was a tough customer, a trait she readily acknowledged. Her toughness was tempered by the hardships she'd suffered in life. She ground her teeth at the thought of past miseries, when she'd had to endure mistreatment from her heartless, unreasonable husband. She could be friendly, but she could also be callous, knowing that it was the only way to survive in this world.

With the best of intentions, Gao Ma urged Xiangzi to start lending money, even offering to help him if he was willing.

"I tell you, Xiangzi, if you keep your money in your pocket, one yuan will always be one yuan. But if you lend some of it out, it will grow. Of course, you have to go into it with your eyes open. You've got to know who you're dealing with and never lend money to someone who might cheat you. If a policeman refuses to pay interest or holds back the principle, go see his superior. One word from you and he loses his job. Find out when he gets paid and show up that day to demand your money. It would be a wonder if he still didn't pay. You can apply this principle to all potential customers. You need to know their background, so you won't have to beg to get your money back. Listen to me and you can't go wrong, I guarantee it!"

Xiangzi's expression amply demonstrated his admiration for Gao Ma without having to say a word. But when he was alone, mulling over what she'd said, his money still felt safer in his own hands. She was right, this was not a way to make more money, but it guaranteed that he wouldn't lose what he had. He took out the money he'd put aside over the past two or three months—all silver dollars—and gingerly turned them over in his hand, one at a time, careful not to make any noise. They were so shiny, so solid, so captivating, he knew he could not bring himself to let them out of his sight, except to buy a rickshaw. To each his own, he was thinking. Gao Ma's ways were not for him.

He'd once worked for a family named Fang, all of whom, even the servants, had opened post office savings accounts. Mrs. Fang had urged Xiangzi to do the same. "You can open an account with only one yuan, so why not give it a try? You know the saying—'Plan for a rainy day instead of hoping the sun will shine.' Now's the time, when you're young and strong, to put some money aside. Not all the 365 days in a year are going to be sunny and bright. Opening an account is easy, reliable, and it pays interest. Besides, you can draw your money out if the need arises. What more could you ask? Go on, get an application, and I'll help you fill it out. It's for your own good."

Xiangzi knew she meant well, and he was well aware that the cook, Wang Six, and the wet nurse, Qin Ma, both had savings accounts; he was tempted to try it for himself. But one day the eldest daughter of the Fang family sent him to the post office to deposit ten yuan. He studied the account book, with its writing and red seals. That's it, that's all there is? Hardly more than a stack of toilet paper! When he handed over the money, the clerk wrote something in the account book and added a red seal. Handing over shiny silver dollars and getting nothing in return but some scrawls in a book had to be a swindle, and Xiangzi was not about to fall for it. He suspected that the Fangs might have some sort of financial arrangement with the post office, which had established moneymaking enterprises all over town, including establishments like the Ruifuxiang Company and Hongji, which is why she was so eager to get him to open an account. But even if that were not the case, his money was better off—far better off—in his hands than in an account book. Money there was just some scribbled words!

Where banks were concerned, Xiangzi knew only that they would have been ideal spots to pick up fares, if the police didn't stop rickshaws from waiting there. What went on inside was a mystery. He was sure of one thing—there was a lot of money there—but he could never figure out why so many people came by to fuss with it. None of this, however, was any of his business, so he put it out of his mind. Many, many things happened in the city that he did not understand, and when he listened in on conversations in teahouses, he was more confused than ever, with one person saying one thing, another saying something else, and none of it making any sense. The best way to keep his head clear was to stop listening and stop thinking about what he heard. Obviously, a bank would be a good place to rob, but he was in no mood to become an outlaw, so keeping hold of his own money was the way to go; let others worry about themselves.

Knowing that he had his heart set on buying a rickshaw, Gao Ma came to him with a suggestion.

"Xiangzi, I know you're against lending money because you're in a hurry to buy a rickshaw, and there's nothing wrong with that. If I were a man who pulled a rickshaw, I'd want to own my own. I'd sing while I worked and not have to rely on anyone else. I wouldn't trade that to be a county magistrate. Pulling a rickshaw is hard work, but if I were a man and I had the strength, I'd do that before I'd take a job as a policeman. They stand out on the street the year-round for a couple of yuan a month, with no chance for any extra income and no freedom. They get fired if they decide to grow a mustache. It's not an appealing job. Now, where was I? Oh, right, if you're in a hurry to buy a rickshaw, I've got an idea. Organize a lending club with ten to twenty people, who each put in two yuan a month. You're the first to use the money. That's forty yuan to add to what you've already got, and you'll be able to buy your rickshaw in no time. Problem solved. Once you have your rickshaw, you form a banking co-op. You won't need to pay interest and it's a respectable thing to do. A new path opens up. If you decide to organize it, I'll be the first to join the club. I mean it. What do you say?"

Xiangzi's heart was racing. If he really could come up with thirty or forty yuan and add it to the thirty that Fourth Master Liu was holding, plus what he'd earned recently, wouldn't he have a total of eighty? That wouldn't be enough to buy a brand-new vehicle, though he could surely afford one that was nearly new. Not only that, but this was the time to get his money back instead of letting Fourth Master Liu hold on to it. A nearly new vehicle was good enough for the time being; when he'd earned enough out on the street, he'd trade it for a new one.

The next question was where to find twenty people. Even if he managed, they'd probably join just to save face. When he needed money, he'd form a club, but what would he do if someone invited him to join their club? With poverty all around, these clubs came and went before you knew it. No man worth his salt goes begging for help. No, he'd buy a rickshaw when he'd earned enough and not before.

When Gao Ma saw that her advice had fallen on deaf ears, she felt like trying to get him moving with a bit of sarcasm. But he was too honest to deserve that. "You know what you want," she said. "The only way to drive a pig up and down an alley is straight ahead. So have it your way."

Without a word in reply, Xiangzi waited till she had left before nodding to himself, as if to acknowledge that his was the proper way to go about it. He was pleased with himself.

Early winter had arrived. At night in the alleys, shouts of honey-roasted chestnuts and salted peanuts were joined by cries of "Chamber pots, oh!" The peddler also carried on his pole earthenware gourd banks. Xiangzi bought a large one. Since he was the first customer of the day, the man did not have change, but then Xiangzi spotted a delightful little chamber pot, bright green with a pursed spout. "Never mind the change, I'll take this, too."

After putting away his gourd bank, Xiangzi took the chamber pot inside. "Still up, young master? Here, I've brought you something to play with."

Everyone was watching Little Wen—the Caos' young son—being bathed, and when they saw the gift, they couldn't help but laugh. Mr. and Mrs. Cao didn't say a word, feeling that while it might not have been the most appropriate gift, it was the thought that counted. They smiled to show their appreciation. Naturally, Gao Ma had to have her say:

"Look at that! I mean, really! A grown man like you, Xiangzi—is that the best you can do? That's disgusting!"

But Little Wen, thrilled with his new toy, scooped some bath water into the chamber pot. "This teapot has a big mouth!" he exclaimed.

That produced even greater laughter. Xiangzi straightened his clothes—satisfied with how this had turned out, he didn't know what else to do—and walked out of the room a happy young man. All those happy faces had been turned his way, a first for him, as if he'd become important in their eyes. With a smile, he took out his silver dollars and dropped them into his new gourd bank, one at a time. Nothing beats this, he was thinking. When I've got enough in there, I'll smash it against the wall—*pow*—and there'll be more silver dollars than pieces of broken pottery.

Xiangzi made up his mind to go it alone. Fourth Master Liu was trustworthy, although they had their awkward moments. There was no risk that Xiangzi would lose the money, but he still had his concerns. Money is like a ring, always better when it's on your own finger. Reaching this decision was an enormous relief. He felt as if he'd tightened his belt around his waist and thrown out his chest so he could stand straighter and stiff.

The days were getting colder, but Xiangzi did not notice, for his resolve pointed to a bright future. He was unaffected by the cold. Ice began to appear on the roads, and the dirt paths froze up. The ground was dry and hard; a yellow cast settled over the arid black soil. Ruts in the road made by passing carts in the morning were crusted with frost, and gusts of wind cut the haze to reveal a high, very blue, and refreshing sky. Xiangzi liked going out early in the morning, to feel the cool wind rush up his sleeves and make him shudder pleasurably, like bathing in icy water. Sometimes a strong headwind made it hard to breathe, but he lowered his head, clenched his teeth, and forged ahead, like a fish swimming upstream. Strong winds stiffened his resistance, as if he were locked in a fight to the death. When a blast of wind took his breath away, he'd shut his mouth for a long moment and then belch, like swimming underwater and then shooting to the surface. One belch, and he was off again, charging ahead; nothing, no force on earth, could stop this giant of a man. Every muscle in his body was taut—he was like an insect besieged by an army of ants, squirming and battling for its life.

He was covered with sweat. When he laid down the shafts, he straightened up, exhaled grandly, and wiped the dust from the corners of his mouth, feeling invincible; staring at the sandy wind whistling past, he'd nod. The wind bent roadside trees, shredded canvas shop signs, ripped handbills from the walls, and blotted out the sun; it sang, it roared, it howled, it resounded, and then it abruptly straightened out and stormed ahead like a terrifying specter, rending heaven and earth. Then, without warning, it turned tumultuous, churning in all directions, like an evil spirit running amok. All at once it gusted from side to side, sweeping up everything in its path: tearing branches from trees, lifting tiles from roofs, and severing electric wires. All the while, Xiangzi, who had just emerged unscathed from the wind, stood there watching. Final victory was his! When the wind was at his back, he needed only to grasp the shafts firmly and let the wind turn the wheels like a dear friend.

Xiangzi was not heedless of the wretched condition of the old, frail rickshaw men whose clothes were so tattered a light wind blew through them and a strong one tore them to shreds. Their feet were wrapped in rags. They waited, shivering in the cold, at rickshaw stands, wanting to be first to shout "Rickshaw!" when a prospective fare approached. Running warmed them up and soaked their tattered clothes in sweat, which froze as soon as they stopped. Strong winds nearly stopped them in their tracks. When the wind came from above, they ducked their heads down into their chests; wind gusting up from below nearly knocked them off their feet. They dared not raise their hands in a headwind, to keep from turning into kites, and when the wind was at their backs, they lost control of both their rickshaws and themselves. They tried every trick they knew, used every ounce of energy they possessed, to pull their rickshaws to their destination, nearly killing themselves for a few coins. After each trip, their faces were coated with dust mixed with sweat, through which poked three frozen red circles—two eyes and a mouth. Few people were out on the streets during the short, cold days of winter, and a day of running might not bring in enough for one good meal. And yet the older men had wives and children at home, while the younger ones had parents and siblings. For these men, winters were sheer torture, and they were no more than a breath away from becoming ghosts, without the leisure and comfort that spirits enjoyed. No ghost ever had to work so hard for so little. Dying on the street like a dog was their greatest hope for peace and comfort. Those who froze to death, it was said, died with smiles on their faces!

How could Xiangzi not see this? But he had no time to worry about them. Their transgressions were the same as his, but since he was still young and strong, he could endure the hardships, unfazed by the wind and the cold. He had a clean room to go home to at night and a proper set of clothes for daytime, which was why he did not see them as peers. He suffered, as did they, but to radically different degrees. For now, he suffered less than they, and he could leave this life behind him in later years, confident that in his old age he would not be reduced to pulling a decrepit rickshaw in constant fear of starving or freezing to death. His present advantages guaranteed his future victory. Chauffeurs who waited in their cars in front of restaurants or private residences would not be caught dead chatting with rickshaw men, for that would be beneath their dignity. That attitude differed little from Xiangzi's attitude toward the old, the sick, and the crippled pullers. While they all existed in hell, they were on different levels. The importance of standing together never occurred to them, as each went his own way, blinded by his hopes and struggles. They all believed that they could single-handedly be set for life with a family and a job, and so they groped their way through the darkness. Xiangzi, who had no thoughts and no time for anyone else, was preoccupied with his own money and his success.

Signs of the approaching New Year's holiday gradually appeared on the streets; on sunny, windless days, even though the air was bracing and cold, the colors were impossible to miss: there were New Year's posters, paper lanterns, red and white candles, silk flowers for the hair, and a variety of sweets, all pleasing to the eye, though somewhat unsettling. Everyone looked forward to a few happy days over the holiday, but they had their concerns as well, some big, some small. Xiangzi's eyes brightened when he saw the roadside displays, with the expectation that the Caos would be sending gifts to friends and family, and each trip would end with twenty or thirty cents for him, to supplement the year-end bonus of two yuan. Even if the tips were small, as long as they trickled in, they added up to a sizable amount. His gourd bank would not let him down! At night, when he had nothing to do, he stared at the new friend that knew how to swallow money but not give it up. "Eat more," he urged it quietly, "eat as much as you can, old friend. When you've eaten your fill, I'll be satisfied!"

The end of the year neared, and before he knew it, it was the eighth day of the twelfth month. Happiness and worries forced people to plan and make arrangements. There were still twenty-four hours in a day, but there was a difference, in that the days permitted no slacking off, for there was always something to do in preparation for the celebration. It was as if time had developed a consciousness and emotions, forcing people to think and to busy themselves at its pace. Xiangzi was one of the happy ones. The flurry of activity, the shouts of vendors, the anticipation of year-end tips and pocket change, the time off, and dreams of good food had him as giddy and hopeful as a little boy. He decided to spend eighty or ninety cents on a gift for Fourth Master Liu. It would have to be small, but the sentiment is what counted. It would serve as an apology for staying away for so long, owing to his busy schedule at the residence; it would also give him an excuse to ask for the thirty yuan the old man was holding for him. Retrieving what was his was worth the expenditure of something less than one yuan. Having made up his mind, he shook his gourd bank and tried to imagine what it would sound like after he added another thirty yuan. With that back in his hands, his worries would be over.

One evening, as he was about to shake his treasure container, he heard Gao Ma call out, "Xiangzi, there's a woman at the door asking for you. I ran into her on my way home, and she asked about you." When Xiangzi came out of his room, she added in a whisper, "She looks like a big black pagoda! Real scary!"

Xiangzi's face turned red as a blazing fire. He knew this meant trouble.

CHAPTER NINE

Xiangzi was barely able to step across the threshold. In a daze, he stood just inside the doorway, where he caught a glimpse of Miss Liu, framed in the light of a street lamp. Apparently, she had just powdered her face, which had a gray-green cast, like a black dew-covered leaf. He had to turn his eyes away.

Huniu wore a puzzling expression. Her eyes revealed a bit of longing for him, but her mouth was twisted into a smirk and the wrinkles on her nose hinted at contempt and anxiety. Her arched brows and outlandishly powdered face gave her a seductive yet domineering appearance. Her lips twitched when she saw Xiangzi come out, and her face betrayed a range of emotions, none seeming to fit her mood. With a gulp, she managed to get her confused feelings and emotions under control. Taking up the social mannerisms she'd learned from her father, a mixture of displeasure and mirth, she displayed her insouciance at seeing Xiangzi with a lighthearted tease:

"Well, aren't you something! Throwing a meaty bun at a dog ensures it'll never return." There was a shrill quality to her voice, much the same tone she used when bickering with one of the rickshaw men. All traces of levity disappeared from her face with this comment, replaced by a sheepish, sordid look. She bit her lip.

"Don't shout!" Xiangzi was able to blurt this out only by concentrating his strength in his lips. Not loud, but forceful.

"I'm not afraid of you!" Huniu hissed with a contemptuous grin, though she did lower her voice a little. "No wonder you've been avoiding me, now that you've got a little bitch of your own! I've always known you were no good. You act like a big, dumb oaf, like a Tartar sucking on a pipe. But you're smarter than you look." The volume had increased again.

"I said don't shout!" Xiangzi was afraid that Gao Ma might be listening on the other side of the door. "Stop shouting, and come with me!" He walked out to the street.

"I'll go anywhere, I'm not afraid, and I'll shout if I want!" Despite her protests, she followed him.

They crossed the street and walked to a path on the eastern side of the park, stopping at the red wall, where Xiangzi—always the country boy—crouched down. "What do you want from me?"

"Me? Hah, I'll tell you what." She stood with her left hand on her hip, her belly protruding slightly. She looked down at him and thought for a moment, as if she wanted to show him some kindness, a bit of pity. "Xiangzi, I need to talk to you. It's important."

Much of his anger dissolved at the gentle sound of his name. He looked up at her. There was still nothing endearing about her appearance, but that "Xiangzi" echoed through his heart, tender and intimate, as if he'd heard it before somewhere, recalling ties of affection that could neither be denied nor severed. He kept his voice low and a bit gentler than a moment before. "What is it?"

"Xiangzi," she said as she bent closer. "It's happened."

"What's happened?"

"This." She pointed to her belly. "So what do we do?"

With a stunned gasp, Xiangzi grasped what she was saying, and thousands of thoughts that had never before occurred to him flooded his head, so many, so urgent, so chaotic that his mind went blank, like movie film that snaps in two. The street was quiet, the moon hidden behind patchy gray clouds, as mild gusts of wind rustled dead branches and dry leaves on the ground; off in the distance a cat screeched. As his mind went from confused to empty, Xiangzi did not hear the sound; head in hands, he stared down at the ground until it seemed to move. No thoughts came to mind, nor did he hope for any; he felt himself shrinking, just not enough to disappear. His entire being, it seemed, was tied up with this painful development. For him, there was nothing else. Now he felt the cold, and his lips quivered.

"Don't just squat there, say something! Stand up!" The cold seemed to affect her as well. She needed to move around.

Stiffly he got to his feet and walked with her, heading north, still unable to come up with anything to say. He was numb from head to toe, like a man emerging from a deep freeze.

"Don't you have any ideas?" She gazed at him, tenderness in her eyes.

There was nothing he could say.

"The old man's birthday is the twenty-seventh. He'll expect you to be there."

"Too busy, end of the year." Even in his confusion, Xiangzi hadn't forgotten his own affairs.

"You're the type that has to be forced to do something. Trying to talk to you is a waste of time." Her voice was rising again, the cold air giving it a crisper edge, and causing Xiangzi considerable embarrassment. "Well, I'm fearless. So what do you plan to do? If you won't listen to me, I won't waste my breath. Come up with something, or I'll stand outside your room and curse you for three straight days and nights! And I'll find you no matter where you go! I don't care who I'm dealing with."

"Stop shouting, won't you?" Xiangzi moved away from her.

"Shouting bothers you, does it? Well, you should have thought about that at the time. You had your fun, and now you want to dump everything on me. Well, pull back your you-know-what and see who you think you're talking to!"

"Go ahead, tell me, I'm listening." Her outburst made Xiangzi, who had been suffering from the cold, suddenly feel hot all over, the heat prickling his skin as it oozed from his frozen pores. His scalp itched terribly.

"That's better. Don't make things hard on yourself." Her lips parted, revealing her canines. "You don't have to feel bad," she said. "I really care for you. You need to keep in mind what's good for you. I tell you, getting pigheaded with me won't do you any good."

"Don't . . ." Xiangzi wanted to say, "Don't slap me, then try to rub the hurt away," but he couldn't recall the whole saying. He knew his share of Beiping wisecracks, but the words often got stuck in his throat. He understood them all right; he just wasn't good at using them.

"Don't what?"

"You first."

"I've got an idea." She stopped and looked him in the eye. "You see, if you send a matchmaker to talk to the old man, he'll say no. He rents out rickshaws, you pull them, and that wouldn't be a good match for his daughter. But that doesn't bother me. I like you, and that's what counts. To hell with all the rest! No matchmaker will get past the old man, because any mention of the word *marriage* will get him thinking about his rickshaws. Even someone above you would be out of luck. So it's up to me, since I chose you. We boarded the train before we bought a ticket. Neither of us can deny what's inside me, but we can't march into the old man's yard and tell him. He's getting more pigheaded all the time, and he might react to our announcement by taking a young wife and driving me out. The old fellow's in great shape for a man in his seventies, and if has a new wife, he could easily father two or three children, believe it or not."

"Let's talk while we walk," Xiangzi said, concerned that the policeman on duty had walked by them twice.

"Nobody can keep us from talking right where we are." She followed Xiangzi's gaze toward the policeman. "You're not pulling a rickshaw, so there's nothing to be afraid of. He can't bite someone's balls off just because he feels like it. Not on your life! He can mind his own business. Now here's what I think. On the twenty-seventh, his birthday, you kowtow to him, then do the same on New Year's, and that'll put him in a good mood. When he's happy, he likes to drink, so I'll have some liquor ready, and once he's good and drunk, you strike while the iron's hot, asking him to be your foster father. After that, I'll gradually let him know that I'm indisposed. He'll ask what's wrong, and I'll remind him of Xu Zhe, who was brought as a prisoner to Cao Cao's camp, and not say another word. He'll really start to worry then, so I'll drop the name Qiao Er—the assistant manager of the undertaker shop east of town—who died recently with no heirs or family and was buried in the potter's field outside Dongzhi Gate. How's the old man going to find out if that's true? This'll put him in a bind, and we can drop a hint that giving me to you would be a good idea. What's the difference between a foster son and a son-in-law? I'll say. That way we'll get what we want without causing a scandal. What do you think?"

Xiangzi said nothing.

Having said her piece, Huniu walked off to the north, head down and looking pleased with herself, as she gave Xiangzi time to think over what she'd said. The wind rose up about them and blew the clouds away from the moon. They'd reached the northern end of the street, where the waters of the Imperial Moat had frozen solid—skirting the red walls of the Forbidden City, silent, gray, flat, and hard. No sounds emerged from inside the wall. The exquisite watch towers, the gold and green memorial archways, the vermillion city gates, and the pavilion at Jingshan Park were silent, as if listening to a sound they might never hear again. The wind blew, like a mournful sigh, snaking through the palace towers and halls, as if wanting to relate tales of days past. Huniu headed west, followed by Xiangzi, to the arched bridge to Beihai. The bridge was practically deserted. Dull moonlight shone down, cold and desolate, on expanses of ice on both sides. Dim outlines of distant pavilions cast dark shadows, as silent as if immobilized in a frozen lake, with only their yellow roof tiles glimmering faintly. Trees rustled slightly, further blurring the moonlight. A white pagoda reaching into the hazy clouds cast a desolate chill on everything, causing the three lakes to reveal the northern bleakness, despite their intricate carvings. As he was crossing the bridge, Xiangzi shivered from the icy expanse below and refused to go any farther. Normally, when he was pulling his rickshaw across the bridge, he concentrated on his feet, afraid of a misstep, as if the sights around him did not exist. Now he was free to look, but the scenery frightened him. The cold, gray ice, the rustling trees, and the deathly pale pagoda were so forlorn they seemed poised to shout hysterically or dance madly. Even the white stones of the bridge at his feet seemed abnormally bleak and so white that even the street lamps were subdued and dreary. He did not want to move, he did not want to look, and he definitely did not want to be with her. Why not just jump headfirst, crash through the ice, and sink to the bottom to freeze in the water like a dead fish!

"I'll see you tomorrow." He turned and headed back the way he'd come.

"That's how we'll do it, Xiangzi," she said to his broad back. "The twenty-seventh!" With one last look at the white pagoda, she sighed and walked off to the west.

Like a man with a demon at his heels, Xiangzi did not look back. Rushing headlong toward the palace area, he was so flustered he nearly crashed into the palace wall. Leaning against it with his hand, he felt like crying. His senses were dulled. "Xiangzi!" came a shout from the bridge. "Come here, Xiangzi, come back here!" It was Huniu.

He took two tortured steps toward the bridge as Huniu, leaning back slightly, walked down to meet him. Her mouth was open. "Come here, Xiangzi, I've got something for you." She was right in front of him before he'd taken more than a few steps. "Take this, it's the thirty-odd yuan we were holding for you. There was some small change, and I added a bit to make an additional yuan. Take it. I'm only giving it to you to show my heart's in the right place. I miss you, I care for you, and I want to look after you. All I ask is a little gratitude. Take it and hold on to it. If you lose it, don't blame me."

Xiangzi took the money—a wad of bills—and stood there at a loss. He didn't know what to say.

"All right, then, I'll see you on the twenty-seventh. No backing out." She laughed. "You're getting the best of everything. Figure it out for yourself." She turned and walked off.

Clutching the bills, Xiangzi followed her with his eyes until her head disappeared on the downward slope of the bridge. Gray clouds slipped in front of the moon again, making the street lamps brighter and turning the bridge extraordinarily white, empty, and cold. He turned and walked off like a maniac, taking long strides. The image of the dreary white bridge was still with him when he reached the gate, as if only a blink in time separated it from him.

The first thing he did back in his room was count the money, once, twice, three times, until his sweaty palms made the bills sticky and hard to count. When he finally finished, he stuffed them into his gourd bank, then sat on his bed and stared blankly at the earthenware container. There was nothing to think about. With money, anything was possible. He was confident that the contents of the bank would solve all his problems, so there was no need to think. The Imperial Moat, Jingshan Park, the white pagoda, the bridge, Huniu, her belly . . . all dreams, and when he woke up, there would be thirty yuan more in his bank, and that was real!

Once he'd gazed at the bank long enough he put it away and decided to get a good night's sleep. He'd sleep away the day's troubles and see what tomorrow brought.

He lay down but couldn't sleep, as all that had happened buzzed into his head, like wasps, one swarm after another, all armed with stingers.

He tried to wipe his mind clean because thinking was a waste of time now that Huniu had closed off all avenues of escape.

Best for him to storm off, but he couldn't do that. He'd rather stand guard over the white pagoda at Beihai than go back to the countryside. What about another city? He couldn't think of anyplace that would be better than Beiping. No, he couldn't leave. This was where he'd end his days.

Once that was decided, why waste time thinking about anything else? Huniu would do what she said, and if he didn't go along with her, she'd badger him mercilessly. There was no place in Beiping where he could hide from her. He'd be crazy to try to give her the slip because that would only anger her and she'd bring Fourth Master Liu into the picture. He'd hire a couple of toughs—no more than that—and they'd take him to a remote spot and kill him.

In his mind he went over the encounter with Huniu, from start to finish, and felt as if he'd fallen into a trap, bound hand and foot. There was no escape. He couldn't fault anything she said, for there were no flaws in her logic. She had cast a fine mesh net from which even the smallest fish could not escape. Since he had no luck analyzing the situation in its details, he decided to look at it in its entirety, and when he did, it pressed down on his head like a millstone. This oppressive weight brought home the reality that a rickshaw man's lot in life can be summed up in two words: hard luck. A rickshaw man, since that is what he was, must stay clear of everything but his rickshaw, especially women, since getting close to one can only end in disaster. Fourth Master Liu and Huniu had both cheated Xiangzi, he with all his rickshaws and she with her smelly cunt. It would do him no good to try to think things through. To accept his fate, he'd have to kowtow to the old man and ask him to be his foster father, and then wait to marry that stinking bitch. Not to do so was suicidal.

When his thoughts reached this point, Xiangzi put Huniu

and everything she'd said out of his mind. He couldn't blame her for what happened; it was just a rickshaw man's lot in life, no different from a dog that expects to be beaten and bullied, even by children, for no good reason. Why cling to a life like that? Give it up and be done with it!

Unable to sleep, he kicked away his comforter and sat up. He felt like getting good and drunk. Why the fuck should he care about this business or about proper behavior! Get drunk and pass out. The twenty-seventh? Not even on the twenty-eighth, and who was going to do anything about it? Throwing the comforter over his shoulders, he picked up the little bowl he used as a glass and ran out.

The wind had picked up a bit, but the gray clouds had drifted away from the moon, which seemed smaller, its beams chilled. Xiangzi, who had just emerged from a warm bed, shuddered from the blast of cold air. The streets were deserted except for a couple of rickshaws, the pullers stomping their feet and covering their ears with their hands. Xiangzi ran straight to a little teahouse on the south side. The door was shut to keep the heat in, with only a tiny window open to make exchanges. He bought four ounces of strong liquor and a packet of peanuts, then carried his bowl of liquor like a sedan-chair bearer, keeping a fast pace without running, not spilling a drop by the time he was back in his room. He scurried back into his bed, teeth chattering. Too cold to sit up. The pungent aroma of the liquor on his bedside table was not pleasant; not even the peanuts interested him. The freezing air hit him like a cold shower, and he didn't feel like sticking his hand out, now that his heart had given up its heat.

Xiangzi lay there for a long time before gazing at the liquor beside his bed. No, he mustn't go down that destructive road over this entanglement; he had to stay away from liquor. Things looked bad, no doubt about that, but there had to be an opening somewhere that he could slip through. And even if no escape was possible, he couldn't let himself wallow in the mud. He had to open his eyes wide and see as clearly as possible how people had managed to beat him down.

He put out the light and pulled the comforter up over his head, hoping that would help him sleep. It didn't. Poking his head out, he saw that the moon's rays had taken on a green cast as they filtered through the paper window facing the courtyard, a sign that daybreak was not far off. The tip of his nose was chilled in cold night air that carried the aroma of liquor. He sat up abruptly, picked up the bowl, and took a big drink.

CHAPTER TEN

Xiangzi was not smart enough to deal with his problems little by little and lacked the boldness to attack them all at once. And so, stymied, he spent his time stewing in his resentments. Like all living creatures, he was thinking only of picking up the pieces after suffering a setback. A fighting cricket that has lost its rear legs tries to crawl on its smaller forelegs. Xiangzi didn't know what else to do but make it through one day at a time, taking things as they came, crawling to wherever his hands and feet would take him, with no thought of leaping ahead.

The twenty-seventh was a couple of weeks off, and that was the only thing on his mind, on his lips, and in his dreams; all day long—the twenty-seventh. Once that day passed, it seemed, his problems would be solved, though he knew that this was wishful thinking. He sometimes tried to think ahead, maybe using some of his savings to go to Tianjin and find a new way to make a living. Could Huniu find him there? In his mind, any place he could reach only by train was too far off for her to track him down! These were comforting thoughts, but deep down he knew it wouldn't work—as long as he could stay in Beiping, he would. And so his thoughts returned to the twenty-seventh, since it was easier to think about things that were close. If he could pass this hurdle, he might be able to put his troubles behind him without having to do anything drastic, and even if this did not solve all his problems, each hurdle brought him that much closer.

So how to get over this hurdle? Two ideas occurred to him: one was to ignore her and refuse to pay respects to her father. The other was to do exactly as she said. Two separate approaches that produced essentially the same result. If he didn't go, she would not let that be the end of it; if he did go, she'd show him no leniency. He recalled his early days with a rickshaw, and how he'd followed the lead of other pullers by taking shortcuts down small lanes and alleys. But he once mistakenly headed to Luoquan, or "Circular" Lane, which, true to its name, brought him back to where he started. Well, he'd done it again, since no matter which way he went, the result would be the same.

Trying to make the best of a bad situation, he asked himself what was wrong with marrying Huniu. And no matter how he looked at it, the prospect sickened him. He shook his head just thinking about how she looked. Forget her appearance and consider her behavior. No self-respecting, hardworking man could hold his head up if he married damaged goods like her and could not face his deceased parents when his time came. And what guarantee did he have that the child in her belly was his? Or that she'd bring the rickshaws along with her? He certainly didn't want to get on the wrong side of Fourth Master Liu. And even if everything went off without a hitch, knowing he'd never get the better of Huniu was more than he could bear. All she had to do was curl her finger to have him running around till his head spun and he did not know in which direction he was headed. He knew what he was up against with her. She was not someone he wanted to start a family with, and that was that.

Marrying her would be the end of him, as he was not a man who held himself in contempt. So he was stuck, no way around it.

Since dealing with her was out of the question, he turned his loathing inward, feeling a need to punish himself. But the truth was, he'd done nothing wrong. It had all been her doing, luring him into her trap. His innocence and decency had been his downfall; people like him always got the worst of it, and trying to sort things out reasonably would be a waste of time.

What really bothered him was that there was no one to whom he could pour his heart out. He had no parents or siblings, and no friends. Most of the time he saw himself as a hardy young man, feet on the ground and holding up the sky, independent and carefree. But now he realized, to his chagrin, that a man cannot live alone, and he began to develop a sense of affection for others, especially his brothers in the trade. If he'd made friends with just a few of them—men like him—he wouldn't have to fear several Hunius, let alone one. His friends would give him advice and take his side. But he'd always kept to himself, and making friends on the spur of the moment was unlikely. He felt a fear he'd never known before. The way things were going, anyone could bully and humiliate him. A man alone cannot hold up the sky!

This fear caused him to start doubting himself. In the winter, when his employer had a dinner engagement or went to the theater, he would take the water bottle out from under the carbide lamp and hold it up against his chest; the water would freeze if left on the rickshaw. He'd sweat after a good run, and the water bottle against his chest would make him shiver until it warmed up. But he'd never felt exploited by doing this, and sometimes it had given him a sense of superiority, since the men who pulled beat-up rickshaws did not have carbide lamps to

begin with. But now he saw things differently. He earned a pittance each month and had to put up with all sorts of degrada-
tions, even holding a water bottle against his chest to make sure
it didn't freeze. His chest—broad and powerful—was less valu-
able than a little water bottle! He'd once thought that pulling a
rickshaw was the ideal profession, for it would make it possible
for him to start a family and earn a decent living. Now he wasn't
so sure. How could he blame Huniu for humiliating him, since
all along he was worth no more than a water bottle?

Three days after Huniu's visit, Mr. Cao was taking in a movie
with friends, and Xiangzi was waiting for him in a little teahouse,
holding the water bottle, which felt like a block of ice, against
his chest. The teahouse door and windows, shut to keep out the
freezing cold, held in the smells of coal, sweat, and the stink of
cheap cigarettes. And still the windows were frosted over. All the
customers, it seemed, were rickshaw men with monthly hires.
Some, their heads resting against the wall, were sleeping in the
warmth of the room. Others were toasting one another with
hard liquor, smacking their lips after each swallow and noisily
passing chilled gas. One was eating a rolled-up flatbread, taking
huge bites that thickened his neck and turned it red. One of the
others was complaining to anyone who would listen how he'd
been on his feet since early that morning and had lost count of
how many times he'd gone from sweat to dry and back again.
Most of the others were sitting around swapping stories until
they heard the man's grumbling. A momentary silence preceded
an outburst of chatter, like birds whose nest has been destroyed,
as the men told of how they, too, had suffered that day. Even the
man eating the flatbread found room in his mouth to free up his
tongue to chew and talk at the same time, the veins standing out
on his forehead. "Just because you've got a fucking monthly

hire, people think you've got an easy time of it! I've been fucking at it—urp—since two o'clock without a drop of water or a bite to eat, and I've taken him from Qianmen—urp—to Pingzimen three fucking times. It's so cold out there my asshole is frozen shut! It's all I can do to fart!" He looked at the other men in the shop, nodded a time or two, and took another bite of his flatbread.

The man's last comment turned the topic to the weather and gave everyone a chance to talk about how they suffered from the cold. Xiangzi listened intently to what they were saying, without adding to the conversation. Despite differences in tone, accent, and specifics, they cursed their lot and complained of the unfairness of life. The voiced complaints fell upon stored-up grievances in his heart, like raindrops soaked up by dry, thirsty ground. He wouldn't have given a clear account of his troubles to these men even if he'd known how, and so could only absorb some of the bitterness of life from what they were saying. These were lives filled with misery, and his was no exception. Self-knowledge made him want to sympathize with them. When they spoke of their sorrows, he knitted his brows, and when they spoke of lighter matters, he grinned. Now he felt like one of them; they were brothers in suffering, and that did not change just because he kept silent. He had once thought that it was these men's constant jabbering that kept them from making a decent living. Today, for the first time, he felt that this was not idle chatter but that they were speaking for him, voicing the bitterness common to all rickshaw men.

The talk was getting especially heated when the door flew open, filling the room with a blast of cold air. All eyes turned angrily to see who the inconsiderate wretch was, and their impatience slowed the newcomer down, as if he were dawdling intentionally. "Hurry it up, my dear uncle," the waiter called out. "Don't let all the warm air out!"

The newcomer—another rickshaw man, probably in his fifties—was in the door before the waiter's plea was finished. He had on a flared padded jacket that was neither short nor long and had holes in the front and in the elbows, where cotton wadding poked through. His face, which looked as if it hadn't been washed in days, had lost its color; his ears, turned bright red by the bitter cold, looked like ripe fruit about to fall from the tree. Tufts of dull white hair stuck out messily from a tattered little cap, frost hung from his eyebrows and short beard. He groped his way to a bench and sat down. "A pot of tea," he said weakly.

This particular teahouse was a gathering place for rickshaw men with monthly hires, and someone like this old man would normally never set foot inside.

The sight of this newcomer added a layer of meaning to what the men had been talking about before his arrival, and none of them felt like saying anything more. Most of the time, the younger, more thoughtless pullers would make fun of a customer like this, but not today.

The old man's tea was still steeping when his head began to droop, lower and lower, until he slipped off the bench and onto the floor.

They all jumped to their feet. "What's wrong?" they shouted.

"Don't move!" the proprietor, who had experience in such things, called out to stop the men from going up to the old fellow, then took charge by loosening his collar and propping him up against a chair by his shoulders. "Some sugar water, and hurry!" Then he put his ear to the man's neck and muttered, "It's not blocked by phlegm."

No one moved, but no one sat down, either. They stood there

blinking in the smoke-filled room, eyes fixed on the door, all seemingly thinking the same thought: "This is what it's going to be for me. One day, after my hair has turned white, I'll collapse and breathe my last on the street."

When the first drops of sugar water touched the old man's lips, he groaned a couple of times and, with his eyes still shut, raised his right hand—which was so dirty it shone as if lacquered—and wiped his mouth with the back of it.

"Drink some of this," the proprietor whispered in his ear.

"Huh?" The old man opened his eyes and, when he saw he was sitting on the floor, drew up his legs in an attempt to stand.

"Take it easy. Drink this first," the proprietor said, taking his hands away from the man's shoulders.

The other men rushed up.

"Ai, ai!" The old fellow looked around and then began slowly drinking from the cup, holding it in both hands.

After finishing what was in the cup, he looked around again. "I've put you all to a great deal of trouble," he said. The words were spoken so gently and kindly it was hard to believe they came from the mouth hidden in that scruffy beard. Again he tried to stand, and this time three or four of the men helped him to his feet. The trace of a smile appeared at the corners of his mouth. "It's all right," he said in the same gentle tone, "Don't trouble yourselves. I can manage. I guess I fainted from being so cold and hungry. I'll be fine now." A smile that even all that grime could not blot out had them believing they were looking into the face of a warm, good-hearted man.

They all seemed moved. The middle-aged man who had been drinking liquor had finished what was in his bowl; his bloodshot eyes were getting moist. "Bring me two more ounces," he said, and when it arrived, even though he was by then noticeably drunk, he went up to the old man, who was now sitting in a chair by the wall, and respectfully held the bowl out to him. "Here, this is on me. I'm already over forty, and I'm not lying when I say that I'm barely making do with this monthly hire. My legs tell me when another year has passed, and in two or three more I'll be like you. You must be about sixty!"

"Not yet," the old fellow said after taking a drink. "Fifty-five. There aren't any fares in this cold weather, and I, I tell you, my belly's empty. But when I get a few coins together, I buy something hard to drink. It warms me up a bit. I was ready to collapse by the time I got here, so I decided to come in and warm up. But it's so hot in here, and me with no food in my belly, that's why I fainted. But I'm fine now, no need to worry. I'm just sorry I put you all to so much trouble."

By now, his dry, brittle hair, grimy face, filthy hands, tattered cap, and lined jacket all seemed to radiate an aura of purity, like a statue of the Buddha in a run-down temple, which retains its dignity even as it crumbles. The men kept their eyes on him, wishing him to stay. All this time, Xiangzi stood stiffly to the side, not saying a word. But when he heard the old fellow say that his belly was empty, he ran outside and returned almost immediately with ten mutton-filled buns wrapped in a cabbage leaf. He held them out to the old man. "Eat these." Then he went back and sat down, head lowered, as if the effort had worn him out.

"Ai!" The old man looked happy but on the verge of tears. He nodded at the men around him. "We really are brothers, aren't we! We can pull a fare till we're ready to drop, and we still won't stand a chance of an extra coin in our pocket." He stood up and headed for the door.

"Eat those first!" the men called out as one.

"I have to go get Xiao Ma first. My grandson. He's outside watching the rickshaw."

"You stay there," the middle-aged man said, "I'll get him. Don't worry, you won't lose your rickshaw around here. The police precinct is right across the street." He opened the door a crack. "Xiao Ma, your grandpa wants you to park the rickshaw over here and come inside."

The old man touched the buns over and over but did not pick any of them up until his grandson walked in the door. "Xiao Ma, my boy, these are for you."

Xiao Ma, a boy of thirteen or fourteen, had a gaunt face and was bundled up against the cold. Two lines of snot ran from his nose, red from the freezing air, down to his upper lip; his ears were covered by tattered earmuffs. Standing next to his grandfather, he held in his right hand one of the stuffed buns, which he'd already begun eating, and reached out with his left for another, and took a bite.

"Slow down," the old man said as he rested a hand on his grandson's head and, with the other, picked up a bun and raised it slowly to his mouth. "Grandpa only needs two of these. The rest are for you. When you're finished, we'll go home. No more work today. If it warms up a little tomorrow, we'll go out early, won't we, boy?"

Xiao Ma nodded in the direction of the buns and sniffled. "Eat three of these, Grandpa, and I'll eat the rest. Then you can ride home."

"No," the old man said, smiling proudly at the men in the room. "We'll both walk. It's too cold sitting up there."

After finishing off his stuffed buns, the old man drank what was left of the liquor while waiting for his grandson to finish the food. Then he took a rag out of his pocket and wiped his mouth.

He nodded to the other men again. "His father went off to fight and never came back. His wife . . ."

"Don't talk about that!" Xiao Ma stopped his grandfather, his cheeks bulging from the buns.

"It doesn't matter—we're among friends." Then he lowered his voice. "He's a serious boy who's determined to make good in life. His mother left us, and now it's just us two and a rickshaw. It's in bad shape, but it's ours, so we don't have to fret over daily rental charges. We earn what we can and struggle to get by. What else can we do?"

"Grandpa." Having finished nearly all the stuffed buns, the boy tugged at his grandfather's sleeve. "We need one more fare today," he said. "We don't have money for a briquette tomorrow morning. It's your fault. We could have made twenty cents by taking that customer to Rear Gate. I wanted to, but you said no. How will we get by tomorrow with no coal briquettes?"

"Leave it to me. I'll get some on credit."

"What about kindling?"

"Yes, of course. Now be a good boy and eat up. We have to be on our way." The old man stood up and walked from man to man, saying, "I've put you to a great deal of trouble, my friend!" Then he took Xiao Ma by the hand, just as the boy stuffed the last of the buns into his mouth.

Some of the customers sat still, while others saw the old man and his grandson to the door. Xiangzi was the first one outside. He wanted to get a look at the rickshaw.

It truly was in sad shape. The paint on the shafts was peeling, and the connecting bar was nearly worn through. The beat-up lamp rattled, ropes tied down the supports for the rain hood. Xiao Ma retrieved a match from inside one of his earmuffs, struck it on the sole of his shoe, and cupping it in both hands, lit the lamp. The old man spat in his hands and, with a sigh, picked up the shafts. "See you later, brothers!"

Xiangzi stood stiffly to one side watching the two of them— one old, one young—and their decrepit rickshaw. The old man muttered as he walked, his voice rising and falling under the flickering street lamp; they moved from light into shadows, and as he watched and listened, Xiangzi was struck by a sadness he hadn't felt before. He saw his own past in the figure of Xiao Ma and his future in the old man. Never before had he so casually let go of money, even a single coin, and yet he was incredibly happy to have bought the stuffed buns for the old man and his grandson. He didn't go back inside the teahouse until they were out of sight. Raucous talk and laughter had already recommenced, perplexing him so much that he paid for his tea and walked out, taking his rickshaw over to a spot outside the cinema to wait for Mr. Cao.

It was intensely cold, with sand swirling in the air. The wind seemed to be racing past overhead, blurring the outlines of stars in the sky, except for a few of the largest ones, which shimmered slightly. There was no wind near the ground, but the freezing cold air was everywhere, opening long cracks in the wheel ruts; the pale earth was as cold and hard as ice. The cold was getting to Xiangzi as he stood in front of the cinema, but he had no desire to return to the teahouse. He needed quiet time to think. The old man and his grandson, it seemed, had dashed his hopes—the old man had said the rickshaw was his. From the first day he'd gone out to pick up fares, Xiangzi was determined to have his own rickshaw; he was still slaving away in pursuit of that goal. Having his own rickshaw, he'd felt, was the answer to all his problems. Hah! Just look at that old man.

Hadn't buying a rickshaw been the reason he did not want

Huniu? First buy it, he'd thought, then start saving money until he could, in good conscience, take a wife. Hah! Just look at Xiao Ma. If Xiangzi had a son one day, things would surely turn out exactly the same.

That being the case, why keep resisting Huniu's threats? Since he couldn't break out of the trap, what difference did it make what kind of woman he married? Besides, she might bring a few rickshaws into the bargain, so why not enjoy a bit of luxury for a change? Having seen through himself, he had no right to look down on others. Huniu was just Huniu, and that was that.

The movie let out, so Xiangzi hurried to hang the water bottle on the lamp and light the wick. Then he took off his lined jacket. Clad only in a thin shirt, he was ready to run like the wind. That would drive away all his thoughts, and if he wound up killing himself in the process, so be it!

CHAPTER ELEVEN

After the encounter with the old man and his grandson, Xiangzi put his hopes aside and decided to enjoy life as long as he could. What good had it done to grit his teeth and make things so hard on himself? The life of a poor man, he now understood, was like the pit of a date, pointed on both ends and round in the middle. You're lucky to get through childhood without dying of hunger, and can hardly avoid starving to death when you're old. Only during your middle years, when you're strong and unafraid of either hunger or hard work, can you live like a human being. Only a fool will pass up the chance to enjoy a bit of life, since, as the saying goes, there are no more inns after this village. Seen this way, even the situation with Huniu was nothing to fret over.

But that resolve lasted only until the next time he looked at his gourd bank. No, he couldn't give in that easily. He was so close to having enough to buy his own rickshaw, this was no time to call it quits. He'd worked too hard to save up what he had. He had to keep at it, he just had to! But what about Huniu? She was still a problem, and then there was that abominable twenty-seventh to worry about.

Frustrated by his worries, he held the bank to his chest and muttered, "No matter what, this is mine, and no one is going to take it away from me!" The money was Xiangzi's safeguard against fear. *Cause me too much anxiety, and that's the last you'll see of me. Money's the fuel that keeps my legs moving.*

The streets were coming alive, with peddlers of sweets made of sticky millet to honor the Kitchen God everywhere and shouts of "Malt taffy, get your malt taffy!" filling the air. Xiangzi had always looked forward to New Year's, but he could not get into the holiday spirit now. The greater the confusion on the street, the tenser he grew, as the fateful twenty-seventh loomed. There were dark circles under his eyes; even the scar on his cheek darkened. He had to be especially careful pulling his rickshaw on slick, crowded streets, but he lacked the energy to deal with that and his problems at the same time. When he concentrated on one, he forgot the other, which inevitably startled him. His body itched like a child's with prickly heat.

East winds swept black clouds into the area on the afternoon honoring the Kitchen God. The temperature climbed. As the lamp-lighting hour approached, the winds turned gentle and snowflakes began to fall, sparsely at first, but enough to worry the peddlers of year-end sweets, who quickly dusted them with white powder, since the combination of warm air and snow-flakes made their wares stick together. The snowflakes turned into ice pellets that fell with a soft rustle and turned the ground white. After seven o'clock, shopkeepers and families at home began honoring the Kitchen God; fine snowflakes merged with the glow of incense and bursts of firecrackers, lending the festivities a somber atmosphere. People out on the streets were on edge as they headed home, on foot or in rickshaws, to perform the rites, but went cautiously, as the ground was treacherously slick. Peddlers, anxious to sell all their sweets, called out frantically, hardly pausing for breath.

As Xiangzi was taking Mr. Cao home from West City at around nine o'clock, they passed through the festivities at the Xidan Memorial Arch and turned east onto Chang'an Street, where the crowds began to thin out. The smooth asphalt roadway was covered by a thin layer of snow that dazzled in the reflected light of street lamps. The headlights of an occasional automobile lit up a long stretch of the road, turning snowflakes caught in the lights into what looked like flecks of gold. As they neared the New China Gate area, a thin layer of snow on the wide roadway gave the welcoming impression that the world had opened up, invested with an air of solemnity. The Chang'an Arch, the New China Gate, and the red walls of Nanhai—the Southern Sea—all wore white crowns, contrasting starkly with their vermillion columns and red walls. In the surrounding stillness they displayed the courtliness of the ancient capital. At that moment, in that place, Beiping seemed to be a city inhabited not by people but by palatial halls and temples and a few old pines whose branches silently received the falling snowflakes. Xiangzi had no time to take in the scenery, and when he saw the snow-covered road ahead, he thought only of getting home as fast as possible. In his mind's eye, he visualized the gate at home at the end of the straight, white, silent road, but he could not run as fast as he wanted, for the snow, while thin, formed a layer on the soles of his shoes. He kept stomping his feet, but a new layer quickly formed. The ice crystals were small but heavy, and they partially blinded him, forcing him to go slow. The cold air kept the snowflakes that landed on him from melting, and before long a layer of ice had formed on his shoulders, annoying him only in the sense that he felt uncomfortably wet. Though there were few shops in the area, firecrackers kept exploding in the distance, and every once in a while a double-pop rocket or a Five-Devils Starburst lit up the night sky. After the sparks died out, the night seemed darker than ever and unsettling. Anxious to get home, Xiangzi heard the firecrackers and saw the sparks in the night sky, but he had to keep his pace frustratingly slow.

What really irritated him was the bicycle that had been following them all the way from West City. When he reached West Chang'an, where the street was quieter, he could hear the tires crunching snow behind him, soft but audible. Like all rickshaw men, Xiangzi hated bicycles. Automobiles were horrible things, yet their engines were so loud you had plenty of time to get out of the way. But bicycles wobbled dizzyingly in and out of traffic. And woe be it to the rickshaw man who collided with one, because it was invariably his fault, at least in the view of the police, who found rickshaw men easier to bully than cyclists. Several times Xiangzi felt like surprising the cyclist by stopping abruptly and sending the little wretch flying. But that would have been a mistake. Rickshaw men had to put up with all sorts of humiliations. Each time he stopped to loosen the ice on his soles, he had to shout, "Stopping!" When they reached Nanhai Gate, the street widened, but the cyclist stuck to him, so angering Xiangzi that he pulled over to brush the snow off his shoulders and then stood there until the bicycle glided past. The rider even looked back at him. Xiangzi took his own sweet time starting out again, giving the cyclist time to get far ahead. "Damn you!" he cursed.

Mr. Cao's humanitarian nature kept him from putting up the padded curtain that served as a windbreaker, and even the canvas hood went up only during heavy rainstorms, all to make it easier on the man in front. Mr. Cao saw no reason to put either one up in such a mild snowfall and far preferred the opportunity to enjoy the sight of the falling snow. He'd spotted the bicycle as well, and after Xiangzi got the curse out of his system, he said softly, "If he hangs around, don't stop at our gate but continue on to Mr. Zuo's house by Huanghua Gate. And don't panic."

Xiangzi started to panic. He was always ready to curse someone on a bicycle, but he'd never considered the possibility that a cyclist was to be feared. If Mr. Cao was unwilling to go straight home, that fellow must have presented a threat. Xiangzi hadn't run more than a couple of dozen steps before catching up with the cyclist, who was obviously hanging back waiting for them. He let the rickshaw go on ahead. Xiangzi took a quick look at him on his way past, and that was all it took: a member of the secret police. He often ran into them in teahouses, and although he'd never spoken to one, he knew them by their clothes and how they carried themselves. Just like this guy. A black overcoat and a felt hat with the brim pulled way down low.

When they reached the intersection of Nanchang Road, Xiangzi sneaked a look behind him as he turned the corner. The man was still there. Suddenly forgetting about the snow on the street, he picked up his pace. Ahead was a long, straight, silvery-white road illuminated by the cold glare of street lamps; behind, a detective on a bicycle. This was a new experience for Xiangzi, and he broke out in a sweat. He turned to look again at the rear entrance to the park. Still there! When they finally reached the gate at home, Xiangzi did not dare stop, yet hated the idea of going on. Mr. Cao said nothing, so he kept running, heading north, and soon arrived at Beikou. The bicycle stayed with them the whole time. Xiangzi turned down a narrow lane. Still behind him! He emerged from the lane. Still there! This, Xiangzi realized, was not the way to Huanghua Gate. He'd taken the wrong lane but wasn't aware of it until he was at the far end. Getting lost like that bothered him.

When they reached the rear of Jingshan Park, the cyclist turned north and headed toward Rear Gate. Xiangzi mopped his sweaty face. The snowfall had lightened considerably and was now a mixture of flakes and ice crystals. He loved the way snowflakes danced so naturally in the air, unlike the ice crystals, which were cold and disagreeable. "Where to, sir?" he turned to ask.

"Mr. Zuo's house. If anybody asks, tell them you don't know me."

"Yes, sir." Xiangzi's heart was pounding, but it was not his place to ask why.

When they arrived at the Zuo home, Mr. Cao told him to pull the rickshaw inside and close the gate behind them. He was as calm as ever, but there was something unsettling about the look on his face as he left Xiangzi with his instructions and went into the house. By the time Xiangzi had parked the rickshaw beside the gate, Mr. Cao had reemerged, along with Mr. Zuo, whom Xiangzi knew. He was one of his employer's friends.

"Xiangzi," Mr. Cao said, speaking hurriedly, "You're to take a taxi home and tell the mistress I'm here. Have her come here, by taxi, but not the one you rode in. Understand? Good. Tell her to bring the things she'll need and those scrolls in my study. Got that? I'm going to phone her, but I'm telling you because she might be flustered and not do as I say. It's up to you to see that she does."

"Why don't I go with him?" Mr. Zuo said.

"No need for that. That fellow might not have been a detective after all, but I have to be careful because of that other business. Would you mind calling for a taxi?"

Mr. Zuo went inside to phone for a taxi, while Mr. Cao gave Xiangzi more instructions: "I'll pay the taxi when it gets here. Tell the mistress to pack up the children's things and the paintings in the study—just those few scrolls—as quickly as possible. The rest doesn't matter. When she's done that, have Gao Ma phone for a taxi and come here. Have you got all that? After they've left, lock the gate and move into the study, where there's a telephone. Do you know how to use one?"

"I know how to take calls but not dial them." Xiangzi did not like taking calls, either, but saying so would only add to Mr. Cao's concerns.

"Good." Mr. Cao continued, speaking rapidly: "Don't open the door for anyone, no matter what. With us gone, you'll be alone, and they'll nab you for sure. If things look bad, douse the lights and go to the Wangs' out back. You know them, don't you? Right. Hide there until this blows over. Don't worry about my things, or yours, for that matter. Just jump over the wall to keep from falling into their hands. If you lose anything, I'll make it up to you. For now, take these five yuan. All right, then, I'll phone the mistress now, but be sure to repeat what I said when you get home. Just leave out the bit about nabbing people. He might not have been a detective, so don't panic."

Xiangzi's head was spinning. There were so many questions he wanted to ask, but he had to concentrate on what Mr. Cao was telling him to do.

The taxi arrived and Xiangzi climbed in awkwardly. Snow still fell, neither more nor less heavily but enough to blur the scene outside the window. He sat up so stiff and straight his head nearly touched the top. He wanted to think things through but could not take his eyes off the arrow on the hood ornament, bright red and quite lovely. He was fascinated, too, by the windshield wipers that swept from side to side, clearing the glass of moisture. They pulled up to the gate just as he was losing interest in all this, and he stepped reluctantly out of the taxi.

Before he could ring the bell at the gate, a man who seemed to come out of the wall grabbed Xiangzi's wrist. His first impulse was to wrench his arm free, but he stopped when he saw who it was: it was the detective they'd seen on the bicycle.

"Don't you recognize me, Xiangzi?" the man said with a smile as he let go of Xiangzi's arm.

Xiangzi gulped, not knowing what to say.

"Have you forgotten how we took you to the Western Hills? I'm Platoon Leader Sun. Now do you remember?"

"Oh, Platoon Leader Sun!" Xiangzi had no idea who he was. When the soldiers dragged him up into the mountains, he hadn't paid the slightest attention to who was a platoon leader and who was a company commander.

"You might not know me, but I know you. That scar on your cheek is a dead giveaway. A while ago, while I was tailing you, I kept looking but couldn't be sure. But there's no mistaking that scar."

"What do you want?" Xiangzi tried again to ring the bell.

"I'll tell you what I want, and it's important. Let's go inside and talk about it." Platoon Leader Sun—now a detective— reached out and rang the bell.

"I'm busy," Xiangzi said as he broke out into a sweat. *I can't get away from this guy*, he said to himself angrily, *and now he wants me to invite him in.*

"You've got nothing to worry about," the detective said with a crafty grin. "This is all for your own good." When Gao Ma opened the gate, the man slipped inside. "Excuse me," he said. Before either Xiangzi or Gao Ma had a chance to react, he pulled Xiangzi in with him. "Is this where you live?" he asked as he pointed to the gatehouse. He stepped inside and looked around. "Not bad, nice and neat," he said. "You've got a good deal here."

"What do you want? I'm busy." Xiangzi had heard enough meaningless talk from the man.

"Didn't I say I've got important business?" Another smile, but the stern tone was unmistakable. "I'll give it to you straight. Your Mr. Cao is a member of an outlawed political party, and when they catch him, they'll shoot him. He won't get away! You and I have had dealings before. You did my bidding at the camp, and besides, we're street people, so I'm here to give you a warning. If you don't get away while you can, you'll be caught in the net with all the others. You and I sell our muscle to make a living, and this case involves others, not us. Isn't that right?"

"I wouldn't be able to face them." Xiangzi was thinking about Mr. Cao's instructions.

"Face who?" Detective Sun was still smiling, but his eyes narrowed. "They're the ones who caused all this, so why worry about them? We shouldn't suffer over what they do. Think for a minute. You've lived like a wild bird all your life; do you think you could stand being locked up in a cage for three months? Not only that—money will take the sting out of prison for them, but you, my young friend, with nothing to offer, might wind up tied to the toilet. But that's just the beginning. They can pull strings and get off with a few years behind bars and make you the scapegoat. We don't look for trouble and we don't cause it, so how fair would it be to wind up with black dates in our chest at the Tianqiao execution ground? You're smart enough not to fight against impossible odds. Face them? Hah! I tell you, my young friend, no one in this world gives a damn about hard-luck guys like us."

Xiangzi was frightened. He could imagine what prison would be like as he thought about how he'd suffered when the soldiers took him. "So I should take off and not worry about them?"

"You can worry about them, but who'll worry about you?"

Xiangzi had no answer for that. He stood there stiffly until he felt his conscience was clear. "All right, I'll take off."

"Not so fast," Detective Sun said with a sneer.

Now Xiangzi was really confused.

"Xiangzi, my young comrade, you are a fool. You don't expect a detective to just let you go, do you?"

"But . . ." Xiangzi was speechless.

"Don't act dumb." Detective Sun's eyes bored into him. "You must have some savings. Let's see what you've got to buy your life with. You make more a month than I do—and me, with a family to feed and clothe. I need to supplement my regular pay. I'm giving it to you straight. Do you really think I can just let you go? Friendship is one thing. If we weren't friends, I wouldn't be doing this for you. But business is business, and if I didn't get something for my troubles, my family would have to subsist on the wind. People who get along like us don't need to waste words—am I right or aren't I?"

"How much?" Xiangzi sat on the edge of the bed.

"Whatever you have. There's no fixed number."

"I'll take my chances with prison, then."

"So you say, but you'll regret it." Sun stuck his hand into his padded coat. "See this. I can take you in right now, and if you resist arrest, I'll shoot. And if I take you in, money will be the least of your problems. They'll strip you and take the clothes off your back. You're a smart boy. Figure it out for yourself."

"If you've got time to squeeze me, why not squeeze Mr. Cao?" Xiangzi's voice broke.

"He's the main criminal, and I'll get a small reward for bringing him in. It'll also be my fault if I fail. But you, you, my young friend, letting you go will be like passing gas, and killing you would be like squashing a bedbug. Give me the money and you can be on your way. Refuse, and I'll see you next at Tianqiao. Don't make trouble for yourself—be a big boy and cough it up. Besides, I won't be able to keep all of what little I get from you. My comrades will lay a claim to some of it, and I might wind up with less than anybody. If you think it's too high a price for your life, my hands are tied. How much do you have?"

Xiangzi got to his feet, his brain about to leap out of his head. He clenched his fists.

"Use those and you're done for. There's a whole gang of us, you know. Now, come on, let's see the money! I'm helping you save face, so now's the time to do the right thing." Detective Sun flashed Xiangzi a sinister look.

"What have I ever done to you?" Nearly in tears, Xiangzi sat back down.

"Nothing. You just wound up in the wrong place at the wrong time. You're either born lucky or you're not, and people like us are at the bottom of the heap. There isn't a thing you can say or do about that." Detective Sun shook his head, as if deeply moved. "All right, let's just say I've wronged you, and let it go at that."

Xiangzi thought hard for a moment and came up with nothing. His hand shook as he took his gourd bank out from under the covers.

"Let's see it," Sun said with a smile. He took it from Xiangzi and flung it against the wall.

Xiangzi's heart broke when he saw the money strewn across the floor.

"That's all?"

Xiangzi said nothing. He was shaking.

"Oh, hell, I'm not out to drain you dry. A friend's a friend, after all. But I want you to know how lucky you are to be buying your life with this pittance."

By now shaking uncontrollably, Xiangzi began rolling up his bedding.

"Don't touch that!"

"But it's cold out there." Flames seemed to leap from Xiangzi's eyes.

"I said don't touch that, and I mean it. Now get out of here!"

Xiangzi swallowed hard and bit his lip as he pushed open the door and walked out.

An inch or more of snow had fallen while he was inside. He started walking, head down. The ground was pristine and white, all except for the dark footprints he left in the snow.

CHAPTER TWELVE

Xiangzi was looking for a place to sit down and think about what had just happened. Even if he only wound up crying, at least he'd know what he was crying about. The changes had come too fast for him. With snow everywhere, there was no place to sit. All the teahouses were boarded up, since it was past ten, but even if they'd been open, he wouldn't have gone in. What he needed was a quiet, out-of-the-way spot, since he knew that the tears could start flowing at any minute.

With no place to sit, he decided to keep walking, slowly. But where should he go? A silvery world offered him no place to sit and nowhere to walk to. The only break in the white expanse came from hungry birds and a solitary man who was sighing in despair.

Where to go? This was the first order of business. A small inn? Out of the question. The way he was dressed, he could be robbed during the night, not to mention all those frightful bedbugs. How about a larger inn? Too expensive. All he had on him were those five yuan, the sum total of his wealth. A bathhouse? But they locked up at midnight, with no overnight accommodations. There was nowhere.

The lack of a place to go drove home the severity of his pre-

dicament. After all his years in the city, he owned only the
clothes on his back and five yuan. Even his bedding was gone.
His thoughts turned to tomorrow. What would he do then?
Pull a rickshaw? That would still leave him with no place to
stay, homeless and his savings gone. Become a peddler? Not
with a measly five yuan as capital. And, of course, he'd have to
buy a carrying pole. He'd never make enough to survive. A
rickshaw man could at least earn thirty or forty cents a day,
while vending required capital, with no guarantee he'd make
enough for three meals a day. He could always spend his capital
and start pulling a rickshaw when it was gone, but that was like
taking off your pants to fart, a waste of five yuan. That was his
last hope, and he mustn't lightly let go of any of it. Take a job
as a servant? He wouldn't know how. Wait on people? He
couldn't do it. Do laundry? Cook? He couldn't do that, either.
He didn't know how to do anything. He was useless, big, rough,
and stupid!

His wandering took him to Zhonghai Lake. He stood on the
bridge, where all he could see anywhere was a blanket of snow,
and only then did it occur to him that the snowfall hadn't
stopped. He reached up to feel his knitted cap—it was wet. The
bridge was deserted; even the duty policeman was nowhere to be
seen. Street lamps appeared to be blinking amid the onslaught
of snow. He looked around at all the snow, his mind a blank.

Xiangzi stayed on the bridge a long time, feeling that the
world had died: no sound, nothing stirred. The gray snowflakes
took this opportunity to speed up their disorderly fall to earth
and submerge the land before anyone was aware of it. Alone in
this hushed moment, he heard his conscience whisper: *Never
mind yourself,* it said. *You have to go back and take care of the Cao
family. Mrs. Cao and Gao Ma are all alone, without a man in the*

house. That five yuan he was holding on to—hadn't Mr. Cao given it to him? Without wasting another minute, he turned and headed back as fast as he could.

There were footprints in the snow outside the gate, and fresh tire tracks on the road. Could Mrs. Cao have left already? Why hadn't that Sun fellow arrested them?

He was afraid to open the gate, in case someone was waiting inside to nab him. He looked around and saw no one. His heart was racing. *Go ahead, give it a try. You've got no home to go back to, anyway, so what if they arrest you!* He gave the gate a cautious push; it swung open, and he took a few tentative steps along the base of the wall. There was a light in his room—*his* room! He felt like crying. He walked up and listened at the window. Someone coughed inside. It was Gao Ma! He opened the door.

"Who's there? Oh, it's you, Xiangzi. You frightened me to death!" Gao Ma sat on the bed, pressing her hands to her chest to calm herself. "What happened to you?"

Xiangzi had no answer. As if he were seeing Gao Ma again for the first time in years, a sensation of pervasive warmth filled his heart.

"I said, what happened to you?" Gao Ma was nearly in tears. "When you didn't come, the master telephoned to tell us we were to go to the Zuos' and said that you were on your way. When you got here, I opened the gate for you, didn't I? But there was someone with you, a stranger. So I turned and went back inside to help the mistress pack. You never came into the house, leaving the mistress and me to grope around in the dark. The young master was sound asleep and had to be taken out of his warm bed. When we were all packed and had the scrolls from the study, there was still no sign of you. Where were you? Tell me that. We were ready to go, so I came looking for you.

You were nowhere in sight. The mistress was so angry—mostly because she was anxious—she was shaking. It was up to me to call for a taxi, but the 'empty city bluff,' keeping people out by leaving the door open, wasn't going to work, so I said, 'You go ahead. I'll keep an eye on the place and come along after Xiangzi gets back. But if he doesn't, well, that's my bad luck.' What do you have to say for yourself? Tell me what happened to you."

No reply from Xiangzi.

"Say something! Don't just stand there."

"You can go now." Finally, Xiangzi managed to speak. "Go on."

"Will you look after the house?" Gao Ma calmed down a bit.

"When you see the master, tell him that the detective nabbed me, but then . . . but then, he didn't after all."

"What's that supposed to mean?" Gao Ma nearly laughed out loud.

"Listen to me." Xiangzi was running out of patience. "Tell the master to leave now. The detective said he was going to be arrested. Mr. Zuo's house is not safe, so he must leave right away. I'll jump over the wall and spend the night at the Wangs'. I'll lock and bolt the front gate. Tomorrow I'll go look for work. I've let the master down."

"I'm really confused now," Gao Ma said with a sigh. "But I'll go. The young master must be half frozen, so I'd better go see how he is. I'll tell the master that Xiangzi said he has to leave right away. Tonight Xiangzi will bolt the gate and sleep at the Wangs' house. Tomorrow he'll go job hunting. Is that right?"

Xiangzi, feeling immense shame, nodded.

After Gao Ma left, he bolted the gate and went into his room. The shattered bank was still on the floor. He picked up one of the large shards and looked at it before throwing it back down. The bedding had not been moved. *Strange! How come? Is it possible that Detective Sun isn't a detective after all? No, that can't be. If Mr. Cao hadn't smelled danger, he wouldn't have abandoned his family to escape with his life. I don't understand, I just don't understand.* Without being aware of it, he sat back down on the bed but immediately jumped up in alarm. *I can't stay here! What if Sun comes back?* Thoughts were racing through his head. *I've let Mr. Cao down, but having Gao Ma tell him to get away makes me feel a little better.* In all good conscience, Xiangzi had done nothing to bring injury to anyone but himself. "My money's gone and I can no longer help Mr. Cao," he muttered under his breath as he gathered up his bedding.

After shouldering his bedroll and dousing the lamp, he went out the back door, then laid his bedroll on the ground and boosted himself up to look over the wall and call out softly, "Old Cheng, Old Cheng!" There was no reply from the Wangs' rickshaw man, so Xiangzi decided to climb over and look for him. He tossed his bedroll over; it landed without a sound on the snowy ground. After picking it up, he walked quietly to Old Cheng's room. There wasn't another sound in the compound, which meant that everyone was asleep, and he couldn't help thinking that being a thief didn't seem all that risky. Emboldened by that thought, he increased his pace. The hard-packed snow crunched beneath his feet. Outside Old Cheng's room he coughed. "Who's out there?" Old Cheng apparently hadn't been in bed long.

"It's me, Xiangzi. Open the door." Xiangzi said this with no trace of panic or urgency. The sound of Old Cheng's reply was like the comforting voice of an old friend.

Old Cheng lit a lamp and opened the door, a well-worn fur-lined jacket over his shoulders. "What is it, Xiangzi? It's the middle of the night."

Xiangzi stepped inside, dropped his bedroll onto the floor, and sat on it without a word.

In his thirties, Old Cheng had prominent muscles—even on his face—that were rock-solid. He and Xiangzi were not close, though they exchanged pleasantries from time to time. On days when Mrs. Wang and Mrs. Cao went shopping together, Xiangzi and Old Cheng went to a teahouse to rest while they waited. Xiangzi did not particularly admire Old Cheng, who ran fast but careened along and did a poor job of controlling the shafts. There was nothing wrong with him personally, but that flaw kept Xiangzi from respecting him.

On this night, however, Old Cheng was everything Xiangzi could want in a friend. He sat there, not knowing what to say but filled with gratitude and affection. Not long before, he had been standing on the Zhonghai Bridge, and now he was sitting in a friend's room. The abrupt change in circumstances erased all that had been in his mind and replaced it with warmth.

Old Cheng went back to bed and pointed to his leather jacket. "There are cigarettes in the pocket. You're welcome to them. They're Estates." Rickshaw men had taken to Country Estate cigarettes as soon as they'd come on the market.

Though he didn't smoke, Xiangzi knew that it would be un-friendly to refuse, so he took one and began to smoke.

"So," Old Cheng remarked. "Did you quit?"

"No." Xiangzi stayed seated on his bedroll. "There's been trouble. The family's left and I don't dare stay there alone."

"What kind of trouble?" Old Cheng sat up.

"I'm not sure, but it's so bad even Gao Ma left."

"You've left the place empty?"

"I locked the gate."

"Oh." Old Cheng mulled this over for a moment. "I'll go tell Mr. Wang. What do you say?" He threw his jacket over his shoulders.

"Hold off till tomorrow. I wouldn't know what to tell him." Being questioned by Mr. Wang worried Xiangzi.

What Xiangzi did not know was this: Mr. Cao gave lectures at a local university, where someone named Ruan Ming was enrolled as a student. Teacher and student had formed a cordial relationship, and Ruan Ming often visited him in his office. Mr. Cao was a socialist, but Ruan Ming entertained a far more radical ideology, though one well within the bounds of their friendship. Age and status, however, did create an occasional clash. As a teacher, Mr. Cao placed professional responsibilities above personal concerns, insisting that his students take their lessons seriously and not use a budding friendship as an excuse to slack off. In Ruan Ming's view, given the chaotic state of the world, young people with lofty ideals ought to be involved in revolutionary activities and not worry about schoolwork, at least for the moment. His relationship with Mr. Cao was based in part on their shared interests, but also on Ruan Ming's hope that the older man's affection for him would ensure his promotion to the next year no matter how bad his test scores were. People like him often betray a shameless side during chaotic times; history is rife with justifiable examples.

Then came the exam, at which Mr. Cao gave Ruan Ming a failing grade. But even if he'd passed him, Ruan Ming's overall grades were not good enough for him to continue. And yet he reserved most of his loathing for Mr. Cao, who he thought had disregarded the concept of "face," which in China is no less important than revolution itself. Ruan Ming had disparaged knowledge in his haste to accomplish other things, and over time this had become so ingrained in his behavior that, like lazy people everywhere, he felt he had to expend little effort in order to be admired and valued, especially since he considered himself to be a progressive. By giving him a failing grade, Mr. Cao was obviously not empathetic toward a young man with lofty ideals, so there was no longer any need to continue the friendship. By pretending to be on good terms with him most of the time, only to embarrass him in the exam, Mr. Cao had shown a sinister side. It was too late for Ruan Ming to improve his grades or to resist expulsion, so he decided to focus his wrath on Mr. Cao. Having failed at getting an education, he would take his teacher down with him. That would not only give him a chance to stir things up a bit, to flex his muscles, but also would let others know that Ruan Ming was not someone you wanted as an enemy. And if he could parlay this effort into membership in one of the new groups that had sprouted up, that would be better than passing the days with nothing to do.

Ruan Ming compiled a list of comments on politics and society from Mr. Cao's lectures and private conversations, and then reported to the Nationalist Party headquarters that Mr. Cao was espousing a radical ideology to all the young minds around him.

Mr. Cao had gotten wind of this but considered it laughable. He knew that his socialist tendencies lacked substance and that his fondness for traditional Chinese painting prevented him from taking forceful actions. How hilarious to be branded as a revolutionary leader! He saw no need to pay attention to such a ludicrous thought, though his students and colleagues warned him to be careful. A calm demeanor is no guarantee of personal safety.

The winter break provided an opportunity to weed out suspect individuals at the university; detectives busied themselves with investigations and arrests. When Mr. Cao sensed that he was being followed, his mood turned from jovial to solemn. He had to think. This would have been an ideal moment to make a name for himself; spending a few days in lockup was simpler and safer than setting off a bomb, and one counted for as much as the other. Time behind bars is capital for important people, but not for Mr. Cao. He refused to try to beat someone at his own game just to build what was at bottom a false reputation. In examining his own scruples, he hated himself for not having what it took to be a fighter, but those same scruples made it impossible to assume the role of a fighter in name only. So he went to see Mr. Zuo.

"If necessary," Mr. Zuo proposed, "you can move in here. They're not about to search my place." He had connections, which always counted for more than the law. "Move in and lie low for a few days to let them think we're afraid of them. We might have to grease a few palms to appease them, but once they've gotten enough face and their pockets are fatter, you can move back home."

Detective Sun knew that Mr. Cao was a frequent guest at the Zuos', which was where he'd go if he sensed he was in danger of being arrested. But Sun's people dared not provoke Mr. Zuo and were only out to frighten Mr. Cao. If they managed to chase him to Mr. Zuo's house, they could put the squeeze on him and gain considerable face in the process. Fleecing Xiangzi had not figured in their plans, but since he'd fallen into their hands so easily, that little bit of money was there for the taking.

Yes, Xiangzi had again been in the wrong place at the wrong time. Tough luck! Everyone could manage, everyone had a crack to slip through, everyone but Xiangzi. He was a rickshaw man, and for him there was no escape. A rickshaw man swallows coarse grains and sweats blood; he depletes his strength for next to nothing; and he stands on the lowest rung of the social ladder, open to assaults by all people, all laws, and all privations.

Xiangzi finished his cigarette but still did not know what to do. He was like a chicken in the hands of a chef, grateful for each new breath, and nothing more. He'd have been happy to talk with Old Cheng if only he'd had something to say, but there were no words to describe his feelings. He'd tasted all the bitterness life had to offer, and yet, like a mute, could say nothing. He'd bought a rickshaw and then lost it; he'd saved up some money and lost that. All his efforts had brought him nothing but torment and humiliation. He dared not provoke anyone, not even a mangy wild dog, and in the end he was so tormented, so humiliated, he could hardly breathe.

Since dwelling on the past would get him nowhere, he needed to think about tomorrow. He could not return to the Cao residence, so where could he go? "I'll spend the night here, how's that?" he said, sounding like a homeless dog that has found temporary shelter from the elements. But even with something so minor, he had to make sure he wasn't being a burden on anyone.

"Sure, stay here. Where else would you go on a snowy night like this? You can have the floor or you can squeeze in here with me, your choice."

The floor was fine with Xiangzi; he did not want to crowd his friend.

Old Cheng easily fell asleep but not Xiangzi, who tossed and turned, his thin mattress feeling like a block of ice, thanks to the cold air coming up off the floor; he pounded his calves to keep them from cramping. Icy wind that blew in through cracks in the door struck his head like needles. Even forcing his eyes shut and covering his head did not work. On top of that, Old Cheng's snores irritated him so much he felt like going over and punching him in the face. And it kept getting colder, until his throat began to itch. Now he was afraid he'd wake up Old Cheng if he coughed.

Unable to sleep, he was tempted to return to the Cao residence and have a look around. He no longer had a job and the place was empty, so why not go back and take a few things? They'd robbed him of the little money he'd worked so hard to save up, all because he was helping Mr. Cao, so why couldn't he steal something for himself as a sort of reimbursement? His eyes brightened at these thoughts, and the cold no longer bothered him. *Go on!* It was an easy way to get back his hard-earned money. *Go on!*

By then he was sitting up, but he quickly lay back down. His heart was racing, almost as if Old Cheng were watching him. *No, I can't become a thief, I can't! It was bad enough disregarding Mr. Cao's instructions and walking away. How could I even think of stealing from him? I won't do it—I'll starve to death before I become a thief!*

But what was to keep other people from stealing? If that fellow Sun went over and took what he wanted, who would know? He sat up again. A dog was barking in the distance. He lay back down, still unable to bring himself to go. If someone else broke in and stole something, that wouldn't be his fault—his conscience was clear, and he refused to sully his reputation no matter how poor he was.

Besides, Gao Ma knew he'd come to the Wang residence, so if something were stolen, he'd be blamed whether he was the culprit or not. Now, having decided not to steal, he was burdened by worries that someone else would break in. If something went missing during the night, he could not wash away the suspicion even if he jumped into the Yellow River. No longer did he feel cold; his palms were actually sweating. What now? Go back and have a look? He didn't have the nerve. He'd bought back his life once already and could not bear the thought of falling into another trap. So he'd stay where he was. But what if something were stolen?

Agonizing over what to do, he sat up again and brought his legs up until his chin was nearly touching his knees. His head drooped and his eyelids felt heavy; but he mustn't fall asleep, no matter how long the night ahead.

One idea after another came and went as he sat for the longest time, until his brain lit up. He reached out and nudged his friend. "Wake up, Old Cheng, wake up!"

"What is it?" Old Cheng could hardly open his eyes. "If you have to go, there's a bedpan under the bed."

"Wake up, I said, and light the lamp."

"Is it a thief?" Old Cheng sat up, still half asleep.

"Are you awake?"

"Yeah."

"Take a good look. This is my bedroll, these are my clothes, and this is the five yuan Mr. Cao gave me. That's all, isn't it?"

"That's all, so what?" Old Cheng yawned.

"Are you awake or aren't you? This is all I have. I haven't taken a single item from the Cao residence, have I?"

"No. People like us, who get room and board, can't have

sticky fingers. If we can handle the job, we do it, and if not, we quit. But we don't take any of our employers' things. Is that what you're getting at?"

"You got it!"

Old Cheng smiled. "There's no mistake. But aren't you cold?"

"I'm all right."

CHAPTER THIRTEEN

The sky seemed to lighten a bit earlier, thanks to the gleaming snow. The old year was coming to an end, and many families had begun raising chickens, whose crows and cackles were more numerous than before. The roosters' early morning crowing lent an aura of snowy abundance to the scene. But Xiangzi could not sleep. Sometime before daybreak he dozed off a time or two, in an uneasy daze, as if floating atop rolling waves. The night kept getting colder, until, finally, when the roosters crowed, he stopped trying to sleep. Not wanting to wake Old Cheng, he curled his legs and covered his mouth with the quilt to muffle his coughs, but he was unwilling to get up. He waited impatiently, sticking it out as best he could. Finally, dawn arrived, and the sounds of wagon wheels and drivers' shouts out on the streets broke the silence. He sat up. Cold as ever, he stood up, buttoned his jacket, and opened the door a crack to peek outside. The snow wasn't as thick as he'd imagined, which likely meant that no more had fallen during the night. A gray sky blurred everything in sight; there were even gray patches on the snowy ground. He saw indentations from the night before, dusted by new snow but clearly his footprints.

Both to keep busy and to erase all traces of his arrival, he found a short broom and, without a sound, stepped outside to cover his tracks. The wet snow made for heavy going—he had to bend over and press down hard as he swept. He cleared away the top layer, but damp snow clung to the ground like a layer of skin. He wound up sweeping the whole yard, straightening up to stretch twice, and piling the snow under a pair of young willow trees. The effort had him sweating and considerably warmed him, which made him feel better. He stomped his feet and released a long, steamy breath.

After walking back inside, Xiangzi put the broom away and decided to roll up his bedding. Old Cheng, who had just awakened, yawned grandly. Before even shutting his mouth, he said, "It must be getting late." The simple statement seemed to have hidden meanings. After rubbing his sleepy eyes, he took out a cigarette from the pocket of his coat and was wide awake after two deep puffs. "Don't go anywhere, Xiangzi. I'll get some water so we can make tea. I'm betting you had a bad night."

"I'll get it," Xiangzi offered. But the words were scarcely out of his mouth when the terror of the night before returned in a flash. His heart skipped a beat.

"No, I'll go. You're my guest." Old Cheng quickly dressed and, without buttoning up, threw his jacket over his shoulders and ran out, a cigarette dangling from his lips. "What? You've already swept the yard? You're really something! Now you have to stay for tea."

Xiangzi began to relax a bit.

Old Cheng returned with two bowls of sweet porridge and an armful of little buns shaped like horses' hooves and oily crisps. "I didn't make tea," he said. "We'll have this porridge instead.

Go ahead, eat up. If there isn't enough, we'll buy some more, and if we don't have the money, we'll put it on credit. People who work hard for a living need good food. Eat up."

The sun was out and their room, while still cold, had brightened up as the two men dug in, not talking as they happily slurped their porridge and finished off all the buns and crisps.

"Well?" Old Cheng said as he loosened a sesame seed from his teeth with a toothpick.

"I should be going." Xiangzi looked down at his bedroll.

"You know, I'm still not clear about what happened," Old Cheng said as he handed Xiangzi a cigarette. "Want to tell me?"

Xiangzi shook his head. But figuring he owed Old Cheng an explanation, he stammered a version of the night's events; it wasn't easy, but he managed somehow to get it all in.

With a look of near disbelief but keen interest, Old Cheng listened in silence. "As I see it," he said, "you have to go see Mr. Cao. You can't leave things as they are, and you can't give up the money. Didn't you say he told you not to stick around if things turned bad? Well, the detective nabbed you as soon as you stepped out of the cab, and whose fault is that? You weren't disloyal, you were just in the wrong place at the wrong time, and you had to save your own skin. If you ask me, you did nothing wrong. Go tell him exactly what happened. I'll bet he'll not only say it wasn't your fault, but, if you're lucky, he'll make up what you lost. Go on. Leave your bedroll here. The sooner you talk to him, the better. The days are short as it is. It's eight o'clock by the time the sun's up. So get going!"

Thoughts swirled in Xiangzi's head, but he still felt he'd somehow let Mr. Cao down. What Old Cheng said, however, made sense. How was he supposed to worry about the Cao family with a detective threatening him with a gun?

"Go on," Old Cheng urged. "I could tell you were confused last night, but who wouldn't be, after what happened to you? Do as I say and you'll be fine. I'm older than you, and I've seen and done more. Now, go on. See there, the sun's up."

Early morning sunlight reflected off the snow to light up the city. A blue sky over a ground covered in white, each bright in its own way, separated by a layer of gold that dazzled the eye. Xiangzi was about to leave when someone knocked at the door. Old Cheng went to see who it was. "Xiangzi," he shouted. "Someone's here to see you."

Wang Er, from the Zuo residence, was stamping his feet in the gateway, his nose running from the bitter cold. Xiangzi had no sooner stepped outside than Old Cheng told them both to come sit in his room.

"You see, I came by to check on the house," Wang said as he rubbed his hands. "But the place is all locked up, and I can't get in. You see, it's damned cold out there! You see, Mr. and Mrs. Cao left this morning for Tianjin, or maybe it was Shanghai, I'm not sure, so Mr. Zuo told me to check on the house. You see, it's mighty cold!"

Xiangzi felt like crying. He'd decided to take Old Cheng's advice and go see Mr. Cao, only to learn that Mr. Cao had just left. Momentarily confused, he managed to ask, "Did Mr. Cao say anything before he left?"

"No, you see, they were all up before the sun was out, no time for talking. The train, you see, was due to depart at 7:40. How do I get into their yard?" Wang Er was eager to be on his way.

"Over the wall." Xiangzi glanced at Old Cheng, as if turning Wang Er over to him. He picked up his bedroll.

"Where are you going?" Old Cheng asked.

"Harmony Shed—it's the only place I've got." That single comment said everything there was to know about his grief, his shame, and his despair. Surrender was the only thing left to him. All other roads were closed. Now he could only trudge through the white snow in search of the dark pagoda that was Huniu. Respectability, ambition, loyalty, and integrity had failed him. Why? Because he led a dog's life.

"Do what you have to do," Old Cheng said. "But Wang Er is your witness that you took nothing from the Cao residence. Go on. Anytime you're in the neighborhood, drop in. Maybe I'll have heard of a job for you. Don't worry about Wang Er. I'll help him get in. Is there any coal in the place?"

"Coal and kindling are in the backyard shed." Xiangzi picked up his bedroll.

By then the snow had lost much of its whiteness. Passing carts had made icy ruts in the streets, while dirt paths were a pitiful patchwork of black and white, thanks to passing horses. But none of this registered with Xiangzi, who hoisted his bedroll onto his shoulder and headed straight to Harmony Shed, not daring to stop, knowing that if he did he wouldn't have the courage to walk in. His cheeks were hot as he entered. He'd prepared what he wanted to say: "I'm back, so do what you want, it's all the same to me." But when they were face-to-face, the words spun through his mind over and over and never left his mouth. He wasn't up to it.

Huniu had just gotten up; her hair was mussed, her eyes puffy, and her swarthy face dotted with goose bumps, like a plucked chicken.

"Well, I see you're back!" There was fondness in her voice and a bright smile at the corners of her eyes.

"Rent me a rickshaw!" Xiangzi kept his head down. Unmelted snow covered the tips of his shoes.

"Go talk to the old man," she said softly, pointing to the east room with her chin.

Fourth Master Liu was drinking his morning tea in front of a brazier with flames that rose half a foot in the air. "So, you're still alive and kicking," he said, half in jest and half in anger. "Forgot about us, I see. But never mind. How long have you been away? How are things? Did you buy your rickshaw?"

Xiangzi shook his head as a pang stabbed into his heart. "I need a rickshaw, Fourth Master."

"Oh? Quit again, did you? All right, go pick one out." Fourth Master reached for an empty bowl. "But first, have some tea."

With the bowl in his hands, Xiangzi stood in front of the brazier and gulped down the tea. The scalding liquid and hot brazier made him sleepy. But when he laid down the bowl and turned to leave, Fourth Master stopped him.

"What's your hurry? You came at just the right time. The twenty-seventh is my birthday, and I'm going to put up a tent for a party. You can help out for a few days and go out with a rickshaw afterward. They"—Fourth Master pointed toward the yard—"aren't reliable. I won't let a bunch of lazy slobs get involved. No, I want you to help. Do what has to be done without me having to tell you. You can start by sweeping away the snow, and I'll treat you to a hot pot at lunchtime."

"Yes, Fourth Master." Xiangzi knew when he was beaten, so now it was all up to father and daughter; they could do with him what they wanted. He was resigned to his fate.

"Didn't I tell you?" Huniu said, coming in at the right moment. "Xiangzi's the one. The rest of them just don't match up."

Fourth Master smiled. Xiangzi's head drooped even lower.

"Come here, Xiangzi," Huniu called from outside. "Take this money and go buy a broom, a good one, bamboo. The yard has to be swept right away because the tent people are coming today." She led him into her room, where she counted out the money and said softly, "Show a little life! You want to get the old man on your side. That'll smooth the way for us."

Xiangzi neither spoke nor got angry. He'd given in completely, mind and body. He'd just get by one day at a time. If there was food, he'd eat; if there was liquor, he'd drink; and if there was work, he'd do it. By keeping busy, he'd get through each day, especially if he could learn from a donkey that turns a millstone—go round and round, oblivious of everything else.

He could not shake the feeling that he'd never again be happy. He swore off thinking, speaking, and losing his temper, and yet there was a heaviness in his chest that went away for a while when he was working but always returned when he had time on his hands—it was soft, but large; it had no definable taste, yet it choked him, like a sponge. He'd keep this suffocating something at bay by working himself half to death so he could fall into an exhausted sleep. His nights he'd give over to his dreams, his days to his arms and legs. He'd be like a working zombie: sweeping away snow, buying things, ordering kerosene lanterns, cleaning rickshaws, moving tables and chairs, eating the food Fourth Master supplied, and sleeping, all without knowing what was going on around him, or speaking, or even thinking, yet always dimly aware of the presence of that spongelike thing.

The yard was swept clean; snow on the roof slowly melted. The man putting up the tent shouted, "Climbing to the roof!" as he erected the framework. He had orders to raise a heated tent that covered the yard, with eaves, railings, and glass-inlaid doors on three sides. Inside were to be glass partitions and screens hung with painted scrolls, the wooden poles wrapped in red cloth, the main and side doors decorated with colorful streamers. The kitchen would be out back. Since this would be Fourth Master's sixty-ninth birthday—one of the celebratory nines—it had to be festive, and a proper tent was the essential first step. Winter days were short, so the tent man was only able to put up the framework, the railings, and the outer skin before darkness fell; the interior decorations and door streamers would have to wait till the next morning. After arguing with the man until he was red in the face, Fourth Master had Xiangzi go make sure that nothing would hold up delivery of the lanterns or the arrival of the cook. Little chance of that, but he was starting to worry. So Xiangzi went, and he'd no sooner returned than Fourth Master sent him to borrow several mahjong sets, so his guests could gamble to their hearts' content. Immediately upon his return, Xiangzi was sent to borrow a gramophone, since a birthday party called for loud music. His feet did not stop moving until eleven o'clock at night. For someone used to pulling a rickshaw, running errands without one was far more tiring. When he returned from his last errand of the day, he—even Xiangzi—could barely lift his feet.

"Good boy! You've done well. I'd gladly give up my last few years if I had a son like you. You've earned your rest. There'll be more to do tomorrow."

Huniu, who was in the room with them, winked at Xiangzi.

The tent man came the next morning to finish the job by hanging painted scrolls on the screens, depicting scenes from the *Three Kingdoms* tales: the three battles with Lü Bu, fighting at Changban Slope, the burning of enemy camps, and others. The stage figures with painted faces sat astride their chargers, swords and spears at the ready, and Old Man Liu was happy with what he saw. Men from the furniture shop were next to arrive. They set up eight tables and chairs, the cushions and covers embroidered with bright red flowers. A longevity shrine was erected in the ceremonial room, with a cloisonné incense burner, candlesticks, and four red rugs in front. When Fourth Master sent Xiangzi to buy apples, Huniu slipped him two yuan and told him to also buy longevity peaches and noodles. The dough peaches were to be carved with the Eight Immortals and would count as Xiangzi's gift. The apples arrived and were set out. Then came the longevity peaches and noodles, which were placed behind the apples. Each peach, painted red and displaying one of the Eight Immortals, was magnificent.

"These are from Xiangzi," Huniu bragged into her father's ear. "See how thoughtful he is!" Fourth Master smiled at Xiangzi.

The calligraphed Chinese word for *longevity*, which, by tradition, would be written by a friend and hung from the longevity altar, had not arrived, and Fourth Master, by nature impatient, was ready to explode. "I'm always the first to contribute to weddings and funerals, but now that it's my turn, I get left in the lurch. Well, fuck them!"

"People won't come till tomorrow, the twenty-sixth," Huniu said to calm him, "so take it easy."

"I want everything ready ahead of time. Doing things in fits and starts annoys me. Xiangzi, see that the carbide lamps are in place. If they're not here by four this afternoon, I'll skin those people alive!"

"Xiangzi," Huniu said to show her reliance on him, "go hurry them up." She made a point of telling him to do things since her father was around. Without a word in reply, he went off to do as he was told.

"I probably shouldn't say this, Father," Huniu said with a little pout, "but if you had a son, and he didn't take after me, he'd take after Xiangzi. Too bad I had to be born a girl. But what's done is done. Having him as a sort of foster son helps. See how he gets everything done without so much as passing gas."

Fourth Master's mind was elsewhere as he listened to his daughter. "Where's the gramophone?" he asked her. "Let's have some music!"

The music that emerged from the well-used gramophone they managed to borrow pierced eardrums like the screeching of a cat when you step on its tail. But Fourth Master Liu didn't care, so long as there was noise.

By that afternoon everything was up and ready, and now it was just a matter of waiting for the cook to arrive the next day. After an inspection tour of the festooned site, Fourth Master nodded his approval. That night he invited the proprietor of the Tianshun Coal Shop to keep the accounts. Proprietor Feng, a man from Shanxi Province who kept detailed and accurate accounts, came to take a look and had Xiangzi purchase two red account books and a large sheet of vermillion writing paper. He cut the paper into strips and wrote the character for longevity on each of them, then pasted them up everywhere. Fourth Master, impressed by the man's attention to detail, offered to invite two more friends to make a foursome for mahjong. Mr. Feng, who was well aware of Fourth Master Liu's skill at the game, said nothing.

Upset over the lost opportunity for a game, Fourth Master summoned some of his rickshaw men. "How about a game of mahjong?" he said. "Any of you got the guts?"

They were eager to play mahjong but not with Fourth Master, since they knew he'd once run a gambling den.

"How do sorry specimens like you manage to stay alive?" Fourth Master sputtered. "When I was your age, not even being broke stopped me. If I lost, so what!"

"Can we play for pennies?" one of them asked.

"Keep your damned pennies—I don't play with children," Fourth Master said as he drained his cup of tea and rubbed his bald head. "I wouldn't play now if you begged me. Tell everyone that guests will be arriving tomorrow afternoon, so bring your rickshaws in by four o'clock. I don't want you elbowing your way in and out while I have guests. You'll get free rent tomorrow, but be back by four. I'm giving you a free day, so I expect good wishes from all of you. Don't disappoint me. There'll be no rickshaws out the day after, my birthday. You'll get fed at half past eight in the morning. Six large platters, two seven-inch platters, four small plates, and a hot pot. That's the kind of treatment you get from me, so I want you to wear long gowns. Anyone who shows up in a short jacket gets booted out. After you've finished eating, make yourselves scarce, since I'll be entertaining friends and relatives with three extra-large bowls, six plates of cold meats, six stir-fried vegetable dishes, four large bowls, and a hot pot. I'm telling you this so you won't gape at the food. Friends and relatives are just that. I don't want anything from you men, but anyone with a heart can cough up ten cents, and I won't consider that an insult. If you prefer to kowtow to me three times instead of giving me money, I'll accept that. But you have to be on your best behavior, understand? If you want to eat here that night, come back after six. You can have whatever's left from the party. But don't come any earlier, got that?"

"What about those of us who work nights, Fourth Master?" a middle-aged man asked. "How are we supposed to be back by four?"

"You can come back after eleven. Just make sure you don't
elbow your way in and out while my guests are here. You pull
rickshaws, and that makes you different from me, understand?"

Speechless, they stood like statues, not knowing how to make
a graceful exit. Fourth Master's tirade had not gone down well.
A day's free rent was all well and good, but the free meal they'd
been promised was anything but, since they'd have to come up
with at least forty cents as a gift. Just as bad was the way he'd
spoken to them, as if celebrating his birthday reduced them to
rats forced to stay out of sight. To top it off, they would not be
allowed to go out at all on the twenty-seventh, one of the busy
year-end days. Fourth Master could absorb the loss of a day's
income, but forcing them to sit around and do nothing an entire day was too much. As they stood there, steaming inside but
not daring to complain, birthday wishes were the furthest thing
from their minds.

Huniu led Xiangzi outside.

The anger percolating in the other men now found an outlet. They turned and glared at Xiangzi's back. Over the past
couple of days, they had concluded that he'd become the Liu
family's running dog, always obsequious to father and daughter, working without complaint and bearing all sorts of grievances, just to be their serving boy. Xiangzi blithely continued
helping out as a way to lessen his own frustrations. He had
nothing to say to the other men at night, but that was not new.
Unaware of how he was suffering deep down, they assumed he
was Fourth Master Liu's puppet and would have nothing to do
with him. What really bothered them was the way Huniu
fawned all over him, and the fact that while they were kept out
of the birthday tent, Xiangzi was guaranteed all he wanted to
eat. They were all rickshaw men, so why the class distinction?

See? Miss Liu is taking Xiangzi outside. They followed him with their eyes, legs itching to move. Finally, somewhat awkwardly, they walked out the door, where they saw Miss Liu and Xiangzi having a conversation under one of the kerosene lamps. They nodded knowingly.

CHAPTER FOURTEEN

The Liu birthday celebration was a roaring success, and Fourth Master was beside himself with joy over all the people who had come to kowtow and wish him a long life. He was particularly pleased that so many old friends had come to congratulate him. Their attendance convinced him not only that the celebration was a success but that he had "made it." These old friends were shabbily dressed, while he was wearing a new fur-lined robe and short jacket. In professional terms, some of them had once been better off than he, but now, after twenty or thirty years, their fortunes were dwindling, and some were even having trouble making ends meet. He looked them over, then turned his gaze to the birthday tent, the longevity altar, scrolls depicting the battle at Changban Slope, the three great bowls of the feast, and the screens, and could not suppress the feeling that he was head and shoulders above any of them. Yes, he had made it. Even where gambling was concerned, he had prepared tables for mahjong, much more refined than common betting games.

That said, in the midst of the raucous celebration, a sense that not all was as it should be gnawed at him. Having gotten used to living alone, he'd assumed that his guests would be confined to shopkeepers and managers, plus some bachelor friends from the old days. He had not expected so many women to show up. Sure, Huniu was seeing to their needs, but he experienced deep feelings of loneliness. He had a daughter but no wife, and Huniu looked more like a man than a woman. If she'd been a man, by now she'd have been married with children, and even as an aging widower, he would not have felt so alone. Yes, he had everything he wanted, everything but a son, and as he got older, his hopes for ever having one lessened. The birthday celebration ought to have been filled with joy, but he was nearly in tears. No matter how much he'd accomplished, with no one to carry on the business, it was all for nothing.

For the first half of the day he was in high spirits, grandly accepting the birthday wishes of his guests, like the warrior who had wrested the grand vessel from the legendary great turtle. But his mood turned sour by that afternoon, as the sight of children hand in hand with women who had come as guests filled him with envy, jealousy even; he would not have felt comfortable getting close to the children. Naturally, he needed to keep a lid on his temper in front of his guests, for as a prominent member of society, he must not disgrace himself; he began to wish that the day, and his unhappiness, would end quickly.

And that was not the only upsetting feature of the afternoon: that morning, while the rickshaw men were enjoying their meal, Xiangzi had nearly been in a fight.

The meal was served to the reluctant rickshaw men at eight o'clock. Though they had been forgiven their rental fee the day before, none had come to the table that morning empty-handed, whether it was ten cents or forty, all destined to fill the celebrant's pockets. On any other day, they were workingmen, while Fourth Master Liu was the shopkeeper; but today they considered themselves to be guests who deserved to be treated better. Worse yet, after they'd eaten, they were to leave the premises and not take their rickshaws out the whole day. At the busy year's end, no less!

Xiangzi knew he would not be vacating the premises with the others, but he chose to eat with them anyway, both to get an early start on the work ahead and to show a bit of solidarity. But he had no sooner sat down than they took their resentment of Fourth Master out on him. "Say," one of them said, "you're an honored guest, what are you doing eating with us?" Xiangzi responded with a foolish grin, missing what was hidden behind the words. Several days of not speaking with anyone had dulled his mind a bit.

Since the men dared not flare up at Fourth Master, their only recourse was to eat as much of his food as possible. There would be no second helpings, but the birthday liquor flowed freely and would serve to quell their discontent. Some drank in silence and some played drinking games; at least the old man couldn't stop them from doing that. Not wanting to set himself apart, Xiangzi drank two cups of the hard liquor. Meanwhile, as bloodshot eyes appeared on the other men's faces, their tongues loosened. "Xiangzi," one of them said, "Camel, this is a sweet job you've got. Food and drink for a whole day just for taking care of the old man and his daughter. You won't be taking a rickshaw out after this—you can be someone's personal attendant." He knew there was more to this comment but wasn't sure what that was. On his first day back at Harmony Shed, he'd told himself to play down his virile approach to the job and leave everything to fate. Let them say what they liked, he'd let it pass. "Our Xiangzi is taking a different path from us. We're outside sweating for a living, but he's got an inside job." That got a laugh out of them, and Xiangzi was sure they were baiting him. But after all he'd suffered, he could easily take a few snide comments. He held his tongue. A man at the next table saw a chance to join in on the fun. "Xiangzi," he said, "one of these days you'll be the boss. I hope you won't forget your pals." Still no reaction. "Say something, Camel!" a man at his table said.

Xiangzi blushed. "How could I ever be a boss?" he said softly.

"Of course you can. Before you know it, cymbals will clash and drums will be thumped!"

Xiangzi was confused. He did not know what they meant by clashing cymbals and thumping drums, but instinct told him it referred to his relationship with Huniu. An embarrassed redness in the face became the white of indignation, as all the grievances he'd suffered raced through his mind and choked his heart. He could no longer quietly stand by, as he'd done for days; he was like water about to burst through a breach in a dam. One of the other men pointed at him and said, "Xiangzi, I tell you, you're like the mute who knows how much he's eaten but won't say. Aren't you, Xiangzi? Come on, tell us."

Xiangzi jumped to his feet, his face deathly pale, and said, "Step outside and say that. I dare you!"

That stopped them cold. They'd been nipping at him, trying to provoke him, but no one wanted a fight.

The silence was a forest where birds go still when they spy a hawk. As he stood there, taller than the others, Xiangzi sensed his isolation, but now that his anger was up, he believed he could handle them all at the same time, if necessary. "Any takers?" he challenged.

"Come on, Xiangzi," they said as one, backing down. "We were just having some fun."

"Sit down, Xiangzi," said Fourth Master, who happened

upon the scene. "As for the rest of you, stop picking on him just because he's a hard worker. Don't get me mad or I'll kick the bunch of you out. Now eat up!"

Xiangzi left the table as the other men picked up their bowls and warily eyed Fourth Master. Munching sounds quickly filled the air; the danger had passed for the birds, whose songs rose again.

Xiangzi crouched down by the gate waiting for someone to come out. If he heard one more snide remark, he would let his fists respond.

He had lost everything, so what the hell!

But the men avoided him as they came out in twos and threes. No fight had materialized, but Xiangzi had vented some of his anger. On second thought, however, he knew that his actions had offended them. Lacking close friends in whom he might confide under normal circumstances, what was he doing making even more enemies? Regret set in as the meal he'd just eaten lay uncomfortably sideways in his stomach. He stood up. To hell with them, he thought. Men who get into fights almost daily and are always one step away from starvation enjoy life, so what is so great about proper behavior anyway? He was beginning to chart a new course for himself, one in direct opposition to that of the old Xiangzi. From now on, he'd start making friends, taking advantage of people whenever he could, drink tea other people paid for, smoke their cigarettes, borrow money with no intention of paying it back, stop making way for cars, piss wherever he wanted, wrangle with the police and not worry if he had to spend a couple of nights in jail. No question about it, that kind of rickshaw man enjoyed life more than he did. All right: since being conscientious, respectable, and ambitious was a waste of time, living like a no-account rascal was not a bad option. Not bad? Hell, it was damn near heroic. Fearing neither heaven nor earth, he'd no longer bow down or suffer in silence. He owed that to himself. Goodness turns a man bad.

Too bad he hadn't gotten into a fight after all. But there was plenty of time for that.

By putting together all he'd seen and heard, Fourth Master knew pretty much what was going on. No one could throw sand in his eyes. Huniu had played the dutiful daughter the past few days. Why? Because Xiangzi was back! Always following him around with her eyes, a sight that made Fourth Master more miserable than ever. Without a son of his own, he was left with no chance of forging a family, and if she ran off with a man, his life's work would be wasted. There was nothing wrong with Xiangzi as a man, but he fell short of what a son or a son-in-law ought to be—a stinking rickshaw man! After struggling all his life, fighting when he had to, and enduring torture, he'd be damned if he was going to let a country yokel get away with his daughter and everything he owned as he neared the end of his life. It might happen but not because of him, someone who, even as a boy, could blow a hole in the ground just by farting.

More people came to offer their congratulations at three or four in the afternoon, but by then he had lost his taste for such niceties. The more they complimented him on his health and good fortune, the less it meant to him.

Most of the guests had left for home by the time the lamps were lit, leaving only a dozen or so close friends who lived nearby. A mahjong table was set up. The old fellow gazed out at the empty tent, painted a soft green by the carbide lamps, and at the tables, now missing their tablecloths, and felt utterly desolate, imagining that this is what his funeral would be like: the tent would become a place of mourning, but there would be no dutiful sons or grandsons in mourning attire kneeling before his coffin, nothing but a few casual acquaintances playing mahjong through the night. He felt like sending the few stragglers on their way as a display of his authority while there was still breath in his body. But he didn't have the heart to take his unhappiness out on friends. So he decided to vent his anger on his daughter, since she was beginning to annoy him. Xiangzi, who was sitting in the tent, struck him as repugnant, his scar looking like a chunk of jade in the lamplight. What a disagreeable couple they made!

On this day, Huniu, who had always been coarse and bad-mannered, savored the role of hostess, in her fine clothes, which earned her the approval of their guests and impressed Xiangzi. She had enjoyed herself all morning, but as the afternoon wore on, exhaustion put her in a foul mood. By that evening, her patience depleted, she could only scowl.

Soon after seven o'clock, Fourth Master could barely keep his eyes open, but he refused to give in to age and go to bed. When his guests invited him to join them in a game of mahjong, he declined, though, insisting that a lack of stamina had nothing to do with it. No, he said, dice games and pai gow were more to his liking, and since his friends did not want to switch, he sat to the side and watched, treating himself to a few more cups of liquor to keep from falling asleep. Over and over he complained that he hadn't gotten enough to eat and that the cook had been over-paid, considering the poor quality of the food. From there he went on to fault everything that had pleased him that morning: the tent, the furnishings, the cook, none of it worth what it had cost him. He had been taken advantage of, cheated from start to finish.

By then, Mr. Feng the accountant had tallied up the gifts: twenty-five birthday scrolls, three offerings of longevity peaches and noodles, a crock of longevity wine, two pairs of longevity candles, and roughly twenty yuan in gift money. Many had contributed, but most for no more than forty cents or ten silver pennies.

The news made Fourth Master's blood boil. If he'd known this beforehand, he'd have settled for some fried noodles with greens. The guests had made a fool of him by coughing up ten cents for a meal with three huge bowlfuls of food. He'd never do this again, no more outrageous outlays! Naturally, they'd brought their friends and relatives along for a free meal. A bunch of baboons and bastards had made a fool of a sixty-nine-year-old man who should have known better. Seething in a slow boil, he could kick himself for the very things that had pleased him that morning, and he expressed his feelings with a string of outmoded street epithets.

Since not everyone had left, Huniu decided to restrain her father to spare the stragglers' feelings. But they were too caught up in their game of mahjong to note the old man's ranting, so she kept quiet. Let him rant. It'll soon pass, since they're ignoring him.

She had not expected him to turn on her. Now, that was going too far! If this was the thanks she got for running around getting things ready for his celebration, she wouldn't stand for it. He had no right to be unreasonable, whether he was sixty-nine or seventy-nine . . . or eighty-nine or ninety-nine . . .

"You're the one who wanted to spend all that money, so what's this got to do with me!" she fired back.

Her counterattack breathed life into the old man. "I'll tell you what it's got to do with you! Everything! Do you think I'm blind to what's been going on?"

"And what is that? After knocking myself out all day, I'm not going to put up with your accusations! Go ahead, tell me, what exactly did you see?" She, too, had gotten her second wind and put her sharp tongue to work.

"You've got envy written all over you. What did I see? I saw through you a long time ago."

"What do I have to be envious about?" She shook her head. "Tell me, what did you see?"

"I saw that—what else?" Fourth Master pointed to the tent, where Xiangzi was sweeping the floor.

"Him?" Huniu's heart lurched. The old man's keen eyes had caught her by surprise. "What about him?"

"Don't play dumb. You know exactly what I mean." He stood up. "I'll give it to you straight—it's him or me. I'm your father, and I've got the right to make you choose."

Things had come to a head much sooner than she'd expected. The old man had seen through her plans before she'd reached the halfway point. So now what? Streaked with powder, her face, flushed a dark red under the lamplight, looked like boiled pig's liver, blotchy and ugly. Weary and irritable, she didn't know how to deal with this. She was confused and upset, but couldn't throw up her hands in defeat. She had to come up with something, and quick. A bad idea was better than no idea at all. She'd never bowed down to anyone before and was not about to start now. Might as well get everything out into the open and let the chips fall where they may.

"It looks like we'd better have it out today. Even if you're right, what are you going to do about it? I'm all ears. You brought this on yourself, so don't accuse me of baiting you!"

The mahjong players must have heard the argument, but to keep from being distracted from their game, they drowned out the heated words by smacking the titles loudly on the table and shouting each move:

"Red!"

"*Smack!*"

Xiangzi, who heard every word, kept his head down as he swept the floor. He knew what he'd do if worse came to worst— he'd use his fists!

"Getting me angry is part of your plan," Fourth Master said, his eyes as round as saucers. "You think I'll keel over in a fit of rage and you can get yourself a man. Well, not so fast. I've got a few years left in me."

"Don't change the subject. Tell me what you're going to do." Huniu's heart was pounding, but there was defiance in her voice.

"What am I going to do? I already told you. It's him or me. I'm not going to let a stinking rickshaw man get what he wants that easily."

Xiangzi threw down his broom, straightened up, and glared at Fourth Master. "Are you talking about me?"

Fourth Master bent over, laughing. "Ha-ha, it seems we have a rebel in our midst. Who else would I be talking about? Now get the hell out of here. I thought you were all right and treated you well, and this is the thanks I get. Have you forgotten who I am? If so, you should have stopped to find out. I want you out of my sight, and I don't ever want to see your face around here again! You were mistaken if you thought you could come here and do whatever you damn well pleased!"

The old man's shouts brought some of the rickshaw men out to see what was going on, while the mahjong players went on with their game, since Fourth Master yelling at one of his employees was nothing new.

There was much that Xiangzi wanted to say, but his mouth was not up to the task. So he stood there silently, stretching his neck and swallowing noisily.

"Get of my sight, I said, get out now! You and your plan to benefit at my expense! I knew all the tricks before you were even born!" While he appeared to be lashing into Xiangzi, the real target of his wrath was his hateful daughter. But even in his anger he could not deny that Xiangzi was a decent and honest young man.

"All right, I'll leave!" There was nothing more Xiangzi could say, so best to get out now; he was sure to lose a verbal sparring match with either of them.

The other rickshaw men had been standing around watching the fun, though when they recalled what they'd been put through that morning, they were happy to see Xiangzi on the receiving end of Fourth Master's tirade. But then they heard him send Xiangzi on his way, and their sympathies returned to their brother, who had worked like a slave for days, only to have the old ingrate turn on him, to tear down the bridge after the river was crossed. That wasn't fair. "What's going on, Xiangzi?" one of them asked. Xiangzi just shook his head.

"Hold on, Xiangzi, don't go yet." Huniu saw what she had to do, now that her plan had fallen apart. If she didn't act fast and keep him from leaving, she could lose the hen *and* the egg. "We're like a pair of grasshoppers tied together by a string, so neither of us can get away. Don't do anything till I work this out." She turned to her father. "You might as well know that I'm carrying Xiangzi's child, and I go where he goes. Now, are you going to let me marry him or would you rather chase us both off? It's up to you."

Things had come to a head much too fast for Huniu, forcing her to show her hand before she was ready, and this new wrinkle obviously took Fourth Master by surprise. Still, he mustn't give in, especially in front of all those people, no matter how things stood. "How could you have the insolence to say what you just said? My face burns with shame, shame for you!" Slapping his own face, he spat, "You haven't an ounce of shame!"

The mahjong players' hands froze. Something was seriously wrong, but they did not know what and kept their mouths shut. Those who didn't stand up sat there staring dumbly at their game pieces.

Huniu's secret was out, and she was glad. "I don't have any shame? Don't get me started on what you've been up to. Your shit stinks worse than mine! This is my first mistake, and it's your fault. A man takes a wife and a woman finds a husband. Someone who's lived sixty-nine years ought to know that. I'm not saying this for their benefit," she said, pointing to the men looking on, "but now everything's out in the open, the way it should be. You've got a tent right there, so make use of it."

"Me?" Fourth Master's face changed from an embarrassed red to an enraged white. He hadn't been a widower all these years for nothing. "I'll burn the damned thing down before I'll use it for you!"

"Fine!" Huniu's lips were trembling, her voice nearly a shriek. "I'll pack up and leave, but first, how much are you going to give me?"

"The money's mine, and nobody's telling me who to give it to." Hearing his daughter say she was leaving saddened Fourth Master, but this was no time to back down, so he hardened his heart.

"Yours? Without me around to help you all these years, you'd have spent it all on whores. Let's be fair." Her eyes sought out Xiangzi. "Say something."

Xiangzi stood there, tall and straight, but there was nothing he could say.

CHAPTER FIFTEEN

Since Xiangzi was not capable of hitting an old man or a woman, his strength lacked an outlet. Trying to turn this to his advantage was an option, but that wasn't like him. He could, of course, simply run out on Huniu, but she had stood up to her father and was willing to run off with him; while there was no way of knowing what was in her heart, to all appearances she was ready to sacrifice herself for him, which forced him into the position of putting up a bold front in the presence of all those people. He had nothing to say, so the least he could do to show that he was a man was to stay put and wait for things to sort themselves out.

Father and daughter, having run out of insults, could only glare back and forth while Xiangzi stood mute to one side. That held true for his brothers as well, no matter whose side they were on. An awkward silence also engulfed the mahjong players. Still, they felt obliged to urge both parties to resolve their differences by calmly talking things out. Trite though their comments were, what else could they do? They were in no position to solve anything, and they knew it. But when it became clear that neither party would give ground, they made themselves scarce at the first opportunity. As the saying goes, "An upright official steers clear of domestic disputes."

Huniu detained Mr. Feng of the Tianshun Coal Shop before he could slip away. "Mr. Feng, you have room in your place, don't you? How about letting Xiangzi stay there for a couple of days? We'll put our affairs together quickly so he won't be on your hands long. Xiangzi, you go with Mr. Feng. I'll come by tomorrow so we can make plans. But I'm telling you, the only way I'll leave this shop is in a sedan chair. He's in your hands, Mr. Feng. I'll come get him tomorrow."

Mr. Feng gulped, wary of taking on the responsibility, but Xiangzi, in a hurry to get out of there, blurted out, "I'm not running away!"

With a final glare at her father, Huniu turned and went into her room, where she bolted the door from the inside and began to sob.

Mr. Feng and the other stragglers tried to get Fourth Master to go to his room, but he asked them to stick around for a few more drinks in an attempt to appear sociable. "Don't you gentlemen worry. From now on, she'll go her way and I'll go mine. There won't be any more quarreling. Once she's gone, I'll pretend I never had a daughter. I've been a man of the world all my life, only to be shamed by the likes of her. Twenty years ago I'd have torn them both apart. But now she's on her own, and I'll be damned if she'll get a cent from me. Not a cent! We'll see how she gets by then. A taste of that kind of life will tell her who's best, her papa or that no-good lover of hers. Stick around for a few more rounds."

But they made their excuses and left as quickly as possible.

Xiangzi went to the Tianshun Coal Shop.

From there, events moved quickly. Huniu rented two small

rooms with a southern exposure in a large, shared-use tenement compound in Mao Clan Bay and hired a man to paper the walls in white, then asked Mr. Feng to write several happiness characters, which she hung here and there. The rooms now in readiness, she went out to arrange for a bridal sedan chair, specifying that she wanted it decorated with stars and accompanied by sixteen musicians, but no gold lanterns or formal escort. That done, she made a red satin wedding dress, rushing to finish to avoid the taboo against doing needlework between the first and fifth days of the New Year holiday. The wedding would take place on the sixth, an auspicious day with no taboo against leaving home. All this she managed on her own, before telling Xiangzi to go out and buy a set of new clothes. "This is a once-in-a-lifetime event," she said.

Xiangzi had only five yuan to his name.

"What?" she remarked, staring at him. "What happened to the thirty yuan I gave you?"

Incapable of making up a story, Xiangzi told her all that had happened at the Cao home, and she stood there blinking, not sure if she should believe him or not. "All right, then," she said. "I don't have time to argue, so we'll let our conscience be our guide. Here's fifteen yuan. If you're not dressed like a proper bridegroom on our wedding day, look out!"

On the sixth day of the New Year, Huniu climbed into a bridal sedan chair and left without a word to her father, no siblings to see her on her way and no good wishes from friends and family; all that accompanied her were drumbeats and the clang of cymbals on streets still festive from the New Year's celebrations. She made her way steadily past Xi'an Gate and Xisi Arch, arousing the envy and stirring the emotions of people in their new clothes, especially clerks in shops along the way.

Xiangzi, his face flushed, was waiting to greet her in a new outfit bought in the Tianqiao district; it included a little satin cap that cost thirty cents. He looked like a man who had forgotten who he was, dumbly taking in what was going on around him, having lost all self-recognition. From the coal shop room, he was abruptly plunged into a bridal chamber freshly papered in white and wasn't sure why. The past was like a coal yard, littered with heaps of black, but now, with a blank look on his face, he was standing in a room so white it nearly blinded him, with blood-red happiness characters on the walls. It was, he felt, mocking him—white, shadowy, oppressive. The rooms were furnished with Huniu's old tables, chairs, and bed. A stove and chopping board were new, and a colorful feather duster stood in the corner. He'd seen the furniture before but not the stove, the cutting board, or the feather duster. The mixture of old and new got him thinking about the past and fretting over the future. At the mercy of others in everything, he was like something old *and* something new, a strange decorative ornament that he himself did not recognize. He could neither cry nor laugh as he lumbered around the warm little room like a caged, fleet-footed rabbit, gazing longingly through the bars and surveying its cramped surroundings, unable to escape. Huniu, in her red dress and heavily rouged and powdered, followed him with her eyes. He didn't dare look at her. She, too. was a strange object, old and yet new. She was a girl, and she was also a woman; she was female, but she looked male; human yet a bit like a wild beast, a beast in a red dress that already had him in its grasp and was getting ready to dispose of him. Anyone could make short work of him, but this beast was especially savage and never let him out of its sight, staring at him, laughing at him, perfectly capable of getting him in a bear hug and sucking out every ounce of his strength. Hopelessly trapped, he took off his cap and stared at the red button on top until his eyes glazed over. When he looked away, the walls were covered with red dots, circling and jumping. The largest of them, and the reddest, right in the center, was Huniu, a revolting grin on her face.

On their wedding night Xiangzi learned that Huniu was not pregnant after all. Like explaining a magic trick, she said, "Would you have gone along if not for this little deception? I don't think so. I stuffed a pillow in my pants." She laughed till she cried. "What a dummy you are! I've done you no injury, so I don't want to hear a word from you. Who are you, anyway? And who am I? I fought with my father to be with you, and you should be thanking your lucky stars!"

Xiangzi went out early the next morning. Most but not all of the shops were open. New Year's scrolls still decorated the doors, but the strings of yellow paper money had been blown away by the wind. Rickshaws were plentiful on otherwise quiet streets, the men more spirited than usual in their new shoes, at least most of them; red paper streamers adorned the backs of their rickshaws. Xiangzi envied these men, with their New Year's spirit, while he had spent the past few days bottled up. They were content with their lot; he had no job to go to and could only stand idly by, which was unlike him. Tomorrow, he was thinking, he'd have a talk with Huniu—his wife. From now on he would have to beg for food from that wife—and what a wife she was. His physique, his strength, all going to waste—useless. His first job was to take care of his wife, that fanged thing in a red dress, that blood-sucking beast. No longer could he lay claim to being a man; he was just a piece of meat. He'd ceased to exist, except to struggle in her teeth, like a mouse caught in a cat's mouth. No, he wouldn't talk things over with her; he'd find a way to escape; as soon as he had a plan, he'd leave without a word. He owed nothing to a crone who would trick him with a pillow. He felt terrible. How he longed to tear his new clothes to shreds and then jump into a pool of clear water to wash away the filth that clung to his body, the unspeakable grime that sickened him. He wanted nothing more than to never see her again!

But where would he go? He had no idea. When he was pulling a rickshaw, his legs went where his passenger told him. Now his legs were free to take him wherever they wanted, but his mind was a blank. At the Xisi Arch he headed south, past Xuanwu Gate. The road ahead was straight, and his mind would entertain no twists or turns. He continued heading south, through the city gate, and when he spotted a public bathhouse, he decided he needed a bath.

After stripping naked, he examined his body and was ashamed. So he went down into the numbingly hot water, shut his eyes, and felt the filth seep out through the pores of his tingling skin. His mind a blank, he could not bring himself to touch his body. Sweat beaded his forehead. Not until his breathing quickened did he lazily drag himself out of the water; by then his body was red as a newborn baby. Unwilling to walk around like that, he wrapped a towel around his waist, but even then he felt unsightly and unclean, despite the drops of sweat raining to the floor. There was, he felt, a stain on him that could not be washed away. In the eyes of Fourth Master, in the eyes of everyone who knew him, he would always be known as a womanizer.

He dressed quickly, before he'd stopped sweating, and ran out, afraid to let anyone see his naked body. A cool breeze greeted him outside and had a relaxing effect. The atmosphere on the streets was even more festive than when he'd gone into the public bath; people's faces had brightened under a cloudless sky. But Xiangzi's mind was as conflicted as ever, and he didn't know where to go next. South first, then east, and south again, he headed for Tianqiao, where, in the days after New Year's, shop clerks congregated at nine in the morning after breakfast, since that was where peddlers of everything imaginable had set up stalls and entertainers put on shows. The place was swarming with people by the time he arrived, attracted by the clamor of drums and cymbals; but he was in no mood to take in the fun. He had forgotten how to laugh.

Comic dialogue performers, dancing bears, magicians, story-tellers, balladeers, drumbeat singers, and acrobats had once brought him pleasure, making him laugh out loud. Tianqiao was half the reason he could not stand the idea of leaving Beiping. Seeing the mats spread on the ground and the crowds forming around them reminded him of so many happy times. But not now. Since he could not share in the laughter, he had no desire to elbow his way into the crush of people. Instead, he needed a quiet spot, away from the crowds, but he couldn't tear himself away. No, he could not leave this bustling, happy place, not Tianqiao and certainly not Beiping. Go away? All roads were closed to him. So he would have to return to talk things out with her—with *her*. He couldn't leave, but neither could he remain idle. He had to stop and think, just as everyone must do when things appear hopeless. After suffering every wrong imag-inable, why should this one be special? He could not change the past, so why not just carry on?

He stood and listened to the clamor of voices and to the drumbeats and crashing cymbals, and as he watched the people and horse-drawn carts stream past, he was reminded once more of those two small rooms. Suddenly, there were no more sounds to be heard, no more people to be seen, nothing but those two white, toasty rooms, with their red happiness scrolls, standing squarely in front of him. He'd only slept there one night, but they were already so familiar, so intimate, that he realized he could not easily rid himself of the red-jacketed woman. In Tianqiao he had nothing and was nobody, but in those two rooms he had everything. There was no way around it—he had to go back. That was where his future lay. Shame, timidity, and sorrow were useless. If he was going to survive, he had to find a place where things were possible.

He went straight home, walking in the door around eleven o'clock. Huniu was preparing a lunch of steamed buns, cabbage with meatballs, and platters with jellied pork skin and pickled turnips. Everything was on the table except the cabbage, which still simmered on the stove and gave off a tempting aroma. She had changed out of her red jacket and was wearing ordinary padded trousers and jacket. But a red velvet flower with a little gilded paper ingot was pinned to her hair. To Xiangzi she seemed more like a woman who had been married for years than a newlywed—efficient, experienced, and at least somewhat self-satisfied. Though she may not have looked like a bride, there was something new in the air: the food on the table, the way the room was arranged, the sweet-smelling air, and the warmth—these were all new to him, and whatever else might be said, he had a home. There was something endearing about a home, and now he did not know what to do.

"Where did you go?" she asked as she scooped up the cabbage.

"I went for a bath." He took off his robe.

"I see. Next time tell me where you're going. Don't walk out with just a wave of your hand."

He didn't respond.

"What's wrong, forget how to talk? I can teach you, you know."

He merely grunted. What else could he do? He knew he had a shrew for a wife, but one who could cook and clean house, who could yell at him one minute and help him out the next, and that made him uncomfortable. He picked up a steamed bun and ate it. This was better food than he was used to, and piping hot. And yet something was missing—it didn't bring as much pleasure as the food he wolfed down most of the time, and it didn't raise a sweat.

When lunch was finished, he lay down on the heated bed, pillowed his head in his hands, and stared at the ceiling.

"Hey, come here and help me wash up," she called from the outer room. "I'm not your housemaid, you know!"

He sat up lazily and looked her way as he went to help with the dishes. Normally ready to help with almost anything, this time he worked with feelings of resentment. Back at the rickshaw shed he'd given her a hand plenty of times, but all he felt now was disgust. He had never hated anyone as much as he hated her. But he couldn't say why that was. He kept his anger bottled up inside, knowing he couldn't break it off with her and that there was no point in arguing. As he paced the floor of the two rooms, life seemed to be one endless grievance.

After she put the dishes away, she took a look around and sighed. "Well," she said with a smile, "what do you say?"

"What do you mean?" Xiangzi was crouched down by the stove, warming his hands. They weren't really that cold, but that was one way to keep them busy. The two rooms really did seem like a home, but he didn't quite know where to put his arms and legs.

"Take me out for some fun. How about White Cloud Monastery? No, too late for that. Let's just go out for a stroll." She wanted to get as much enjoyment out of this new marriage as possible. The wedding itself hadn't been anything to brag about, but the freedom to do as she pleased felt good, so why not have a grand time with her new husband, at least for a few days? In her father's home she'd always had food to eat, clothes to wear, and money to spend, but she'd lacked the companionship of a man; now she looked forward to strolling the city's streets and temple fairs with Xiangzi at her side.

Xiangzi said no. In the first place, he considered walking in public with one's wife shameful. Second, the only thing you could do with a wife like this was keep her hidden at home. This was nothing to be proud of, but the less she was in the public eye the better. To top it off, he was sure to meet acquaintances out there, since there wasn't a rickshaw man anywhere in West City who didn't know all about Huniu and Xiangzi. The last thing he wanted was for people to whisper behind his back.

"Let's talk things over, all right?" He remained crouching by the stove.

"What's there to talk about?" She walked up to him.

Xiangzi rested his hands on his knees and stared at the flames. After a long silence he managed to say, "I can't sit around with nothing to do."

"You live to suffer!" She laughed. "Your hands itch if you can't pull a rickshaw for one day, isn't that right? Look at my father. After he was too old to keep living only for pleasure, he opened a rickshaw shop. He doesn't have to pull a rickshaw, doesn't have to work at all. He gets by on his wits alone. You could learn a thing or two from him. What's so great about pulling a rickshaw anyway? We can continue this conversation after we've enjoyed a bit of life. Nothing has to be decided immediately. What's the rush? I'm not going to argue with you over the next few days, so please don't pick a fight."

"I want to talk things over first." Xiangzi was not going to back down. Since he could not pack up and leave, he had to find something to do, and that meant taking a firm stand. He did not want to keep swinging back and forth, getting nowhere.

"All right," she said as she moved a stool up next to the stove, "let's hear what you have to say."

"How much money do you have?"

"I knew it. That's exactly what I expected to hear. You married me for my money."

Xiangzi felt like he was choking. He swallowed hard. Old Man Liu and all the men at Harmony Shed thought he was money-hungry and that he'd taken up with Huniu only for what he could get. And now she was saying the same thing! After losing his rickshaw and all his money, he wound up subjugated by what little money she had. Even the food he ate was hers to dispense. He could hardly keep from grabbing her around the neck and throttling her! Choke her till he saw the whites of her eyes. Then, once she was good and dead, he'd slit his own throat. They both deserved to die. He was no more human than she, and he deserved to die, too. What right did they have to go on living?

Xiangzi stood up to go out, regretting having come home.

Huniu softened her attitude once she saw the look on his face. "All right, I'll tell you. I started out with about five hundred yuan. The sedan chair, three months' rent, the papering, the clothes, and what I gave you, altogether nearly a hundred, which leaves four hundred. I tell you, there's nothing to worry about, so let's enjoy ourselves while we can. You've been sweating away in front of a rickshaw for years, and you deserve to have a good time for a change. And me? I've been a spinster all this time, and I'm ready for some fun. We'll keep at it till the money's gone, then go to the old man and get some more. I'd never have left home if not for the fight we got into that day, but I'm not mad anymore, and he is, after all, my father. I'm all he's got, and he's always liked you, so we throw ourselves at his feet and apologize, and he'll be in a forgiving mood. It's foolproof! He's rich, and we stand to inherit his money. There's nothing unreasonable or improper about that. It's better than being a slave for somebody else. You go over in a few days. Now, he might refuse to see you, so you return a second time. That will give him enough face to come around sooner or later. Then I'll go and sweet-talk him, and I wouldn't be surprised if he asked us to move back. When that happens, we can throw out our chests and not have to worry about anyone looking crooked at us. But if we stay here and try to stick it out alone, we'll always be on people's blacklist. Am I right or aren't I?"

This was all new to Xiangzi. Since the day Huniu had come to the Cao house looking for him, his only thought had been that, after they were married, he'd get her to buy him a rickshaw and he'd be back on the street. Spending his wife's money was not honorable, but since their relationship was the kind he couldn't talk about, what did it matter? That she might have other ideas never occurred to him. He could hold his nose and do as she said, but that was not in his nature. As he mulled over what she said, he realized that if someone steals money from you, there is nothing you can do about it. And when someone gives you money, you have no choice but to take it, and from that moment on, you are no longer the master of your own as-pirations and strength: you belong to someone else. You are your wife's plaything and your father-in-law's servant. A man alone is nothing—a bird, perhaps, that falls into a trap when it tries to feed itself. But if it's content to be fed, it must live in a cage and sing for its food until the day it's sold to someone else.

He did not want to go see Fourth Master. He had a physical relationship with Huniu but not with the old man. She'd tricked him, and he refused to go to her father with his hand out. "I can't sit around doing nothing" was all he said. Best to avoid wasting breath or getting into an argument.

"A man born to suffer," she taunted. "If you want to keep busy, open a shop."

"Not me," Xiangzi replied tensely, the veins in his forehead standing out. "I can't make money doing that. I pull a rickshaw. I like pulling a rickshaw!"

"Well, I tell you, I'll not have you pulling a rickshaw. I won't let you climb into my bed all sweaty! You see things your way, I see them mine, and we'll find out who comes out on top. You got yourself a wife, but I paid for it, every cent of it. So who do you think ought to listen to whom?"

Once again, Xiangzi could say nothing.

CHAPTER SIXTEEN

Xiangzi's period of idleness lasted till the fifteenth day of the first month, the day of the Lantern Festival, when he could no longer endure it.

Huniu, who was in good spirits, busied herself boiling glutinous rice balls and making dumplings, visiting temples during the day and viewing colorful lanterns at night. Xiangzi had no say in anything as she plied him with all sorts of tasty treats, some bought on the street and others homemade. The compound was home to seven or eight families, most of whom packed a dozen or more people into a single room. Among them were rickshaw men, street vendors, policemen, and servants, all caught up in activities of one kind or another, with no time to relax. Even children were put to work, fetching gruel in the mornings and scrounging for bits of coal in the afternoons. Only the very youngest were free to play and tussle in the compound, their bare bottoms turned red by the freezing air. Ashes from stoves and dirty water were unceremoniously dumped in the middle of the compound and left there; the water froze on the ground and served as a skating rink for the raucous children when they returned from their coal collecting. The days were hardest on the elderly and the women. The old folks, hungry and in need of warm clothing, lay on their ice-cold brick beds, waiting for their younger kin to bring home a bit of money so they could eat. Sometimes their wait was rewarded, sometimes not. If they returned empty-handed, the angry young men were just looking for an excuse to start an argument. Meanwhile, the famished old folks had no choice but to swallow their tears. The women not only had to take care of their elders and their children but also deal with the family's wage earners as well. And being pregnant did not free them from their duties, even though they had to get through the days with chunks of corn bread and bowls of gruel; no, it was still their duty to go fetch gruel from the public canteens and perform whatever other odd jobs cropped up. Then, after the old folks and children were fed and put to bed, they washed and mended clothes under the weak light of an oil lamp. Clad in rags and with a bowl or less of gruel in their stomachs, the heavily pregnant women did their work only after everyone else was fed, with wind whistling in through holes in one wall and carrying all the warmth out of the tiny rooms through cracks in another. Riddled with disease, these women had lost most of their hair before they reached the age of thirty, but they worked on, from sickness to death, when they were buried in coffins paid for by charitable people in the community. Girls of sixteen or seventeen, having no trousers to wear, simply wrapped a tattered cloth around themselves and did not venture outside—for them the rooms were virtual prisons where they helped their mothers with their chores. If they needed to visit the latrine, they first made sure that the compound was deserted before slipping outside unnoticed. They did not see the sun or blue sky all winter long. The ugly ones would take over for their mothers in time, while the decent-looking girls knew that sooner or later they would be sold by their parents to enjoy a good life, as they say.

Huniu felt smug about living in such diminished surroundings. As the only resident of the compound who had no need to worry about food or clothing, she was free to take strolls and enjoy life. With her head held high, she came and went as she pleased, comfortable in her superiority and happy to ignore her poor neighbors for fear of being contaminated by them. Peddlers who came to the compound sought out customers to buy their cheap fare: meat pared from bones, frozen cabbage, raw bean juice, mule and horsemeat. But after Huniu moved in, peddlers of sheep's head, smoked fish, buns and pastries, and spicy fried tofu began shouting their wares at the compound gate. As Huniu carried her purchases back to her rooms, nose in the air, children would stick their thin, dirty fingers in their mouths when she passed by, as if she were royalty. Intent on enjoying the fruits of life, she could not, would not, dared not witness the suffering of others.

As someone who had been born to poverty, Xiangzi took a dim view of her behavior; he knew what it was like to suffer and had no appetite for the expensive food she brought home. What disturbed him even more was the realization that she was plying him with good food to keep his mind off going out to pull a rickshaw, like fattening up a cow to get more milk. He was little more than her plaything. Out on the street, he'd seen a scrawny old bitch set her sights on a strong, well-fed male when she needed a lackey. He not only hated this life but also was worried about what he was becoming. A man who sold his muscle had to keep fit at all costs; good health was everything, and at this rate, one day he would be reduced to skin and bones, an empty hulk. The thought made him shudder. Pulling a rickshaw was the only way he could survive. Out all day running, he'd return home at night and sleep like a baby, dead to the world. By not eating her food, he'd stop being her plaything. There was no way around it—no more compromises. If she'd buy him a rickshaw, well and good; if not, he'd rent one. And that is what he did, without telling her.

On the seventeenth day of the month he started pulling a rickshaw again, an all-day rental. After two long hauls, he experienced something for the first time ever—leg cramps and sore hips. He knew why and consoled himself by attributing it to a three-week layoff. A few more hauls to limber up his legs and he'd be back.

He picked up another fare, this time as part of a group of four. When they were all ready, they chose a tall forty-year-old to take the lead. He smiled, well aware that the other three men were fitter than he, but he gave it his all, unwilling to use age as an excuse for slowing the youngsters down. After they'd run nearly half a mile, the men praised him: "How's it going? Getting tired? You're doing fine!"

He called back breathlessly, "I have to keep the pace up with fellows like you behind me." He was running at such a fast clip that even Xiangzi had to work hard to keep up. But the old fellow had a funny way of running: quite tall, he had trouble bending at the waist, so his torso was like a block of wood that forced him to lean forward and stretch his arms behind him. It looked more like dragging something along than running. Since his back was straight as a board, he had to swing his hips from side to side, while his feet, which barely cleared the ground, twisted their way forward at a good pace. It was obviously hard work. People had to hold their breath as they watched him take corners, seemingly caring only if he, and not his rickshaw, safely made it through.

When they reached their destination, he laid down the shafts of his rickshaw, hurriedly straightened up, and grimaced as beads of sweat dripped noisily to the ground from his nose and earlobes. His hands shook so badly he could hardly hold the money he was given.

A bond formed among the men, who parked their rickshaws together, dried themselves off, and began a round of banter. All but the older man, who kept to himself for a few moments, racked by dry coughs; after spitting out gobs of white phlegm, he recovered enough to join in the conversation.

"I'm beat," he said. "My heart, my hips, my legs, they all pretty much fail me. I try to stretch, but my legs don't want to move. That's got me plenty worried."

"Not the way you were running a minute ago," a short twenty-year-old said. "You can't call that slow. You've got no reason to feel bad. Look at the three of us—we were sweating right along with you."

Even those consoling words were not enough to keep him from sighing.

"But you make it hard on yourself the way you run," another one said, "and that's no joke for a man your age."

The tall fellow smiled and shook his head. "There's more to it than age, my friends," he said. "I tell you, men in our line of work have no business starting a family, and that's the truth." Having gotten their attention, he lowered his voice and said, "Once you've got a family, you're on the go day and night, never a minute to yourself. Just look at my hips—stiff as a board, no spring in them at all. And if I grit my teeth and start running hard, I nearly cough my lungs out and my heart feels like it's about to burst. Take my word for it, for men like us, spending the rest of our lives as fucking bachelors is the only answer. Even those fucking sparrows are free to pair off, but not us. And then there are the kids, a new one every year. I've got five, all waiting to be fed when I get home. Rickshaw rents are high, food's expensive, and there isn't enough work to go around. What's the answer? Bachelorhood. Go visit a whore when you feel the need, and if you wind up with syphilis, so what. Everybody's got to die sometime. This business of starting a family, you wind up with more mouths than you can feed, and you can't die in peace." He turned to Xiangzi. "Am I right or aren't I?"

Xiangzi nodded.

A man looking for a ride walked up, and after the short fellow got the price he was looking for, he handed the fare over to the tall fellow. "You take him, old friend. You've got five kids at home."

"All right," he said with a smile. "I'll take this one, though I shouldn't. But I can buy some more flatbread to take home. See you later, friends!"

As he watched the man run off, the short fellow muttered, "A fucking lifelong bachelor, no wife to share a bed, while those rich bastards have four or five women to wrap their arms around!"

"Never mind them," one of the others piped up. "People who do what we do have to be careful. What the tall guy said was right. What does marriage get us? A good time? No! It's nothing but trouble. You gnaw on hard corn bread day in and day out, and are squeezed from all sides. That'll finish off even the strongest among us."

With this comment, Xiangzi picked up his shafts. "I'm heading south," he said in a conversational tone. "There's no business here."

"See you later," the two youngsters said.

Appearing not to have heard them, Xiangzi walked off, striding purposefully. His hips ached, they really did. At first he planned to knock off for the day, but he couldn't face the idea of going home. It wasn't a wife who was waiting for him—it was a blood-sucking demon!

The days were getting longer. He made a few more rounds and it was still only five o'clock. After turning in his rickshaw, he killed some time in a teahouse, until a couple of bowls of tea spiked his appetite and he decided to get something to eat before going home. Once he'd finished off twelve ounces of meat-filled pastries and a bowl of red-bean millet congee, he belched loudly and then headed slowly home, where he knew a storm awaited. But he didn't care, for he was determined not to argue with her. He'd go straight to bed and be back on the street with his rickshaw tomorrow, whether she liked it or not.

When he walked in the door, Huniu, who was sitting in the outer room, looked at him, her face a study in unhappiness. Xiangzi pulled a long face and thought about pacifying her with a friendly greeting. But he couldn't do it. Head down, he went to bed. Without a word from her, the room was as silent as a cave deep in the mountains. Elsewhere in the compound, the neighbors' coughs and conversation and the crying of children were crisp and clear and yet seemed to come from a distant mountaintop.

Without a word, like a pair of big, voiceless turtles, they lay down in bed and slept awhile. Huniu broke the silence after they awoke. "What were you doing out there all day?" Clearly irritated, she tried to make it sound light-hearted.

"I took a rickshaw out," he mumbled sleepily, as if something were caught in his throat.

"I see! You just don't feel right unless you stink of sweat, you miserable wretch. Instead of eating the meals I cook for you,

you're out in town having a great time. Don't push me too far. My father came from a shady background, and there's nothing I won't do. If you go out again tomorrow, I'll hang myself and show you I mean what I say."

"I can't sit around doing nothing."

"You're not going to go see the old man?"

"No."

"Stubborn ass!"

Xiangzi could hold out no longer. He had to say what was in his heart: "I'll keep at it till I have enough to buy my own rickshaw, and if you try to stop me, I'll leave and never come back."

"Hah!" she snorted, the drawn-out sound swirling around in her nose. She needed no words to express her arrogance and her contempt for Xiangzi, but there was more to it than that. She knew that while he was simple and honest, he was strong-willed, and men like that mean what they say. After all she'd gone through to land him, she couldn't let go now. He was an ideal mate: honest, hardworking, healthy, and strong. Given her looks and age, finding another gem like him would not be easy. She had to know when to be hard and when to be soft, and now was the time to take the pliant approach. "I realize you're ambitious, but you need to know how much you mean to me. If you're not willing to go see the old man, why don't I go? I'm his daughter, after all—so what if I lose a bit of face."

"Even if the old man wants us back, I'm still going to pull a rickshaw." No use holding back now.

Huniu held her tongue, never imagining that Xiangzi could be that clever. The words were so simple, but there was no mistaking that he'd no longer fall into one of her traps. He was nobody's fool. With this in mind, she knew she'd have to tread more carefully if she was going to hold on to this big fellow—

this big creature—who could buck and kick if pushed too far. She had to back off to keep from losing something she'd fought so hard to get. To hold on to him, she'd alternate between loosening her grip one minute and tightening it the next. "All right, if you want to pull a rickshaw, I can't stop you. But promise me you won't take a monthly job. I want you to come home every evening. You see, one day without you drives me out of my mind. I want you to promise me you'll come home early every evening!"

Xiangzi recalled what the tall fellow had said that day. Staring into the darkness, he could see clusters of rickshaw men, peddlers, and coolies, all with bent backs, dragging their feet. That would be him one day. But he could not keep fighting with her. He'd won a victory by getting her to agree to his demand to pull a rickshaw. "I'll only take odd fares," he promised.

Despite what she'd said, she was in no hurry to go see Fourth Master Liu. They had always had their share of arguments, but things were different now, and the storm clouds would not disperse with a simple apology. She was no longer considered a member of the Liu family, since a married daughter's relationship with her parents is never as close as before. If she went straight to him, and he turned her away, denying her claims to an inheritance, there'd be nothing she could do about it. Even if an outsider tried to smooth things over between them, in the end, all the mediator could do was advise her to go home—her new home.

Xiangzi went out with his rickshaw, while Huniu stayed home to pace the floor. Each time she decided to go see the old man, she could not make the effort to dress up for him. What a dilemma! For her own comfort and enjoyment, she had to go, but that would mean a loss of face. If the old man had cooled down and she could get Xiangzi to return to Harmony Shed, there would be a job for him that did not entail pulling a rickshaw; eventually, the two of them would take over the business. That thought brightened her mood. But if the old man refused, it would be more than just a loss of face; she'd end up being the wife of a rickshaw man for the rest of her life. Her? Not on your life! That would make her no different from the women who lived in their compound, and that thought immediately darkened her mood. She was beginning to regret marrying Xiangzi. For all his ambition, if her father refused to give in, he'd spend the rest of his life pulling a rickshaw. At this point, she was ready to call it quits and go home by herself; she couldn't give up everything she'd had for him. But on second thought, she was enjoying hard-to-describe happiness with Xiangzi. As she sat vacantly on the edge of the brick bed, wondering what the future held, she reflected upon the joys of married life. She couldn't put her finger on them, sensing only that they meant something to her. She was like a large red flower blooming in the pleasant warmth of the sun. No, she liked Xiangzi too much to give him up, ever, even if that meant begging on the street while he went out with his rickshaw. Look at those other women in the compound—if they could put up with that life, so could she. To hell with it, she wouldn't go back to the Liu home after all.

Not once since leaving Harmony Shed had Xiangzi ventured back to Xi'an Gate Road. Over the past couple of days he had confined his work to South City; there were too many Harmony Shed rickshaws in West City, and meeting up with any of them would be painfully awkward. But on this day, after turning in his rickshaw, he purposely walked past the yard's gate for no other reason than to take a look. With Huniu's vow still ringing in his ears, he wanted to see if he had the guts to go in if she was eventually able to talk the old man around. First he needed to know what it felt like to walk down this street again. With his hat pulled down low, he kept his distance to avoid running into anyone he knew. From where he stood, he could see the light above the doorway, a sight that saddened him for some reason. His thoughts carried him back to his first days in the yard and to his seduction by Huniu, as well as to the night of the old man's birthday celebration. The scenes floated in front of his eyes, as clear as on the days they'd occurred. Other scenes, equally clear but shorter, were intermingled in the tableau: the Western Hills, camels, the Cao residence, the spy . . . strung together in all their fearful clarity. And yet, he felt lost, as if he were looking at these images without understanding that he was in their midst. When he realized his involvement with them, confusion set in, as the scenes began to swirl around helter-skelter in his mind, until they were just a blur. Why, he wondered, had he suffered all those indignities? The amount of time the events occupied seemed quite long and yet amazingly short, and he lost track of his age. He was, he felt, much, much older than when he'd first arrived at Harmony Shed. Back then, he had been filled with hope. And now? Nothing but a gut of worries. He didn't know why that was, but the pictures in his head did not lie.

Harmony Shed was just up ahead. He stopped across the street and stared woodenly at the bright light in the doorway. Suddenly something caught his eye: the golden characters above the door were different. Though illiterate, he knew what the first character in the word for harmony looked like: it was two lines that met near the top [人], not crossing and not a triangle. But that simple yet strange symbol had been replaced by another, even stranger one [仁], and why was that? He looked at the rooms to the east and the west—two rooms he'd never forget. Both were dark.

He stood there until his patience ran out and he started for home, head held low, thinking as he walked, Could the place have shut down? He'd have to ask around, but no need to say anything to his wife, not yet. When he walked in the door, Huniu was dispelling her boredom by nibbling on melon seeds.

"Late again!" She did not look happy. "I tell you, I don't know what I'll do if this keeps up. You're out all day long, and I can't leave the house for a minute. With all these paupers in the compound, I'd be sure to lose things. From morning to night, I've got no one to talk to, and I can't stand it any longer. I'm not made of wood, you know. You have to think of something because this has to stop."

Xiangzi held his tongue.

"Say something. Why must you always try to make me mad? Do you have a mouth or don't you? Well, do you?" The words were coming faster and sharper, like a string of firecrackers.

Again, Xiangzi said nothing.

"How's this?" Clearly on edge, she wasn't sure how to deal with him. With a look somewhere between tears and laughter, she had to fight to keep from exploding. "We'll buy a couple of rickshaws, and you can stay home and live off the rent. How's that?"

"Two rickshaws won't bring in more than thirty cents a day," Xiangzi said with slow deliberation. "We can't live on that. But we'd do all right if we rented one and I took the other one out." The mere mention of buying rickshaws drove all other thoughts out of his mind.

"What good will that do? You still won't be home."

"How's this, then?" Talk of rickshaws got Xiangzi thinking. "We'll rent one for a whole day. I'll take the second one out for half a day and rent it out the second half. If I take the early shift, I'll be home by three in the afternoon, and if I take the night shift, I'll go out at three and be home that night. That'll work."

Huniu nodded. "I'll think about it. If I can't come up with a better plan, we'll do it your way."

Xiangzi could not have been happier. If this worked out, he'd be back to pulling his own rickshaw, even though it would be a gift from his wife. But he'd work hard and save up until he could buy one himself. All of a sudden, he was beginning to see a good side of his wife, and he smiled. It was an innocent, heartfelt smile that seemed to erase all his pain and suffering and create a brand-new world, as easily as changing clothes. He was thrilled.

CHAPTER SEVENTEEN

Little by little, Xiangzi pieced together what had happened at Harmony Shed: Fourth Master Liu had sold off some of his rickshaws and turned the remainder over to an established yard in West City. Xiangzi guessed that the old man had reached the age where he felt he could no longer run the business without his daughter around to help, and had decided to sell it off and enjoy life with his earnings. What he was unable to learn was where the old man had gone.

Xiangzi wasn't sure if he should be happy or unhappy. Viewed from the perspective of his ambitions and resolve, the news that Fourth Master had abandoned his daughter meant that her plan had fallen through and now he could earn his keep by pulling a rickshaw—he was free to be his own man. Still it was a pity that Fourth Master had liquidated the business and left him and Huniu out in the cold.

But that is how things stood, so why let it bother him? Truth is, it mattered little. His strength belonged to him alone, was how he figured it, and by working hard, food would not be a problem. So he broke the news to Huniu, simply and without a show of emotion.

To her, it mattered a great deal, for her future suddenly became painfully clear—her life was effectively over! Consigned to being the wife of a rickshaw man from now on, she would never leave this paupers' compound. The possibility that her father might remarry one day had crossed her mind in the past but not that he would leave without a word. Had he remarried, she could have fought for her share of his property, and might even have struck a deal with her stepmother to gain some advantage. The possibilities were endless, as long as the old man held on to his rickshaw business. But what he'd done—converting his holdings into cash—and how he'd done it—sneaking off with the money—caught her unprepared. The idea behind her quarrel with him had been a quick reconciliation, since they both knew that Harmony Shed could not operate successfully without her. The flaw in her plan was exposed when he unexpectedly sold off the business.

Spring was in the air. Buds on the trees were turning red. But there were no trees or flowers in their compound to herald spring's arrival. First the winds poked holes in the icy ground, released fetid odors from the stinking earth, and blew rubbish and litter over to the bases of walls, where they swirled in little eddies. For the residents, each season brought its share of troubles. Only now did old folks venture outside to soak up a bit of warmth; only now did the young women wipe off a bit of the soot from their noses and expose skin turned red from the cold; only now did mothers take a chance on sending their children out into the yard to play; and only now did those children run around trying to fly kites made of scraps of paper without fear of chapping their grubby hands. But the public kitchens stopped giving out gruel, shopkeepers no longer sold on credit, and charitable people retied their purse strings, all handing the suffering masses over to the sun and the breezes of spring. With the wheat

still young and green, and grain stores nearly depleted, prices
soared. And as the days lengthened, old-timers could not turn in
early to trick their empty stomachs with dreams. So the arrival
of spring actually made life harder for people who lived in the
compound. Lice that had survived the winter were especially
savage; they crawled out of the padded clothes worn by the very
old and the very young to get a taste of spring.

Huniu's heart was chilled as she watched the ice melt in the
compound and saw the tattered clothing, smelled the motley
mixture of warm odors, and listened to the sighing of old
people and the howls of children. People stayed indoors during the winter as the filth was sealed up in the ice. Now it
began to emerge and things returned to their original form;
earth peeled from bricks in crumbling walls that seemed ready
to fall to the ground on the first rainy day. Pitiful little paupers'
flowers that brought color to the compound only succeeded in
making it uglier than in the winter. Ugh! She now faced the
reality that this is where she would live out her life. What little
money she had would not last forever, and Xiangzi was only a
rickshaw man.

After telling him to stay home and watch the place, she went
to see her aunt at Nanyuan—Southern Park—to find out what
happened to the old man. Fourth Master had indeed been by,
her aunt said, around the twelfth day of the new year, both to
thank her and to tell her he planned to go to Tianjin or Shanghai to relax and enjoy himself. He'd spent his whole life in
Beiping, to his shame as a so-called man of the world. It was
time to see the sights while there was still breath in his body.
Besides, he'd said, he couldn't bear to stay in the city after the
way his daughter had disgraced him. That was all the aunt could

tell her. Maybe, she added, he really is off somewhere, or maybe it was all talk and he's lying low somewhere, who knows?

When she returned home, Huniu threw herself down on the bed and sobbed. This time it was not an act—she wept until her eyes were red and puffy.

After drying her tears, she said to Xiangzi, "All right, be pig-headed and have it your way! I placed my bet on a losing number. As they say, marry a rooster and spend your life as a hen. There's nothing more I can say. Here's a hundred yuan, go buy a rickshaw and start pulling it."

She had decided to hedge her bets after talking about buying two rickshaws, one for him to pull and one to rent out. Now her plan was to buy one for him to pull but hold on to the rest of the money, for that was the source of her power. What if she gave it all to him and he had a change of heart? No, she had to take precautions. The departure of Old Man Liu had taught her a lesson: she could rely on no one but herself. Who knew what tomorrow would bring? She wanted to enjoy life, and money was the key. Having gotten used to snacking on little treats, she'd keep doing that as long as she could. They could get by on Xiangzi's earnings—he was, after all, a first-class rickshaw man—and spend her money as she liked. She would live for the moment. One day the money would run out, but no one lives forever. Marrying a rickshaw man—she'd had no choice—had been bad enough, and the thought of being forced to go to him with her hand out was too humiliating for words. Her mood brightened a bit. Facing a bleak future was no reason to hang her head now. It was like looking into a sunset—though darkness has settled in the distance, it is still light enough close by to walk a few more steps.

Xiangzi saw no need to argue with her, since she'd given her approval to buy a rickshaw. He could surely earn sixty or seventy cents a day pulling his own rickshaw, enough for them to get by. Suddenly he felt pretty good about things. He had suffered in pursuit of buying a rickshaw, and now that he'd achieved that, what more was there to say? To be sure, two people living off the earnings of one rickshaw would be tight, and the danger existed that they would not be able to save up enough to buy a new rickshaw when this one wore out, but given the difficulties involved, buying just the one was good enough for now. Better not to think too far ahead.

As luck would have it, one of the compound residents, Er Qiangzi, had a rickshaw for sale. The year before he'd sold his nineteen-year-old daughter Fuzi to an army officer for two hundred yuan. For a while he'd spent lavishly, redeeming everything he'd pawned and buying new clothes for his family. His wife was the shortest, ugliest woman in the compound: protruding forehead, high cheekbones, hardly any hair, buckteeth, and a face full of freckles—a truly disgusting sight. She had cried over the loss of her daughter till her eyes were red, but that did not keep her from wearing her new blue dress. After selling his daughter, Er Qiangzi, a violent man, took to drinking, and later, once he was drunk, with tears in his eyes, he began looking for trouble. For his wife, a new dress and good food to eat hardly made up for enduring twice as many beatings as before. Er Qiangzi, who, at the age of forty, vowed never to pull a rickshaw again, bought a pair of baskets and a carrying pole with which to peddle an assortment of goods—melons, fruit, peanuts, and cigarettes. After two months, he made a rough calculation and saw that he'd not just lost money, he'd lost a great deal of it. Pulling a rickshaw was what he was good at; he had no head for business.

Pulling a rickshaw was all about getting fares, whereas there were tricks to peddling that he could not master. Men who pulled rickshaws knew that their lives revolved around credit, and he could not find it in him to say no when his friends wanted to buy now, pay later. But getting them to settle up was harder than he'd thought. As a result, good customers were few and far between, and good friends could not pay off their debts. How could he not lose money? And the more he lost, the more heavily he drank, leading to confrontations with the police and ugly scenes at home with his wife and children. All because of alcohol. Regret and wrenching sadness set in when he sobered up, realizing that he was squandering money he'd gotten by selling his own daughter, and that he had turned into a drunk and a bully. What kind of man was that? At such times, he'd spend all day in bed, trying to dream away his sorrows.

He decided to give up peddling and go back to pulling a rickshaw. No sense throwing away what money he had left. So he went out and bought a rickshaw. Altogether unreasonable when drunk, when sober he was all about keeping up appearances, so he put on stylish airs. With a new rickshaw and natty clothes, he considered himself to be an elite rickshaw man, one who drank the best tea and pulled only high-class passengers. He would take a spot at one of the stands, showing off his new rickshaw and clean, white pants and jacket, and chat with the other men, seemingly too good to vie for fares. One minute he'd dust off his rickshaw with a new blue whisk, the next he'd stomp his white-soled shoes on the ground or stare at the tip of his nose and stand there with a smile, waiting for someone to come up and admire his rickshaw. An endless conversation would begin immediately. This could go on for days. When he did get a good fare, his legs were incapable of matching his rickshaw or attire.

He could barely run, which upset him so much he'd start thinking about his daughter again and would have to drink to forget. And so it went, until all he had left was a rickshaw.

Around the time of the winter solstice he got drunk once again. The minute he walked in the door at home, his sons— one thirteen, the other eleven—ran off to hide from him, but not before he angrily gave them each a kick. When his wife complained, he kicked her in the belly. She fell to the floor and lay there without making a sound for a long moment, throwing their sons into a panic. One picked up a coal spade, the other a rolling pin, and they fought off their father. In the scuffle they stepped on their mother. Neighbors, hearing the commotion, rushed over and pinned Er Qiangzi to the brick bed, while the boys went crying to their mother. Er Qiangzi's wife regained consciousness but was unable to walk again. Then, on the third day of the twelfth lunar month, she breathed her last, still wearing the blue dress bought from the sale of her daughter. Her distraught parents insisted on taking their son-in-law to court, relenting only after friends intervened and Er Qiangzi agreed to arrange a decent burial. After giving the family fifteen yuan, he pawned his rickshaw for sixty. New Year's came and went, and Er Qiangzi had hopes of ridding himself of the rickshaw, though he was too strapped to redeem it. So he went out and got drunk and hatched a plan to sell one of his sons. There were no takers. Next, he went to see Fuzi's husband, who refused to recognize this so-called father-in-law. And that put an end to his plans.

Knowing the rickshaw's history, Xiangzi had no interest in buying it; there were plenty of rickshaws for sale, so why buy a jinxed rickshaw acquired through the sale of a daughter and sold because of a wife's murder? Huniu saw it differently: she figured they could buy this nearly new rickshaw for a little more than eighty yuan, a bargain considering that it came from the renowned Decheng Factory and had only been in use for six months or so—its tires looked brand-new. Rickshaws that were only two-thirds new went for fifty or sixty! This was too good a bargain to pass up, especially since she knew that money was short after the New Year's holiday, and he would not try to raise the price. He needed the money. So she went to look the rickshaw over and bargain with Er Qiangzi. The deal was struck while Xiangzi stayed home, and there was nothing he could say, since it wasn't his money. He could only wait to take the rickshaw out on the street. When Huniu brought it back, he inspected it carefully. It was a good, strong rickshaw in fine shape. And yet, it made him uncomfortable. What disturbed him most were the colors—pitch-black, with nickel alloy fittings. Er Qiangzi had thought that the contrast—black and white—gave it a classy look. But it reminded Xiangzi of mourning garb in a funeral procession, and he would have preferred new fittings in bronze or soft yellow, to give it a livelier appearance. But he said nothing to Huniu, knowing the sort of reaction he'd get.

The rickshaw attracted a great deal of attention when Xiangzi took it out. He hated it when people called it "the little widow," although he tried to put that out of his mind. But the rickshaw followed him around all day, keeping him on edge, as if at any moment something bad might happen. When thoughts of Er Qiangzi and his sad fate popped into Xiangzi's mind, he felt as if he were pulling a coffin behind him, not a rickshaw, and he often saw ghostly shadows on the rickshaw, or so it seemed.

But nothing happened, despite his constant worries. As the weather warmed up, he changed his padded clothes for an unlined shirt and trousers; Beiping springs are notoriously short, and the days became irritatingly long and wearying. He would go out early in the morning, and by four or five o'clock in the afternoon he was finished for the day, though the sun was still high in the sky. He'd pulled enough fares, yet was not ready to go home, so he dithered, feeling unsettled, one long, lazy yawn after another.

However weary and bored Xiangzi was during those long days, it was worse for Huniu, who was maddeningly lonesome at home. She could warm herself by the stove in the winter and listen to the wind whistling outside, dejected to be sure but comforted by the thought that it was better than going outside. But now that the stove had been moved under the eaves, she had too much time on her hands. The filthy, treeless yard was submerged in a pall of rank odors, but if she went out for a stroll, she would not be able to keep an eye on her neighbors. Even shopping trips had to be kept as short as possible. She felt like a bee trapped in a sealed room, able to see sunlight through the window but unable to fly out. She had nothing in common with the women in the compound, who talked only of family affairs, while she was an unrefined woman who had no interest in such things. Their grumblings stemmed from the bitter lives they lived, and it took little to bring tears to their eyes. Her complaints, on the other hand, were a product of the dissatisfaction with what life had dealt her; she had no tears to shed, venting her frustration instead in cursing and quarreling. There was no basis of understanding between her and them, so best to mind her own business and not even talk to them.

Then, in the middle of the fourth month, she found a friend. Er Qiangzi's daughter, Fuzi, came home. The man in her life was an army officer who set up a simple home wherever he was sent and spent a hundred or two to buy a large plank bed, a couple of chairs, and a young girl, all he needed to live enjoyably for a while. Then, when his unit was transferred, he picked up and moved on, leaving everything, the girl included, behind. Spending a hundred or two for the better part of the year was worth it, since hiring a domestic to wash and mend his clothes, cook his meals, and perform a myriad of little chores would easily cost ten yuan a month, food included. But marrying a girl brought him a servant *and* someone to share his bed, a girl guaranteed not to pass on a venereal disease. If she pleased him, he could buy her a nice dress at a cost of one yuan or less. If not, he'd leave her at home stark naked, and there was not a thing she could do about it. Then, when it was time to leave, he unemotionally abandoned the bed and chairs, leaving her to find a way to come up with the rent for the last two months, most likely more than she could get by selling the bed and chairs.

After disposing of the furniture and paying the outstanding rent, Fuzi returned home with nothing but a cotton dress and a pair of silver earrings.

As for her father, upon selling his rickshaw, Er Qiangzi paid off the pawnshop, with interest, and wound up with slightly more than twenty yuan. At times he bemoaned his fate of losing a wife at middle age, but gained no sympathy from anyone. That drove him to drink, and the more he drank, the greater his self-pity. He began to treat money with hostility, spending it with wild abandon. But there were other times when he told himself he ought to go back to pulling a rickshaw and bring his sons up properly, so they might have a future. With the two boys on his mind, he would rush out and madly buy all sorts of food for them, and then watch them wolf it down with tears in his eyes. "Poor motherless children," he'd mutter, "ill-fated sons. Your father works like a slave for you. It means nothing to me if I go hungry, so long as you have food to eat. Eat up. And don't forget your old papa when you grow up!" Slowly but surely, the twenty yuan ran out.

Broke again, drink was his only refuge, and that led to fits of temper, times when he could go a day or two without a single thought for his sons. Left to their own devices, the boys had to find a way to earn enough to buy food. So they began running errands at weddings and funerals and digging in garbage carts for scrap iron and paper they could sell for a few flatbreads or some sweet potatoes, which they'd gobble down, skins, roots, and all. If all they managed to earn was a small coin, they'd spend it on peanuts or broad beans, not enough to stave off hunger but something to chew on at least.

When Fuzi returned, they wrapped their arms around her legs and wordlessly smiled up at her with tears in their eyes. With their mother gone, she would have to take her place.

Er Qiangzi showed no emotion over his daughter's return; all she meant to him was another mouth to feed. But the happiness in his sons' eyes made it clear how important it was to have a woman in the house—to cook and do the laundry. So he said nothing, content to let things take their course.

Fuzi was not bad-looking. She'd left home a small, thin girl but, after living with the army officer, had put on weight and grown taller. There was nothing special about her, but she was attractive, with a round face and long neat eyebrows, and was seemingly in robust good health. She had a short upper lip that rose up when she pouted or smiled to reveal a row of even white teeth. Those teeth had been the officer's favorite feature. With a silly, slightly vacant look, her open mouth proclaimed her lovely innocence, and this expression endowed her with the look of a flower, so common in attractive girls born to poverty: once they have a bit of fragrance or color, they are taken to be sold at the market.

Huniu, who generally ignored her neighbors, found a friend in Fuzi. To begin with, she was a pretty girl in a flowery dress. Then, too, since she had been married to an army officer, she'd seen a bit of the world. That was enough for her. Women do not make friends easily, but when they choose to, it happens quickly. Huniu and Fuzi were fast friends within days. Any time Huniu, who was an inveterate snacker, had some melon seeds or the like, she would call Fuzi over to share them. And as they laughed and chatted, Fuzi would smile her foolish little smile and talk to Huniu of things the other woman had never heard before. Living with the officer had not been easy or pleasant, but when he was in a good mood, he'd taken her to a restaurant or to a show, which provided her with many tales that piqued Huniu's interest and aroused her envy. There were things Fuzi would rather not have talked about, degrading things, but for Huniu they were a joy to hear. When she begged her to go on, Fuzi found it hard to refuse, no matter how embarrassed she might be. She'd seen pornographic pictures; Huniu hadn't, and she begged her to talk about them over and over. Huniu did not just admire and envy Fuzi. She was jealous of her. After hearing such stories, she would think about herself—her appearance, her age, her husband—and feel that life had passed her by. Having already been denied her youth, she could entertain no hopes for the future. As for the present, she had only heartless Xiangzi, and the greater her disappointment in him, the keener her admiration for Fuzi. Admittedly, the girl was pitifully poor, but the joys of life had not completely escaped her in her estimable travels, and she could die on the spot with no regrets. In Huniu's view, Fuzi represented the life women deserved to enjoy.

Huniu seemed not to notice Fuzi's troubles. The girl had come home with nothing, yet she had to care for her two brothers—since her father had no interest in doing that himself—so where was she going to get the money to feed them?

It was left to Er Qiangzi to come up with an idea while he was drunk: there's one way you can feed your brothers if you really care that much for them. Look at me, I work like a dog day in and day out, but I can only do that on a full stomach. If I don't eat, I don't work. You could laugh if I dropped dead out there, but what good would it do you? Instead of idling around, you've got something to sell, so what are you waiting for?

She looked at her drunken, irrational father, then at herself, and finally at her famished brothers. All she could do was cry. But her tears did not move her father and could not feed two boys who looked like starved rats. No, something more practical was required. In order to feed her brothers, she had to sell her own flesh. As she hugged the younger of the two, her tears fell on his hair. "I'm hungry, Sister," he said. Sister! Sister was a piece of meat to feed her brothers.

Instead of commiserating with Fuzi, Huniu was willing to help by lending her money to make her presentable. She could pay it back out of her earnings. She was also happy to let the girl use one of her rooms, since her own place was so dirty. There was plenty of space in the two rooms, and they were in decent shape. Xiangzi was out during the day, and she was eager to help a friend. It would also give her a chance to see some things that were new to her, things she missed and could never do, even if she wanted to. Her only condition was that Fuzi give her twenty cents each time she used the room. Friends are friends, but business is business. She would have to keep the room neat and clean for Fuzi's use, which would entail an expenditure of both effort and money. After all, brooms and dustpans aren't free, are they? She was willing to charge so little only because Fuzi was a friend.

Fuzi's teeth showed as she swallowed her tears.

The effect of this on Xiangzi, who was told nothing, was the loss of a lot of sleep, as Huniu attempted to recapture her youth on his body.

CHAPTER EIGHTEEN

By June the compound was silent during the day. The children went out early with their splintered baskets to scavenge the area, returning with what they could find by nine o'clock, when the blistering sun had begun to crack the skin on their scrawny backs, and eat whatever their parents had for them. Then the older boys would buy—if they could scrape together even a bit of cash—or steal chunks of ice to resell. If no money was to be found, they'd go in groups down to the moat for a bath, stopping along the way to pilfer a few lumps of coal at the train station or catch dragonflies or cicadas to sell to the children of the rich. The younger children, who dared not wander far from home, would play with locust beetles near the compound gate or dig up larva. With the children and the men all away from the house, the women stayed indoors, naked to the waist, unwilling to go outside, not out of a sense of shame but because the sun-baked ground burned the soles of their feet.

The men and children trickled back shortly before sunset, when the walls cast their shadows and cool breezes rose up, while the stored-up heat turned the rooms into steamers. They sat outside waiting for the women to cook the evening meal. The yard would be as lively as a marketplace but with no wares to sell. A day's heat and empty stomachs had pushed the men's tempers to the boiling point. One careless word could easily lead to a beating—children or wives, it made little difference—or at the very least an angry outburst. This would last till dinner was over, when some of the children would fall asleep in the yard and others would run out to play in the street. When they had a meal under their belts, the men's mood would improve enough for some of them to gather in threes and fours to complain about the day's hardships. For those who had nothing to eat, it was too late to pawn or sell anything—if they had anything to pawn or sell in the first place—so they would throw themselves down on their beds, ignoring the heat, and lie there in morose silence or fill the air with their curses. Teary-eyed women would visit neighbors and, if they were lucky, return with crumpled twenty-cent notes. Clutching the treasured notes in their hands, they'd buy some cheap fixings for a pot of gruel to feed their families.

This was not the sort of life Huniu and Fuzi led. Huniu was pregnant—this time for real. Xiangzi went out early, leaving her to get out of bed by eight or nine o'clock, in accord with the mistaken belief that pregnant women should move around as little as possible. But that belief was only one reason for her indolence; pregnancy was also a status symbol. While the neighbor women had to be up working early, she could lie in bed doing nothing as long as she wanted. When night fell, she took a stool out onto the street to enjoy the evening breezes and not go back inside until almost everyone else was asleep in bed. It was beneath her to engage any of them in conversation.

Fuzi also spent her mornings in bed, but for a different reason: she was afraid of the looks the men in the compound gave her, so she did not leave the house till they had all gone to work.

Then she either visited Huniu or went out for a walk alone, since she was her own best advertisement. At night, in order to escape notice by her neighbors, she roamed the streets, not stealing back home until they were all in bed.

Among the men, Xiangzi and Er Qiangzi were the exceptions. Xiangzi hated the idea of walking into the compound and shuddered at the thought of entering his own room. The unending talk in the compound always put him out of sorts, and he longed for a quiet place to be by himself. At home it seemed to him that Huniu was truly living up to her name. He nearly choked on the heat, the oppressive atmosphere, and the tigress who lived there the moment he walked inside. Before Huniu had someone to keep her company, he had been forced to come home early to avoid an argument. But now that she had loosened her grip on him, he could, and did, stay out late.

As for Er Qiangzi, who stayed away most of the time, his daughter's trade shamed him too much to show his face in the compound. But since he was incapable of supporting his children, he could not stop her from doing what she did. Best for him to stay away. The phrase "out of sight, out of mind" said it best. Some of the time he deeply resented his daughter; if she had been a man, she would not have made such a spectacle of herself. Why, as a female, had she been born into this family? Other times he took pity on a daughter who was forced to sell her body in order to feed her brothers. But resentment or fondness, what difference did it make? When he was drunk and broke, he neither hated nor pitied her, but came to her for money. At such times he saw her as a wage earner, and as her father, he had the right to claim some of her earnings. He also had to keep up appearances, and since everyone else looked down on her, he must do the same. Cursing and verbally abus-

ing her as he pressed her for money would show everyone that
he—Er Qiangzi—knew how shameless his daughter was.

So he yelled at her, and she bore it. Huniu, on the other
hand, sent him away with curses, but only after he'd gotten what
he came for—more money to drink away. If he'd ever seen this
with a clear head, he'd probably have drowned or hanged himself.

The sun scorched the earth on the fifteenth of June as soon as
it rose in the morning. A suffocating gray vapor, neither cloud
nor mist, hung low in the sky. Not a breath of wind anywhere.
The sight of the reddish-gray sky convinced Xiangzi that he
ought to take the night shift, going out to pull his rickshaw after
four in the afternoon. If business was slow, he could stay out all
night. Working at night was more bearable than suffering
through the day.

But Huniu wanted him out early so he wouldn't be around if
Fuzi had a client. "You might think it's better inside, but by
noon the walls will be too hot to touch," she said.

Without a word, he drank a ladleful of water and went out.

Willow trees lining the street drooped as if sick, dusty leaves
curling at the tips, branches hanging limp. The parched roadway
gave off a white glare while dust swirled above the dirt paths and
merged with the gray vapor to form a cruel veil of sand that
seared people's faces. No place escaped the dry, blistering heat or
oppressive air that turned the ancient city into a blazing kiln.
People could hardly breathe; dogs sprawled on the ground, pink
tongues lolling from their mouths; mules and horses flared their
nostrils; peddlers' voices were stilled; road surfaces cracked.
Even brass signs above shop doors seemed to be melting. Except
for the unnerving clanging of a hammer in the blacksmith shop,
the streets were deathly quiet. Even knowing they wouldn't eat if

they weren't out running, men who pulled rickshaws could not muster the energy to take on fares. Some parked their rickshaws in the shade, raised the rain hoods, and dozed, while others escaped the heat in teahouses or came out without their rickshaws to see if there was any reason to work that day. Those who picked up passengers, including the best-looking and youngest among them, preferred walking to running hard, even if they lost a bit of face in the process. Every drinking well was a lifesaver; they never passed one by, even if they'd only run a few steps, and if they missed one, they drank greedily from troughs set out for mules and horses. Then there were those who walked along until heatstroke or a case of cholera sent them pitching to the ground, from which they never rose again.

Xiangzi, too, was intimidated by the heat, which seemed to wrap itself around him after he'd taken only a few steps with his empty rickshaw. Even the backs of his hands were sweating. But that did not stop him from responding to a potential fare—maybe running would stir up a slight breeze. But when he started off, he realized that no one should be out working in such crippling heat. The air was too hot to breathe and his lips burned as he ran. He wasn't thirsty, but the sight of water made him want to drink. Yet as soon as he stopped, the searing heat blistered the skin on his hands and back. His clothes stuck to his body by the time he'd managed to get where he was going, so he tried fanning himself with a rush fan, but all that did was assault his face with hot wind. He'd drunk water every chance he had, and still he went to a teahouse, where he drank two cups of hot tea, which made him feel a little better. The tea went in, the sweat oozed out, as if his body were an empty chamber that could not retain a drop of water. He was afraid to even move.

After sitting there awhile, he grew restless. He didn't dare go back outside, but he had nothing to do, and he felt as if the weather was spiting him. No, he thought, I won't admit defeat. This was not his first day out, and certainly not his first summer day, and he refused to waste a whole working day. But his legs did not feel up to the task and he was listless, like one who is sweating after a hot bath that has failed to invigorate. So he sat a while longer, but since even that made him sweat, he might just as well go out and give it another try.

He realized his mistake the moment he stepped outside. The gray vapor had dissipated, lessening the oppressive feeling, but the sun was beating down so savagely that no one dared look up. The sky, the rooftops, the walls, even the ground, were dazzlingly white, tinged with red. Wherever you looked, up or down, the world was like a fiery mirror on which every ray of sunlight seemed focused, turning everything it touched into flame. In that engulfing whiteness, every color hurt the eye, every sound grated on the ear, and every smell carried with it a stench from the steamy ground. The streets, all but deserted, appeared wider than before, an expanse devoid of cool air, and so white it made him shudder in fear. Xiangzi didn't know what to do as he plodded along in a daze, head down, pulling his rickshaw behind him, heading nowhere and reeking of sticky sweat that covered his body. Before long, his shoes and socks stuck to the soles of his feet, as if he'd stepped in mud; it felt terrible. When he spotted a well, he drank; though he wasn't thirsty, he savored the refreshing coolness of the water as it slid down his throat into his stomach. His pores contracted and he shivered, an enormously pleasant feeling. He belched several times, nearly bringing the water back up.

After walking awhile, he sat to rest, too lazy to look for fares, all the way to noon. Not particularly hungry, he thought about getting something to eat anyway, except the sight of food sickened him. His water-filled stomach made an occasional gurgling sound, like the sloshing of water in a mule's stomach.

Xiangzi, who had always feared winter more than summer, never imagined that summer could be so unbearable. This was not his first summer in the city, but it was easily the hottest in memory. But had the weather changed or had he? Suddenly, his mind cleared and his heart seemed to chill. His body, it was his body that had weakened. Fear gripped him, but there was nothing he could do. He could not drive Huniu away, and one day he would be just like Er Qiangzi or that tall fellow he'd met that day or Little Ma's granddad. He was doomed.

He caught another fare at one o'clock that afternoon, the hottest time of the hottest day of the year, but he was determined to take the customer where he wanted to go, the searing sun be damned! If he managed to pull this off, he'd know he was still fit. But if he couldn't, all he could say was he'd be better off crumpling to the burning ground and dying.

He'd taken only a few steps when he felt a bit of cool air, like the breeze that seeps in through the door of a hot, stuffy room. It must be an illusion, he thought. But then he saw the branches of roadside willows rustle as people swarmed into the street from the shops, covering their heads with rush fans and looking all around. "A breeze! A real breeze!" they shouted, jumping up and down. The willows had become angels bearing heavenly tidings. "The willows are swaying! Bring us more cool winds, old man in the sky!"

It was still miserably hot, but people were breathing more easily. The cool wind—what little there was of it—brought them hope. After the wind gusts, the sun beat down less fiercely than before. The sky, now bright, now a bit darker, looked as if a cloud of flying sand were floating by. Then the winds increased, bringing joyful news to the dormant willow branches, which waved in the air and seemed to grow longer. A strong draft darkened the sky and filled it with stirred-up dust. When that began to settle, dark clouds appeared in the northern sky. Xiangzi, who was no longer sweating, looked to the north and stopped the rickshaw to put up the rain hood. He knew that summer rains came quickly and waited for no one.

The rain hood was barely up when another blast of wind brought the dark rainclouds rolling in to cover most of the sky. The merging ground heat and cool air stank from the dry earth, feeling cold and hot at the same time. The southern half of the sky was bright and sunny, the northern half blanketed with dark clouds and threatening the worst. Panic was in the air. Rickshaw men struggled to put up their rain hoods, shopkeepers hurriedly took down their signs, peddlers hastily packed up their stalls, and people out on the street ran for cover. Another blast seemed to sweep the streets empty of shop signs, peddlers, and pedestrians, until the only things to be seen were willow branches dancing wildly in the wind.

The roadways turned dark even before the rain clouds covered the sky, turning a steamy, bright midday into a dark night. The winds brought raindrops crashing to earth, as if searching for something. Lightning cleaved the northern sky, creating blood-red scars. The winds were dying down, but the whistling sound made people tremble. Then it passed, leaving behind a sense of uncertainty; even the willow trees waited for what they feared might come next. More lightning, this time directly overhead, illuminating a squall of shiny white raindrops that thudded into the steamy ground. Large drops falling on Xiangzi's back made him shudder. Then, as dark clouds filled the sky, the rain stopped. But only for a moment. The next blast of wind, the strongest yet, spread willow branches straight out, sent dirt flying, and brought down more rain. Wind, earth, and rain mingled in a cold, swirling gray mass that moved in all directions at once, swallowing everything in sight and making it impossible to distinguish trees from the earth or clouds. It was noisy, misty chaos. When the wind had passed, only the pounding rain remained, producing an impenetrable curtain, a mass of streaking water that sent countless projectiles surging up into the sky from the ground and spawned thousands of waterfalls cascading down from rooftops. Earth and sky merged as rain streaming from the sky formed a watery world on the ground with rivers of dark gray and murky yellow and an occasional flash of white.

Xiangzi was drenched—not a dry spot on his body. His hair was sopping wet, despite the straw hat he wore. Sloshing through ankle-deep water made for hard going, especially with rain pummeling his head and his back, hitting his face from all sides, and soaking his trousers. He could neither raise his head nor open his eyes, and he had so much trouble breathing he had to stop walking. He could only stand there, having lost his sense of direction. Dazed, all he felt was the bone-chilling water washing over him. A tiny bit of warmth remained in his heart as his ears filled with the sound of the downpour. He wanted to put his rickshaw down, but where? He felt like running, but the water held his legs fast. So, by now all but done in, he slogged forward, one foot ahead of the other, head down. For all he knew, his passenger had died in his seat, since no sound emerged as he was carried slowly along through the water.

When the rain began to let up, Xiangzi straightened up a bit and, exhaling heavily, said, "How about finding shelter for the time being, mister?"

"Keep moving!" the man said with a stomp of his foot. "You can't leave me stranded here!"

Xiangzi contemplated putting his rickshaw down anyway and finding a place to get out of the rain. But since he was soaked to the skin, he knew that if he stopped he'd likely begin to shiver, so he clenched his teeth and started running, putting the depth of the water out of his mind. The sky turned dark for a moment, then brightened, as the blinding rain recommenced.

When they reached their destination, his passenger gave him the fare, not a penny more. Xiangzi said nothing, since life for him had ceased having any meaning.

The rain stopped and started again but not as heavily. Xiangzi made it back home, where he sought the warmth of the stove. He was shaking like a wind-blown, rain-soaked leaf. Huniu prepared a bowl of sweet ginger water, which he mindlessly gulped down before climbing into bed. His mind was blank as he slept fitfully, the rain sounding in his ears.

By four in the afternoon, the clouds had grown weary and emitted only an occasional weak bolt of pink lightning. Then those in the western sky began to break up, their black crests inlaid with streamers of gold. White mist rushed along beneath them. Lightning moved south, producing muted claps of thunder. Then the sun peeked through, turning the wet leaves a golden green. A double rainbow appeared in the east, the ends buried in dark clouds, the arches holding up a patch of blue sky. The rainbows were short-lived, as the clouds vanished and everything—sky and earth—was washed clean, emerging from the darkness as a cool and beautiful new world.

Colorful dragonflies flitted about the puddles in the compound yard.

But only the barefoot children who chased after the dragonflies had time to enjoy the clear sky, now that the rains had
stopped. Part of the rear wall in Fuzi's room had collapsed, and
she and her brothers were busily covering the spot with the
straw mat from their brick bed. The same had happened at several places in the compound wall, but people were too busy
cleaning up their rooms to worry about that. Occupants of
flooded rooms with low thresholds were bailing out the water
with dustpans and chipped bowls, while others were trying to
repair crumbling walls open to the outside. In other places,
water poured in through holes in the ceilings, soaking household items that were quickly moved up near the stoves or up
onto windowsills to dry out. While the rain was falling, they
had taken shelter in rooms that could easily have collapsed
around them, burying them alive and sending them on their
way; now, the danger passed, they assessed the damage and sal-
vaged what they could. In the wake of the storm, the price of
grain might drop a bit, but that could not compensate for their
losses. They paid rent, but no one ever came to make repairs on
their rooms, unless, that is, they were no longer livable. Then a
couple of brick masons would come by to patch them up with
mud and broken bricks, which would last until the next time
they crumbled. If the family refused to pay their rent, they
would be evicted and their belongings held back. No one cared
if the run-down houses were death traps. Living in decrepit,
dangerous houses served them right if that was the best they
could afford.

Sickness was the worst thing the storm left behind. Whole
families trying to earn a bit of money were often caught outside

in a sudden downpour. The bodies of people who lived by their strength in the summer were forever covered with sweat and ravaged by cold northern rainstorms that were sometimes marked by walnut-sized hailstones. Icy raindrops pelting open pores laid the people low with fever for at least a day or two. There was no medicine money for sick children; rain that made the corn and sorghum grow also had the power to carry away the sons and daughters of the poor. It was worse when the grownups got sick. Poets sing the beauty of pearl-drenched lotuses and double rainbows, but for the poor, when the head of the household took to a sickbed, the family went hungry. A rainstorm added to the number of prostitutes and thieves and increased the prison populations; better for the children of the sick to turn to these vices than starve. The rains fell on rich and poor alike, they fell on the beautiful and the ugly, but there was no fairness in their effect.

Xiangzi fell ill, but in that compound, he was not the only one.

CHAPTER NINETEEN

Xiangzi lay in a daze for two days and nights. In the grip of panic, Huniu went to the Temple of the Matriarch to pray for a magic cure, which consisted of a bit of incense ash and a handful of medicinal herbs. It seemed to work, since he opened his eyes as soon as she poured the mixture down his throat. But almost immediately he closed his eyes and began muttering incoherently. That convinced Huniu that it was time to call a doctor, who inserted a pair of acupuncture needles and prepared a dose of Chinese medicine. This time Xiangzi awoke. "Is it still raining?" he asked, wide-eyed.

A second batch of medicine was prepared, but he refused to take it, in part because of the cost but also because he was ashamed to have been laid low by a summer storm. To prove he had no need for the bitter medicine, he insisted on getting out of bed and dressed. But he'd barely sat up when it felt as if a huge rock were crushing down on his head; his neck went limp, he saw stars, and he fell backward. This time he drank down the medicine without an argument.

Altogether, he was bedridden for ten days—days of anxious torment. Every once in a while he buried his face in his pillow and sobbed silently. Knowing he could not earn a thing in bed, he was forced to let Huniu pay all the bills. But when her money ran out, his rickshaw would be the sole means of support, and he could not make enough to cover her extravagant spending and her habit of snacking, especially with a child on the way. His imagination ran wild while he was confined to bed, and the more he brooded, the harder it was to cure what ailed him.

After the worst had passed, he asked Huniu, "What about the rickshaw?"

"Don't worry," she said, "I rented it to Ding Si."

"Oh!" That worried him. What if Ding Si damaged his rickshaw? But since he was sick in bed, they'd have to rent it out. They couldn't let it stand idle. He did some silent calculations: on a normal day he could bring in fifty or sixty cents by pulling the rickshaw himself, barely enough for two people for rent, fuel, rice, oil, and tea—clothing was extra—if they watched their money carefully, something Huniu was not doing. Now, with only ten cents coming in each day from the rental, they had to make up the lost amount from their savings, not counting the cost of medicine. What if his illness dragged on? No wonder Er Qiangzi turned to drink and his down-and-out friends committed all kinds of outrages. Pulling a rickshaw was a dead-end trade. No matter how hard you worked or tried to better yourself, you cannot marry, get sick, or make a false move. "Hah!" he muttered as he thought back to his first rickshaw and the money he'd put aside. Who had he offended? It had been taken from him for no good reason, though he had neither married nor fallen ill. Good or bad, it made no difference, death claimed you in the end, whether you saw it coming or not. This thought turned his melancholy to despair. To hell with it! Why not just lie here, why try to get up in the first place? So he lay there, his mind a blank. But not for long. He felt he had to get up and do the only thing he knew how to do. It might be a dead-end, but his heart was still beating, and he would keep his hopes alive until they laid him in his coffin. For the moment he was still too weak to stand. He turned to Huniu.

"I knew that rickshaw was bad luck," he said pitifully.

"You're supposed to be getting better, not talking nonsense, you and your rickshaw!"

Xiangzi said nothing. She was right. Ever since the very first day he had believed that a rickshaw was everything. If only. . .

Once he was on the mend, he got out of bed and looked in the mirror. He hardly recognized the man looking back at him. Scruffy beard, sunken temples and cheeks, a pair of hollowed eyes, even wrinkles spidering his scar! The room was stuffy, but he didn't dare go out in the yard, partly because his legs were still rubbery but also because he didn't want to be seen. Everyone in the compound, like the men at the rickshaw stands in East and West City, knew that Xiangzi was one of the hardiest men around, not the sickly creature he'd become. No, he couldn't go outside; but the room was sweltering. How he wished he could eat himself back to health and go back out with his rickshaw. But the ravages of illness came and went at will.

After being laid up for a month, Xiangzi took his rickshaw out, mindless of whether he was completely recovered or not. He pulled his hat down low so no one would recognize him when he ran more slowly than before. The words *Xiangzi* and *speed* were inseparable, and he knew that people would laugh at him if he made a show of loping along.

Though his body had not yet healed, he took on as many fares as he could to make up for what the illness had cost him; his sickness returned in a matter of days. And this time his troubles were compounded by dysentery. He slapped himself in frustration, but that accomplished nothing. His stomach was caved in; his bowels were loose. By the time his dysentery was under control, his legs were so weak he could hardly get up from a squat, let alone run. So he took another month off, though he knew that Huniu's money was quickly running out.

On the fifteenth of August, Xiangzi was determined to take his rickshaw out again. He vowed that if his illness returned, he'd end it all in the river.

Fuzi had visited him often during his first illness. For someone who could never best Huniu in an argument and who had such a gloomy outlook on life, Xiangzi enjoyed his occasional chats with Fuzi. That did not sit well with Huniu. Fuzi was her friend when Xiangzi was out, but with him at home, she was—according to Huniu—a shameless harlot. And so, after demanding that Fuzi return the money she'd lent her, she sent her away: "Don't come back here anymore!"

So Fuzi lost a place to entertain her clients. Her own room was so shabby—her bed mat still hung over the crumbled wall—she had no choice but to go to register at the escort service. But the service, which specialized in schoolgirls and girls from good families, rebuffed her. With good connections and steep prices, they had no use for such common goods. Now what? She considered going to one of the brothels, since she had no capital and no ability to work for herself, but there she'd have to turn over her earnings and lose her freedom. Then who would look after her brothers? Death was the easy way out of this living hell, and that did not frighten her, but now was not the time—she was determined to do something nobler and more courageous than die. There was plenty of time for that after she'd seen to it that her brothers could survive on their own. Death would come sooner or later, but she wanted her death to be the salvation of two young lives. After thinking things through, she saw only one path open to her: to sell herself cheaply, since no one who came through her door would be willing to pay a high price. All right, then, anyone was welcome, as long as he paid. She could stop worrying about nice clothes or cosmetics, for no one who paid so little could expect much in the way of appearances. All they cared about was the little bit of pleasure their money bought; her youth alone made it a bargain.

By then, Huniu, big with child, was having trouble getting around and was afraid of losing the baby if she went shopping. With Xiangzi out all day and Fuzi no longer willing to come by, she was as lonely as a caged dog. That loneliness increased her bitterness, for she believed that Fuzi was selling herself so cheaply to spite her, and that was unendurable. So she began sitting in the outer room with the door open, waiting. When she saw men approach Fuzi's room, in a loud, abusive voice she said things that made the men uncomfortable and embarrassed Fuzi. She took malicious pleasure in the decline of Fuzi's business.

Fuzi knew that at this rate, the other residents of the compound would gradually align themselves with Huniu to drive her out. She was afraid, but dared not get angry. People who have fallen as low as she know that anger and tears serve no practical purpose. So, brothers in tow, she went to Huniu and knelt at her feet. She said nothing; the look on her face said it all. If this act did not save the situation, she was prepared to die, but would take someone with her. The noblest sacrifice of all is to endure humiliation, and the noblest endurance of humiliation is in preparing to resist.

This put Huniu, who was caught off guard, in a bind. She could not fight the girl, not in her condition, and since a physical response was out of the question, she squirmed out of the awkward situation by telling Fuzi that it had all been in fun. Imagine Fuzi taking it so seriously! That did the trick; they were friends again, with Huniu back to supporting the younger woman in her calling.

Since he again began taking out his rickshaw soon after the Moon Festival, caution had become Xiangzi's new watchword. One illness on top of another had taught him that he was not made of steel. He still hoped to make as much money as possible, but the setbacks had taught him an important lesson: a man alone is the embodiment of weakness. Any man worthy of the name must grit his teeth to survive, but even then he might wind up spitting blood. No longer bothered by dysentery, Xiangzi still suffered occasional stomach pains. Sometimes, when he was loping along and wanted to test his legs with a bit of speed, his stomach would twist into knots, forcing him to slow down, even stop, lower his head, and bear the contractions in his gut as best he could. He didn't do badly when he was on his own, but when he was part of a group and pulled up abruptly like that, the others wondered what was happening, and he was mortified. If he became a laughingstock in his twenties, what would he be like in his thirties and forties? The thought made him shudder.

A monthly hire would have put less strain on his body, since there would be rest breaks between trips. He could run fast and then take a long break, which was easier than picking up fares all day. But Huniu was not going to let go of him, that was a certainty; marriage had cost him his freedom, and the woman he'd married was a shrew. What rotten luck!

Six months passed, from autumn to winter, with Xiangzi somehow getting by half the time and struggling the rest, avoid-

ing careless mistakes without slacking off, in the grip of dejection but determined to dig in and keep fighting. Dig in. No
longer could he blithely take things as they came. He still earned
more than most rickshaw men, passing up no fares except when
his stomach acted up. He refused to employ the tricks some men
used; he never demanded exorbitant fares, switched fares midway, or waited for customers that paid well. It was tiring work,
but it made for a steady income. And by avoiding all forms of
deception he stayed clear of danger.

And yet he never earned enough to put a little aside. He took
the money in with his left hand and paid it out with his right,
just about breaking even each day. Saving a bit was out of the
question. He knew how to economize, but Huniu knew only
how to spend. Her confinement was due early in the second
month of the new year, and when she began to show, at the beginning of winter, she thrust her belly out as a sign of her importance. A glance at her bulging abdomen was all she needed to
stay in and let Fuzi do the cooking; the leftovers were fed to her
brothers, which was an added expense. And, of course, Huniu
snacked between meals, increasing the girth around her middle.
She felt she mustn't deny herself the treats she deserved; besides
spending her own money on little tidbits, she had Xiangzi bring
something home every day. Whatever he earned, she spent; she
pegged her demands on his fluctuating earnings, and there was
nothing he could say. Her money had gotten them through
when he was laid up, and now it was his turn to spend on her.
Holding back even a bit drove her straight to her sickbed. "Carrying a child is a nine-month illness, something you'll never understand." That was the truth.

Huniu got more demanding as New Year's approached. Since
her movements were restricted, Fuzi was sent out to buy things

for her. However much she hated being stuck in the house, she pampered herself too much to go outside. She was bored to tears, and her only recourse was to treat herself to the things she liked, though she insisted they were for Xiangzi, not for her. "Why don't you try some," she said, "after working so hard? You haven't completely recovered, and it's already the end of the year. If you don't eat, you'll wind up skinnier than a bedbug." Xiangzi did not argue with her—he didn't know how—so she prepared whatever it was and ate two or three large bowlfuls. Then, when she was finished, she'd sit there, bloated and complaining that it was a problem with her pregnancy.

After New Year's, Huniu kept Xiangzi from going out at night, afraid that the baby might come when he was away. Only now was she reminded of her true age, though she would not reveal it. She stopped saying, "I'm just a tiny bit older than you" to Xiangzi, which had always annoyed him. Life is perpetuated by the birth of sons and daughters, and he was secretly pleased, despite the knowledge that a child was one thing he did not need. Yet even the hardest-hearted man will, if he closes his eyes and reflects, be moved by that simple, magical word *Dad*, when it refers to him, whatever else he might think. Xiangzi, a rough, clumsy man, could see nothing in himself to be proud of. But that wonderful word made him feel respectable; it did not matter that he had nothing, since a child of his own gave value to his life. Then he considered Huniu, who was no longer just "one" person, and vowed to do what he could for her, wait on her as best he could. Disagreeable though she was, in this situation she deserved credit. And yet he'd run out of patience with her mercurial temper. She would change her mind on a whim and make absurd demands on Xiangzi, who had to go out to make a day's wages and then rest in the evenings. Even if she spent his earnings foolishly, he needed a good night's sleep so he could go out the next day and do it all over again. But she not only kept him home in the evenings, she made it impossible for him to get a decent night's sleep, and he was helpless to change matters. He plodded woozily through each day, like it or not, by turns happy, anxious, and dejected. There were times when he was ashamed of his happiness, times when he was comforted by his anxiety, and times when he was happy to be dejected. His emotions were a jumble, and as a simple man, he lost the ability to figure out which way was up. Once he even took a passenger past his destination after forgetting the address he'd been told.

Around the time of the Lantern Festival in the middle of the first lunar month, Huniu, having reached the point where she could hold out no longer, sent Xiangzi for a midwife, who saw that it was not time and explained to her the signs of imminent labor. Huniu held on for two more days before raising another row, demanding that the midwife return. Still too soon. By then she was screaming tearfully that she wanted to die, that she was in unbearable agony. Xiangzi, feeling helpless, could only indulge her by not taking his rickshaw out.

By the end of the month, even he could tell that the time had come. Huniu no longer looked human. When the midwife arrived this time, she hinted to Xiangzi that owing to the mother's age and the facts that this would be her first child, that she had been sedentary for so long, that the fetus was especially large, and that she had eaten far too much greasy, fatty food, it was likely to be a difficult birth. Those factors eliminated any hope that things would go smoothly. She had not seen a doctor, who would have helped her correct the position of the fetus, and the midwife lacked the skill to do that. But she knew enough to say, "I'm afraid we might be in for a tough time."

In the compound it had become customary to talk about the birth of a child and the death of a mother in the same breath. But the danger for Huniu was greater than for the other women, who remained active up till the day the babies came, and who kept the size of the fetus down by eating less. Their babies came easily; the danger they faced came from a lack of care after childbirth. It was the opposite for Huniu, whose advantages in life would prove to be her downfall.

Xiangzi, Fuzi, and the midwife attended her for three days, during which she called upon all the deities she could think of and made countless vows. All wasted. Finally, her voice nearly gone, she could only call out softly, "Mother!" There was nothing the midwife could do, nothing anyone could do, so Huniu told Xiangzi to go to Desheng Gate and fetch Granny Chen, an old medium who spoke through a Toad Spirit. Granny Chen demanded five yuan to come, so Huniu took out her last seven or eight yuan and handed them to him. "Go ahead, Xiangzi, and be quick about it. Never mind the money. When I'm better, I'll be a good wife to you. Now go!"

Granny Chen arrived in the company of her acolyte, a jaundiced forty-year-old man, when it was time to light the lamps. In her fifties, she was dressed in a blue silk jacket, wore a red pomegranate flower in her hair, and was draped in gold-plated jewelry. The first thing the hawk-eyed woman did after walking in the door was wash her hands; then she lit some incense, kowtowed, and sat in front of the incense stand staring intensely at the burning tips. Suddenly, without warning, her body quaked with violent spasms, her head drooped, her eyes snapped shut, and she remained motionless for what seemed like a long time. They could have truly heard a pin drop in the room. Even Huniu clenched her teeth to keep from making a sound. Granny Chen's

head rose slowly before nodding to the people in the room as her
acolyte grabbed Xiangzi to get him to kowtow. Now, Xiangzi
could not say if he believed in spirits, but what harm could a
kowtow do? So he began, unsure of how many times he banged
his head on the floor. When he stood up, he looked expectantly
at the piercing eyes and the glowing incense tips and smelled the
fragrant smoke, vaguely hoping that something good would
come of all this. His palms were sweaty as he stood there in a bit
of a daze.

The Toad Spirit spoke in an ancient, shaky voice, "No, no, it
doesn't matter, draw a charm to hasten, hasten, hasten the delivery!"

The acolyte quickly handed a sheet of thin yellow paper to
the spirit, who grabbed a handful of incense sticks, wetted the
paper with spit, and began to draw.

When she finished, she muttered something about a previous
life, wherein Huniu had incurred a debt to her child, who was
making her suffer. Poor, bewildered Xiangzi understood little of
what she said, but he was afraid.

Granny Chen yawned grandly, shut her eyes for a moment,
and then snapped them open, as if waking from a dream. She
seemed pleased when the acolyte told her what the Toad Spirit
had said. "The Toad Spirit must be happy today, for it has spoken. She told Xiangzi to make Huniu swallow the magic charm,
along with a pill she handed him.

Granny Chen then eagerly waited to see what effect her
charm produced. Meanwhile, Xiangzi was expected to feed her,
a task he entrusted to Fuzi, who went out and bought some
sesame cakes fresh from the oven and a jellied pig's elbow.
Granny Chen grumbled over the lack of wine to wash it all
down.

Huniu had swallowed the charm, but even after the medium and her acolyte had finished eating, she writhed in agony on the bed. That went on for another hour, until her eyes rolled up into her head. Undaunted, Granny Chen calmly told Xiangzi to light another stick of incense and kneel in front of it. By then, his faith in Granny Chen had pretty much vanished, but since he had spent five yuan on her, he might as well give it a try, since he certainly couldn't attack her physically. Besides, what if it actually worked?

Kneeling before the stick of incense, his back straight, Xiangzi had no idea who he was praying to, but he concentrated on being devout. As he watched the flickering flame, he talked himself into seeing something shadowy in the red glow, and he began to pray. The incense burned lower, gray streaks spreading across the red tip; his head drooped and he rested his hands on the floor as a hazy sense of weariness overcame him, after three days with hardly any sleep. When his head pitched forward, he awoke with a start. The incense stick had burned all the way down. Without knowing if this was the time he should stand up or not, he braced his hands on the floor and got slowly to his feet on legs that were slightly numb.

Granny Chen and her acolyte had stolen away as he slept.

With no time for enmity, Xiangzi rushed over to check on Huniu, aware that he could expect the worst. She had deteriorated to the point of being unable to speak. The midwife told him to rush her to the hospital, that there was nothing more she could do.

That heartbreaking news drew a mournful wail from Xiangzi; Fuzi, too, was sobbing, but she knew she had to keep a clear head. "Don't cry, Elder Brother Xiangzi, I'll go."

Without waiting for a response, she ran out, drying her tears.

After an hour, she returned out of breath. Supporting herself on the table, she was racked by coughs before she could speak. A visit by the doctor would cost ten yuan for a quick examination, she reported. The childbirth would cost twenty more. And a difficult delivery would require taking the patient to the hospital, which would mean much more money.

"What should we do, Elder Brother?"

There was nothing they *could* do but wait for death to claim whom it would.

Ignorance and cruelty had brought them to this point. Where there is ignorance and where there is cruelty, there will be other reasons.

At midnight, Huniu delivered a dead infant and then stopped breathing.

CHAPTER TWENTY

Xiangzi sold his rickshaw.

Money trickled through his fingers like water. The deceased had to be taken out and buried, and even the death certificate cost money.

As he numbly watched people scurry about, Xiangzi was good only for handing out money. His eyes were frighteningly red, with yellow mucus collecting at the corners. He heard nothing as he mechanically submitted to the demands of the milling crowd, not knowing what he was doing.

Only as he followed Huniu's coffin out of the city did his mind clear a bit, though he remained unable to gather his thoughts. Xiangzi and Fuzi's two young brothers were the only mourners, each with a handful of spirit money to appease demons blocking the way on the road to the grave.

Numbly he looked on as the pallbearers placed the coffin in the ground. He did not cry, for a fire blazing in his chest had dried all his tears, making crying impossible and irrelevant; as he stood there staring into space, he could not have said what they were doing. Finally, when the head bearer came up to announce that they had finished, the thought entered his head to go home.

Fuzi had the rooms ready for his return. He threw himself

down on the bed, too tired to move. His eyes were too dry to close, so he looked around the room, then quickly averted his eyes, not knowing what to do with himself. He went out, bought a pack of Yellow Lion cigarettes, and sat on the edge of the bed and lit one. It brought him no pleasure. As he watched blue smoke rise from the tip of the cigarette, the tears finally came. He was weeping not only for Huniu but for all that had happened. This is what years of diligence and hard work in the city had brought him! Just this, just this! He wept silently. A rickshaw, a rickshaw had been his rice bowl. He'd bought one and lost it. He'd bought another and sold it. Time and again he'd reached up only to be thrown back, as by a ghostly apparition that forever eluded his grasp. He'd suffered so many hardships and wrongs, and yet had come up empty. Nothing, he had nothing, had lost even his wife. Huniu had been a shrew, but without her, how could he have a home and family? Everything in the room was hers, but now she was lying in a grave outside the city wall. As his bitterness swelled, blazing anger again dried his tears. He smoked his cigarette with fury; the more the act gnawed at him, the more furiously he smoked, until it burned all the way down. Then he held his head in his hands and, the acrid taste burning his mouth and his soul, he felt like screaming until he could spit out the blood in his heart.

At some point, Fuzi had walked into the outer room and was standing by the chopping board, watching him warily.

When he looked up, he saw her, which brought more tears. He was so miserable he'd have wept at the sight of a dog, at any living object to which he could pour out his grievances. He'd have liked a bit of sympathy. But there was too much to say, more than his mouth could handle.

"Brother Xiangzi!" She stepped toward him. "I've tidied the place up."

He nodded without thanking her—conventional manners in the midst of sorrow are empty gestures.

"What do you plan to do?"

"Huh?" At first he didn't comprehend what she said, but when the words registered, he shook his head. He hadn't thought that far ahead.

She stepped closer and blushed, showing her front teeth, but said nothing. Modesty had been a victim of the life she led, but as a decent young woman at heart, she knew what to do when confronted by something so important. "I was thinking . . ." That was all she managed to get out, though there was so much more she wanted to say. Again she blushed, and the words vanished beyond recovery.

People seldom tell each other the truth, but a woman's blush says more than words. Even Xiangzi knew what she meant. She was the most beautiful woman he'd ever known; her beauty reached into her bones. Had her body been covered with rotting sores, to him she'd still have been irresistible. Pretty, young, and diligent. If Xiangzi wanted to remarry, she'd be an ideal wife. But it was too soon to be thinking of that, too soon to be thinking of anything. Yet she was obviously willing and had been forced by her drastic situation to raise the issue. How could he refuse? She was a good person and had been so helpful; he could only nod, yearning to take her in his arms and cry on her shoulder to wash away his troubles, then start life anew with her. He saw in her all the comforts a man could and should receive. Though he was someone not given to speaking, the mere sight of her made him want to say everything that was in his heart.

Nothing he might say to her would be a waste of breath. He could ask for no better reply than a nod or a smile, and he would feel that he had a home.

At that moment, Fuzi's second brother ran in. "Sister," he shouted. "Father's here!"

With a frown, she went over and opened the door. Er Qiangzi had walked into the yard.

"What are you doing in Xiangzi's rooms?" He stumbled toward her with a wicked glare. "You can't sell yourself enough as it is. What's the idea of giving it away to Xiangzi, you cheap slut!"

Hearing his name, Xiangzi came outside and stood beside Fuzi.

"You there, Xiangzi." Er Qiangzi tried to throw out his chest but was too unsteady to even stand straight. "Are you a man, or aren't you? Take advantage of some people if you want, but who do you think you are to try that on her?"

Xiangzi had no desire to fight with a drunk, but a bellyful of anger forced his hand. He stepped up. Four bloodshot eyes met and seemed to emit sparks. Xiangzi grabbed Er Qiangzi by the shoulders, lifted him off the ground like a rag doll, and flung him across the yard.

A guilty conscience, aided by alcohol, sparked an attempt at rage. But Er Qiangzi was not as drunk as he pretended, and being sprawled on the ground sobered him up completely. Though he'd have liked to fight back, he knew he was no match for Xiangzi. Yet quietly leaving the scene was not an option, so he sat there, not yet ready to stand up but knowing he'd have to sooner or later. His mind a tangle of thoughts, he had to say something. "What business is it of yours what I say to my children? Hit me? You'll fucking pay for this!"

Saying nothing in reply, Xiangzi waited for the man to get up and fight.

Fuzi stood there in tears, helpless. Reasoning with her father would be a waste of time, but she didn't want to see him beaten, either. Managing to dig up some small change from her pockets, she handed it to her brother, who was normally fearful of getting too close to his father. But seeing him knocked to the ground gave him a dose of courage. "Here, take this and get out of here!"

Er Qiangzi squinted as he took the money and grumbled, standing on shaky legs, "I'll let you bastards off this time, but get me mad enough and I'll cut your damned hearts out." When he reached the street, he turned and shouted, "We're not finished, Xiangzi. We'll settle this one day!"

Once he'd gone, Xiangzi and Fuzi walked back inside.

"There's nothing I can do," she said under her breath, summing up her distress and incorporating her boundless hopes in Xiangzi: if he'd have her, she could leave that life behind.

This episode opened Xiangzi's eyes to some dark shadows in Fuzi. He still loved her, but supporting her brothers and her drunken father was beyond his means. He still had trouble believing that Huniu's death had freed him, for she'd had her strong points, most prominently her willingness to help him financially. However certain he might be that Fuzi would not sponge off him, it was just as true that no one in her family could contribute any income. Love or no love, for a poor man, money talks. Lasting love can sprout and grow only in the homes of the rich.

He began packing his things.

"Are you moving out?" Fuzi asked, her lips turning white.

"Yes." He hardened his heart. In this unfair world, a poor

man retains what little personal freedom he is entitled to only by being hard-hearted.

With a quick glance at him, Fuzi lowered her head and walked out. She felt neither hatred nor resentment, only despair.

Huniu's jewelry and finest clothing had been buried with her, leaving only some well-worn clothes, a few pieces of furniture, and the pots, pans, and dishes behind. After putting aside the generally presentable clothing, Xiangzi sold everything else to a scrap dealer for something over ten yuan. In a hurry to get rid of all that stuff, he'd accepted the man's first offer without holding out for a better deal. After the man took everything away, what remained in the room were Xiangzi's bedding and the few items he'd held back, all lying on the bare brick bed. He felt better seeing the room empty, as if freed of his bonds; now he could get as far away from there as he wanted. But then he recalled those sold-off objects. The table that had sat by the wall was gone, but little square marks left in the dust by its legs remained, reminders not only of things but also of a person, now vanished like a dream. Good or bad, without those things and that person, his heart had no resting place. He sat on the edge of the bed and took out his pack of Yellow Lions.

A crumpled bank note came out with the cigarettes. Absentmindedly, he removed all the money from his pockets. Over the past few days, he hadn't gotten around to figuring out how much he had. There was a little bit of everything, from foreign money to ten-cent bills, one-cent bills, and small coins. It was a large pile that added up to less than twenty yuan. Together with the ten yuan he'd gotten from the scrap dealer, he had a total of slightly over thirty. His entire worth: thirty yuan plus a little.

After laying it out on the bare bed, he stared at it, not knowing whether to laugh or cry. The room was empty except for

Xiangzi and that pile of crumpled, filthy money. The meaning of it all escaped him.

With a sigh, he scooped up the bills and coins, and then picked up his bedding and the clothes he'd put aside to go looking for Fuzi.

"These are for you. I'll leave my bedding to look for work at the rickshaw sheds. I'll be back to get it." This he said in one breath, afraid to look her in the eye.

Her only response was a muffled assent.

Xiangzi found work and returned for his bedding. Fuzi's eyes were red and swollen from crying. Not knowing what else to say, he forced himself to utter, "Wait, wait till I'm back on my feet. I'll be back. I will be back!"

She nodded but said nothing.

After taking a day off to rest, Xiangzi was back pulling a rickshaw, but not with the fire of earlier days. He didn't loaf on the job; he just took each day as it came. After a month of getting by, his mood had lightened. His face had filled out somewhat but wasn't as ruddy as it had been; it had a sallow cast that gave him a look somewhere between robust and frail. His eyes were bright but absent any expression, as if filled with lighted energy but seeing nothing. His spirit was like a tree after a storm, standing quietly and timidly in the sun. Taciturn to begin with, now he was all but mute. Tender green leaves filled the branches of willows in the warm air. Sometimes he pulled his rickshaw out into the sun and, head down, muttered to himself, lips barely moving. At other times he lay on his back and slept under the sun. He didn't speak unless he had to.

By then he'd picked up the smoking habit. Anytime he was alone on his rickshaw, he'd reach under the footrest, take out a cigarette and light it, then enjoy a leisurely smoke, eyes fixed on the smoke rising from the tip of his cigarette. Then he would nod, as if he'd had some sort of epiphany.

He still ran faster than most rickshaw men but not like before. He was careful when he took corners or negotiated a slope, up or down. More careful than he needed to be. When challenged to a race, no matter how intensely he was provoked, he kept his head down and his mouth shut as he ran on at a steady pace. It was as if he'd figured out what this business of pulling a rickshaw was all about and had abandoned any thoughts of gaining glory or praise from it.

But back at the rickshaw shed he actually made some friends. Not that he gave up his disinclination to talk, but even a silent wild goose keeps to the flock. His loneliness would have crushed him without a circle of friends. Whenever he took out a pack of cigarettes, he first passed them around. And if one of his new friends was embarrassed to take the last cigarette in the pack, he'd simply say, "There are more where they came from!" No longer did he shy away from watching the other men gamble, and some of the time he joined in, not caring whether he won or lost; he just wanted to show that he was one of them and acknowledge that after days of pulling a rickshaw, there was nothing wrong with a little amusement. When they drank, he drank—not much—and he sometimes went out and bought the liquor and snacks to go with it. Things he'd looked down on in the past now seemed perfectly reasonable. The course he'd chosen had not worked out, forcing him to admit that the others had been right all along. In the past, he'd ignored his social obligations whenever someone had a funeral or a wedding; now he'd kick in forty cents or whatever his share of a joint gift might be. And that wasn't the end of it: he made a point of participating in the wake or offering his congratulations, for he had come to realize that these gestures were an essential component of human relations, not a waste of money. The wails and joyful outbursts were genuine, not an act.

But he would not touch those thirty-odd yuan, which he clumsily sewed into a piece of white cloth and kept next to his skin at all times. He did not want to spend it, even though he was no longer saving up to buy a rickshaw. He kept it with him, just in case, knowing that the next calamity could be right around the corner, and that he had to be prepared for the possibility of an illness or some other sudden catastrophe. He was not made of steel—he knew that now.

Shortly before the beginning of fall he landed another monthly hire. His duties at this new manor were lighter than those he'd worked at in the past; he would not have taken the job otherwise, having learned the virtue of discernment. He'd take on a monthly hire only if it suited him. If not, he'd continue picking up stray fares. He no longer felt a fire in his belly to work at one of the manors. Finally realizing the importance of good health, he understood that a rickshaw man could drive himself mercilessly—as he had once done—and kill himself in the process, all for nothing. Experience teaches a man how to cut corners in life, because you only live once.

This job was located in the vicinity of the Yonghe Lamasery. His employer, a fellow in his fifties named Xia, was an educated, cultured man with a wife and twelve children. He had recently taken a concubine, without his wife's knowledge, and had installed her in this quiet part of the city. Only four occupants lived in the new household: Mr. Xia, his concubine, a maidservant, and the rickshaw man—Xiangzi.

Xiangzi was happy with his new job and the surroundings. It was a six-room house—three for Mr. Xia, a kitchen, and two for the servants. The yard was small, with a young date tree standing against the southern wall, which, at the time, had produced a dozen or so half-ripe dates on its top branches. To sweep the yard, it took him no more than a few swipes with the broom to go from one end to the other. There were no plants to water, and though he was tempted to prune the tree, he knew that date trees tend to grow crooked, so he left it alone.

There were few other responsibilities. He took Mr. Xia to work in the yamen early in the morning and picked him up to return home at five in the afternoon. As if he were in hiding, Mr. Xia would not leave the house again that day. The new Mrs. Xia, on the other hand, went out often, but was always back home by four o'clock to give Xiangzi time to pick up her husband. That was the last chore of the day. Even better, she confined her trips to the East Gate Market or Sun Yat-sen Park, which gave Xiangzi plenty of time to rest. For him the job was child's play.

Mr. Xia was a stingy man who never spent a cent without having to. Wherever he went, he sat rigidly in the seat, looking straight ahead, as if the streets were devoid of people and objects. His wife was the opposite—she went out shopping every two or three days, and if she bought food that was not to her liking, she gave it to the servants. And she would turn usable items over to them when she wanted to get money from her husband to replace them with new ones. To all appearances, Mr. Xia's purpose in life was to expend all his energy and spend all his money in the service of his concubine. She was his life, his only enjoyment. All the money that left his hand passed through hers on the way out. He seemed pathologically incapable of spending it, let alone giving it away. Word had it that his first wife and twelve children, who lived in Baoding, could go four or five months without seeing a cent of his money.

Xiangzi disliked the way Mr. Xia sneaked around like a thief: hunched over, neck drawn into his shoulders, eyes cast down, eerily silent. A committed penny-pincher, he never laughed, and he rode in his rickshaw like a scrawny monkey. He did speak, once in a blue moon, but what he said was invariably offensive. Only he was an educated, cultured gentleman; everyone else was a useless bastard. People like that had always disgusted Xiangzi. But a job was a job, and all that mattered was that he got paid every month. Besides, the man's concubine was a generous woman who often gave him food and other things. *Let it go at that,* he concluded. *I'll pretend I'm pulling a thoughtless monkey.*

In Xiangzi's eyes, the concubine was simply a woman who provided him with small change, not someone he admired. She was prettier than Fuzi, and she smelled wonderful, with all the perfume and powder she used. How could Fuzi compare with someone who dressed in silks and satins? But despite her beauty and delicate makeup, there was something about her that reminded him of Huniu. It wasn't her clothes or her looks; no, it had more to do with her attitude and her behavior, though Xiangzi had trouble putting it into words. He just felt that she and Huniu were—it was the only expression he could think of—the same sort of goods. She was young, no more than twenty-two or -three, but she had the airs of an older woman, not those of a recent bride. Like Huniu, it seemed, she'd never known a time of girlish modesty or gentleness. Her hair was permed, she wore high-heeled shoes, and her clinging dresses showed off her figure to great effect. Even Xiangzi could see that, stylish though she was, she lacked the grace of most married women. But she didn't appear to have been a prostitute, and Xiangzi could not figure her out. She intimidated him, the way Huniu had, but since she was younger and prettier than Huniu, it was, if anything, worse. She personified all the harsh feminine qualities and malice he'd ever experienced, and he averted his eyes when she was around.

His fear of her increased the longer he worked there. Mr. Xia hardly ever spent any money when Xiangzi was around, though sometimes he bought drugs in a pharmacy. Xiangzi had no idea what the drugs were, but they made them a happy couple whenever he brought some home, and Mr. Xia normally a man who could hardly draw a full breath, would be full of energy. That would last two or three days, until Mr. Xia reverted to his sickly old self, even a bit more bent at the waist, like a fish bought at the market that would thrash around in a pail of water for a while before giving up the fight. Whenever Xiangzi saw Mr. Xia looking like death warmed over, he knew it was time to visit the pharmacy again. He did not like Mr. Xia but could not help feeling sorry for the scrawny monkey each time they headed for the pharmacy. Then when they returned home, drugs in hand, Xiangzi would think of Huniu and be miserable for some strange reason. He didn't want to think bad thoughts about the deceased, but when he looked at himself and then at Mr. Xia, his resentment of her returned. He was not as strong as he'd once been, and for that Huniu had been largely responsible.

He considered quitting, but to do so over something so trivial did not make sense. As he puffed on a Yellow Lion, he muttered to himself, "Worrying about other people is a waste of time."

CHAPTER TWENTY-ONE

When chrysanthemums came on the market, Mrs. Xia bought four pots, one of which the maidservant, Yang Ma, broke, for which she suffered a severe tongue-lashing. Having come from the countryside, Yang Ma saw nothing special in flowers and houseplants. But through her own carelessness, she had broken something belonging to her employer, however inconsequential, and took the abuse without a sound. At first. But when Mrs. Xia went on relentlessly, calling her a country bumpkin and a useless savage, she could not keep her temper in check and out it came. Now, when country folk get worked up, self-control goes out the window; Yang Ma responded to Mrs. Xia with the vilest curses. Hopping mad, Mrs. Xia told Yang Ma to roll up her bedding and clear out.

Xiangzi stood by without intervening in the blowup. His tongue never served him well in such situations, especially when the argument involved two women. And when he heard Yang Ma call Mrs. Xia a cheap whore, a stinking cunt ridden and fingered by a thousand men, he knew she could not possibly hold on to her job, and that he'd likely be fired too, since Mrs. Xia would not want a servant around who knew about her background. After Yang Ma left, Xiangzi waited to hear that he was dismissed. He figured it would happen as soon as a new maid-servant was hired, and that did not bother him in the least. Experience had taught him that jobs came and went, and there was no need to get worked up over it.

But after Yang Ma left, Mrs. Xia treated Xiangzi with surprising courtesy. With no maid in the house, she had to go into the kitchen to do the cooking, so she sent Xiangzi to the market. When he returned, she told him what to peel and what to wash while she chopped the meat and boiled the rice, talking to him the whole time. She was wearing a pink chemise over a pair of dark trousers and white satin embroidered slippers. Xiangzi did his work clumsily, head down to avoid the temptation to look at her. He breathed in her perfume, which seemed to be telling him he must look like a bee that is drawn to a flower.

Knowing how dangerous a woman can be, Xiangzi also knew that they aren't all bad. One Huniu was all it would take any man to both fear and cling to women. With Mrs. Xia, who was superior to Huniu, that prospect was intensified. He sneaked a look at her. Though she was as much to be feared as Huniu, she was in many ways more desirable than his wife had ever been.

If this had been two years earlier, Xiangzi would not have had the nerve to look, but that bit of social convention no longer concerned him. In the first place, he had been seduced once and his self-control had suffered from that seduction. Second, he had gradually come to fit into the "rickshaw man" groove of behavior. What the average rickshaw man considered proper he did, too. Since hard work and self-restraint had brought him only failure, he had to concede that the other men's behavior and attitude had been right, and he was determined to be a "rickshaw man," whether he felt like it or not. You travel with the crowd or not at all. Now, any poor man knows that getting away with something is a good thing, so why had he passed up all those opportunities to do exactly that? He'd looked at her. So what! She was just a cheap woman, and if she was willing, he could not refuse her. It might have been difficult to believe that she could lower herself for him. But who could say? He would not make the first move and didn't know what he'd do if she dropped a hint or two. But she had already opened the door a crack, which was the only reason he could think of for her sending Yang Ma on her way and not hiring another maid right away. Just so he could help out in the kitchen? Then why the perfume? Xiangzi entertained no illusions, but deep in his heart a choice was forming and hope was sprouting anew. He seemed caught up in a wonderful yet unreal dream; knowing it was only a dream, he was nonetheless set on seeing it through to the end. A life force inside compelled him to admit that he was not a good person; hidden in this admission was the source of great pleasure—and maybe great troubles. Who knew? Who cared?

A ray of hope stoked his courage, and that little bit of courage created heat that ignited his heart. There was nothing cheap or demeaning here. Neither he nor she could be considered low-class. Carnal desire is common to all.

But then a note of fear reawakened his judgment, and that judgment put out the fire in his heart. He was tempted to get out of there as fast as he could, for there could only be trouble here; by taking this road he would make a fool of himself.

Hope one moment, fear the next, as if he were suffering from the alternating chills and fever of malaria. He felt worse now than he had when Huniu had entrapped him in his innocence. Then he'd been like a bee that falls into a spider web on its first venture out of the hive. Now he knew the virtues of caution and the risks of boldness. For some strange reason he wanted to take this to its logical conclusion, yet he was fearful of falling into the trap.

He did not look down on this concubine, this unlicensed prostitute, this beauty, who was everything and nothing. If he wanted to defend this view, the person to be looked down on was that hateful scrawny monkey, Mr. Xia, who deserved retribution for being such a disgusting human being. With a husband like him, she could not be faulted for anything. And with an employer like him, he—Xiangzi—could do as he pleased. His courage returned.

But she showed no sign of being aware that he had looked her way. When lunch was ready, she ate in the kitchen, alone. And when she finished, she called out to Xiangzi, "Come and eat. When you're finished, you can do the dishes. This afternoon, when you go to pick up Mr. Xia, swing by the market to buy groceries for dinner. That will save you a trip. Tomorrow's Sunday, so my husband will be home, and I can go out and hire a new maid. Know anyone? A good maid is hard to find. But eat your lunch before it gets cold."

She'd spoken so easily and naturally. Her pink chemise—in Xiangzi's eyes—suddenly did not seem so outrageous. Disappointment set in and then chagrin, as he realized that he really was a bad person, not a man with clear aspirations. Somehow he managed to finish off two bowls of rice, overcome by feelings of dejection. He went straight to his room after washing the dishes and chain-smoked Yellow Lions.

That afternoon, as he was bringing Mr. Xia home, he was struck by intense feelings of disgust for the scrawny monkey and would have liked nothing more than to get up some speed, then let go of the shafts and send the man crashing to the ground. Only now did he understand what had happened once when he was working for a wealthy family. The master had caught his third concubine having dubious relations with his son, who had then thought seriously about poisoning the old man. Back then, Xiangzi had thought that the young master was too young to know what he was doing; now, however, Xiangzi understood that the old man really did deserve to die, though he personally had no desire to commit murder. To him, Mr. Xia was repugnant and loathsome, yet he had no way of making him pay for these ugly qualities. All he could do was jerk the shafts up and down to make it an uncomfortable ride for the scrawny monkey, who never said a word, which made Xiangzi feel that he himself had gotten the worst of it. Never before had he done anything like that, and though he had his reasons for doing it this time, that was no excuse. Feelings of regret instilled in him a sense of detachment. *Why make things hard on myself? No matter how I look at it, I'm a rickshaw man. I need to do my job and not think about anything else.*

That calmed him. He put the incident out of his mind, and on those occasions when he was reminded of it, he found it ludicrous.

Mrs. Xia went out the next day to hire a maid and returned later in the day with a trial maid in tow. Xiangzi knew what he could expect, and the whole affair left a bad taste in his mouth.

After lunch on Monday, Mrs. Xia sent the trial maid packing, complaining that she wasn't clean enough. Then she sent Xiangzi out to buy a pound of chestnuts.

When he returned with the still-hot chestnuts, he stood outside her door and said he was back.

"Bring them in," she said.

She was sitting at her vanity powdering her face when Xiangzi walked in. Still wearing the pink chemise, she had changed into a pair of light green pants. She turned to face Xiangzi when she saw him in the mirror, and smiled. He saw Huniu in that smile, a young and beautiful Huniu, and stood there stiffly. His courage, his hopes, his fears, and his caution, all gone, leaving only a heated breath that supported his body—it could swell up, it could shrink. This breath dictated whether he went forward or retreated; he had no will of his own.

The next evening he returned to the rickshaw shed with his bedding.

What Xiangzi had once considered the most fearful and shameful of things he now shared openly and jokingly with his friends: he could not urinate.

His friends eagerly gave advice on which drugs to use and which doctor to go to, none of them seeing anything shameful about his predicament. With plenty of sympathetic advice, a bit of embarrassment, and considerable pride, they related their own experiences with the problem. Several of the younger men had paid to get the disease; some of the slighter older men had picked it up free of charge. Some of those with monthly hires spoke of experiences that differed in degree but were similar in nature, while others, who had no firsthand experience, related tales of their employers that were worth telling. Xiangzi's sickness caused them to open their hearts to him and treat him as one of their own. Forgetting his shame, but taking no pride in what had happened to him, he took his sickness in stride, treating it as if he'd caught a cold or suffered a bit of heatstroke. Regret set in when there was pain, but once that passed, memories of the pleasure returned. He was not going to get excited over this, for he had lived long enough to know how little life was worth, and getting excited over such matters never accomplished a thing.

The little bit of medicine and prescriptions cost over ten yuan but did not get to the root of his problem, since he quit taking the medicine as soon as he was a little better. On overcast days or during seasonal changes, when his joints began to ache, he would take a few more doses or tough it out, not caring one way or the other. Life was already unimaginably bitter, so why worry about his health? That was just the way things were. If even a fly can enjoy life in a privy, a grown man like him ought to be able to do at least as well.

After the illness had passed, Xiangzi was a changed man. He was still as tall as before, but his fighting spirit had died. He let his shoulders sag and kept a cigarette dangling from his drooping lips. He often stuck an unlit butt behind his ear, not because it was a convenient place to keep it but to make him look tough. He still wasn't much of a talker, but when he did speak, he larded his speech with street slang, caring only about the effect, not his lack of fluency. As his will deserted him, his appearance and attitude grew sloppy.

And yet, he wasn't so bad when compared to other rickshaw men. When he was alone, he thought back to what he'd been like before and longed to stop the downhill slide he was on. He knew he could be better, and while that might not do him any good in the end, there was nothing noble in self-destruction. At such times, thoughts of buying another rickshaw crept in. He had already spent ten or more of his thirty yuan on his illness, a waste of money. But with twenty yuan he wasn't nearly as hopeless as the penniless men whose poverty had them firing a gun with an empty chamber. With that thought, he felt like throwing away the half-smoked pack of Yellow Lions and giving up smoking and drinking altogether. He'd tighten his belt and go back to saving money. Saving money meant buying a rickshaw, and that led him to guilty feelings about Fuzi. After leaving the compound, he hadn't been back to see her, not once. And during all that time, he'd not only failed to better himself but had even contracted a shameful disease!

But when he was with his friends, he continued to smoke and, when he had the chance, drink with them, putting Fuzi out of his mind. He was never one to take the lead in what they did, but he didn't shy away from joining them, either. Having a good time with his friends was the only way he could put the hard day's work and the bellyful of grievances behind him, for a while, at least. That momentary pleasure banished his lofty ideals, which were replaced by a desire to have a bit of fun and then sleep like the dead. Who wouldn't prefer that to a meaningless, painful, hopeless way to live? Only the poisons of tobacco, liquor, and women have the power to dull life's toxic cankers. Fight poison with poison. Everyone knew that it would one day eat into the heart, but who could come up with a better way out?

A lack of will to do better only increased Xiangzi's self-pity. Once proudly fearless, he now sought only comfort and ease. He stopped taking his rickshaw out on stormy days and took off two or three days at the first sign of soreness. Self-pity made him stingy, unwilling to lend out a cent of his savings, keeping it for a rainy day. It was all right to treat his friends to a cigarette or a drink, but he kept his savings to himself, since he was in greater need of coddling and pity than anyone. The more time he had on his hands, the lazier he grew, and the only way to lessen his boredom was to entertain himself with amusements or to treat himself to some good food. When it occurred to him that he was wasting time and money, he consoled himself with his latest mantra, culled from personal experience: "I tried to make something of myself, and what did it get me?" No one could dispute the logic or offer a reasonable explanation, so what was to keep him from sinking lower and lower?

Laziness can make a person hot-tempered, and Xiangzi mastered the technique of belligerence. No longer did he meekly knuckle under to his passengers or to the police or, for that matter, to anyone. He had never been treated fairly as a hardworking rickshaw man. Finally appreciating the value of his sweat, the less he shed, the better. No one had better try to take advantage of him. He'd park his rickshaw anywhere he pleased, whether it was legal or not, and if a policeman tried to get him to leave, he was quick to argue and slow to move. When it was clear he'd have to move on, the argument grew heated and vile. If the policeman argued back, well, why not let his fists do the talking? He knew his strength would not fail him, and after beating up the other man, a few days in the lockup was nothing to worry about. Fighting made him confidently aware of both his strength and his ability, and displaying his might on another man's body made it seem as if the sun shone especially bright, just for him. Never in the past had he entertained the thought of saving up his strength to do well in a fight. But that's what it had come to, and what pleasure he derived from it. That struck him as quite comical.

Xiangzi refused to be intimidated, not just by the policemen he encountered but also by automobiles that drove up and down the Beiping streets. He never made way for cars that roared toward him, sending dust flying, no matter how threateningly they honked their horns or how their occupants cursed and screamed. Only when they slowed down to avoid a collision did he move out of the way to avoid choking on the dust. The same held true when they came up from behind, for he knew they would never deliberately run into him. Why in the world, then, would he move to the side and eat their dust? The traffic police were concerned only about clearing the way for automobiles so they could raise as much dust as possible, but Xiangzi, who was not a policeman, had no interest in letting them roar by. He was, in the eyes of the police, a hard nut to crack, someone to be provoked at their peril. Sloth is the natural result of unrewarded hard work among the poor, reason enough for them to be prickly.

The passengers he hauled received no special treatment from Xiangzi. He took them where they wanted to go and not a step farther. If they said the entrance to an alley, then expected him to take them down the alley, not on your life! He was ready to meet his disappointed passengers glare for glare, and he always won, since he knew his nicely clad riders were afraid of getting their foreign suits dirty. He also knew how unreasonable and cheap these men—most of them, at least—were. All right, he was ready. The moment they popped off, he reached out, grabbed the sleeves of their fifty- or sixty-yuan suit coats, and decorated them with a big black handprint. It was not a free gift, for they still had to pay him. If they doubted his strength, their sore, skinny arms told them all they needed to know.

He still ran fast, but breakneck speed did him no good. If his passenger told him to speed up, he'd slow to a shuffle and demand, "You want speed? What'll you pay for it?" He sold blood and sweat, not courtesy. No longer did he hold out hope that a generous tip awaited him at the end of a run. The price—what he thought was fair—had to be settled before he put his muscle to work.

A rickshaw was nothing to be pampered. No longer did he fancy buying one of his own, nor did he care about those owned by others. They were just rickshaws. When he pulled one, he ate and paid the rent; when he didn't, he paid no rent, and as long as he had enough money to buy food, why worry about it? That was the relationship—the only relationship—between man and rickshaw. He was not one to deliberately damage one of them, but he saw no need to go all out to take care of one, either. From time to time, he was involved in an accident with another rickshaw, but he was no longer hopping mad when that happened. He'd calmly take it back to the owner's shed, and if he was told to pay fifty cents for the damage, he'd hand over twenty. What if the owner demanded more? Easy—he'd threaten to settle the matter with his fists, and he was happy to oblige if the owner was up for it.

Experience is the soil of life; it determines what a man will become. A peony will not grow in the desert. Xiangzi fell into a rut, neither better nor worse than any other rickshaw man, just an ordinary member of the trade. Not only did that make for a more comfortable life, but it also gained him acceptance from his peers. All crows are black, and he had no desire to be the only one with white feathers.

Another winter arrived, bringing a yellow sandstorm from the desert that in a single night froze many people to death. Xiangzi reacted to the howl of the wind by burying his head under the covers and staying there until it stopped. With a reluctant grumble he got up, not sure if he wanted to go out or take the day off. Although he was deterred by the thought of grasping those icy shafts, his greatest fear was the choking, nauseating blasts of wind. Dusk usually calmed the gale-like winds, and by four that afternoon, they had died out completely, as patches of sunset pink peeked through the evening haze. He forced himself to take his rickshaw out, tucking his hands into his sleeves and pushing the crossbar ahead with his chest, plodding along listlessly, a cigarette dangling from his lips. Darkness fell, and he decided to haul a couple more fares before knocking off for the day. He didn't even feel like lighting the lanterns until four or five policemen along the way finally got him to comply.

In front of the Drum Tower he stole another man's fare under the street lamps and began hauling his passenger to East City. Without even taking off his padded robe, he loped along, knowing how pathetic that looked, but so what! Would he get anything extra by doing a better job of it? He wasn't pulling: he was just going through the motions, and even when his forehead was beaded with sweat, he didn't stop to take off his robe. What difference did it make? When he turned down an alley, a dog that must have reacted to the sight of a rickshaw man running in a padded robe nipped at his heels. Xiangzi stopped, grabbed his whisk broom, and took off after the dog. Even after the dog had run off, he waited, in case it dared come back. It didn't. "Fucking cur!" he cursed spiritedly. "Think I'm afraid of you?"

"What the hell kind of rickshaw man are you?" his passenger asked angrily.

It was a familiar voice, and Xiangzi's heart skipped a beat. The alley was pitch black, and the lantern beams, though bright enough, pointed down, making it impossible to see the man's face. He was wearing a hooded winter hat that hid his features, all but his eyes. Xiangzi was still trying to recall where he'd heard that voice when the man asked, "Aren't you Xiangzi?"

Now he knew. It was Fourth Master Liu! Stunned, he went hot all over and didn't know what to do.

"Where's my daughter?"

"Dead!" Xiangzi stood there glued to the spot. Did he say that, or was it somebody else?

"What? She's dead?"

"Yes, she's dead."

"Anybody who falls into your fucking hands is sure to die!"

Xiangzi suddenly found himself. "Get down! I said get down! I'd knock you down from there if you weren't so old. Now get down!"

His hands shaking, Fourth Master climbed down. "Where's she buried? Tell me that."

"That's none of your business!" Xiangzi picked up the shafts and walked off.

After putting some distance between them, he turned to look. The old man—a big black shadow—was still standing there.

CHAPTER TWENTY-TWO

Xiangzi had forgotten where he was headed as he strode forward, head high, both hands gripping the shafts, eyes blazing, mindless of direction or destination. Happy and care-free, he felt as if he had disgorged all the bad luck that had come his way since marrying Huniu onto Fourth Master Liu. Disregarding the cold and forgetting to look for fares, he single-mindedly walked on, as if somewhere up ahead was the place where he would rediscover his old self, that happy-go-lucky, clean and honest, ambitious, hardworking Xiangzi. The vision of the old man standing in the middle of the alley made anything he might say unnecessary. Triumphing over Fourth Master was the ultimate victory. He hadn't raised a hand against him, hadn't given him the boot, but the old man had lost his only close relative, while Xiangzi remained free and perfectly at ease. No one could say that vengeance wasn't sweet. If the news did not kill Fourth Master outright, it would surely hasten his death. He had everything; Xiangzi had nothing. But Xiangzi could happily pull a rickshaw, while the old man could not even learn where his daughter was buried. All right, old man, even with your piles of money and prodigious temper, you are no match for a poor rick-shaw man who can barely manage two meals a day.

As his spirits soared, he felt like singing a song of triumph in a booming voice to let the world know that Xiangzi lived on and had claimed his victory.

Cold night air seemed to peel away the skin of his face, but to him it was bracing; chilling rays of light from street lamps actually warmed his heart. He was surrounded by light that brightened his future. Not having smoked for many days, he didn't miss it at all. From now on, no more tobacco and no more alcohol. Triumphing over Fourth Master gave Xiangzi the desire to start life afresh, to once again strive to better himself. He'd beaten Fourth Master once and for all. The old man's curses had the effect of highlighting Xiangzi's sense of accomplishment and filling him with hope. Now that he had spat out that last malevolent breath, he would henceforth breathe in only fresh air. Just look at those hands, those feet. He was still young, wasn't he? He would always be young. Huniu was dead, Fourth Master would soon be dead, but Xiangzi was very much alive; he was happy and he had ambitions. Yes, Xiangzi would live on. All evil people will die unmourned. The soldiers who'd seized his rickshaw; Mrs. Yang, who'd withheld food from her servants; Huniu, who'd deceived and oppressed him; Fourth Master, who'd been contemptuous of him; Detective Sun, who'd swindled him out of his money; Granny Chen, who'd made a fool of him; Mrs. Xia, who'd tried to seduce him . . . They would die, all of them, while faithful, honest Xiangzi would live on forever!

But, Xiangzi, from now on you must always do your best! he cautioned himself. *Why wouldn't I want to do my best? I have the will, the strength, and my youth.* In defense of himself, he replied, *Once I'm happy, no one can stop me from marrying and enjoying success at my trade. After what's happened to me lately, who could keep from going downhill in dejection? But that's all in the past.*

Tomorrow you will all be introduced to a new Xiangzi, even better than before, much better!

His legs seemed invigorated by his muttering, as if to prove that it was not meaningless talk. *I've got what it takes to carry this out. So what if I was sick or that I contracted a social disease? This change of heart will make me well and strong again. No problem!* He had worked up a sweat and a thirst. Thoughts of finding something to drink woke him up to his surroundings—he'd arrived at Rear Gate. Rather than go to a teahouse, he parked his rickshaw in the lot west of the gate and summoned a boy selling tea from a clay pot; he drank two bowls of an insipid liquid that passed for tea but tasted like dishwater. It was terrible, but he vowed that that was what he'd drink from then on; no more wasting money on good food and drink. Having made up his mind to live austerely, he decided to get something to eat— something that did not go down easily—to mark the beginning of a new life, dedicated to hard work and privation. He bought ten leathery, crusty griddlecakes filled with cabbage leaves and managed to get them down, despite the foul taste. Then he wiped his mouth with the back of his hand and asked himself, *Where to now?*

He could think of only two people he could go to and count on. To fulfill his promise to make something of himself, he would have to go see them both—Fuzi and Mr. Cao. Mr. Cao was a wise man who would be forgiving and helpful; he would tell Xiangzi what to do. After taking Mr. Cao's advice on dealing with the outside world, he'd go to Fuzi, who would be his helpmate at home. It was a flawless plan.

But had Mr. Cao returned home? Never mind, he'd go to Beichang Street the next day and ask around. If there was no news, he'd check with Mr. Zuo. Once he found Mr. Cao, his problems were solved. *All right, then,* he said to himself, *I'll haul fares tonight, and then go find Mr. Cao tomorrow. After that, I'll give Fuzi the good news that I had made a mess of things, but that's all in the past. Now it's time for you and me to set out on life's road together.*

Xiangzi's plans lit up his eyes as he searched the area for fares like a hawk, and when he spotted one he nearly flew to it. He was out of his padded robe even before settling the fee, and once he started out, though his legs lacked the power of earlier days, he ran all out, spurred on by a heat that coursed through his body. The same old Xiangzi. When he ran like that, no one could keep up with him. He overtook every rickshaw ahead, like a man possessed. Sweat streamed from him. His body felt lighter after his first trip, and there was renewed spring in his step. He wanted to keep running, like a fine racehorse that paws the ground when it hasn't run enough. He did not quit for the day until one in the morning, when he returned to the shed with the day's rent, plus ninety cents.

He went straight to bed and slept till daybreak. Then he rolled over and did not open his eyes again till the sun was high in the sky. There is nothing sweeter than a good rest after a hard workout. He got up and stretched, limbering up his cracking joints. His stomach was empty; he was famished.

After getting something to eat, with a little laugh he said to the shed boss, "I have something to do, so I'll be taking the day off." He had it all worked out: he'd take care of his personal business today and start his new life tomorrow.

First he headed to Beichang Street to see if Mr. Cao had moved back, intoning a silent prayer as he walked: *Please, Mr.*

*Cao, be there, don't let me come up empty. If things go bad at the
beginning, nothing will come out right in the end. Heaven won't
desert Xiangzi, now that he's turned his life around, will it?*

He rang the bell at Mr. Cao's gate with a trembling hand. His
heart nearly leaped out of his breast as he waited for someone to
come to a gate he knew so well. He had no time to think about
all that had happened; he just wanted to see the gate open to a
familiar face. He waited, beginning to suspect that there was no
one home. Why else would it be so dreadfully quiet? Suddenly,
there was a noise on the other side; it gave him a momentary
fright, like hearing something stir when you are keeping vigil at
a bier. The door opened, its creaky hinges accompanied by the
dearest, most affectionate sound he could have hoped for: "Oh!"
It was Gao Ma.

"Xiangzi, how long has it been? Look how thin you are!" She,
on the other hand, had put on weight.

"Is the master home?" was all he could say.

"Yes, but aren't you something! You can ask about the master
but pretend we don't know each other, not even a 'How do you
do?' Always the timid carpenter, too scared to saw wood. Come
in. How've you done for yourself?"

"Not so good." He smiled.

"Master," Gao Ma said outside the study. "Xiangzi's here."

Mr. Cao was moving some narcissus plants into the sunlight.
"Come in!"

"Go on in. You and I can talk later. I'll go tell the mistress
you're here. We often talk about you. A fool and his dumb luck."
She walked off talking to herself.

Xiangzi entered the study. "I'm back, Master." He wanted to
ask how the old man was doing but couldn't get the words out.

"Ah, Xiangzi." Mr. Cao, who stood there in a mandarin jacket, was wearing a kindly smile. "Sit down, um . . ." He thought for a moment. "We've been back quite a while. Old Cheng told us you were—let's see, Harmony Shed, I think. Gao Ma went looking for you but didn't find you. Sit down. How've you been? How about work?"

Tears were about to spill out of Xiangzi's eyes. He was incapable of telling people what he felt because that was written in blood and buried deep in his heart. It took a moment to calm down and try to turn that blood into simple words that would flow from his heart. It was all right there in his memory, and once he arranged it, little by little, he could narrate a living history. How significant it would be he did not know, but all the wrongs he'd suffered were clear and distinct.

Mr. Cao could see that Xiangzi was deep in thought, so he sat down to wait quietly for him to say something.

For what seemed like a long time, Xiangzi just stood there with his head bowed. Then he abruptly looked up at Mr. Cao, as if to suggest that he would say nothing if no one was interested in hearing him out.

"Go ahead, say it." Mr. Cao nodded.

So Xiangzi told what had happened to him, starting with how he'd come to the city from the countryside. He hadn't planned on mentioning such trivial facts of his past, but skipping them would have made it difficult to put the rest of his life in context. His memory was formed by blood, sweat, and suffering, and mustn't reveal itself lightly, leaving anything out. Every drop of sweat, every ounce of blood, flowed from his life, so everything that had happened was worth relating.

How he worked as a coolie laborer immediately after coming into the city, and then began pulling a rickshaw. How he scraped together enough to buy his own rickshaw, and how it was lost . . . he told of his life all the way up to the present. Even he was surprised by how much he had said and how natural it had felt. One after another, events in his life seemed to leap from his heart, each finding the words appropriate to its description. One sentence followed another, all honest and true, all endearing and tragic. He was powerless to keep the events bottled up, and so the words were unstoppable, with no hesitation or confusion. He seemed to want to empty his heart in one prolonged breath. A sense of relief built as he spoke, quickly forgetting himself, since he was now part and parcel of his narration. He was there in every sentence—ambitious, wronged, hardworking, degraded, all him. When he finished, his brow was sweaty, his heart empty, comfortably empty, the sort of comfort someone feels after passing out and coming to covered in a cold sweat.

"Now you want me to tell you what to do, is that it?" Mr. Cao said.

Xiangzi nodded. Now that he'd said his piece, he was reluctant to say more.

"You still want to pull a rickshaw?"

Again Xiangzi nodded. It was all he knew how to do.

"Well, since that's what you want," Mr. Cao said slowly, "you have two choices. One is to save up to buy your own rickshaw, the other to rent one from someone else. Don't you agree? Since you have no savings, you could borrow money to buy a rickshaw, but you'd have to pay interest on the loan, so what's the difference? You're better off renting one for now and finding a monthly job. It's steady work with a place to stay and free food. Your best bet would be to come work for me again, but since I sold my rickshaw to Mr. Zuo, you'd have to rent one. What do you say?"

"That sounds wonderful!" Xiangzi stood up. "Have you forgotten that other affair, sir?"

"What affair is that?"

"That time you and the mistress moved in with the Zuos."

"Oh, that!" Mr. Cao laughed. "I forgot that long ago. I was on pins and needles then, so the wife and I went to Shanghai for a few months. We really didn't have to, since Mr. Zuo took care of everything. That fellow Ruan Ming is an official now, and he doesn't seem inclined to give me any trouble. But you don't know about any of this, so don't give it another thought. Let's talk about you. What about that Fuzi you mentioned—what's her situation?"

"I don't know."

"Off the top of my head, I'd say you can't afford to marry her and find a place to live; you don't have enough for the rent alone, let alone the coal and lamp oil you'd need. Finding work, with you pulling a rickshaw and her working as a maid for the same household, would be harder than you think. Don't get me wrong, but I need to ask: Is she trustworthy?"

As his face reddened, Xiangzi stammered, "She only did what she did because she had no choice. She's a good person, I'll stake my life on it! She . . ." His heart was tied up in knots, as a welter of emotions came together, then flew apart and rushed out. He was at a loss for words.

"If that's the case," Mr. Cao said hesitantly, "I guess I can put you up here. I have a vacant room; whether for you alone or the two of you, it makes no difference. Do you know if she can wash and mend clothes? If she can, then she can help Gao Ma. The mistress is going to have a baby soon, which will be too much for Gao Ma to handle by herself. The girl will get room and board but no wages. What do you say to that?"

"That would be wonderful." Xiangzi wore a childishly innocent smile.

"But first I have to check with the mistress. This isn't something I can decide on my own."

"I understand. If she has any concerns, I'll bring Fuzi over to let her see for herself."

"Good." Mr. Cao also smiled, pleasantly surprised by Xiangzi's grasp of the situation. "All right, then, I'll mention it to the mistress, then you bring Fuzi over in a couple of days. If the mistress gives the nod, that's how we'll do it."

"May I go now, sir?" Xiangzi was anxious to find Fuzi and give her the unimaginably good news.

It was nearly eleven o'clock when Xiangzi left the Cao house, the most captivating time of a winter day. It was a beautiful day, not a cloud in the blue sky, with the sun shining down through the cool, dry air, bringing with it a refreshing warmth. The crisp sound of roosters' crows, dogs' barks, and peddlers' shouts carried a long way; noise made on one street could be heard clearly on the next street over, like the cries of a crane raining down from the sky. The rain hoods on rickshaws were pulled back; the brass fittings sparkled. Camels walked alongside the pavement, slow and steady; automobiles and trams sped up and down the streets. People and horses on the ground and birds passing overhead lent the ancient city a bustling tranquility, joyously chaotic and joyously serene. The blue sky overlay all the sound and the richness of life below, surrounded by trees standing tall and silent.

Xiangzi felt as if his heart were soaring into the sky, where it wheeled along with the pigeons. He had everything: a job, wages, and Fuzi. Those few words had solved all his problems. It was more than he'd dreamed of. What a crisp, clear sky, just like the straightforward, easygoing people of the north. When good things happen to a man, even the weather cooperates. He could not recall a more captivating winter day. To celebrate his happiness, he bought a frozen persimmon, and when he bit into it, the freezing juice seeped down to the roots of his teeth and spread all the way to his chest, making him shudder. He finished it off in a few bites, numbing his tongue and gladdening his heart. As he strode off, in his mind's eye he could see the compound, the little room, and his beloved Fuzi. If only he could sprout wings and fly to her! One sight would erase all the bad things that had happened and give him a new start in life. He was even more expectant now than he'd been when he went to see Mr. Cao. The older man was his friend and master, each of them helping the other. But she was more than a friend; she was going to give herself to him, and two people would emerge from their hell on earth, wipe away their tears, and walk forward hand in hand. What Mr. Cao said had moved him, but Fuzi could move him without saying a word. He had spoken openly and honestly with Mr. Cao and planned to open his heart to Fuzi when he saw her, saying things he would never say to another living person. She was his life; without her, nothing would have any meaning. He could no longer labor just to feed himself. He must rescue her from the room she lived in so they could be together where it was warm and clean, as happy and respectable and affectionate as a pair of lovebirds. She could stop worrying about Er Qiangzi and her two brothers and become Xiangzi's partner. Er Qiangzi could take care of himself, and her brothers could manage by pulling a rickshaw in tandem or find another trade. But Xiangzi could not do without her. He needed her in every aspect of his life—physical, emotional, even his work— and she needed a man like him.

His impatience nearly drove him to distraction, but he was happy with knowing that Fuzi was the finest woman anywhere and the ideal match for him. He'd been married once and had had an illicit affair, had been in contact with the beautiful and the repulsive, the old and the young, but none of those women had found a place in his heart—they were just women, not true companions. Granted, she was not the chaste maiden he'd dreamed of, but that only made her someone to pity and the ideal person to help him. A naïve country girl might be wholesome and unspoiled, but she would not have Fuzi's ability and intelligence. And what about him, a man whose heart was stained? They were well suited, neither one better nor worse than the other, like two cracked urns that both held water and stood side by side.

However he looked at it, it was an ideal match. With this in mind, he turned to more practical matters. First, he would ask Mr. Cao for a one-month advance on his wages so he could buy her a padded gown and some decent shoes before he took her to see Mrs. Cao. Presentably dressed in a new gown and plain but clean shoes, spotless from head to toe, given her appearance, her youth, and her impressive manner, she would, without question, win over Mrs. Cao.

When he arrived, drenched with sweat, at the neglected gateway, it was like a long-delayed homecoming. He found the dilapidated gate, the crumbling wall, and the gateway arch, topped by patches of dead grass, so deeply endearing. He passed through the gate and went straight to Fuzi's room, opening the door without waiting to knock or calling to her. He recoiled from what he found. A middle-aged woman was sitting on the brick bed, wrapped in a tattered quilt in the unheated room. Xiangzi stood dumbfounded in the doorway. "What's wrong with you?" the woman asked. "Has somebody died? What's the idea of barging into somebody's home? Who're you looking for?"

Xiangzi didn't know what to say. The sweat on his body turned cold. With his hand on the beat-up door, he didn't dare give up hope. "I'm looking for Little Fuzi."

"Don't know her. Come back tomorrow, and next time, don't just barge in on people. Little Fuzi or Big Fuzi, never heard of her."

He sat dazed in the gateway for a long time, his mind emptied even of a sense of why he was there. Slowly it started coming back, but limited to thoughts of Fuzi, who walked pointlessly back and forth in his head, like a paper figure in a twirling lantern, first one way and then the other. He seemed to have already forgotten about Fuzi and him, as her image slowly shrank and his heart returned to normal. At that moment the sadness hit him.

When confronted by something that could turn out either good or bad, people will always hope for the best. Maybe she moved, nothing more than that. It was all his fault—why hadn't he come to see her more often? Shame spurred him into action, wanting to make amends for his failure. First, he had to ask around. So he went back into the compound to get answers from an old neighbor. He left disappointed but still hopeful. Without pausing to eat, he went looking for Er Qiangzi, either him or the two boys. It shouldn't be hard to find one of them, at least, out on the street.

He asked everyone he met—at rickshaw stands, in teahouses, in other tenement compounds, wherever his feet took him—but by the end of the day, there was no news.

That night he returned to the rickshaw shed, exhausted, but he couldn't stop thinking about what had happened. After a day of disappointments, he held out little hope for the days to come. The poor die easily and are just as easily forgotten. Could Fuzi already have left this world? But if not, could Er Qiangzi have sold her again, this time to some faraway place? That was possible and, if anything, worse than if she were dead.

Xiangzi's friendship with tobacco and alcohol was rekindled. Without cigarettes, how could he think? And without alcohol, how could he forget?

CHAPTER TWENTY-THREE

Xiangzi walked down the street, shaken to the core, when he spotted Little Ma's grandfather. Wearing clothes that were even thinner and more ragged than before, the old man no longer pulled a rickshaw. Now he was carrying a large earthen jar on one end of a willow shoulder pole and on the other a frayed ingot-shaped basket filled with sesame cakes, oil fritters, and a brick. He remembered Xiangzi.

Once they started talking, Xiangzi learned that Little Ma had died more than six months before. So his grandfather had sold the rickety rickshaw and begun selling weak tea and sesame cakes at rickshaw stands. He was as friendly and pleasant as ever, but his back was badly bent and his eyes watered in the wind, turning his lids red, as if he'd been crying.

Xiangzi bought a cup of his tea and revealed some of the things that had happened to him.

"You thought you could make it on your own, didn't you?" the old man said, reacting to Xiangzi's sad tale. "That's what everybody thinks, and what no one manages to do. I was young and strong once, and ready to take on the world. But look at me now. Would you call me strong? Even for a man of steel there's no way out of the net we're all caught in. Good intentions? A waste of time. Good is rewarded with good, and evil with evil, they say, but don't you believe it! When I was young, I was known as a warmhearted, helpful person who always looked out for others. Did that do me any good? None. I even saved someone from drowning once and one from hanging. My reward? Nothing. I tell you, I could freeze to death one of these days. I now know that for poor, hardworking people there's nothing more difficult than making it on their own. How far can a man alone leap? You've seen grasshoppers, haven't you? Left alone, one of them can hop great distances. But if a child catches it and ties it with a string, it can't even move. Yet a swarm of them can consume an entire crop in no time and no one can do a thing about it. Am I right? With all my so-called virtues, I couldn't even keep a little boy from dying. When he got sick, I didn't have money to buy medicine and watched him die in my arms. There's nothing more to say, nothing. Tea! Who wants hot tea?"

Now Xiangzi understood. Fourth Master, Mrs. Yang, Detective Sun . . . none of them received the punishment they deserved from being cursed by Xiangzi, and in the end, his ambition got him nowhere. By relying on himself alone, he wound up like the grasshopper tied with a string, just like the old man said, and what good did having wings do him?

He lost interest in going back to Mr. Cao. If he did, he'd be back to trying his hardest to succeed, and what good would that do? Better to drift through life and not worry about it. When there was nothing to eat, he'd take out a rickshaw, and when he had enough to feed himself, he'd take a day off and worry about tomorrow later. That wasn't just a way to get by, it was the only way. Why work hard and save up to buy a rickshaw just so someone could take it away? Better to enjoy life while he could.

If he managed to find Fuzi, he'd try again, if not for himself, then for her. But that wasn't happening, and like the old man whose grandson had died, who was he living for? Warming up to the old man, he told him about Fuzi.

"Who wants a bowl of hot tea?" the old man called out before he gave Xiangzi a bit of advice. "The way I see it, one of two things happened. Either Er Qiangzi sold her to be someone's concubine or she's been sent to the White Manor. The second possibility is more likely. Why do I say that? If, as you say, she's been married before, finding a man who'll want her now won't be easy. Men expect their concubines to be virgins. So I'm guessing she wound up in the White Manor. I'm nearly sixty, and I've seen a lot in my time. If a healthy young rickshaw man doesn't show up on the street for a couple of days, you'll find that he's either landed a monthly job or he's made his way to the White Manor. And if the wife or daughter of one of the rickshaw men disappears all of a sudden, chances are that's where you'll find them. We sell our sweat; our women sell their bodies. That's something I know. Go look for her there. I hope I'm wrong, but . . . Tea! Who wants a bowl of hot tea?"

Xiangzi ran out of Xizhi Gate without stopping.

After passing through Guanxiang, he was struck by the emptiness of his surroundings, with spare roadside trees on which no birds perched. The trees were gray, the ground was gray, and the houses were gray, all standing silently under a dreary sky. Looking out beyond the gray vista, he could see the cold, barren Western Hills. He guessed that the squat building just beyond the wooded area north of the railroad tracks must be the White Manor. Nothing moved among the trees, and as his gaze drifted north, he spotted some uneven clumps of withered cattail reeds standing in marshy land on the far side of Wansheng Garden. There were no people outside the White Manor, no sound, no movement anywhere, and he wondered if it really was the infamous brothel. He found the courage to walk up close, where he saw reed curtains hanging in front of the doors; they looked new, a slightly glossy yellow. He had heard men say that in the summer the women sat outside, baring their breasts to entice men passing by. Prospective guests would sing bawdy songs in loud voices as a sign that they were old hands at this. Why was it so quiet now? Had they closed for the winter?

As he stood there puzzled, a curtain near him parted and a woman's head appeared. He was startled by how much she looked like Huniu. *I came to find Fuzi,* he said to himself. *Wouldn't it be bizarre if I found Huniu instead!*

"Come on in, silly boy." She sure didn't sound like Huniu—raspy, more like the old man who sold wild herbs at Tianqiao. Hoarse and urgent.

The room was empty except for the woman and a small brick bed that had no mat; the fire burning under the bed gave off a noxious smell. A well-used quilt covering it was as greasy as the bricks themselves. The woman, who looked to be in her forties, had neither brushed her hair nor washed her face. She wore a pair of lined trousers under an unbuttoned blue padded jacket. Xiangzi had to duck to get through the door and was immediately caught in a bear hug. Two huge, pendulous breasts were pressed up against him.

Xiangzi sat on the edge of the bed since the ceiling was too low to let him stand without bending his head. He was glad he'd run into this woman, for he'd heard people talk about someone called Flour Sacks, and this must be her. The name obviously came from her large breasts, which she could fling over her shoulders. That was one of the tricks her guests invariably asked her to show them. But her fame was not limited to her enormous flour-sack breasts—she was the only independent operator in the place, here because she wanted to be. Married five times, she had, in short order, reduced all five of her husbands to shrunken bedbugs before they died, which is why she gave up on marriage and came here to enjoy what she liked to do. As an independent operator, she was also free to speak her mind, and was the one to go to when you wanted to know anything about the White Manor, while all the other women would divulge nothing about the place. Her reputation spread, and she welcomed the curious. But her answers did not come free of charge; the "tea money" she earned made her the best-paid woman in the house and the most engaging. Xiangzi knew this, so when he handed her the tea money, Flour Sacks brought an end to the enticements. He came straight to the point and asked her if she knew Fuzi. She said no. But when he described her, she knew who he was talking about.

"Yes," she said, "there was someone like that. Young, two nice, white, protruding teeth. That's right, we called her Tender Morsel."

"Which room is she in?" There was a wild gleam in Xiangzi's eyes.

"Her? Long gone." Flour Sacks pointed outside. "Hanged herself from a tree."

"What?"

"Tender Morsel hit it off with the other girls right away, but the life was more than the poor little thing could take. One night, soon after the lamps were lit, I recall it like it was yesterday, I was sitting outside with two or three of the other girls. Ai, just about this time. A man came up and went straight to her room. She didn't like to sit in the doorway with the rest of us, even got a beating for it when she first came. But after she made a name for herself, we let her sit alone in her room, because some of the men wanted her and nobody else. After about the time it takes to eat, the man came out and headed straight for the woods. We didn't think anything of it and nobody went in to see if she was all right. But when the madam came to collect the money, she found the man lying on the bed without a stitch of clothing, dead drunk. Tender Morsel had taken off his clothes, slipped into them, and run off. She knew what she was doing. She'd never have gotten away in the daylight, but since it was dark and she was wearing the man's clothes, she fooled us all. Well, the madam sent people out looking for her, and when they entered the woods, they found her hanging from a tree. They cut her down, but it was too late. I tell you, her tongue wasn't hanging out and she didn't look half bad. She had that fetching look, even in death. In the months since, the woods have stayed quiet, and she hasn't come out to frighten us. Such a good girl . . ."

Without waiting for her to finish, Xiangzi stumbled back to the road and went over to a tidy little graveyard with a dozen or so graves surrounded by pine trees that dimmed the already faint sunlight. He sat on the ground strewn with dry grass and pine needles. The only sounds were the mournful cries of gray magpies. This could not be where Fuzi was buried, he knew that, but tears streamed unchecked down his face. Gone, everything gone. Even Fuzi was in the ground. He had tried so hard, so had she, and all he had left were some useless tears, while she was now a hanged ghost. Wrapped in a straw mat and buried under an unmarked mound somewhere—that was where a life of hard work and struggle had taken her.

Back at the rickshaw shed he went to bed and slept fitfully for two days. He had no desire to go see Mr. Cao, or even to write to him. Mr. Cao could not save him now. After getting out of bed, he took a rickshaw out, his mind a blank. He gave up thinking and hoping, putting up with the grind only to fill his stomach. When that was done, he went back to bed. What could he gain by thinking or hoping? He spotted an emaciated dog crouching beside a sweet potato peddler's pole, waiting for cast-off peelings and roots, and realized that he was just like that dog, a day's work devoted to the accumulation of scraps. He thought only of living from day to day. Why think of anything else?

Mankind had managed to rise above wild animals, only to arrive at the point where people banished their fellow-men right back into the animal kingdom. Xiangzi lived in a cultured city but, through no fault of his own, had himself become a two-legged beast. No longer a thinking human being, even if he killed someone he could not be held accountable. Having given up all hope, he began a downward spiral that carried him to society's lowest rung. He ate, he drank, he whored, and he gambled. He turned lazy and crafty, now that his conscience had been taken from him. All that remained was a big, tall, flesh-covered frame, just waiting to rot away and be buried in an unmarked grave.

Winter gave way to spring, and nature's gift of sunlight clothed the people. Xiangzi rolled up his padded clothes and sold them so he could treat himself to some decent food and drink. What good were winter clothes, since he had no plans to see another winter? He'd enjoy himself today, for tomorrow he'd be dead. To hell with winter! If he was unlucky enough to still be around when winter returned, he'd deal with that then. In the past, his thoughts had covered the range of his life to that point; now he was concerned only with the present. Experience had taught him that tomorrow was but an extension of today, a continuation of the current wrongs and abuses. Selling his padded

clothes boosted his spirits. What was wrong with having spending money, and what was gained by saving for the next winter,
with winds that choked the life out of you?

His thoughts gradually turned to selling more than his padded clothes. Anything he didn't need at the moment he sold,
happily seeing his possessions turn into cash, which he then
spent. That insured that his money would not fall into other
people's hands. He'd buy those things again if the need arose,
unless he didn't have the money; in that case, he'd simply do
without. He could also save time and money by not washing his
face or brushing his teeth. Who was he trying to look presentable for, anyway? Wearing tattered clothes didn't matter as long
as he could satisfy his hunger with buns stuffed with braised
pork. With some solid food in him, even if he died he wouldn't
end up like a starving rat.

Xiangzi, the once-presentable Xiangzi, had fallen as low as he
could go; he was now just another skinny, dirty rickshaw man.
He stopped bathing and washed neither his face nor his clothes.
He often went a month or more without shaving his head, and
he no longer cared if the rickshaw he pulled was new or old,
only that the rent was cheap. When he had a fare, he might stop
midway and pass him off to another puller if there was benefit
to be gained; if the passenger objected, Xiangzi would fix him
with an angry glare and follow that up with his fists if necessary.
Spending a couple of days locked up didn't bother him in the
least. If it was just him with a fare, he went slow, not wanting to
waste even a drop of his sweat. But when it was a group run, if
he felt like it, he'd run as fast as he could just to leave the others
behind. At such times he delighted in a bit of mischief, like cutting in front of other rickshaws or turning sharp corners to make
the runners behind him swerve or stumble, or to catch the ones

ahead off guard. He had once thought that pulling a rickshaw was in fact transporting a human being, and that he could accidentally kill that person if he wasn't careful. Now he flirted with danger whenever he could, since it made no difference to him if he killed someone. After all, everyone has to die sometime.

He reverted to his tight-lipped ways, never speaking unless he absolutely had to. He ate, he drank, and he made mischief. Speech is how human beings exchange ideas and express feelings. But he had no ideas to exchange and no hope to give voice to, so what good was speech? All day long his mouth remained tightly shut, except when he negotiated a fare. It seemed to be put there only to eat, drink tea, and smoke. Even drunk, he had nothing to say; he would merely seek out a remote spot to weep alone. Just about every time he got drunk, he went to the place in the woods where Fuzi had hanged herself to cry. From there he'd go to the White Manor to spend the night. He'd wake up sober, broke, and, once again, diseased. No regrets. If he regretted anything, it was always trying to better himself and insisting on being cautious, honest, and sincere. His regrets all belonged to the past; there was nothing to regret in the life he led now.

Anytime he could gain some small advantage he did so: he smoked other men's cigarettes, passed off counterfeit coins for purchases, gobbled up extra pieces of salted greens when he bought a bowl of fermented bean curd, and charged passengers more for using less energy, all of which pleased him enormously. His gain was someone else's loss, and that was how it should be, a form of revenge. Slowly but surely, he took this philosophy to greater extremes: he borrowed money with no intention of paying it back and was ready with a shameless excuse if pressed for the money. At first, his friends lent him what he asked for, having no reason to doubt him and knowing that he'd always been respectable and trustworthy. He exploited the remnants of this character trait to borrow from everyone he could think of; it was like finding money on the street, and he spent it immediately. When someone came to get their money back, he struck a pathetic pose and begged for more time, and if that didn't work, he went out and borrowed twenty cents to pay back the fifteen he owed, and drank up the rest. After a while, his sources dried up, so he turned to deception to get what he needed. He visited the home of everyone he'd ever worked for and made up a sad story; master or servants, it made no difference. If they wouldn't give him money, he asked for some old clothes, then immediately converted them into cash, which he smoked or drank up. He lowered his head and thought hard, trying to come up with a better way than pulling a rickshaw to lay his hands on more money. Less effort and more money, that was the way to go. He even went to see Gao Ma at the Cao home and waited across the street until she came out to do the shopping. He spotted her and rushed up with a warm greeting.

"Hey, you scared me! I didn't know who you were at first, Xiangzi! What happened to you?" Her eyes were as wide as if she'd seen a wild animal.

"Don't ask." Xiangzi hung his head.

"I thought you had it all worked out with the master. Why did you leave and not come back? I asked Old Cheng if he'd seen you, but he said no. Where have you been? The master and mistress have been worried about you."

"I was sick, nearly died. Would you ask the master to help me out for now? I'll come back when I'm better."

Xiangzi delivered his simple yet moving prepared speech.

"The master isn't home. Why don't you come in and talk to the mistress?"

"No, not the way I look. You tell her for me."

Gao Ma returned with two yuan. "This is from the mistress. She told you to use it to buy some medicine."

"I will. Thank her for me." He was already planning where he'd spend it when he took it from her. As soon as Gao Ma's back was turned, he was off to Tianqiao, where he spent an enjoyable day.

Once he'd made the rounds of all his former employers, he went back for a second round, but the results this time were disappointing. Obviously, this was not going to be a long-term solution, so he had to come up with another way to make money that was easier than pulling a rickshaw. In days past, pulling a rickshaw had been the only trade he could count on; now, there was nothing he hated more. For obvious reasons, he couldn't just walk away, but as long as he could eat three meals a day, he didn't touch a rickshaw. He'd grown lazy, but his ears were sharper than ever, and he never missed an opportunity to show up where there was money to be made: joining a citizens' parade or a protest rally, anything at all, as long as he was paid. Thirty cents, even twenty, for marching around all day holding a banner was still better than pulling a rickshaw. The earnings were meager, but little effort was involved. Holding a small flag, he kept his head down and silently followed the crowd, a cigarette dangling from his lips, a half smile on his face. When everyone else shouted a slogan, he opened his mouth wide, but no sound emerged; he wanted to save his voice. He refused to put himself out for anything; he'd done that before and look what it got him. If there was any sign of danger during one of the loud demonstrations, he was the first to bolt, running as fast as his legs would carry him. He could take his own life if he felt like it, but he wasn't about to sacrifice it for anyone else. Someone who strives only for himself knows how to destroy himself—the two extremes of individualism.

CHAPTER TWENTY-FOUR

Another season for pilgrims to burn incense at mountain temples arrived, bringing with it the blistering heat of summer.

Peddlers of paper fans suddenly appeared out of nowhere, drawing the curious with strings of clanging bells tied to boxes slung over their shoulders. Vendors hugging the roadsides hawked piles of green apricots, eye-catching red cherries, rose-petal dates attended by swarms of honey bees; glass noodles in large porcelain bowls gave off a milky glare, while sellers of puddings and bean-starch noodles displayed their wares neatly on carrying poles, offering a range of condiments. People had changed into light, garish clothes, creating a colorful tableau on the streets, as if rainbows had fallen to earth. Street cleaners were hard at work sprinkling the streets and roads with water, but they were frustrated by dust that continued to fill the air to the displeasure of everyone. And yet willow branches and swallows that swayed and darted amid the fine dust somehow instilled in the populace a sense of freshness and rebirth. They yawned lazily, exhausted yet happy in the perplexing weather.

Rice-sprout dancers, lion dancers, and other performers at the various fairs headed up the mountain, heralding their passage with the clanging of cymbals and the pounding of drums, troupe after troupe carrying baskets on shoulder poles and hoisting apricot-yellow banners into the air. An air of strange agitation filled the city, instilling in the people vague feelings of intimacy amid the lingering sounds and dust. Those who took part in the fairs or just went to watch experienced the same enthusiasm, piety, and excitement. During troubled times, superstition spawns bustling activity, and the ignorant find consolation only in self-deception. The array of colors and sounds, the pristine clouds, and the dusty streets imbued the populace with energy and drive. Some climbed the mountain, some visited temples, and others took in flower shows . . . those too poor to do any of that could still stand by the road and watch the excitement or recite a Buddhist chant or two.

The arrival of summer awoke the ancient city from its dreamy spring lethargy. Amusements were everywhere as people looked for things to do. The heat accelerated the blooming of flowers and the growth of grasses and trees along with the enjoyment of the people. Green willows and new reeds at Nanhai and Beihai Lakes drew youths to their shores to play their mouth organs; boys and girls rowed boats into the shade of overhanging willows or in among tender lotus leaves, where they sang love songs and kissed with their eyes. Gorgeous peonies and camellias brought forth self-styled poets and scholars to stroll unhurriedly in the parks and cool themselves with expensive paper fans. When they tired, they sat at the feet of red walls or beneath pine trees to drink cups of green tea and dream their melancholy dreams, taking time out to steal glances at the daughters of rich families and courtesans from north and south who passed by. The cool breezes and warm sun at those once-remote spots attracted visitors like butterflies. People with parasols came to view the peonies at Chongxiao Buddhist Temple, the reeds at Taoran Pavilion, and the mulberry woods and rice paddies at the Museum of Natural History. Even the solemnity at the Temple of Heaven, the Confucian Temple, and the Yonghe Lamasery was interrupted by a bit of bustling activity. Hikers and students made treks to the Western Hills or hot springs, even to the Summer Palace to stroll the grounds, gather up things they found, or write their names on rocks. Even the destitute had places to go: Huguo Temple, Longfu Temple, White Pagoda Temple, the Temple of the Earth God, and the flower market all came to life around this time. The streets were lined with captivating plants and flowers, and for only a few cents you could take a bit of beauty home with you.

At stands where fermented bean curd was sold, salted vegetables as fresh and enticing as large flowers were sprinkled with red chili peppers. Eggs were cheap, and when they were fried nice and brown, they made your mouth water. There was a flurry of activity at Tianqiao, where tea sheds were erected with new mats, one after the other. White tablecloths and sing-song girls in colorful dress faced the distant ancient pines above the walls of the Temple of Heaven. Drums thudded and cymbals clanged until seven or eight o'clock at night, the disturbing sound crisp and clear in the heated night air. Prostitutes had no trouble advertising their wares—a simple flowered dress of imported cotton that showed off their curves did the trick. Those who preferred quieter surroundings had places to go as well. There was Jishui Shoal, outside the Temple of Long Life, the kilns in the eastern suburbs, and White Bridge in the western suburbs, all ideal fishing spots where tiny fish set the reeds swaying gently when they bumped into them. When the fishing was done, a meal of pig's head, stewed bean curd, clear liquor, and salted beans at a rustic teahouse was an intoxicating end to a day. Then it was time to gather up the fishing poles and the day's catch, walk along the willow-lined shore in the setting sun, and stroll home through the gates of the ancient city wall.

Good times, bustling activity, and color and sound were everywhere. The abrupt early summer heat was like a magical charm that bewitched the old city. Disregarding death, disaster, and hardships, it would flex its muscles, when the time was right, and mesmerize the vast populace, who would, dreamlike, sing its praises. Filthy, beautiful, decrepit, lively, chaotic, peaceful, and charming, that was the magnificent early summer city of Beiping.

This was the time when residents looked for something newsworthy to relieve their boredom, something they could read two or three times with relish, and exciting enough to want to see whatever it was for themselves, a pleasant diversion during the long, refreshingly sunny days.

And here it was! The trams had barely left the depot when the paperboys were shouting the news: "Read all about it, Ruan Ming to be executed! Read all about it, Ruan Ming to be paraded at nine o'clock!" One coin after another fell into the little grubby hands. News of Ruan Ming filled newspapers on the trams, in the shops, and in the hands of pedestrians: Ruan Ming's photo, Ruan Ming's background, fonts large and small, pictures and captions, page after page of Ruan Ming. Ruan Ming was on the trams, in pedestrians' eyes, on the people's lips, as if no one but he existed anywhere in the old city. Ruan Ming would be paraded today and then shot. Worthwhile news, an ideal news item. Pretty soon not only would people be talking about Ruan Ming, they'd be able to see him. Women dressed in a hurry and old folks went out early on shaky legs to avoid being left behind. Even schoolchildren dreamed of skipping half a day's classes to broaden their knowledge of the world. By half past eight the streets were filled with people—excited, expectant, jostling, noisy, waiting impatiently to witness this living news item. Rickshaw men forgot to look for fares, shops were in turmoil, street vendors lost interest in hawking their wares, as everyone waited in tense anticipation for the prison truck and Ruan Ming. History is replete with the likes of the rebel leaders Huang Chao and Zhang Xianzhong and the bloodthirsty Taipings, who not only slaughtered victims but also took pleasure in seeing people slaughtered. A firing squad seemed too commonplace, nowhere near as much fun to watch as the death of a thousand cuts, beheadings, or skinning or burying alive; the mere sound of these punishments produced the same shuddering enjoyment as eating ice cream. But this time, before they shot him they were going to parade him through the streets; whoever thought that up was to be congratulated, since this was a rare opportunity to feast their eyes on a half-dead, trussed-up man in the back of a truck. That was the next best thing to being the executioner himself. Such people are not burdened by a sense of right and wrong, an understanding of good and evil, or a grasp of what is true and what is false; they cling desperately to their Confucian ethics so they will be thought of as civilized. And yet they enjoy nothing more than watching one of their own being sliced to ribbons, gaining the same cruel enjoyment as a child does killing a puppy. Given the power, they would happily decimate a city, creating mountains of breasts and bound feet severed from women. There can be no greater pleasure. But that power is denied them, and the next best thing is to watch the slaughter of pigs, sheep, and people to satisfy their craving. If even this is beyond their reach, at least they can vent their fury by subjecting their children to threats of a thousand cuts.

In the east, a red sun rose high in the cloudless blue sky as light breezes rustled the leaves of roadside willows. People filled a large patch of shade on the east side of the street, shoulder to shoulder—young and old, male and female, the ugly and the handsome, the fat and the skinny, some dressed with a modern flair, others in traditional mandarin jackets, but all chatting and smiling with keen anticipation and casting frequent glances to the north and south. If one person turned to look, everyone followed, hearts racing. Slowly the crowd edged forward until they formed a lopsided human wall, heads bobbing. A throng of police emerged to maintain order; they held people back, they shouted, and here and there they grabbed one of the grimy children and slapped him around, to the boisterous delight of the people. The waiting crowd endured legs aching from standing so long, unwilling to leave for home, and the latecomers pressing forward, which led to heated confrontations, not with fists or feet but with angry curses, as neighbors egged them on. Fidgeting children were rewarded with resounding slaps; pickpockets had a field day, eliciting loud curses from their victims. Clamor, shouting, and arguments failed to thin out the crowd; the more people who came, the more tenaciously everyone dug in, clear evidence that no one was leaving until they'd seen the half-dead prisoner.

Suddenly, the people fell silent, as a unit of armed police was spotted a ways off. "Here they come!" someone shouted, sparking a renewed outburst of noise. The mass of humanity inched forward, as if a switch had been thrown. Here he comes! They're here! Eyes lit up, tongues wagged, and a loud din arose from within the sweaty, smelly crowd of civilized inhabitants who hungered to witness the killing.

Ruan Ming, a squat man, was sitting in the truck, hands tied behind him, looking like a sick monkey. His head was bowed. A two-foot-long white placard giving his name and crime stuck up behind him. Shouts from the assembled mass came in waves as they curled their lips and voiced their disappointment: That's him, that little monkey? That's what we came to see? Head down, white-faced, and not a sound! Time to taunt: "Come on, folks, cheer him on!" Shouts of "Bravo!" erupted up and down the lines, the same cries with which they applauded their favorite actress on the opera stage but now scornful, malevolent, and disagreeable. That elicited no response from Ruan Ming, who did not look up. Never expecting such a weak-kneed prisoner, some in the crowd were so annoyed they elbowed their way up to the side of the road and spat at him. And still he neither moved nor made a sound. The onlookers were starting to lose interest but not enough to leave. What if all of a sudden he shouted, "I'll come back in twenty years, better than before!" Or what if he asked for a couple of pots of liquor and some meat to go with it? No one budged. Let's see what he's going to do! So after the truck passed, they fell in behind it. He's not doing anything now, but who knows, when he reaches the memorial arch he might take a deep breath and sing some lines from *Silang Visits His Mother*. Follow him! Some would go all the way to Tianqiao. He hadn't done anything admirable or satisfying, but at least the people could see him take a bullet, and that alone would make the trip worthwhile.

During all this excitement, Xiangzi walked slowly, head down, hugged the wall at Desheng Gate; when he reached Jishui

Shoal, he stopped and looked around. Seeing that he was alone, he tiptoed slowly up to the water's edge, where he found an old tree and leaned up against it. He sat down once he was sure there was no one else around. But each time the reeds rustled or a bird cried out he jumped to his feet, sweating nervously; he'd look and listen for a moment before slowly sitting back down. This happened several times before he got used to seeing the reeds move and hearing the birds twitter. Vowing not to jump up again, he sat there and stared blankly at a ditch beside the lake, where tiny fish swam, their eyes like pearls, schooling and swimming away, this way and that, some bumping into the tender reeds and others sending bubbles to the surface. Tadpoles that had grown legs stretched out in the water at the ditch's edge, their little black heads bobbing, when suddenly they and the small fish were swept along by a rush of water and swam with the current, tails wriggling. Another school took their place, struggling against the current to stay put. A crab scurried past as the water calmed and the fish came together to nibble at green leaves or water grasses. Slightly larger fish hid at the bottom, rising until their backs broke the surface but quickly returning to safety, leaving little ripples on the surface. A kingfisher skimmed above the water, sending all the fish, big and small, diving for cover beneath the duckweed. Xiangzi's gaze was fixed on all this activity, but he saw nothing. He picked up a stone and tossed it into the water, raising a series of ripples and parting clumps of duckweed. The movement startled him, and he jumped to his feet.

After sitting back down, he reached a big black hand into his waistband to feel around. He nodded, waited awhile, and then took out a stack of bills, which he counted before carefully putting them back.

All Xiangzi had on his mind was the money—how to spend

it, how to keep it a secret from others, and how to enjoy it in safety. He was no longer his own man; he now belonged to money and could only do its bidding.

The source of that money dictated how it would be used. He could not spend it openly. It and the man in whose hands it rested must be kept in the shadows. While other people were out on the street watching Ruan Ming, Xiangzi was lying low in this secluded spot beneath the city wall hoping to find an even quieter and darker place. No longer could he show his face in town, now that he had sold out Ruan Ming. Even resting up against the city wall, with no one else around as he stared at the gently flowing water, he dared not raise his head, so as to keep from seeing the ghostly apparition that he feared was following him. While Ruan Ming might be lying in a pool of his own blood at Tianqiao, to Xiangzi, he was not dead but lived in the stack of bills tucked into his waistband. He felt no remorse, just fear, afraid of a ghost that followed him everywhere with no reprieve.

After becoming an official, Ruan Ming had begun to enjoy the very things he had once fought against. Money leads people into society's evil domains; they cast off their noble ideals and travel willingly to the depths of hell. He began wearing fancy Western suits, visiting prostitutes, gambling, and taking up the use of opium. When his conscience caught up with him, he laid the blame for what he had become on the evil nature of society. While admitting that his behavior had been wrong, he was powerless to resist society's seductive pull. And so he continued, until his money ran out, and he was reminded of the radical thoughts he had entertained as a student. But rather than translate these thoughts into action, this time he was more interested in translating them into money, much the same as trying to translate his friendship with his teacher into a passing grade without working for it. Moral integrity has no place in the philosophy of a lazy man; sooner or later anything that can be converted to cash will be sold. Ruan Ming took what was offered; someone eager to promote revolution cannot be choosy in finding fighters for the cause and must hope that those who come forward are like-minded. But people who take what is offered are expected to produce results, regardless of how they do it, and reports must be submitted. Ruan Ming had to produce something to show for the payment he accepted, so he involved himself in organizing rickshaw pullers.

Xiangzi had become an old hand at waving flags and shouting slogans by then, and that is how he met Ruan Ming.

Ruan Ming sold ideas for money; Xiangzi accepted them for the same reason. Ruan Ming knew that if the need arose he could sacrifice Xiangzi. Xiangzi, on the other hand, never entertained such a thought, and yet that is precisely what he did—he betrayed Ruan Ming. People who do things for money fear being confronted with more of it. Loyalty cannot be built on money. Ruan Ming believed in his radical ideas and used them to excuse all his evil actions. Xiangzi listened to everything Ruan Ming proclaimed and found it reasonable, yet he envied the man's extravagant lifestyle: "If I had the money, I'd enjoy life, for a few days at least, like that Ruan fellow!" Money diminished Ruan Ming's character; it enticed Xiangzi. He sold the man out for sixty yuan. Ruan Ming sought the strength of the masses. Xiangzi set his sights higher: he wanted more enjoyment out of life, just like Ruan Ming. Ruan Ming spilled his blood for payments received; Xiangzi stuffed the money he received into his waistband.

He sat there until the sun sank in the west, dressing the duckweed and willows in red and gold light. On his feet again, he headed west, hugging the city wall. Accustomed to cheating for money, this was the first time he'd sold a man's life. To top it off, he had found Ruan Ming's exhortations perfectly reasonable. The vast expanse at the base of the wall and its towering height instilled dread in him as he walked. He even gave crows scavenging piles of garbage a wide berth for fear of startling them into inauspicious caws. He sped up when he reached the western wall and slipped out through Xizhi Gate like a dog that has stolen food. He craved a place where he could be with someone who would help dull his emotions and deaden his fears; the White Manor beckoned.

By the early days of autumn Xiangzi's sickness had ended his days as a rickshaw man, but even if that had not been the case, he had lost the trust of anyone who might rent him a rickshaw. He found work as a night watchman for a little shop, earning two coppers a night and a place to sleep. His daytime jobs provided him with a daily bowl of thin porridge. Begging on the street was out of the question, for no one would take pity on a big fellow like him. And he had never learned how to scar himself up enough to tug at the heartstrings of pilgrims at the city's temples. He didn't have what it takes to be a thief, and besides, thieves banded together in gangs with tight connections. He had no one to rely on but himself if he was to eat. He would work for himself until the day that work killed him. He was waiting for that last breath, for he was already one of the walking dead, with individualism as his soul. That soul would one day accompany his body into the ground.

Ever since the city of Beiping was chosen as the nation's capital, its pomp and ceremony, its handicrafts, its cuisine, its language, and its police structure had slowly spread in all directions, searching out and fostering people who aspired to achieve the dignity and resources of the Emperor. Beiping's mutton hot put was now served in the Westernized city of Qingdao; doleful cries of "Hard dough—pastries!" were heard late at night in the bustling city of Tianjin; in Shanghai, and Hankou, and Nanjing, the police and yamen runners spoke the Beiping dialect and ate flatbreads stuffed with sesame paste. Scented teas originating in the south came north to Beiping, where they were smoked twice and returned to the south. Even pallbearers sometimes rode the train to Tianjin or Nanjing to help carry the coffins of the rich and powerful.

But Beiping was beginning to give up its pomp and ceremony: glutinous cakes were now available in shops after the Double Ninth Festival, on the ninth day of the ninth month; peddlers of sweet dumplings once sold only on the fifteenth day of the first lunar month began showing up at markets in the fall; shops that had been around for hundreds of years celebrated anniversaries by passing out handbills announcing grand sales. Economic pressures forced pomp and ceremony to look elsewhere, since decency and honor could not fill anyone's belly.

Weddings and funerals, however, retained most of the traditional rites and practices. These joyful and mournful events still seemed noteworthy enough to warrant a degree of grandeur. The paraphernalia, musicians, bridal sedans, and coffin shrouds were not available in every city. Longevity cranes and lion dogs that led funeral processions replete with paper figurines of people, chariots, and horses, or the dignitaries and twenty-four musical instruments in weddings still evoked an aura of power and prestige, reminiscent of the prosperity and spirit of more peaceful times.

Xiangzi relied on the remnants of such rites and customs to

get through the days. In wedding processions he held up ceremonial parasols; for funeral corteges he carried wreaths and
scrolled elegies. He neither took pleasure in nor cried over his
role in such processions, for which he received ten cents or
more. He dressed in green robes supplied by funeral homes or
blue ones from bridal shops and wore ill-fitting caps, all of
which hid the rags he wore underneath and gave him a bit of
respectability. When a rich and influential family arranged the
event, everyone in the procession had to shave their heads and
wear boots, giving Xiangzi a rare opportunity to walk with a
clean head and feet, though his unspeakable sickness slowed
him down. He would shamble along by the side of the road
holding up a banner or a pair of scrolled elegies.

Even at such trivial tasks, Xiangzi was not particularly good.
His best years were behind him. A rickshaw had not provided
him with a family or a lasting trade, and everything he did,
along with all his hopes, had turned into: "So what!" He put his
large body only in the service of carrying a flying-tiger pendant
or a pair of short scrolls. He refused to hoist the heavy red parasols or solemn tablets. Competing with old men, children, even
women was not beneath him, just so long as he did not get the
worst of any situation.

He shuffled along slowly, laboriously, carrying his light burden, head hung low, bent at the waist, a cigarette butt he'd
picked up off the ground dangling from his lips. When everyone else stopped, he kept walking, and when they were off
again, he stopped where he was for a while. He seemed not to
hear the signaling gongs and never paid any attention to the
distance between him and those in front or back or whether he
was aligned in his row. He just plodded along, head bowed, as if
in a dream or pondering some arcane truth. Rustic curses from

the mouths of the red-clad gong beater or the procession stew-
ard, who carried a silk streamer, all seemed directed at him:
"You son of a bitch, I'm talking to you, Camel! Stay in line,
damn it!" They fell on deaf ears. The gong beater came up and
hit him with the gong hammer, but he merely rolled his eyes
and looked around through a veil of haze. Ignoring the man's
curses, he kept his eyes glued to the ground to see if there were
any butts worth picking up.

Respectable, ambitious, idealistic, self-serving, individualis-
tic, robust, and mighty Xiangzi took part in untold numbers of
burial processions but could not predict when he would bury
himself, when he would lay this degenerate, selfish, hapless
product of a sick society, this miserable ghost of individualism,
to rest.

HARPER PERENNIAL MODERN CHINESE CLASSICS

RICKSHAW BOY • A Novel
Lao She

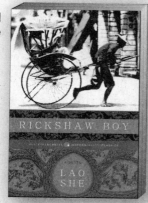

ISBN 978-0-06-143692-5 (paperback)

First published in 1937, this classic Chinese novel
is the story of Xiangzi, an honest, serious country
boy, who works as a rickshaw puller in Beiping.
A man of simple needs, Xiangzi's great ambition
is to one day buy his own rickshaw and keep his
earnings for himself. After years of grueling work,
Xiangzi realizes his dream, only to have it stripped
away through a series of tragic events that are
beyond his control.

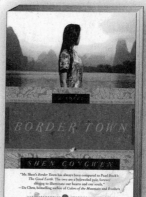

BORDER TOWN • A Novel
Shen Congwen

ISBN 978-0-06-143691-8 (paperback)

Cuicui, a young girl coming of age during a time
of national turmoil, dreams of finding true love,
but is also haunted by the death of her grandfather,
a poor and honorable ferryman who is her only
family. As she grows up, Cuicui discovers that life is
full of the unexpected and she alone will make the
choices that determine her destiny. First published
in 1934, this beautifully written novel is considered
Shen Congwen's masterpiece.

THE ANCIENT SHIP • A Novel
Zhang Wei

ISBN 978-0-06-143690-1 (paperback)

Originally published in 1987, two years before the
Tiananmen Square protests, Zhang Wei's award-
winning novel is the story of three generations
of the Sui, Zhao, and Li families living in the
fictional northern town of Wali during China's
troubled post-liberation years. Translated into
English for the first time, *The Ancient Ship* is a
revolutionary work of Chinese fiction.

HARPER ● PERENNIAL

Available wherever books are sold, or call 1-800-331-3761 to order.